FOREVER DREW

A. K. STEEL

Forever Drew

Copyright ©2021 by A. K. Steel

All rights reserved. No part of this book may be reproduced or transmitted in either electronic, paper hard copy, photocopying, recorded, or any other form of reproduction without the written permission of the author. No part of this book either in part or whole may be reproduced into or stored in a retrieval system or distributed without the written permission of the author.

This book is a work of fiction. Characters, names, places and incidents are products of the author's imagination. Any resemblances to actual events, locations, or persons living or dead is purely coincidental.

The author acknowledges the trademark status and owners of products referred to in this fiction which have been used without permission. The publication and use of these trademarks is not authorised, associated with, or sponsored by the trademark owners.

Published by A.K. Steel

Edited by Contagious Edits

Blurb by Contagious Edits

Cover Design by Opium House Creatives

Cover Photo by Michelle Lancaster www.michellelancaster.com

www.instagram.com/lanefotograf.

Cover Model tommyfierce.

ABOUT THE BOOK

I write fairytales, but I certainly don't live in one.

A long time ago I met my knight in shining armour. The dreamy Drew Walker. Drew showed up in the right place at the right time to free me from my train wreck of a life. I was stripping at a local club, on the run from my ex-boyfriend, a thug for one of Sydney's largest criminal empires.

I fell for him quickly, but the timing wasn't right and tragedy struck, destroying our chances of finding happiness together. We parted ways, and I thought that would be the end.

Five years later, across the busy room of a local bar our eyes lock. He smiles, flashing his cheeky charismatic dimples and it's like no time has passed. Except we're both different now. He has found fame as Australia's sexy bad-boy pro surfer, and I'm just a humble librarian with big dreams of being an author.

Could this be our second chance at happiness together? Or are too many ghosts from the past still haunting us to ever really be able to hold onto the love we have for each other?

Is the past lost to me forever, or could Drew be my happily ever after?

* Content warning: contains elements of violence and sexual abuse.

PROLOGUE
JENNA

My heart hammers in my chest, and I feel the familiar uncomfortable churn of my belly. I can't believe I'm back doing this again. This was not my plan. I had hoped I could get a job as a waitress or in one of the cute boho retail shops along the main street. But just my luck, no one was hiring, and I couldn't afford to wait. I needed a job and fast. The life I'm trying to flee was dangerous, and in all honesty, in the end, I was scared for my safety. I had seen too much and was afraid I was next. I probably am if my ex-boyfriend manages to track me down. I just pray that I'm far enough away that he won't.

It's been six months since I've needed to work, but the shitty circumstances of the past few weeks have brought me back to the only job I seem to be able to get. One I'm good at —and why wouldn't I be? I've been doing it since I was 15, and the moves come naturally.

This club is different to most I've been in; the room surrounding me is set up like a circus tent, with a high ceiling of yellow-and-red-striped shiny satin fabric. There's a circular stage in the centre of the room where two girls are hanging from long silk apparatuses attached to the ceiling. I stand and watch in awe from the doorway to the change room.

"Aerial acrobatics," says one of the other girls, making her way past me to start her shift, in a sparkly next-to-nothing outfit.

"They're amazing," I murmur in wonderment. I could stand here and watch them all day, their strong bodies twisted in silk as they twirl around. These girls are gorgeous and toned, with flashy sequined costumes that leave little to the imagination. They're more like gymnasts than strippers.

But we're all strippers here, no matter how talented they are with their acrobatic routine.

This is my first night at this club. I've been in training with them all week, learning the dance routines. The manager here has very high standards with her dances, so the routines need to be perfect. I have no idea why; from my experience, men couldn't care less how well we dance. They're here for the booze, tits, and arse. But I need this job, so I have learnt my routine carefully from Ariel, one of the other girls who has been here a few years.

It's been nice getting to know Ariel this week. I don't have any other friends in town yet, and she's been kind, taken me under her wing, so to speak. So caring that she heard my sob story and offered me her spare room to stay in until I'm back on my feet. She's stunning, with long strawberry-blonde hair and sparkling green eyes. Her name was picked from her resemblance to the Little Mermaid.

As I watch, a rowdy group enters the club and heads straight for the roped-off area down the back, where I'm working tonight. I take a deep breath, trying to mentally prepare myself for the night ahead. *You've got this, just like riding a bike*, I joke to myself, trying to get my nerves under control. Ariel grabs my hand and drags me to the bar alongside her. She motions for two shots, and the bartender places them on the bar.

She holds the glass up to me. "Come on, this'll help. I can see how nervous you are." She has been such a lifesaver this week, and she's right, I'm nervous as hell.

I glace at the clear liquid in the shot glass. Tequila. I'm not sure if this is a good idea but I throw it back, and it burns my throat.

She does the same, then motions to the bartender for another two. We tip them back in unison, and she pulls a face. I giggle at her. I like this girl. She's fun and easy-going, everything I'm not. I feel the tingle of warmth radiating through my body already. Much better.

"You good now, girl?" She smiles.

I nod. "Let's do this."

"Good. It's our lucky night; we have a buck's party of young sexy rich guys to dance for in the private room."

I follow her through the back onto the smaller stage and take my place on the pole. As the music starts, we move, and for the most part it comes back to me.

I should feel lucky, because this club is different to any I worked for in Sydney. The manager is nice and actually gives a shit about the girls who work here. I pay attention to the music and follow the moves Ariel taught me. I think I'm nailing it. My confidence starts to return, and I'm relaxing. I can do this.

This isn't my chosen profession, but things in life haven't always gone my way. Or ever, really, starting with being dumped on a doctor surgery doorstep when I was six months old, with a note saying that my parents had both died and I needed someone to take care of me. To this day I have no idea if they actually died or if they just didn't want me, but that was the start of the series of unfortunate events that has been the life of Jenna West.

I came to work as a stripper when I was 15 because I had no other options. I couldn't stay at the foster home I had been placed in. Things had gotten out of hand with my foster brother, and it got to the point where the home that was supposed to be my secure place in this world didn't feel so safe anymore, so I ran away. While on the streets, I met a girl who was a little older than me, and she hooked me up with the job. I was too young to be working in a club at the time, but armed with a fake ID, they didn't think twice about giving me the job.

So I was a stripper. The money was decent enough, and I was able to survive on my own just fine. I was doing okay until I met Vinnie. I kinda knew he was going to be trouble right from the beginning. He was one of the heavies for Mr Donovan, the owner of the club where I worked. Mr Donovan was a big name in the city, mostly because he owned half of it. He was the one everyone bowed down to, so Vinnie had a lot of power, and he knew it.

I should have known better than to get involved with him, but he was nice to me and offered me a place to stay. He didn't want me to strip anymore, so he paid for everything and took care of me. It seemed like a sweet deal, and for a while it was—until I walked in on him murdering some poor young guy.

The scene was horrific and still plays over in my head when I close my eyes, even now a few weeks later. I can't unsee it, it was so awful. Tears instantly prick at my eyes, and I blink them away. I can't cry now, I need to focus on what I'm doing. I can't fuck this job up, I really need it.

I always knew Vinnie was one of the heavies for Mr Donovan, but I had no idea he took things that far. It scared the shit out of me. I wasn't hanging around another day, so I grabbed the few important possessions I had—which weren't many, they all fit in a small backpack—and I got the hell out of there. It was like déjà vu, running from my foster home all over again.

So now I'm back where I started all those years ago; 22 years old, not a cent to my name and still dancing for money. I just pray Vinnie doesn't give a shit that I'm gone, cause if he wants to find me, I'm sure he will, and I don't even want to think of what will happen then.

Ariel suggested a disguise to make me feel more comfortable, so I'm wearing a lolly-pink bobbed wig and Barbie-pink lippy, the best I could do to disguise myself with hardly any cash to splash on an outfit.

I run my hands seductively over the red sequined outfit I have on. I can't help but snap out of my thoughts when one of the guys from the party takes a seat directly in front of me. He's easy to dance for: young, cute, maybe mid-20s, and longish, sandy-blond hair with a curl to it and a sexy-as-fuck simile with dimples. He's dressed in black jeans, a white T-shirt, and a leather jacket. He looks good enough to eat. But it's his kind blue eyes that keep me focusing on him, and my first-day jitters disappear.

There are plenty of other girls dancing here tonight, but he hasn't taken his eyes off me. They're a piercing blue, gorgeous, the kind of eyes you could get lost in. He's seriously dreamy. The type of guy that would never look at me twice unless I was on a pole.

And there it is, that slap back to reality. I know who I am, and I wouldn't normally be worth his time of day. Yet he watches my every move tonight.

My group's turn on the stage is done, and it's time for us to make the rounds, offering lap dances. I sway my way over to him, hips moving to the music. "Hello, handsome," I purr, placing my hand on his shoulder. Faking every bit of confidence I don't have.

Close up, he smells divine. He is so good I'm thinking this must all be just a figment of my imagination, some sort of mirage I've made up to get me through my shift—or maybe those shots of tequila were stronger than I thought.

He relaxes back in his chair, getting comfortable as I move around him. That smile, man, he's something else.

"What's your name, gorgeous?" he asks, his deep voice making my insides somersault. He reaches out, playing with the tassels on my outfit. His hungry eyes roam down my body, starting with my breasts, then all the way down my legs.

I'm surprised by his question; most guys don't care what my name is. "I'm Bambi," I say, batting my eyelashes. It's the most ridiculous name, but all the girls here have names from either Disney films or children's stories. Weird, but it's fitting for me, I guess.

"Of course that's your name." He smirks.

I move around him, dropping to my knees then slowly running my hands up his legs. As I stand, my breasts are just millimetres from his face. "Named after the beloved childhood character, because I too am an orphan." Why did I just tell him that? It's his eyes, they have me under a spell. He asks a question and I want to tell him everything, but I really need to shut the fuck up.

His face drops as he takes me in, his gaze questioning. "Oh, that's a sad story."

"Least that's what I was told anyway. I have no idea what happened to my parents, really." Why am I telling him my sob story? Because I secretly want to be saved by a gorgeous man like him. Rescued like a stray cat, taken home and cared for, loved. I really have hit an all-time low when all a handsome man like this has to do is ask me a few questions and I'm ready to go home with him. You'd think I would be more wary after the last situation and where that got me, but nope, still hoping for a saviour.

"That's awful!" I see the pity in his eyes, and I need to change the subject, get his eyes back on my body, not looking so sad. The poor man is here to be entertained, but he's going to go home feeling as depressed as I am.

"I guess, it was a long time ago now." I shrug, lifting one leg over his lap so I'm standing but straddling him. I run my hands up my body, starting with my tummy, until I reach my breasts. I squeeze them together and his attention is back where it should be, on my tits. Good. I was blessed with amazing breasts, totally out of proportion to my thin frame. They've gotten me every job so far.

I roll my hips towards his cock. He's hard and massive, I can feel it through his jeans.

"What's your real name?" he asks.

I laugh at his question. "You know I can't tell you that. What's yours?"

"Drew." He pauses, watching me. "Tell me, what's a lovely girl like you doing dancing in a strip club, anyway?"

I turn away from him, so I'm almost sitting on his lap, my arse rubbing up against his hardened length. My head falls back, resting on his shoulder as I move on his lap. He is so chatty.

"Why do you assume this isn't what I want to be doing? There's a lot of girls who love this job, and we make a shitload of cash."

"I don't know, I just don't see it for you. You seem smart," he whispers, and I'm so close to him when he talks, I can feel his warm breath on my neck.

It's confusing. Being so close to his body has me thinking all sorts of naughty thoughts that I don't normally have while doing this job. But his words are pissing me off. Who does this guy think he is, sitting here, all judgemental about my life choices? Bet he has never had to struggle a day in his life.

"Thanks, guess I should take that as a compliment," I say, the sarcasm dripping from my every word.

"Sorry, I didn't mean to offend you or anything. You just don't look that happy to be here."

Oh, he's just trying to be nice. "Don't worry about it. I guess you're right, it's not my life ambition to strip forever. It's just a placeholder until something better comes along."

I turn back to him again, facing him. "You could try something else," he suggests.

"Not that simple. I just moved here and no one else is hiring. I've tried. Why do you care, anyway? Most guys I give a lap dance to just want to ogle my body, not give me career advice."

"I don't know. I was watching you up on the stage earlier. You just seem like you're going to be someone important in my life, and I want to help you."

My heart kicks up a beat. He wants to help me. What a strange thing for him to say. I take a step back from him, not quite knowing how to react. Am I being pranked or something? Can he read my thoughts screaming *help me*? I'm one more bad mistake away from ending it all. Or have I just got to the point where the deep depression I'm in is written all over my face, even when I'm trying to plaster on my best smile? And to say I'm going to be someone important in his life? I doubt that!

"You got all that from watching me dance for you? I must be better than I thought. What, has it been a while since you got laid or something, you getting desperate? There are girls here who will help you out with that if you need," I offer sweetly.

He pulls me back towards him, our faces so close. "I don't have any trouble getting laid, sweetheart, trust me."

"Okay, if you say so, handsome." Over his shoulder, I get the nod from my manager. I need to move on to someone else. "As lovely as it's been dancing for you, Drew, I'm being told I need to continue on. Enjoy your night," I whisper into his ear.

As I try to slip away, he grabs my wrist. "I'm not finished with you yet," he protests, his voice low and growly. I glance back to the guard watching me and smile so he knows I'm okay.

"If you're lucky, I might come back." I give him a wink and pull out of his grip, sauntering away before security causes a scene. I can feel Drew's eyes on me the whole time I do. I would have liked to keep talking to him, it was nice to have a conversation, but I move on to the next guy, doing my routine.

I try to black out the way Drew just made me feel. What was that? I'm so used to being treated like shit that some good-looking guy says a few nice things to me and I go all mushy again, ready to make another mistake. I need to get my head together, toughen up a bit. I can't afford any more bad decisions.

This next guy I dance for is younger, but he couldn't care less about my life, and he's handsy, digging his fingers into my arse. I take a step back, glaring a warning at him. I need to keep my distance from him. I scope the room for that security guy and notice he's watching. He nods to Ariel, and she grabs my hand, and I dance with her, keeping our distance from the guy.

As we dance, I can't help but glance in Drew's direction. He's now talking with two other guys about his age, and they're all looking back at me. I feel a little uneasy. Something about the way one of them is looking at me isn't right. Has Vinnie worked out where I am already? No, he couldn't have. I'm just being paranoid.

Drew smiles over to me. "Bambi." He gestures with a wave for me to come over to where he's standing with his group. "Come meet my friends."

I wonder what they want. I whisper to Ariel, "Come and save me if I give you the signal."

"No worries, honey." She takes over with Mr Handsy.

I sway my hips as I walk towards them. I twirl a strand of my wig around playfully, my eyes never leaving the three of them. They're all tall and handsome, the other two in suits. They look like they have money, intimidating standing as a group. One has dark hair and is unshaven, the other is more clean-cut looking with light brown hair—he's the one I don't like the look of. The way he assesses me makes my palms sweaty.

Drew introduces the other two. "This is Fraser and Blake. They're here for the buck's party as well; it's one of their business partners that's getting married."

I nod, standing back from them a little. "Nice to meet you, boys." I'm still wondering why I've been called over.

"Drew tells us you're new to the area," says Blake, the one who scares the shit out of me.

I play with the fringing on my costume, trying to look away from his steely gaze. "Yeah, just been here a few weeks." What's it to him, anyway? I'm really regretting saying anything to Drew. What if it was some sort of a trap?

"You on the run from your boyfriend or something?" Blake asks.

My eyes dart to him then to Drew. What does he know? I suddenly get the urge to run, but where am I going to go? If Vinnie has sent a guy to find me, there will be nothing I can do. I look back at Drew, but he looks uncertain of what his friend is talking about.

"Ah, why would you ask that?" I can feel my hands start to tremble. I don't like where this is going at all.

"Because my dad is Max Donovan, and he sent me to find you," he says, and the fear I felt when he first looked at me all makes sense. I can see it now, the family resemblance is there. He is fucking Mr Donovan's son—I'm so screwed.

I need to get out of here. I take a step back and bump into Drew. With the three of them all standing so close to me, I have no chance to run. I look over to security. He can see my discomfort and is on his way over. I give him a wave and the best smile I can muster to say I'm fine. I don't need to draw any more attention to myself. I have to talk myself out of this somehow.

"W-Why? I'm not who you think I am, sorry. I have no idea who that is, you must have the wrong girl."

Drew's eyes flick to Blake. He looks confused, and I get the feeling he has no idea what's going on. "What are you talking about, Blake? Who's your dad?" Drew asks.

Blake ignores Drew, keeping his attention on me. "Why do you seem like you're about to run then?"

"Blake, stop it, you're scaring her," says Drew. I like how he sticks up for me against this arsehole. It's not going to save me if Vinnie gets a hold of me, though.

And he's right, I am scared. If they take me back to him, I have no idea what he will do to me. I have seen too much and then running from him; he is going to be beyond furious. I can feel tears pricking my eyes as they dart between Blake and Drew. What do I say so they believe me and let me go? I try and look as calm and happy as I can. I don't want them to know how they're affecting me. "I'm just confused. I don't know who you're talking about," I mutter.

Blake's face softens a little. "Bambi, I'm not going to tell them where you are. I don't work for my dad. I'm nothing like him. But I just wanted you to know, they're searching the town for you. You're not safe working somewhere like this. They'll find you here. It's only a matter of time; my dad knows everyone in this line of business." He has a warmth to his eyes, I see it now. Something tells me I can trust him, but I'm scared to trust anyone at this point. I have been wrong so many times in the past.

I can hear my pulse pounding in my ears; it's making it hard to think. They're looking for me here? I don't have anywhere else to go. I can't hold the tears back any longer, and I can feel the trickle as the first escapes down my cheek. I wipe it away. "You don't understand. I don't have any choice. I have to dance. I need the money. No one else is hiring, and this is all I know. What am I supposed to do?" I spit at Blake. Someone like him would never understand. He would have had all the money in the world when he grew up, with a dad like his.

"We can help you find you something different," he offers with total sincerity. "You can't work here."

I want to believe him. But I don't know if I can even trust any of them. He could be pretending to help me, to lure me into a trap. But I have no one else, and I'm so frightened right now I can't even think straight. The way Drew looks at me, I feel like he's a decent guy. I fucking hope I'm right. "You can't let him find me. I don't want to go back to him. He's dangerous. I... I saw things. I can't go back. Please don't tell him where I am."

"I won't, *we* won't, you can trust us," Blake says.

"How do I know that? I don't know you," I cry.

"Man." The other guy, I think his name was Fraser, knocks Blake on the arm, tilting his head towards the door. "Is that your dad?" he whispers, but I hear him, and I follow his line of sight.

Fuck, it's Mr Donovan. I'm screwed.

"You have to be fucking kidding me," chokes out Blake. "Drew, your jacket, get it on her now. Cover her up and get her out of here."

I need to run away from all of them. "I can't go with him. I don't know any of you, I'm not going anywhere. Besides, security won't just let me slip out of here with you, it's going to cause a whole big scene," I protest. They can't tell me who I'm leaving here with, I don't even know if I can trust them.

Blake rests his hand on my shoulder, and I flinch. "We have to get you out of here. Seriously, if you don't want him to find you tonight, you need to get out of here now. We'll deal with security."

Before I can plead my case again, Drew wraps his jacket around me, then takes my hands. I look up into those gorgeous eyes. I want to believe I can trust him, that he will save me from this living hell I'm in. "Come with me. You can come back to my place. My dad and brother are both cops in this town. I promise you can trust me. I will keep you safe. You can't stay here," Drew begs me.

I have no other choice. I have to trust him.

I glance between the guys in front of me and over to the door, where Mr Donovan and now Vinnie—oh fuck, he's here as well, and they're talking to the bouncer. I'm out of here, it really is the only option. I look back to Drew. "Okay, Drew, I trust you." He takes me by the hand.

"Is there a back door?" Blake asks, and I nod. "Take her home, Drew. I—."

Those are the last words I hear from Blake as I'm ushered farther down the back of the club by Drew, and their words are drowned out by the music.

We make our way past the changing rooms, and I remember I need to grab my stuff. "Wait, I need my bag." I don't want to come back here again, so I need to get it now.

"Be quick," says Drew nervously. He waits by the dressing room door as I run through as quickly as I can and grab my bag and the dress I came in, throwing it over my head. Ariel comes running through the door.

"What's going on?"

"I'm sorry, I have to go. That guy out there talking to the bouncer, he's the one after me."

"Okay, you get out of here, I'll see you at my place later." She hugs me.

"I'll let you know."

I rush back to Drew, and we sprint for the back door, pushing it open into the cool night air and the back alley of the club.

Outside, it's eerily quiet in comparison to the blaring music. We hurry down the darkened street. My body is shaking, and he notices.

"You're cold. Here, let me warm you up until I can get you home. It's just a short walk to my parents' place." He puts his arm around me, and I let him. I'm wearing next to nothing, even with my dress over the top, and I'm freezing—or maybe it's the shock of it all. How did Vinnie find me so quickly? I knew this would happen. I'm never going to be safe from him.

We stop walking when we arrive in front of a beautiful Queenslander-style home; this must be his parents' house.

"Are your parents home?" I ask tentatively. I don't have the energy for dealing with parents tonight.

"Yeah, but it's late, they'll be in bed." He tucks a strand of my wig behind my ear.

The wig—what use would this have been, anyway. I tug it off and let my hair out. It's long and falls down my back. "I should just keep walking to my apartment," I say, running my hands through my hair.

He takes me by the hands and offers a warm smile. "You're not going anywhere by yourself tonight. Those guys Blake was taking about, they might have your address. You're staying with me until I know your place is safe for you to return."

"I don't know about that, Drew, I don't want to impose. This is your parents' house, and you don't even know me."

"I know enough. You can stay in my bed tonight, I'll take the couch, and in the morning my dad will be able to help you. We can work out a plan so they don't find you. I promise I won't let anything happen to you. You will be safe here with us."

He rubs his hands up and down my arms, trying to comfort me. I look up at him. "Why are you helping me?"

"Because you need a hand. I would do the same for anyone if they were as down on their luck as you. It's the way I've been brought up, and my parents would kill me if I didn't. It's what us Walkers do." He cups my face, running his thumb over my lip. It sends a thrill right through my body. His touch is electric, energising, and I don't know if it's the adrenaline rush, but I want this man so badly I can taste it.

I bite the inside of my mouth to stop myself from acting on my impulse and just kissing him. He lowers his hands and laces our fingers together. "And I told you earlier, you're someone important to me, I know it already."

"Drew Walker, you might just be the sweetest guy there ever was."

He grins. "What's your real name? I can't introduce you to my parents in the morning as Bambi."

"It's Jenna, Jenna West."

He smiles and pulls me into his chest, and I let him. I need to feel the comfort of another human. After everything I've been through, the warmth of his body and the small gesture of a hug and knowing someone in this fucked-up world actually cares enough to go out of their way for me, it means everything.

While we stand in his parents' front yard, his arms wrapped around me, I go over his words in my head. *You're someone important to me.* Such a strange thing for him to say when we have literally just met, but I can feel it too. He's going to be someone important in my life as well.

CHAPTER ONE

JENNA: FIVE YEARS LATER

I watch Ivy's daughter, Harmony, play on the rug in front of us. She has little unicorn and fairy figurines lined up on the carpet, talking to herself as she moves them around. She's the cutest kid ever, with a fantastic imagination; it's wonderful to watch her play.

We have just finished dinner and we're enjoying a wine before I head off back to my boring townhouse all alone. Ivy's daughter is so sweet. I've always wanted kids of my own, and I know I'm youngish still, but with the bad luck I've had, I feel like I'm never going to settle down and get married, so the thought of babies of my own seems like an almost impossible dream.

Ivy's not married either. She's a single mum to an adorable five-year-old, and she's one of the best people I know. We've been in each other's worlds since just after Harmony was born, when she moved into the townhouse next to me. I feel so lucky to have been a part of her life, since I have no family of my own to speak of. Having these girls in mine is such a blessing.

There are three townhouses in our block, and to the

other side of us is Fay. She is a retired artist in her 60s. Never having had a family of her own, she is also a part of our little Broken Point girl gang. We have dinner once a week and coffee on as many occasions as we can. I do also like to drop in on Ivy's pancake Sundays whenever I get the chance.

I drain the rest of my wine. "I guess I better go home." I let out a long exhalation. I couldn't really be bothered to move.

"You can stay. I just have to get Harmony to bed then we can watch a movie?"

I smile at my friend. I'm so lucky to have her. But tonight, I need to be alone. "Nah, thanks, but I hear a book calling my name."

"Suit yourself." She shrugs, helping Harmony pack away her toys.

"Night, hun," I say, wrapping her in a hug and making my way to the door.

"See you on Sunday for Harmony's birthday." She smiles sleepily and yawns.

"Looking forward to it." I blow her a kiss and turn to walk home to my townhouse. It's Friday night and I have nothing on, as usual. Dinner with my bestie and her daughter is about as exciting as it gets for me these days, such a contrast to my colourful past. Not that I'm complaining, this life is wonderful in comparison.

Today, while I was as work at the library, I was dreaming about curling up with a good book boyfriend and a glass of red. I need a little escape into a romantic imaginary world with a happily ever after. I let myself in and drop my bag and keys on the kitchen table. I live alone, and everything in my place is just the way I like it—organised, clean, and tidy. I'm a little obsessive about it, but this place means so much to me, because I never thought I would have a home of my own, and now that I do, I like to make sure I take good care of it.

This place was only just built before I moved in, so it's still very fresh and modern. The surfaces are timber, the walls an off-white. The furniture is comfy and homely, eclectic pieces gathered from all over. I love it, I feel so safe here.

I pour a large glass of wine and head upstairs to the home office I have dedicated as a library for all the books I have collected over the last five years. These magnificent distractions from reality are my most prized positions. As a kid I didn't have many belongings; it's hard to own much when you get sent to a new foster home every six months or so. So, when I moved into this place and could finally have my permanent home, I started my collection. So far, I have filled one entire wall. I had a friend of mine and the builder of these townhouses, Blake, build floor-to-ceiling bookshelves for me to eventually fill. I met Blake and his wife Indie when all the shit happened with Vinnie, and they have been close friends ever since.

Books are my life now. I work at the local library, and in my spare time I write stories, some of them short, others like my current project are novel length. They're not something I'm writing to publish or anything, they're just for me, my way of escaping.

I run my hands along the spines of my romance section, trying to decide who I want as my date for this evening, stopping when I come to a black velvety-feeling book with some flowers on the cover. This is the one. I hold it up, smelling the pages, and as I do, a folded piece of paper floats to the floor. I bend down to pick it up, unfolding it. It might have been a while since I saw this piece of paper, but I know the words written on it without even reading it. It's a letter from the only man I have ever loved—Drew Walker.

I sit on the plush carpet, cross-legged, pulling on my tortoiseshell reading glasses and scanning over his words; I know every word off by heart, but it's been a while since I read it. I had forgotten I hid this particular letter here. I have them all. Every single letter he ever wrote me, but this one is special, and it breaks my heart every time I read it.

Drew was my friend after all the shit with my ex, Vinnie, just like Blake. But with Drew, things were different, right from the start. He was a truly special person in my life, and when you have lived a life like mine, where you stay nowhere for long, you don't find friends like that every day. He was the sweetest, and to this day, I still think he's the best-looking man on the planet, with his curly dirty-blond hair, blue eyes, and those dimples. Even the thought of him has me all hot and bothered.

He travels a lot for work because he's a professional surfer, so for a while, when he was away on the world surfing tournament, we would write each other letters. It's so old-fashioned, I know. We could have sent email or text, but it was cute. He knew how much I liked the written word, so he attempted to keep in touch in the best way. And with every letter, I fell for him more and more.

I run my thumb over his words. This was the last letter he sent before the accident. The car accident that in a cruel twist of fate freed me from my arsehole ex, who I was on the run from, and killed Fiona, the woman who was meant to marry Drew's brother.

That day will forever be etched into my soul, it was devastating. And that's why I did what I did. He came home to see me, straight to the hospital off his flight to make sure I was okay, and I broke his heart. But I had to. How could we stay in each other's lives when I was the reason his sister-in-law died? Surely, every time his family looked at me, all they would be able to see was that I was the reason Fi was dead—and I wouldn't blame them, they would be right. If I hadn't run from Vinnie in the first place, he wouldn't have been speeding through town after abducting me. I was in the car boot when the car we were in ploughed into her car, and she was killed by the impact. She was eight months pregnant at the time, though somehow the baby survived.

The guilt still kills me, even today, that the poor child has to grow up without his mother, just like I did. That was why I told Drew we couldn't ever see each other again. I had fallen for him, so much that I knew I was in love with him. But I couldn't be selfish. His family needed time to grieve without me there as a constant reminder.

He was upset with me, but he didn't fight it; he walked out the door to my hospital room, and I haven't seen or heard from him since. It was the right decision, even though I still miss him and wonder what we could have been if things had worked out differently. It was the right choice at the time.

Reading this, I can't help but wonder about what he's doing now. Probably still surfing the world. I bet he never thinks about me, like I think about him. Why would he? I told him to move on, and I'm sure a catch like him did.

For a while after we parted ways, I stalked his Instagram account. It was a connection with him. I could see what country he was in, where he was ranking, but after a while, I found it was hurting more than helping. He always looked like he was having so much fun. A new beautiful girl hanging on his arm every other week, it was too hard to take.

After having time to reflect on everything, I knew how majorly I had fucked up. I'm pretty sure he could have been my one. By the time I came to that realisation it was too late for me to fix it, so I knew I needed to let any thought of him go. I stopped following him on social media, and that must have been when I put this letter in here as well. I have a vague drunken memory of knowing I had to hide it from myself.

I refold the letter and place it back in the front of the book, then move over to my comfy armchair, pulling a fluffy blanket over my lap. I open to the first page and start to read.

Normally I would fly through this book. One of the girls I work with, Olive, carries on about me being the fastest reader in the world and how I should go for a Guinness World Record. I don't know about that, but I'm normally a lot faster than I am tonight. This story is one of my favourites, but I keep losing my place and reading the page, only to realise I haven't taken any of it in, so I read it again, only to repeat the same process five minutes later. My mind is too distracted thinking about Drew—dreamy Drew Walker. I sigh. I put the book down, taking a big sip of my wine.

I wonder what he is doing right now. What exciting country is he hanging out in, surfing? I know I shouldn't, but tonight I can't help myself. I'm curious to see if he's still single, travelling the world, or if he has found his perfect match and settled down. The thought of that has me feeling a little uneasy. I know I'm the one who let him go, so I should hope that he is happy with his life, that he has moved on, but I don't. I hope that he is as lonely as I am, out there somewhere, wondering about me. I think that makes me an awful person, but I can't help it. I never moved on from him, not even close.

I've tried a couple of times. I have been on disastrous

dates with no spark, no connection, no conversation. No one compared to him and the way I felt when we were together. It's so strange, we never even got close enough to kiss. I don't know why. We were close so many times, but we would get interrupted. I think he was too worried about me and my situation to push it, and I was too shy to try anything with him, but I didn't need to. The connection we had was so strong that I didn't need any physical contact to know he was my perfect match.

I pick up my phone and type his name into the search box on Instagram. Drew Walker. The first image that comes up is from the lighthouse here in Byron. The next is a house I recognise as his parents' house, then the beach here in Broken Point. My heart kicks up a beat. He's home in Byron —by himself, it would seem from the pictures. There is no sign of a girl. That's not what I was expecting at all and doesn't help me. Now I know he's so close by and the possibility of us running into each other is real.

Drew

The ocean is crystal clear and glassy, not even a breath of wind. I lie on my board waiting for the next wave to roll in. Conditions today are perfect for a cruise surf while I wait for my two nephews to arrive for their surfing lesson. Both my sister Elly and brother Theo have five-year-old boys. While a little young, both of them are keen to be top surfers just like their Uncle Drew—and why wouldn't they want to be like me? I'm pretty sick. So while I recover from my knee surgery, I've offered to give them some lessons. Just easy stuff for now, learning how to paddle out, water safety, how to read the waves. But they have been loving it, and truth is, it's just what I need as well.

After crashing out in the finals last year and destroying my knee, I have been lost. Surfing has been my whole life for as long as I can remember, and when I was handed the news that my knee needed to be operated on, I thought it was all over. I don't know anything else; what the fuck am I supposed to do with my life if I don't have surfing and the world tour? The doctor might as well have told me I had some sort of terminal disease, because it sure as hell felt like a death sentence.

But that was 18 months ago now, and the surgery went better than expected. I'm a quick healer so my recovery has been fast. I'm back in the water, training, getting my body back in peak condition so I can try and win a wild card and get back in. I stayed away as long as I could, but I need the water. I need to ride the waves, it's in my blood. My surgeon warned me to give it longer, but I know my body. I have already missed a season, and I need to get back on the tour before I'm too old and that title I have been working towards my whole life is out of my grasp forever.

I can see my twin sister Elena—or Elly, as we all call her—walking up the beach with her son, Cooper. I better catch a wave in. That little dude is full of energy, and he won't want to be kept waiting for long.

I glance over my shoulder, waiting for the right wave to ride in. As I see it, I paddle madly. The wave starts to pick up and I paddle faster, and my board rises in the water as the wave starts to pick me up. I pop up to standing, and I ride the wave in to the shore, showing off a little for Coop. I know he'll be impressed. I jump into the water as I get closer in. Tucking my board under one arm, I wade through the shallows to where they're standing on the beach.

Elly shakes her head. "You're doing alright for someone who's not supposed to be riding waves at the moment. How's the knee?"

"The knee is fine, Sis, don't need you worrying about me as well. Mum is doing enough of that for everyone."

"I bet. You looked comfortable out there. You must be getting better, it's good to see."

"Thanks." I bend down so I'm at eye height with Cooper. He has spiky blond hair and blue eyes; he looks just like me at the same age. I mess up his hair. "And how are you today, little buddy, you ready for your lesson?"

"Sure am! I have been watching YouTube clips of you when you were younger. You were sooo good, I want to be just like you."

"We better get started then, you have a lot to learn." I look back to Elly. "Have you heard from Theo, are they coming?"

She looks back up the beach, then shrugs. "I think so."

As she answers, Jasper, Theo's little boy, comes running out of the beach path towards us, with Theo following closely behind carrying his board. Jasper is a cutie, with strawberry-blond hair and a scattering of freckles across his nose. He's not loud and full of energy like Coop, he's more reserved, but when you get him talking about something he's keen on, he won't stop, and he likes surfing as much as Coop.

He throws his arms around me in a hug. "Uncle Drew! Aww, you're all wet," he complains, shaking his hands off.

"Yeah, I've been in already." I laugh. "Why don't you two go and get wet, then you can come back up here and we can revise what we learnt last week."

The boys run down to the water, splashing through the shallows, giggling at each other. Theo drops Jasper's board on the sand and sits down, running his hand through his hair. He looks all hot and bothered.

"What's going on with you?" I ask, throwing him a look.

"Nothing, we were just running late," he mutters.

"Yeah, and? You look weird," says Elly. She must be noticing the strange smile on Theo's face, just like I have. Something is definitely going on with him. I haven't seen that goofy look on his face in a long time.

"And nothing, just been an interesting afternoon. Sorry we're late," he huffs.

Yeah, right, I don't believe it's nothing for a second. But the kids are on their way back out of the water, so it can be left until later.

"Come on, boys, line up your boards on the sand and lie down." I go over the skills we learnt the week before and some more water safety, then we take one board down to the water to do a little practice in the smaller waves. They're both picking it up quickly but need to be better at swimming before I take them any further. We make our way back up the beach to where Theo and Elly sit talking.

"Go say thank-you for your lesson, Cooper," Elly tells him.

"Thanks, Uncle Drew, that lesson was sick!"

"No worries, little dude. See you back in the waves, same time next week." I give him a wink.

Elly and Cooper head for home, walking up the beach. Or should I say Cooper runs and Elly speed-walks to keep up with him. They live not far from here. I take off and walk toward Theo's car with him and Jasper, board under my arm.

"So, are you going to tell me why you've been wearing that stupid grin on your face since you got here or what?"

"He's just happy he didn't kill the pretty lady's cat," says Jasper.

I raise a brow at Theo, silently asking him to elaborate. I have no idea what Jasper is talking about. But the look makes sense if a pretty lady is involved.

"We nearly had an accident on the way over here," Theo says. "A little ginger cat ran out in front of our car. Luckily, I didn't hit it. The lady and her daughter had just got it today, so they were very happy she was okay."

"Still doesn't explain the smile, unless it's got something to do with Jasper's comment about *the pretty lady*."

Theo gives me a look but doesn't respond. Instead, he rests Jasper's board against his car, opening the door for Jasper to get in.

Jasper rolls his eyes. "He was talking to her for forever, that's why we were late," says Jasper, his words exaggerated.

"That makes more sense, Jas, your dad can talk too much." I mess up his hair, and he nods.

"Why don't you hop in the car, Jas, get yourself strapped in." He does as Theo suggests, leaving the two of us to talk.

"So, what's the go? She must have been alright, hey?"

"She was more than alright. I have never met anyone quite like her before." He sighs, and I wonder what his problem is if he likes her so much. It's not like he has any issues getting what he wants when it comes to chicks.

"Well, I'm sure you gave her your number, and with the luck you have, she'll be regretting her poor life choices by the weekend."

"Hilarious." He opens the car boot, sliding the board through, slamming it closed. "She's not like that, she's different. She's a single mum, and her daughter goes to school with Jasper."

I nod, only half believing him. If that is the case, though, good for him. Theo's fiancée, Jasper's mum, was killed in a car accident when she was pregnant with Jasper, five years ago. They managed to save him, but it was too late for his mum. Theo has been raising Jasper on his own ever since. I'm not quite sure how he does it. He copes a lot better than I would. Kids are fun to play with and all, but that's why I'm the fun uncle. I hand them back when any of the real work has to be done.

He opens his door, sitting in his car, then turns back to me. "We're on for this Saturday night, right?"

"Yeah, for sure."

I wave them both goodbye and walk toward my place, board under my arm. It's just a short walk from the beach. That's one of the reasons I bought my block of land in the first place; I need to be close to the beach, and from my place, I can hear the rumble of the waves crashing to the shore and smell the salty water when I wake up in the morning.

My block of land now has a massive house on it that Elly's husband Fraser and a friend of mine, Blake, built for me a few years back. More than what a single guy really needs, but I had the money, so why not have an awesome beach house, with five bedrooms, three bathrooms, a games room, and a pool? There is also a large garage to house my favourite toys, my three cars and motorbike.

I push through the side gate and go round the back to hose off my board. Resting it on the side of the house, I strip off my board shorts and jump under the outdoor shower to rinse off the sand before I head inside.

Thinking about what happened with Theo's fiancée, Fiona, makes me think about *her*, Jenna, the only girl I have ever wanted anything more with. She was perfect—shy, beautiful, intelligent... and damaged. Even if we didn't meet under the best circumstances, the months following that night were the best of my life. I got to know her, like really *know* her, and I fell for her, hook, line, and sinker.

I have never been the type of guy to want a relationship, but with her, I was starting to hope that would be possible. I could see it, our future, and it was going to be perfect. She wasn't friends with me because of the money or the fame, like most of the girls I came across; she was friends with me because we connected on a deeper level.

I kept my distance from her for months, even though I wanted more. I kept it to just friends because I knew what she had been through. The men in her life had only ever taken advantage of her and treated her poorly, and I wasn't going to be one of them. Of course I craved more with her. I had from the first moment I saw her, but I knew she was fragile. She had been through a lot, so I wasn't going to push it. She needed a friend, and that was exactly what I was going to be, the best damn friend she ever had. I could hang on and wait until she was ready for something more.

That was... until the accident that killed Fiona.

That accident not only ruined Theo's life, but it destroyed any chance there could ever be for me and Jenna. After Elly rang me to tell me about the accident, I was on the first flight home. I went straight to see Jenna in the hospital as soon as I got in, but she didn't want to see me. She blamed herself for what happened. It didn't matter how many times I told her it wasn't her fault, she couldn't accept it. The way she saw it was Fiona died because she had run away from her ex, Vinnie. He had kidnapped Jenna, the car they were travelling in was the one that collided with Fiona. So it was all her fault.

Except it wasn't! No one else saw it that way. Vinnie was a criminal, a filthy scum-of-the-earth thug. He was to blame, not her. But that was it for us, she wanted nothing to do with me anymore. She said it was for the best that we go our separate ways, that I move on with my life, but I could never see it that way.

At first, I was angry at her for throwing away what we had, but after a while, I was just sad. For her, for what she had been through. She deserved a better life than the one she had lived. In the few months we had known each other, she let me in so much, and I got the impression that was rare. I wish things had been different, but I learnt a few hard lessons that year, and sometimes it doesn't matter how much you want something, it's just not meant to be.

So, I moved on with my life as best I could. I blocked Jenna out, any sign of her from my life removed. I went back to the same life I had before I met her, but I wasn't the same. Surfing, travelling, never staying in one place for too long, sleeping with anyone I could, and partying harder than I ever had before. Anything I could do to forget she ever existed. It didn't help me forget about her, because no matter how hard I tried, nothing in my life compared to how I'd felt when we were together.

But the lifestyle I chose to help me move on gave me a new bad-boy reputation, and the sponsors lined up to have my face and name attached to their brand. Cobie, my manager, loved me for it. I was making us both more money than I had in the past, and it's the reason I have the life I do now. Jenna saying goodbye to me changed me, and I will never be the same again because of it.

I finish showering off, grab my towel, and slide open the back door. I need food, I'm starving. I head straight to the kitchen and open the fridge door, grabbing all the makings for a supper sandwich: salami, ham, tomato, cheese, and baby spinach—yum. I place it all on the counter and get to work.

As much as I don't want it to, my mind wanders back to her. I may have deleted all of the photos I had of her, but I don't need them. I can remember every little detail about her. She was the most beautiful girl in the world. Long, slim legs with the perfect tan, big tits... Fuck, I wish I had gotten my hands on those when I had the chance. Her long chestnut-brown hair, big doe eyes with thick black lashes, but it was her smile, honest to God, my heart would slow and the rest of the world would black out. It would be me and her and that was it. She is perfection.

I wonder if she's still living in the townhouse Blake and I helped her buy. If she is, she lives not far from me. I've made a habit of peeking at her place when I drive past, hoping to catch sight of her. Or maybe we'll bump into each other down the beach, things like that happen. But that would probably be all kinds of awkward now that it's been so long. What do I even say to her after five years? I'm sure she has moved on with her life, happy with a husband and a baby or some shit like that. A girl like her wouldn't have stayed single for long. At least I hope she's happy, it's what she deserves.

CHAPTER TWO

JENNA

My head is all over the place tonight. I don't know why, but I've been feeling like shit all week. Out of sorts, not like myself, like I need to let loose and have some fun. I'm sick of being at home alone, reading about other people having adventures or meet cutes where they fall hopelessly in love. I need some excitement in my life, or maybe just something totally out of character for me, like a drunken hook-up that I can conveniently forget about tomorrow and go back to my normal boring existence.

Luckily for me, I'm out at our popular beachside pub with my two besties, Ivy and Penny, and the chances of a random hook-up are high… if I don't chicken out like every other time I've amped myself up for something fun, like sex with a stranger. I have nearly done it a handful of times, but every time, as the night progresses, I talk myself out of it.

This is a monthly event for us girls, but normally Penny is the only one getting lucky, and with the kinds of adventures she has, she more than makes up for us. Ivy and I normally end up heading home earlyish after a meal and a few drinks, jealous of what we're missing out on.

Ivy mouths the words to the song that is blaring as we dance, her smile a little more lopsided than normal after a few too many margaritas with dinner. I feel like she's in the same mood as me. She has this boho beauty vibe going on tonight, luxurious long honey-blonde hair that reaches her waist. Pale baby-blue eyes. At first glance, she appears like a relaxed hippy type, but she's anything but chill. I guess it's hard to be when you're the sole parent with all the responsibilities lumped on you day after day. Most of the time, she runs on anxiety and coffee. I'm pretty sure that's why she teaches yoga, to keep her demons under control, but I know her better than anyone, and it's a challenge for her.

Tonight, we're both feeling sorry for ourselves, desperate and dateless, but it's our own fault, neither one of us has tried to rectify our sad situations. We have been this way since we met five years ago. At dinner tonight, I admitted to her how I have been feeling lately, and her solution was to drink up and have a fun night dancing. Can't say it was terrible advice. I sway to the music, feeling the buzz from the cocktails, and it has me smiling happily to myself for the first time in a while. My body feels alive tonight, the warmth from the alcohol making me feel like I could do anything.

Penny must see something shiny. She turns to us with a wink before she weaves her way through the dancefloor to check it out. The girl's a ditz, bright and bubbly and so much fun to be around, but she flits from one thing to the next looking for entertainment. She won't sit for too long, and she's the same with her guys. Moves from one bad choice to the next, never taking life too seriously.

Actually, it's surprising that she and Ivy are friends, now that I think about it. They're complete opposites, but I guess somehow, they even each other out. They both teach yoga at the Lotus Studio, and that's how Penny came to be a part of our awesome little girl gang. Her hair is like her personality, a bouncy, crazy, messy mass of dark blonde curls, with sun-kissed highlights. It's fitting, because she's our ray of sunshine, radiating warmth and happiness. Her eyes, hazel with flecks of green, are large and bright. Tonight, she's in a red playsuit with ridiculously tall heels. She flicks her hair over her shoulder and stops when she reaches the bar. Probably after some guy she has spotted.

Man, I wish I had just a pinch of her confidence. I would love to have the guts to go up to a guy, tell him what I want for the night, then slip out of here with him. No looking back, no regrets. It's never going to happen, but a girl can dream.

I scan the pub. It's the usual type of crowd we get when we have our monthly night out, pretty casual. Being so close to the beach, most tourists wander over for dinner and drinks when they're finished with the beach for the day. The rest of us locals make more of an effort, but it's still nothing fancy, just guys in jeans and button-downs or tees and chicks in summer dresses. I close my eyes, feeling the music vibrate through my body as I move to the beat of the song.

Ivy grips my arm, squeezing hard enough to get my attention. "What?" I say, a little irritated. I rub my arm where it feels like she's left a mark.

She looks panicked and tilts her head in the direction of the bar. I follow her line of sight to see Penny talking to two guys at the bar.

She buries her head in her hands, giving it a shake. "It's him," she mouths.

I look to see what she's talking about. "Who?"

She leans in to talk into my ear so I can hear her over the

music. "The guy who nearly ran over my cat at Harmony's birthday party." Now that she says it, I do recognise the tall blond guy Pen is talking to. Ivy has been crushing on him ever since he nearly ran over her cat last weekend. Penny is playing it up with these guys. She is her usual flirty self, touching his arm as she talks. There is another guy with him, but I can't quite see him through the crowd as someone is standing in front of him.

I smirk at her. "Now's your chance then. Go have some fun for once, girl. This must be some sort of fate that you're both here tonight. I'd take it as a sign and go get me a piece of that fine body."

She tilts her head, taking him in, watching as he talks to Pen. "He is mighty fine."

"Godlike, even." I giggle at the nickname she has given him.

She gives me a serious look then bursts into laughter herself. "I'm not going to live down saying that, am I?"

"Not likely, but it's a pretty accurate assessment. He's gorgeous! And his eyes are fixed on you, hun. This is your chance."

I can see the blush rise as she stares back at him, it's so cute. I so want this for her. She deserves to have a bit of fun in her life, a break away from all the responsibility.

Penny moves aside, looking our way and talking to the second guy. As soon as I register who she's talking to, I freeze. I know that face, that cheeky grin, that longish curly hair, broad chest. As much as I have tried to forget him, erase him from my thoughts, he still frequents my dreams, even now, five years since I saw him last. I swallow the lump in my throat. Drew Walker, sexy bad-boy pro surfer, and now it all makes more sense: the guy staring at Ivy is Theo Walker, his brother. I thought I recognised him the other day, but I couldn't place him. I don't know whether to run and hide or throw myself at Drew's feet and beg for his forgiveness.

I knew he was home from the surfing tour and that this very situation could play out, when we run into each other. It's going to be awkward as fuck, how could it not be. He recognises me too, and I'm surprised to see his famous cheeky grin, dimples and all, when he makes eye contact, rather than a scowl of hatred like I deserve. He's so dreamy, and in my tipsy state, I don't want to run and hide.

I know his reputation these days has him painted as a bad boy, always partying with a hot new girl on his arm, but knowing all that doesn't stop that familiar pull I have towards him. And the overwhelming desire I have to roll around naked with him.

I want to see how this is going to play out tonight—hopefully like my dreams. His hands on my body, cock buried deep inside me, while I scream his name on repeat as he gives me the most earth-shattering orgasm of my life. It's been a long five years, and at this point, I'm pretty sure I will combust if he just touches me.

DREW

I'm out with my brother, Theo, and his two work mates, Talon and Sean. After I have smashed him at a few rounds of pool, we're at the bar topping up our drinks. Theo has attracted the attention of a bouncy girl with blonde curls. She's standing in front of us with a look of determination on her pretty face.

"Evening, boys, I'm Penny," she purrs flirtatiously, with a broad smile full of perfectly straight teeth.

"Hi, Penny, I'm Theo, and this is my brother, Drew."

I give her a nod as I try to look around her in the direction she came from.

"Who's your other friend, the brunette?" I ask Penny.

Theo looks back over at them, inspecting the two girls on the dancefloor. His eyes widen, and I know he sees what I see. It's her. I thought it was at first glance but wondered if my eyes were playing tricks on me because I've been thinking about her so much lately.

Penny flicks her hair over her shoulder, "Oh, that's Jen, come and introduce yourself. She's cute and just as single as Ivy." She touches Theo on the arm as she says Ivy's name. He looks a little distracted, and I'm not surprised. The last time he would have seen Jenna was the night his fiancée, Fiona, was killed.

"Jen as in Jenna?" I ask just to make sure, but I know who she is. I could never forget that face, and the pull to go to her immediately is strong, even from this far away.

"Did Ivy send you over?" Theo asks, his eyes fixed on the attractive blonde.

The two of them talk about Ivy, and I tune it out. All I can do is watch Jenna. She is just as perfect as I remember her. Her long, chestnut-brown hair is straight tonight, her skin tanned. She smiles over to me, and even from here I can see the blush rise to her cheeks.

I thought when I saw her again, I would feel hurt or angry or maybe nothing, it has been a long time. I've spent the last five years trying to block her from my memory and get over her by getting on every other chick I could. But all the feelings I had for her are rushing back to me. She was the one. I know it without a doubt. Now she's here in the same place as me. I want her more than ever before, but that won't happen. I can't go back there. Falling for her only ends in heartbreak, and I will not let myself go through it again. I can't. I shake my head and look away, trying to refocus on what the others are talking about.

"Oh, you have no idea, honey. I've known Ivy for five years, and I don't think she's even been on one date. But my girl's got a crush on you, big time. She has been calling you *the god* all week." She laughs again.

I pretend to choke. Is this chick for real? "What did you do to this girl?"

Theo chuckles. "Oh, really? That's good to know." He turns to me. "I haven't done anything yet, we just talked. I guess I'm just that good!"

Penny nods with a cheeky smile. "She hasn't stopped all week, really she hasn't."

"What are you ladies drinking?" Theo asks Penny. He looks impressed with himself. She has inflated his ego even more. Great, that was the last thing he needed.

The bouncy blonde leans over the counter, ordering drinks for herself and her two friends, openly flirting with the bartender as she does. The bartender places the drinks on the bar as she waits for Theo to pay.

"You boys should come and join us. If you're waiting for Ivy to give you a written invitation, it's never going to happen," she says as she bounces away with the drinks Theo paid for.

Jenna and Ivy glance back over to us, taking their drinks from Penny. Jenna's eyes again come to settle on mine, and she smiles over at me— if I didn't know better, I would think seductively. She is flirting with me from across the room, giving me that look girls do when they want you to fuck them senseless.

God, she is sexy. The way her full lips shape into that inviting smile stirs something in me I haven't felt since she ended it. I have been with many chicks over the years, so many I can't recall names, much less the number it would have been, but no one has ever made me feel the way Jenna can with just a hint of a smile. My heart rate increases, and I know I need to get a handle on this situation before it gets out of control. I will not go there. *She is not for you, Drew, and she never will be*, I remind myself.

Theo gives me a look and I know what he's thinking before he says it. "You okay if I head over there? You know, with Jenna being there, will it be weird?"

"Yeah, I'm good with it if you are. I have some unfinished business with her anyway." God, what am I even saying? I can't finish what I want to with her, that would be really fucking stupid after all this time. *Get your cock and your mind under control before you head over there. She is not for you.*

"Okay." He gives me a look as he orders us two beers from the bar. Two of his workmates, Talon and Sean, join us after finishing up their game of pool. Theo, Talon, and Sean are all detectives at the local station, and tonight is a pretty usual occurrence for us. Whenever my twin sister Elly or Mum can have Theo's little boy for the night, we make the most of it.

The girls have made their way over to a free table. "Boys, we're heading over there," Theo calls to his workmates, pointing to the group of giggling girls as we head towards them. Geez, she must be drunk. Maybe that's why she's eyeing me like she wants to eat me.

"Evening, ladies, can we join you?" Theo turns on the charm, and I have to stop myself from scoffing at him.

Ivy, the girl Theo has a thing for, eyes us both suspiciously. "Well, it's our girls' night, so normally no boys allowed, but I guess since you bought us the drinks." She laughs at herself, clinking her drink with Jenna. Yeah, I would say they have all consumed a fair amount of alcohol tonight. But I like this girl, quite the smart-arse towards Theo. That is just what he needs to bring him down off his high horse.

Jenna looks between Theo and me, a little unsure, and I guess I would be too if I were in her shoes. But she has nothing to worry about, I'm not here to hate on her. I'm a lover, not a fighter. *You're not here to love her either*, I remind myself.

The other boys catch up to us and arrive at our table, drinks in hand. "This is Sean, Talon, and my brother Drew." Theo introduces us to the girls, but I need no introduction to the girl sitting in front of me.

Jenna has grown up a lot since I saw her last. She was always stunningly beautiful, but somehow, she is even better than I remember, her curves showcased so nicely in that white low-cut dress she's wearing. My cock is hard at the sight, and I will it to get with the no-touch policy I have in place for this girl. But the thing that worries me the most is the way I can't seem to drag my eyes away from her, even though I know I should. I'm just here to catch up with an old friend, but the way my body reacts to her is going to make resisting the temptation for something more very hard indeed.

The girls offer a little wave hello, and Penny gets up so we can slide in; I make sure I'm sitting next to Jenna. It's quite a snug fit on the bench seats, but I'm not complaining. I'm close enough to be able to take in her scent. It's intoxicating, a mix of something fruity. She hasn't said a word and neither have I, but her eyes haven't left mine, and she plays with her bottom lip, biting it a little. It's sexy as hell, and she is definitely flirting with me. I'm surprised; in the past we never got past the friendship zone. We were close, really close, but the timing just wasn't right, so I didn't push it and neither did she.

I know for my own sanity I should go and look for someone easy to satisfy my appetite tonight. That was the plan for the night originally, but as soon as I laid eyes on her, any other girl in the room paled in comparison, and I knew that was never going to happen.

I lean into her ear, so she can hear me over the music. "You seem surprisingly happy to see me."

She smiles and places her hand on my leg, her fingers running up the seam of my jeans playfully. "Always happy to see an old friend, Drew. If I'm being honest, I was wondering how long it would take for us to run into each other when I heard you were home. I'm glad we did."

"You knew I was home?" I say, surprised she was keeping tabs on me. Last I checked, she didn't give a damn what I was doing. Or where I was, for that matter.

"People talk. Gossip about one of our biggest surf stars travels fast around these parts, you should know that."

Flattery, she knows how to get to me. "Biggest surf star, hey?"

She shrugs. "Well, that's what the people say when they talk about you, anyway. I mean, I wouldn't know about any of that, surfing's not really my thing. But I have heard the rumours. You have quite the reputation for yourself these days." She pokes at my thigh. "What was that article saying? Something about the bad-boy surfer caught at it again." She shakes her head. "You're one naughty boy, Drew Walker."

She's killing me. This is not the Jenna I remember, all shy and stuff. She is pushing my buttons, and it's making it hard not to respond in a way that ends with me bending her over this table and fucking her stupid. I'm not loving that she has read some article about me, though. Most of what is said in the tabloids is total shit, and the rest is not anything I would want her to know about me or the way I live my life. But something about it seems to have ignited a fire in her.

Ivy and Theo get up and head towards the dancefloor. It's a great opportunity to distract her from where this little chat is heading. "You want to join your friend?" I ask, hoping she says yes.

She nods, and I offer my hand, pulling her to standing and leading her to the dancefloor with me. The music is loud pumping through the pub, and we move to the beat. It's fast and fun, her dance moves fluid like she is one with the music. Man, it's sexy as fuck and so much more dangerous than just talking. I know I shouldn't go there, but it takes me back to the night we met when she danced for me. Fuck, it was the hottest lap dance I have ever had. Her perfect body moving around me in the tiny sparkly number she had on—it's not something I will ever forget.

Theo leans into me. "Drew, I'm taking Ivy out the front for some fresh air. You guys alright?"

I glance at Ivy; she doesn't look well, her face very pale. Theo has his hands full. He'll be lucky if she doesn't puke. "All good, mate, see you later." He escorts her through the crowd out the front of the pub. I lean in to whisper to Jenna, "Looks like you're stuck with me for the night. How much did your girl have to drink? You on some crazy bender or something?"

"No, just a little tipsy, letting loose for a change, having a bit of fun. You know how that is, don't you, Drew?" She has stopped dancing and stares up at me. Her tongue licks over her top lip seductively.

I could kiss her and show her how much fun we could really have. I would show her the fucking time of her life, the kind of fun that would leave her unable to walk tomorrow. I run my hands through my hair, taking a step back from her. No, not going there, no matter how much I want it, that would be a mistake. "Do you want to get out of here? It's too loud and I'm hungry."

"I could eat." She smiles, and I know she isn't talking about food. Who is this Jenna and why is she making it so damn hard for me to resist her tonight? I take her hand, leading her back towards the table. Penny, Talon, and Sean are playing some sort of drinking game. Jenna grabs her bag.

"You getting out of here, Jen?" Penny asks her.

"Sure am. I'll see you later," she slurs. I think food is a good idea; she is more than a little tipsy.

We hit the cool night air and it's refreshing after the humidity of the dancefloor. I wrap my leather jacket around her arms, and she smiles up at me gratefully. The sense of déjà vu isn't lost on her either. As we walk up the street, she slips her hand into mine and I let her.

"I have missed you, so much."

"I've missed you too." Holding her hand, her body so close to mine. It may have been a while since I've seen her, but with her, the instant familiarity is there, our closeness back to how it was immediately. It makes me realise how much I have really missed her.

"I wasn't sure you would be happy to see me," she says softly.

"Honestly, I wasn't sure how I felt at first, but what happened between us back then, well... it's in the past. You were going through a really hard time, and as tough as it was, now that I've had time to process, I get it. Yeah, maybe I expected to be a little angry when I saw you again, but I'm just happy to see you. Looks like you're doing well."

"Thank you, I am, thanks to you and Blake for all your

help back then." She stops walking and turns to me, taking both my hands. "Drew, I have wanted to get in contact so many times over the years. There are so many things I want to say to you, but it's hard to put into words. What you did for me... and I... I'm so sorry." Her voice cracks, and I can see the well of tears she is trying to hold back. The last thing I want is for her to be sad.

"Hey, it's okay, don't get upset, it's all fine now. I'm just glad to see you're doing so well." I tuck some stray hair behind her ear and cup her face. She is so beautiful. Her eyes look down to my mouth, then back to my eyes as she blinks away the tears.

I lost track of the number of times we have been in this same position, our faces just inches apart, so close I could just kiss her if I wanted to. Take those plump red lips with mine and show her just what she has been missing out on. Is that what she wants? The way she's looking at me, I feel like it is, but when it comes to her, I don't want to do the wrong thing. Maybe I'm reading her wrong. She has been drinking as well.

Also, do I want to put myself back in that position again? Last time, nothing actually happened between us. We spent every spare minute we could with each other, shared our hopes and dreams for the future, as well as our fears, but we never actually did anything physical... and she still destroyed me. It's best I don't go there with her, no matter how much I want to in this moment, looking into her eyes. I pull away, dropping her hands, and turn to keep on walking.

"Sorry, I'm being silly, it's the margaritas. They make me cry every time," she says, a little embarrassed.

"Don't worry about it." We're out the front of the kebab shop. "You want one?"

"Sounds perfect. Just whatever you're having. I'm going to sit down for a sec out the front."

I order our food, two doner kebabs with all the trimmings and a bottle of water for her; she needs it after all those cocktails. I take our food out to where she's found a park bench that faces out to the street, and I take a seat beside her, handing her the water.

"Thank you so much. How did you know I needed water?"

I raise a brow. "Just a hunch."

She drinks half the bottle and screws the lid back on, taking her wrap from me. Unravelling it, I bite into mine—so good. Greasy and just what is called for tonight. We sit for a while in comfortable silence while we eat; the street is still busy with cars going by and pedestrians walking about. "So, are you still at the library?" I ask, directing the conversation back to safe territory.

She looks up from her food, licking her lips, and I wish she wouldn't. "Yes, still working there."

"That's good, must have been the right job for you." I already knew that from the last time I talked to Blake. I don't ask him anymore, but he likes to give me updates on her anyway. While she couldn't see me anymore, she managed to keep her friendship with him. Knowing that kind of stings, but I guess their friendship was different to ours.

"Yes, I love it there. My home away from home. Books were my first love and being surrounded by them every day makes me very happy." She looks down at the ground, then back at me. "How long until you can surf again? I mean, your leg looks okay now."

"You really have been doing your research on me." I laugh. "I'm surfing again, just not competing again yet.

There is a local comp I can do next month if I'm feeling up to it. I might."

"You love competing, you must be finding it hard to be stuck in one place, not travelling round doing all your comps."

In the past, that would have been a correct assessment of me, but something has changed for me now after having this time off. "Yeah, it's not easy, but this time being home has felt different. I'm not itching to leave again so soon like I used to every time I came home. I think even if I qualify and I get back on the tour, this might be my last year. I'm ready to stay put for a while. Make a life for myself here. Maybe try something different." I'm not even sure why I just told her that. The thought has crossed my mind a bit over the last six months, but nothing is set yet. Well, it wasn't until I saw her tonight, anyway. How can running into her make me want to stay when I never have before?

CHAPTER THREE

JENNA

I HOP OUT OF THE SHOWER, THROW MY TOWEL AROUND myself, fix my make-up, and brush my hair into a high ponytail. I'm running late for my class, but the woman staring back at me doesn't look like she cares like she normally would. She looks happy, carefree, even. The smile on my face is massive. Last night was amazing. Dreamy Drew is back in my life, and this time he wants to stay here in Byron permanently. I was so surprised to hear him say that, but it makes my heart happy to know he'll be around, and seeing him just makes it all the more obvious how much I have missed having him in my life.

We spent the entire night together, walking round town, catching up on the time we've lost, eating ice cream then sitting in another bar and drinking some more. He is just how I remember, so much fun, and I couldn't get the smile off my face all night. It was wonderful. The only thing that has me question myself is at one point I was sure he was going to kiss me. I was positive; the moment was perfect, but before anything happened, he pulled away and the moment passed.

Probably for the best, I guess. Maybe I hurt him too much last time, and he can forgive me enough to be friends, but I have destroyed any chance of anything else. I'm sure this is the way things are supposed to be between us, but there is this niggling part of me that wants it to be so much more with him, a little voice coming from within that tells me maybe I can change his mind. Maybe this could be something more this time? I'm not really sure how. I'm not like Penny, I can't just put myself out there and ask a guy for what I want. Truth is, when it comes to men, I'm pretty clueless.

When I was younger, I had a few boyfriends, and things were not what I would call ideal relationships. Then there was Vinnie, and that was a whole other type of messy. I attract the wrong type of man, that's for sure. I wouldn't say I have a bad-boy complex, because they always seem okay to start off with, then once they have me sucked in, I see the real side of them and everything turns to shit.

That was, until Drew. He was so different from everyone else, and I haven't had anyone special in my life at all since him. No one ever compared to him, so what was the point in trying? If I gave in and went on a date, it never progressed to a second one. And after a while I just gave up. I was happy with my life the way it was, mostly. There are perks of not dating—no drama, no arsehole to run from scared for my life. Really, I have so many reasons not to date.

But sometimes the loneliness creeps in. I have been by myself my whole life, so it's not like that's anything different, and if anything, I have the girls now, so I'm not completely alone, but that nagging feeling that it would be nice to have someone special in my life, it's there, and it sits like a rock in the pit of my stomach.

I want more.

I chuck on my pale pink zip-up sports bra and shorts then throw over a white hoodie, grab my boots, and run out the door. I quickly jump in my black VW Golf and check the time. Shit. I really am late: class starts in ten minutes. I speed the whole way there and pull up just in time to open the studio. There are a few girls lined up waiting for me. And I feel terrible, I'm never late. They don't look too bothered, leaning against the brick wall, chatting amongst themselves.

"Afternoon, girls, sorry I'm late. Hope you've all had fun weekends," I call to them as I open up the door and flick on the lights. They filter in, throwing down their bags and getting themselves ready as I get the music sorted and the room set up. "Start your warm-up, the same as last week. I'll just get my boots on." I pull on my boots and zip them all the way up and move to the front of the class to stretch at the ballet bar. This dance studio caters for lots of different types of dance; there's a barre class that is mainly done at the ballet bar, a boot-camp type class, and then there's the class I teach. Pole dance.

"Okay, everyone, take your position at the pole and we can get started moving through the dance I showed you last week." I know it seems weird that I teach a pole-dancing class now that I have my life all pulled together and all that. But I started dancing when I was so young. It's a part of me, and a few years back, I was feeling a little lost, I was really missing the dancing side of stripping.

I didn't want to dance for sleazy guys or anything, and I didn't need the money, but I loved the empowering feeling of moving to the music and how strong my body felt after. So, I looked into classes. I turned up to the first class and the instructor was the redheaded girl I worked with at the strip club, Ariel—or Mia is her actual name. I took one look at her and nearly ran for it. I hadn't seen her since I moved my stuff out of her place years before, but she stopped me, talked me into staying and giving it a go. She owns this studio and is an amazing dancer.

Once I took a few classes with her, she offered me the Sunday class to teach. I wouldn't have thought I had the confidence to do it, but I love it, and it's like my little secret. I just tell Ivy and Pen I'm at a dance class when they ask why I can't catch up on a Sunday arvo. They have no idea about my past, and I would prefer to keep it that way.

These girls are a beginners' class, but we have been together for a few months now so they're getting pretty good. We run through our routine, stopping the music to slow down the harder parts when they need.

"Right, girls, from the top one more time." I play the music, and everyone takes their spots as we flow through the dance moves again.

The hour disappears fast. "Excellent class today, girls, I'm so proud of how far you've all come. Don't forget to do your cool-down stretches." I make my way back over to the bar.

They follow me then gather their belongings and filter out until it's just me. I sit to take off my boots and check my phone for the fiftieth time today. I don't know why but I keep hoping Drew might have texted me, but nothing. We exchanged numbers last night, and I kinda got the impression that he would call me or text me, but maybe I was wrong. I look up from my phone to see Mia waltzing through the door. She's a fresh burst of energy, looking stunning as always in a cute workout outfit, her long red hair in a high pony, swishing from side to side as she moves.

I run over to her and hug her. "I feel like it's been forever since I saw you last," I tell her.

"That's why I'm here. You want to go for a drink or something? We haven't caught up in ages, and I feel like you have a lot to tell me." She raises a knowing brow.

I eye her suspiciously. What is she on about? "What gives you that feeling?"

"I saw you last night, missy. Who's the hottie?" She pokes me in the arm.

My eyes widen. I was drunk, but I wouldn't have been that drunk that I forgot I saw her, would I? "Where did you see me?"

"I have eyes everywhere." She laughs as she links arms with me, and we walk out of the studio.

I lock the door and we continue to walk up the street. "Can we get coffee? I don't think I can go for another drink just yet, after last night." My tummy is still not right from the amount of alcohol I consumed, and even though it's Sunday afternoon, I really want to make the most of a quiet night at home writing. I have a crazy number of ideas flowing, and I need to get them down, but I'm so tired from last night. If I don't have coffee now there is no way it's going to happen.

"That big of a night, was it?" She giggles at me. "I'm happy for you, Jen, you need to get out and enjoy yourself more. You're too young to be sitting round the house reading your life away."

"I enjoy reading." I pout.

"You know what I mean."

Ouch. We run straight into a man. Or he runs into us. He mustn't have been looking where he was going, and we were distracted talking. His hands land on my shoulders as he steadies himself and stops me from falling on my butt.

"Are you fucking kidding me? Watch where you're going," yells Mia.

The man keeps his head down, his black hoody shadowing most of his face. His eyes dart to me then he turns away. "Sorry, ladies," he mumbles as he keeps moving down the street. It's the strangest thing.

I get a flashback to my past from the sound of his voice and the small glimpse of his green eyes I got. It must be in my head. I'm overtired and my hangover has my mind playing tricks on me, because it couldn't be who I think it is. He lives in Sydney, and I haven't seen him since I was just fifteen. I turn back, trying to see if it was him, but whoever it was is gone.

"Let's go in here," Mia says as we stop in front of a coffee shop.

"Yeah, I like this place." We walk through the door to a cute little coffee shop and place our order at the counter, then take a seat near the window, looking out over the street. I watch the people and cars go by.

Mia grabs my hand across the table. "Sooo, tell me all." She grins.

"There's not that much to tell, really. I ran into an old friend, we caught up over a few drinks, end of story."

"He didn't look like a friend from where I was standing. You too looked very cosy. Walking hand in hand."

Of course she had to have seen us when we were holding hands. I don't even know why we were holding hands. That was weird. There is something so comforting and familiar about him, even though it had been a while, I just had to touch him. I sigh loudly. "I wish he was more than a friend."

Her brows knit together. "What's the problem then? Is he married or something?"

Does he have a girlfriend, or worse, did he get married? "Nah, he's single, I think." I didn't actually ask him if he was or not. I just assumed he was because of all the things I've read about him lately. They all imply he's single and making the most of it, which really should be a huge red flag. *Stay away from him, he's not the man for you, Jenna. He gets around and will never be the boyfriend you're dreaming of having all to yourself.* But how do I stay away from him, when every fibre of my being craves him? From the moment I locked eyes with him last night, he is literally all I can think about.

"Then you should totally be all over that then." She smirks at me. I know what she's thinking, I need to get out there and stop being a boring old lady before it's too late and I'm old. But I'm not like her, all gorgeous and confident. And this situation is not an easy one to tackle.

"It's complicated, we have a history." The barista brings over our drinks and I sip on mine, still people watching on the main street. "Anyway, enough about me, what's going on with you?"

"Well, okay, but you do really need to put yourself out there, honey, before you get too old."

I give her a look of annoyance. I have heard that line a million times before from her.

She shrugs and starts to talk about her ideas to expand the studio. I try to listen intently like a good friend should, but my mind is running through everything that happened last night. Should I have just been brave, reached up and grabbed his handsome face and kissed him like I wanted to? Or does he have a significant other, and that's why nothing happened? That would make sense, but he didn't say anything about another girl. Hmm, where would that leave us if something did happen?

Theo seemed okay with me, not strange at all, but I think that's just because he was so fixated on Ivy. The rest of Drew's family probably still despises me for what happened. I would.

I take another sip of my coffee and almost spit it straight back out when I see him standing right in front of the window where we're sitting. Cheeky, dimply grin and all. I cough to stop myself from choking.

"Are you alright?" asks Mia, giving me a concerned look.

I nod my head, turning away from the window. "Yeah, sorry, just went down the wrong way." I try to catch my breath.

"Yeah, or it's because you just spotted that sexy son of a bitch you were with last night." She hits me on the arm.

"No, that's not it." I shake my head, trying to look extra convincing.

"Oh, good, because he's coming our way." She smirks. She is loving watching me squirm. She knows how terrible I am with guys. "Lucky you look extra hot today in that cute outfit."

I look down at what I'm wearing. Oh, hell no. I'm sitting here in just my fitted shorts and sports top. I was so hot after class I didn't even throw on my jacket. I look around for my zip-up hoody, but I must have left it in the studio. Damn it.

"Jenna," comes his familiar deep voice.

I swivel in my chair to face him. He is as hot as ever in a pale blue T-shirt and faded jeans. How can he make something so simple look so unbelievably gorgeous? "Drew." I offer a small smile. I feel so awkward today. I have lost all my courage now that I'm sober.

He looks between me and Mia. "Sorry, this is a friend of mine, Mia. She owns the dance studio where I teach a class." He raises a brow in my direction and holds out his hand for her to shake.

"Hi, Drew, aren't you just yummy," she says.

Oh, my God, she didn't just say that. I shake my head at her.

"Hi, nice to meet you, Mia." He smiles, removing his hand from her grip. He's being all charming. He knows he's hot. He probably gets that kind of reaction all the time.

I narrow my eyes at her, giving her the signal not to say anything to embarrass me in front of him any further. She is so forward, she and Penny would get on like crazy; glad they've never met, that would be all too much. "Mia," I growl at her.

She shrugs it off. "What, he is." She pats the empty seat between us. "You should join us, Drew. Jenna was just telling me all about last night. What are the chances of you running into each other twice in two days? This must be fate. Do you believe in fate, Drew?" She tilts her head, waiting for his response.

I give her a filthy look. Why did she just say that?

He looks uncomfortable, and of course he is. Who wouldn't be right now? I know I am. "Yeah, I'm not sure about fate, but it's pleasantly unexpected," he says, his eyes dropping to me again. The way he looks at me has my lady parts throbbing with desire. I want to taste what he has to offer so badly.

I swallow the lump in my throat. Sure, it must be my turn to talk. I have no idea how long I have been just staring at him, probably with my mouth open, drooling. "I'm sure Drew has better things to do with his afternoon than listen to you jibber jabber on about nonsense."

His eyes roam up my body slowly; he's taking in every inch of me. I'm sure he's probably wondering why I'm half naked, sitting in a coffee shop. Why didn't I bring my jacket? "That's okay, I have nothing on for a bit, I'll just go order. I'd love to hear your opinion on fate, Mia." He walks to the counter and places an order.

I hit Mia on the arm. "Why did you do that to me?" I cry dramatically.

"Oh, come on, you two are adorable. I'm just helping my shy little friend finally get lucky after all these years. You can thank me later."

"It's not like that with Drew," I say through gritted teeth as he makes his way back to our table with some sort of a green juice in a glass.

He sits in the empty seat next to me. "So, Mia, what kind of dance studio do you own?"

Oh shit, I don't want him to know that. I throw her a look, and she smiles back at me sweetly.

"Oh, you know, just a dance-to-be-fit studio, kinda like a gym, but we dance instead." She looks down at her phone. "Is that the time? I would love to sit and chat, but I've got a class to teach." She pushes her chair back, kissing me on the cheek. "Good luck, hun," she whispers into my ear. "Nice to meet you, Drew. See you two later." She waves as she slips out the door. I'm going to be having words with her next time I see her, leaving me like this, and she most definitely does *not* have a class to get to.

I look back at Drew and offer a small smile. This is more like how I imagined it would be when I saw him again, awkward. I don't know what to say. The alcohol must have been giving me some much-needed confidence last night. But in the light of day, with just a coffee in hand, I have lost my voice. I just watch him sipping his drink, hoping to God he'll do the talking for me.

Drew

This is the Jenna I remember. Reserved, quietly taking everything in. You can almost see her brain ticking as she overthinks and internalises everything. It's so hard to know what's on her mind because she holds her cards close to her chest.

She smiles at me sweetly. I need to say something, but I'm a little lost for words myself with that hot outfit she's wearing. Wow! A little zip-up crop top and tight shorts, sportswear from the dance class she's just done, I assume, but fuck, she looks good. She has the perfect hourglass figure; the little top accentuates her big tits, small waist, her legs are toned, and her tan is glowing. It's hard not to visualise her dancing around in that, it would be fucking sizzling to see.

My mind can't help but wander. Man, the things I want to do to her. I don't even care that there are people in this café, I just want to take her right here on this table. I would unzip that top and take her big juicy tits into my mouth before she would straddle my lap, riding my cock until she's screaming my name. My brain tells me not to go there, but my body isn't listening. It's like all the years of wanting this girl have built up so much that I'm going out of my mind with crazy hunger for her. I went home last night and jerked off twice just to get my blue balls under control.

I need to talk to her to break this tension and stop staring at her like some weirdo. "Last night was fun, I'm glad I ran into you."

"So much fun, you're a bad influence, though. I never drink like that. I had to sleep half the morning to recover." She giggles.

"I was going to say the same to you. You drank a lot more than I did." I sip on my drink. "I like that you teach a dance class, that's new."

She shrugs, looking a little embarrassed, but I don't know why. From what I've seen, she's good at dancing, or maybe that's why. "Yeah, it's a bit of fun. Dancing is something I have always been okay at."

I remember how skilled she was at dancing. Thoughts of her on that pole, moving around me in that skimpy sequined outfit, still stay with me to this day, but I'm not going to tell her that. "Yeah, I know, you sure could move last night."

"Ha, yeah, thanks. Dancing with you was fun until Ivy got sick." She drops her gaze back down to her coffee, pulling back from me again.

"Have you heard how she is today?" I ask.

"Yeah, talked to her this morning. She's fine. Got home before we did. She is crushing on your brother, hey. I think they would be cute together."

"Don't think you can call Theo cute, but yeah, I can see them together. They're a good match, both with kids and all that."

"How is the rest of your family?" she asks, her expression unsure, like the question makes her uncomfortable.

"Pretty much the same." I check my watch. She has just reminded me I have surf lessons with my nephews then dinner with my family. "I'm sorry but I have to get going."

She looks disappointed, and I feel bad because I would like to stay and talk to her. "Oh, okay, of course. It was good to see you again."

"I'm sorry. I don't really want to go. I could stay and talk to you all day. But I have to meet Elly and Theo at the beach. I'm giving their kids a surf lesson. Why don't you come to family dinner tonight? I'm sure everyone would love to see you again." She has been to our Sunday dinner heaps of times. My family adores her.

She looks at me, unsure, scrunching up her nose. "I'm sure they wouldn't."

I take her hand across the table, reassuring her. "My family have always adored you, especially my mum. She would love to see you."

"Don't they hate me?"

She really believes they hate her, after all this time she still thinks that. They never hated her. "No one hates you. What happened that day wasn't your fault. We have been over this. No one has ever blamed you, Jen. You should come to dinner, you'll see."

She thinks for a second. "Maybe another time, I'm tired from last night. Someone kept me up way past my bedtime, and I have some work to do." She smirks, lightening the mood that has become heavy.

I'm disappointed but I get it. Maybe she needs more time to process seeing my family again, and I don't want to push it. "Okay, then can I take you for dinner this week so we can catch up properly?" I'm not even sure why I'm asking her. I don't know where I'm going with this, but I can't help myself. I want to see her some more, and dinner as friends is safe. What can it hurt? "Not like a date or anything, just two old friends hanging out."

"That sounds nice. Wednesday maybe? Tuesday, I have dinner with Ivy and the girls, and Thursday I look after Ivy's daughter Harmony while she teaches at the yoga studio."

"Wednesday works for me. I'll pick you up from your place at say six?"

"See you then." I reluctantly let go of her hand and leave

her sitting at the table. I look back at her before I walk out the door; she's staring out the window, and I wonder what she's thinking. Is she feeling this pull to me like I am to her? I don't even know how I'm going to wait till Wednesday to see her again, but maybe it's a good thing. I need to cool off a bit, get my head together and my raging cock under control before I take this further than I should. The last thing I need this year is to get involved with a girl like Jenna. This can only be a rekindled friendship, nothing more. I have to concentrate on winning the comp this year. That is my number-one priority. It's what I have worked towards my whole life, and this might be my last chance.

CHAPTER FOUR

JENNA

I've hardly slept since Sunday. When I'm not working at the library, I've been pouring myself into this new book I'm writing. The characters are constantly talking to me. I'm currently sitting in my home office, having not long ago arrived home from work. My little notebook I take with me everywhere is open, with all the ideas I jotted down today while at the library, and I'm madly typing away. My fingers are struggling to keep up with the speed of my thoughts.

Romance isn't my normal genre, but it's all just clicking for me with this story, and the characters are so clear. When I close my eyes, I see them playing through the scenes like it were a movie. The leading male is so swoony, a knight in shining armour right from the start, trying to save my leading lady from her tragic life. Yeah, his physical description resembles a sexy surfer I know all too well. Tall, athletic build, blond, totally dreamy of course, and always there to help her whenever she needs. Which is a lot, because she is a hot mess. She is blind to his awesomeness and keeps him at arm's length because she's so afraid of getting hurt. She's a fool, and if she doesn't work it out soon, he'll end up with someone else, probably someone more suited to him, and it will all be too late. I'm not sure how it's all going to end yet, but that's the general idea of the plot, and the rest will develop as I write.

I check the time on my computer. Drew will be here soon to take me to dinner. I really need to stop writing and get ready. He was very clear that it's not a date, just dinner between friends, but I can't help but feel a little disappointed by that. I know it's my own fault.

I'll just type a few more lines... I'm putting off getting ready because I have no idea what to wear. But it's more than that as well. I have that sick feeling in my stomach, the one I get when I need to make a decision on something and can't quite work out what the best thing is to do. It's making me feel frozen to my desk chair.

I feel so safe within the four walls of my cosy home office, in my own little imaginary world. Here I'm in control of it all. Out there in the real world, things can go wrong, and for me, they often do. And since I saw Drew on Sunday, I've just been feeling like I have wasted so much time. Why did I even let him go? It was such a mistake, and seeing him again only highlights that for me even more.

How do I go to dinner with him tonight and not tell him how I feel? I want to tell him that he is the only one for me and has been for sooo long, but I'm scared for his reaction. If he rejects me and only wants to be friends, I will forever hate myself for saying anything and destroying the fact we could have been friends again. But if I say nothing, we could go on with our lives, alone and never really finding true happiness, because for me, I know no one else will ever compare with the way he makes me feel, and that would be a terrible lonely existence. All because I was too scared to be honest.

I run my hands through my hair and take a deep breath. You can do this, Jenna, go and make yourself irresistible for him so he takes the decisions away from you. If he would just give me a sign that he wants something more, then I wouldn't have to agonise over all of this so much. *Stop thinking and go and get ready*, I yell at myself. Sometimes I'm so frustrating.

I run up the stairs to my room and sift through all the clothes in my walk-in wardrobe. I groan in frustration. I have no idea what to wear. I want to look good. I want his eyes to be on me like they used to be, making me feel like I'm the most important person in the world. But I don't want to go over the top and look like I'm trying too hard either.

I pull out a white off-the-shoulder top and a pair of nice black shorts. Simple and understated, but I'll look nice enough. The weather is still warm out so this will be perfect. I dress then make my way into the bathroom to fix my face. Once my make-up is perfect, I brush my hair and decide to leave it down rather than my usual high pony. My hair is really long now and flows down my back, straight and thick. I glance in the mirror once more, applying a little red lipstick, then that will have to do.

I still have ten more minutes until he's supposed to be here, and that's lucky, because I have a few more ideas I need to jot down in my notebook.

I hear a car pull up and check—sure enough, it's him. I take a deep breath, grabbing my purse from the sideboard, then head out the front. He makes his way out of his fancy-looking black Audi; I have no idea what type it is, but it looks very expensive and new.

I know I sound like a lovesick teen when I say this, but

he looks seriously dreamy tonight. Black jeans, T-shirt, his hair a little wet and still curled at the ends from a recent shower—or fresh from a surf, knowing Drew. His smile has an air of mischief as he takes me in, and I feel the heat between us instantly.

The way he looks at me makes me feel like I'm all his. Like I'm someone so important to him and he just can't get enough of me. I'm sure I'm not just imagining it. Am I? No one else has ever looked at me like this, but he does, and I melt into a puddle every time. I really hope this isn't all just in my head. Because if it is, I know for a fact that it will break my heart again, already.

CHAPTER FIVE

DREW

I PULL UP AT JENNA'S HOUSE. IT'S WEDNESDAY, AND I'M here to take her to dinner. I have been looking forward to seeing her again since Sunday. I'm fresh from a late surf, I just needed to clear my head before I saw her, but it's totally useless now. Any clarity I had is gone at the first sight of her.

She makes her way down the driveway carefully, and I get out of the car to greet her. Fuck, she's gorgeous. Her outfit suits her curves perfectly, and those legs of hers, so long and toned in those shorts. Her hair is down and flows over her bare shoulders, just the way I like it, and her lips are the same shade of red they always are. It sounds corny as fuck, but her beauty still takes my breath away every time I see her.

I've spent many years travelling to all sorts of countries and been with lots of different girls, but I have never seen anyone who even comes close to completely bringing me undone like she does. I can deny myself the satisfaction of ever really having something with her, tell myself it's because I need to focus on my career, but deep down, I know I'm in so much trouble when it comes to Jenna.

"Hi, Drew," she says shyly.

"You're so stunning, Jenna." That wasn't even what I meant to say, it just slipped out. I'm amazed every time I see her, my body reacts to her. I kiss her cheek and take her hand, leading her to the open door of the car. Suddenly I feel out of my depth, all the normal charm I have with women gone. With her, I don't even know how to act.

You're just friends. Get a fucking grip and act normal.

I open her door and she hops in.

"Nice car," she says.

"Thanks, it's one of my favourites."

She gives me a questioning look. "How many do you have?"

"A few." I shrug like it's nothing, but I love my cars and bike. Anything fast, really.

As I lean in to close the car door, my eyes drop to her cleavage, and she catches me checking her out and gives me a little smirk. Shit, I need to get my desire for her under control before this gets out of hand. No distractions this year. I'm just reconnecting with an old friend. We didn't do anything back then, and I can keep this relationship platonic now, as well.

I close her door and make my way round to my side of the car, giving myself a second to calm down. I hop in and she watches me, her head tilted, taking me in. She looks like she wants to say something, but she doesn't. She just smiles, then glances out the front window. The car already smells like her perfume.

I take off down the street, turn the corner, pulling into my driveway.

She turns to me, confused. "Why are we at your place?"

"You really have been very thorough with your stalking, Miss West."

She smirks. "I was just curious where you were living when I heard you were home, and Blake told me. No stalking needed." She brushes her hair over her shoulder, and it takes everything I have to concentrate on her face. I'm like a horny teenager. All I can think of is getting her naked and relieving this ache I have inside whenever she's close to me. "Did you build here so you could be close to me? Cause that's sweet if you did," she teases.

I ignore her question. She's clearly joking with me, but she's not that far away from the truth. I found this block of land on one of my trips home. I was heading to my sister Elly's place; she lives just up the road from here, and I took a detour to drive by Jenna's house just to see if I could catch a glimpse of her. I didn't, but I found this empty block of land for sale. It was perfect and so close to the beach as well, so I bought it. Knowing I would be close to her was a bonus.

"I was going to take you out for dinner, but it's such a nice night I thought why not order dinner from that kiosk and sit at the beach to eat. What do you think?"

"Sounds perfect. You going to give me a tour of the palace first?" She raises a brow.

"The palace?"

"Well, it's kinda massive and fancy. It's like the nicest house in the street, Drew, you have to give me a quick tour. I have been wondering if the inside is just as amazing as the exterior."

"A tour of the house it is—but food first, I'm starving. I'll bring you back here after if you like."

"I would. Thank you."

We both hop out of the car, and I pull the wine and the rug out of the boot and we walk towards the kiosk. After ordering our food, we set up at a sheltered spot near the dunes. For such a warm night I'm surprised not to see many other people around. Other than an elderly couple walking their dog a bit farther up, we have the beach to ourselves.

"This was a good idea. I haven't had fish and chips in ages, and I love the way they have these little takeaway containers with the compartments, and even salad on the side. It's so fancy."

"It's pretty fancy, for dinner at the beach, I guess." She is so easy to impress, happy with takeaway at the beach, and that's one of the reasons I like her so much. She's not trying to be anyone or anything and I can relax around her. Everything just feels real. When I'm on the tour, everyone is trying to be something else, including me, and it's exhausting.

"You're so different from all the people I normally hang with, it's refreshing spending time with you."

She's picking at her chips but looks up at me, confused. "How is that? Cause I'm boring?"

"No." I laugh. "Not boring. You're just yourself, not trying to be something you're not in order to impress or get my attention."

"Is that what people are normally like with you? Fake?"

I shrug. "Pretty much. Most of the time it feels like they all just suck up to me because they want something from me."

"It must be kind of nice having all that attention, though. It can't be all bad. You would never feel lonely with everyone loving you so much."

"I feel lonely all the time, Jen. Yeah, maybe I used to enjoy the attention when I was younger, but the older you get, the more you see it for what it is. No one really cares about you. When you drop off the top of the ranks because of an injury, you see who your real friends are, and I really don't have many."

"That's sad, Drew. I never really saw it like that. You're lucky, though, you have such a supportive family. They will always be there for you. I wish I had that."

I feel bad now, I shouldn't have said that, knowing what she has been through as a kid. And even now; she has no family. It would still be hard as an adult. I couldn't even imagine it. I have always had family around me—even in the womb I had Elly. I have never even been all alone in this world. "I am really lucky. I'm sorry, Jen. I must look like such a dick complaining about feeling lonely. I didn't mean I don't have wonderful people in my life. I can't even imagine what it was like for you when you were growing up. Not knowing your parents, living in foster homes."

"Yeah, it was lonely, really lonely." She picks at her food and looks out to the water. I eat some of my barra—it's not half bad.

But now I'm just feeling bad for her, and I wish there was some way I could make her feel better. "You know you will always have me to come to if you ever need anyone. I know we haven't been in contact for a while, but I don't want that to happen to us again. You will never be all alone again, you will always have me, Bamb."

She nibbles her bottom lip; she looks like she is about to cry. "Bamb... you haven't called me that in so long."

"Ha, yeah, I know."

"Thanks, Drew, it means a lot to know I have you. I had some really nice times growing up as well. There was one lovely older couple, Keith and Shirley, I lived with for a bit when I was quite young, they were wonderful. Their own kids had all grown up and left so they had a lot of time to spend with me. I was with them longer than any of the other families. Shirley would take me to the vintage shops to look for hidden gems. She always used to find the best stuff, designer handbags or vintage jewellery. And they loved listening to music. They would dance together, and by the way they used to look at each other, I remember thinking that's what it must be like to be truly in love. They were the closest thing I had to a real family and the only time in my life when I didn't feel alone."

"What happened to them, why didn't you stay with them?"

"She got sick, cancer, so they couldn't take care of me anymore. I was placed in a new home."

"I'm sorry, that must have been awful." I take her hand in mine and lace our fingers together. She glances over to me. I can see she's back there reliving these memories; she looks like a lost little girl.

It hurts my heart to think of what she must have been through. I remember what she was like that night when we ran away from the strip club. On the outside, she had put up a wall of strength to protect herself. But after weeks of us spending so much time together, she finally let me in. She fell apart, she couldn't be strong anymore, and she let me be the one to help her through it. I know more about her than anyone. Well, I did, but I guess that was a long time ago now.

When she looks up at me like this, I feel like I can see into her soul. I want to take her into my arms and love her the way she deserves. Tell her I can take care of her forever. But the memory of what it felt like when she told me she never wanted to see me again stops me dead in my tracks. I have never felt pain like that before, and I couldn't go through it again if she doesn't want the same as me. I would be back to where I was all those years ago, a broken man. And I can't let that happen again. I have too much to achieve this year, and getting distracted by her won't help me win the title I so desperately want.

Jenna

Sitting here on the beach with Drew like this, it's almost too much. He is too perfect, too kind to me after what I did to him. No other man has ever listened to me like he does, but I can see he is different to the man I knew back then. He is here for me, but distant at the same time, not letting me get too close to him. He has a wall up. I get it, it's my own fault. He was the only man who was ever actually paying attention to me because he genuinely cared about me, and I threw all that away because I couldn't deal with the guilt. I had hoped time would have healed the wound, but being here with him now, I can see that mistake will be one I have to live with forever. I don't think there is any coming back from it.

I offer him a small smile, not really knowing what else to do. "Thank you for this tonight, it's so nice to have you in my life again. I have really missed you."

"I've missed you too. You will always be someone special to me, Jenna."

A stray tear slips from my eye. This man kills me with his kindness. "Just like you said to me that first night. You are the only one who has ever said those words to me."

"That you're special?"

I fiddle with my hands, feeling silly for saying it out loud, but it's true. "Yes. I mean, I know Ivy and Penny appreciate me, but no one has ever said that I'm special to them."

He squeezes my hand and looks out at the water. We both sit in silence for a while, lost in our own thoughts. "Come on, it's getting cold. You want to come back to the palace, as you called it? I'll give you the tour and maybe we can watch a movie? I'll let you pick. I think I still have Casablanca somewhere in my collection."

I smile at him. "Sounds perfect. I can't believe you remember what my favourite movie is after all these years."

"How could I forget? You watched it weekly!" He laughs as he stands, brushing off the sand and holding his hands out to help me up. I place my hands in his and he pulls me up to standing. Neither of us let go, we just stand there, the sound of the waves crashing to the shore the only noise I can hear. His intense gaze melting me more as each second goes by. I lick my lips, willing him to kiss me, to give me what I have always wanted from him. But just like the other night, the moment passes, and he pulls away. My heart sinks, deflated, as the hope fades. I internally kick myself as I follow him down the sandy path away from the beach and towards his house.

How stupid I am for thinking this could ever be something different between us. We are friends, and I should feel lucky that he even wants that.

He gives me the grand tour of his place, going from one massive room to the next. It's all hard timber floors and marble bench tops, decorated perfectly with beautiful art on the walls. I would guess thanks to his sister and Indie, because I don't see Drew as having the best sense of style. It has a masculine but homely feel to it.

"This house is insane, Drew. You must have got some pretty good sponsorship deals over the years to be able to afford this."

"Ha, yeah, I guess, but mostly I've been good at investing what money I made, so it paid off. I have two other investment properties here in town as well." I can see how proud of himself he is, and he should be. Other people in his position would have spent it all, but he has been saving and building a future for himself.

"Whoa, I'm super impressed, all that in five years. Last time I saw you, you were living with your parents. No interest in anything like property."

"A lot has changed since you last knew me."

He says it as more of a statement, but I want to know what he means by it. "What else has changed?"

"It doesn't matter. Why don't we get that movie set up before it's too late; you have work tomorrow, don't you?"

"Yeah, I guess I do." I sigh, wishing I could just skip work for once and stay here with him all night.

He leaves the kitchen and walks back into the media room, flicking on the light. I wonder what he meant that a lot has changed. He mostly seems the same. Maybe he does have a girlfriend or something, or he's hiding some illegitimate kid or something crazy like that and is just waiting for the right time to tell me. *Jenna, don't let your imagination run wild. He probably didn't mean anything too much by it.*

"Are you coming?" he calls from the other room.

I catch up with him and he's already made himself comfortable on the soft leather lounge, remote in hand, a fluffy blanket lying next to him. He pats the spot beside him, and I go to him, kicking off my shoes. He spreads the blanket over our legs and we both relax back into the plush sofa. I'm so close to him I can smell his intoxicating scent, but I'm also acutely aware of the distance that is between us. We have spent many nights like this curled up watching a movie, but this feels different. Maybe that is what he was talking about when he said he's changed. He had to change because of me.

I turn my head to look at him. I need to see his reaction to the question I'm about to ask. "Drew, did you ever think about me over the years?"

He looks at me but doesn't respond.

"I only ask because I thought about you. A lot. Sometimes so much I stalked you on the socials. Your life always looked like so much fun, like you were having such a blast. I was a little jealous." I laugh to hide the truth of how I feel about it. Seeing his life in photos was so hard it almost felt like what we had meant nothing, even though I know it did.

"I thought of you all the time. To be honest, I didn't want to, but you're difficult to forget." We're face to face. His look is so intense, the cheeky Drew is nowhere to be seen. For the first time, I can see the truth in his eyes: he's still so hurt. "You broke my heart, Jenna. For a long time, I thought I would never be able to get over you. Yeah, I was having fun while I was away, but I was just doing whatever I could to forget about you. Block out the memory of what we had, because if I let myself think about you too much, I would fall apart again."

This is the most honest he has been with me. I'm the reason he was out partying. I was right, it was because of me he changed. "That's what you meant earlier, isn't it? You're not the same person anymore because of me?"

"My life wasn't the same without you in it. I didn't cope well, and yeah, it changed me. I won't make the mistake of falling for someone again." He turns to look at the screen. He can't even look at me anymore. "That's why this time we can only be friends." And now I know why. He's making it clear what this is, but he can't even look me in the eye when he says it.

I take in his expression; his face is stony cold. I knew I hurt him. I hurt myself, but to say he won't ever fall for someone again, that's ridiculous! You can't just block yourself off from everything so you never get hurt again.

"We were only friends back then as well, Drew. You can't stop yourself from falling for someone because you don't want to get hurt. The heart wants what it wants." I know I might be pushing him too far by saying that, but it's true, and I need to know exactly where we stand before I go getting my hopes up for something more.

He runs his hands through his hair. He doesn't want to have this conversation, I can tell, but tough, I need to have it. "Not mine. I have very successfully avoided that from ever happening again, and I will continue to."

"By sleeping around and never getting close enough to anyone to actually have feelings?" I scoff.

He snaps back to look at me. "That's right."

He's annoyed at me already, but I can't help but push a little more. I narrow my eyes at him. "But you won't ever sleep with me? Because we're friends and that would make things complicated."

"I think that's for the best, don't you?" He raises a brow.

"If that's what you want." My voice is barely a whisper now. It's hard to agree with him when it's the complete opposite of what I want.

"That's what I want." He says it with absolute certainty.

"Okay, I understand," I say sadly. I do, but it hurts, and I have to concentrate on the movie in front of me to stop the tears that threaten to escape at his rejection. It sounds so silly even when I say it to myself, but this man has a reputation for sleeping around. He has just admitted that's what he does. But he will never lay a finger on me. Ever. I feel a pinch of jealousy towards all the other woman who have filtered through his life. I may be the one he shares so much with, but the one thing I really crave from him, true intimacy... I know I will never be able to have it, and it's all my fault.

CHAPTER SIX

JENNA

I SCAN THROUGH THE LAST OF THE OVERNIGHT RETURNS and load them onto my trolley, ready to put them away, when Olive, our other librarian, knocks me on the arm, causing the pile of books I was balancing to tumble to the floor.

"Sorry, Jen, I didn't mean to do that." She drops to her knees with me, and we collect up the mess of books, loading them back onto the trolley.

"It's okay. I was in my own little world. Why did you bump into me, anyway?"

"I have this for you. Some guy just delivered it."

She hands me a yellow envelope. I inspect it. Nothing but my name written on the front in bold black letters. I open it to find a photo of a little boy. He would be probably three, and he is kneeling down next to a baby in a bassinet; the baby looks to be a girl, dressed in a pink jumpsuit with little flowers all over it. She also has a headband with a bow sitting in amongst her brown curls. She would be about six months old, I guess.

"Who delivered this?" I ask Olive.

She shrugs. "Some guy in a suit."

I scratch my head. I need more information, this is odd. "What did he look like?"

"Sorry, I didn't take a lot of notice." She gives me a worried look. "He was in a rush and just asked me if I worked here. I said yes, so he handed me the envelope and said, 'Give this to Jenna.' What's in it?" She glances over my shoulder.

I show her the photo. "I don't get it. Why is this for me? Who are these kids?"

She studies the photo. "Very odd. You said you don't know anything about where you came from... maybe one of your birth parents is trying to get in touch with you or something?" she suggests, her eyes looking hopeful.

I narrow my eyes to her. "Did the guy look old enough to be my dad?" I ask.

"Nah, the guy would have been like early thirties I'd say, at most."

A brother? No one has ever tried to contact me before, and if it is my brother, this is a funny way of telling me. I slip the photo in my notebook I keep behind the counter. "So random." I shake my head, getting back to work stacking the books again. Pushing the trolley out into one of the aisles, Olive follows me.

"What's going on with the hot surfer you keep daydreaming about?" She bats her lashes at me dramatically. Olive is fairly new at the library, but we made an instant connection. She brings some fun to the normally mundane routine we go through daily. She's pretty, with long jet-black hair that she always wears in a side braid with a fringe at the front, green eyes, and a scattering of freckles across her otherwise porcelain skin. She is also about thirty years younger than the last librarian, Doris, who worked here before her, and it's nice to have someone my age around.

I narrow my eyes at her. "How do you know I'm daydreaming about him?"

"Um, because you have been talking about him pretty much constantly for a month now. It's all Drew this and Drew that. And you're in your own world like heaps more than usual."

"I am not."

"You so are, Jen." She laughs.

"I could just be planning my next book or something," I say, playing with the books in front of me.

"Yeah, but you're not, I can tell. Spill, come on, what's the latest? Has he kissed you yet?"

I let out a long exhalation. "Drew and I are friends, and that's okay. That's all we ever were, so why would we be anything different now, just because I wish it was something more?" I have had so much time to reflect on the poor decisions I've made over the years while working here, or when I go home to my lonely apartment, and letting Drew go was one of the worst.

It's been a month since we ran into each other at the pub. That night was perfect. Since that first night, we've seen each other as much as we can. He takes me to dinner, movies, swims at the beach... it's all wonderful, but it's all as friends. And he has made it very clear that it will stay that way.

Olive clicks her fingers in front of my face, and I realise I must have zoned out again. Maybe she's right, this daydreaming about him is getting out of control! "So, if he hasn't kissed you, kiss him. You said so yourself, he wanted a relationship with you five years ago. Make it happen, girlfriend."

I shrug. "Oh, I don't know. I think I missed my opportunity. This time when we reconnected, I thought things might be different between us. That night after the pub, I was almost begging him to kiss me, but that might have just been the effect of the margaritas, because nothing happened. But when I had an honest conversation with him about it, he said nothing will ever happen between us in that way. I hurt him too much, so he's decided never to fall for anyone ever."

She pulls a face.

"I know, right? Like you can control falling for someone. The thing is, it might have been what he said, but it's not the way he's acting. Since that night when we talked about it, he's been his normal self. The way he looks at me, I know he wants more. I'm sure it's not just in my head." This is the stuff I would normally run past Ivy, but she is a little distracted at the moment with Theo, and I feel like it's all a bit close to home, so it's nice to have Olive to talk it out with. She has a fresh opinion on everything.

"Very odd. I would say he is just confused. Maybe you just need to make a move on him, see what happens?"

"I can't after what he said. He made it clear nothing will ever happen between us."

She smirks at me, looking in the direction of the door. "Maybe, but if a guy as hot as him was spending as much time with me as he is with you, I wouldn't wait for him to catch up with the program, I'd be all over that."

I turn to see why she's smirking and sigh because what else can I do. Drew has just walked through the door to the library holding what appears to be two motorbike helmets. He's wearing a white T-shirt, jeans, and a leather jacket, and the temptation to bite him is real. He looks tasty. What the actual fuck is wrong with me! He's so hot, I want to sink my teeth into him. This isn't the first time he has visited me at work; actually, he has made quite a habit of dropping in to see me here.

"Ladies." He smiles, and it reaches those dimples. I can practically feel myself drooling all over the stack of books in front of me. *Get it together, Jenna, you're just friends. He doesn't want anything more from you, so you need to control yourself.*

"Hi, Drew," Olive purrs, trying to look busy behind the counter, stacking some books. "To what do we owe the pleasure?"

"I was just out for a ride, and I thought it's close to lunchtime so I might take you to lunch?" He glances my way.

"You thought that while you were out for a ride with two helmets? Strange, but okay." I smile, biting my lip playfully.

"Fine, so I planned to come and take you for lunch. Sue me, I'm hungry and I knew it was your lunch time."

Olive nudges me in the arm again. "She was just about to go, your timing is perfect."

Of course he has a motorbike. He is all about the adrenaline rush, but the idea is a little scary to me. "I've never been on a motorbike before," I say, knowing I sound so lame, but I'm a total scaredy-cat when it comes to things like this. I don't do rollercoasters or even waterslides. I like my limbs intact and no broken bones.

"Your part is easy, you just have to hang on. I'll take care of the rest." He hands me the helmet. I look it over like it's going to bite me. I really don't know if I can do this. But something about Drew has me pushing myself out of my comfort zone.

"Okay," I say tentatively.

Olive hands me my purse from under the counter. "Have fun, kids."

I pull a scared face at her, and she laughs as I follow Drew out of the building. His bike is parked right out front, all polished black metal and leather. "I didn't know you had a bike."

"I have lots of fun toys I have yet to show you." The way he says it is all flirty. He's different today, he's all excited or something.

Holy hell, the way he looks at me is pure sin. Is he talking about his dick? Because, man, I want to see that toy, like, really badly. And if he isn't, that's just mean, saying it like that. Maybe I should offer to ride that instead, because getting on this bike scares the shit out of me. I would much prefer to take his body for a spin.

He looks me over, and I know it's because I'm just standing here frozen in fear on the sidewalk. He takes my helmet and brushes the hair out of my eyes, then pushes it down onto my head. "There, now you're ready to go. Don't be frightened, just hold on to me. I'll look after you. It's fun, I promise." He chuckles.

This is not funny at all. And as far as me having a good time doing this, I highly doubt it. He leads me to the bike and jumps on; I follow, throwing my leg over the other side. Luckily, I have on my black three-quarter skinny jeans today. This would not work in one of my pencil skirts. I feel super awkward. "Where do I hold on?" I ask.

He takes my hands and wraps them around his waist. "Don't let go."

"I won't." Oh God, I'm never going to want to let go. His body is warm under my arms, and I'm so close to him I can smell his aftershave mixed with the scent of leather. It's one lethal combination for my senses. It has me fantasising all sorts of dirty things. I really do need to stop reading kinky books while I'm hanging out with him, because something about this whole get-up has my mind running wild with scenarios.

He revs the bike into action and takes off up the road. I close my eyes, too scared to look where we're going. I just cling to him, trying not to scream in his ear. When we stop at a traffic light, I take a breath for what feels like the first time since I hopped on the bike.

"Keep your eyes open this time." He laughs.

"How do you know I had them closed?"

"Just a hunch. It's more fun when you can see the scenery whooshing past."

"I'll try, but I'm not making any promises. I'm not brave like you."

He gives me a squeeze on the leg. "Good girl." Then we're off again. This time I keep my eyes open. I'm not sure if it's worse being able to see us weaving through traffic or not. Luckily, it's not long before he pulls up out the front of a cute little restaurant in one of the back streets. I have been here before; the food is to die for. Fresh Asian-inspired food. I already know exactly what I'm going to order.

He helps me off the bike and takes my helmet. I tell him, "Good choice, I love this place."

"Thought you might." He smiles cheekily.

"Who have you been talking to?" I laugh.

Drew

We take our seats in a little courtyard off to the side of the restaurant and wait to be served. I haven't been here before, but this place is trendy-looking. A recycled-brick wall runs down one side with a vine climbing to the top and over our heads, lush ferns in planter boxes all around, and timber tables with brightly coloured chairs in greens and oranges. I can see why she likes this place. It has a cool relaxed vibe, my kind of place.

It's been a couple of days since I've seen Jenna and sitting across from her at the table after just having her arms wrapped around me on my bike is harder than I thought it would be. Her fingers gripping my shirt as she held on, I could feel her tits pressed into my back, her warm body so close to mine, and now my mind is imagining all the things it shouldn't when she can only be a friend.

I bet she's just as turned on as I am... the blood would be pumping through her veins with the adrenaline rush from riding on a motorbike for the first time.

She narrows her eyes at me. "What's going on with you today? You're like an excited little puppy."

"I can assure you nothing about me is little, Jenna." And I have gone and done it again, said what I was thinking without using my Jenna filter. Over the last month, I have tried my best to keep the attraction I feel towards her to myself. But every time I see her, it's harder. The need to fuck her is very real, and I don't know how much longer I can convince myself that I can't go there, just to protect myself from getting hurt by her again.

She shakes her head at me with a smirk. "Okay, I believe you. But what's going on?"

"Okay, so I wanted to tell someone. I just got the best news. I competed in a trial comp over the weekend, and I got the call today. I have been accepted into the World Surfing Tour again as a wild card! They only give out three a year, so this is like pretty sick news."

She blinks, staring at me for a second, then jumps out of

her chair to throw her arms around me. "Oh, wow, Drew, that's fantastic news! I'm so happy for you, we need to celebrate."

I can think of so many ways I would like to celebrate with her. "Yeah, it hasn't sunk in yet. I really thought after my injury it was going to be over for me, but this is another shot at the title I have been working towards my entire life."

She lets me go and slides back into her seat as the server comes to take our order. I can see Jenna is in her head thinking, worrying.

"What can I get you today?" the server asks.

I was too excited to tell Jenna my news, so I haven't looked over the menu, but Jenna orders straight away. This is one of her favourite restaurants, according to Ivy.

"I'll have the rice paper rolls, the chicken, pork, and veggie—oh, and I'll have that nice satay sauce on the side as well. Thanks." She smiles at him.

"That sounds good, I'll have the same," I say, not bothering to look at the menu. I'll trust her taste.

"Won't be too long," he says with a nod, leaving us again.

"So, when will you have to leave?" She is playing with her bottom lip, biting it nervously, and I wish she wouldn't because it keeps drawing my attention to her full, luscious lips and how much I want them on mine. Why is she nervous about my leaving? Is she really worried about me going away? I think I already knew she would be, that's why I wanted to tell her first. We have become really close again, and it's going to be challenging not seeing her all the time when I do go.

"Not for a few weeks. But after every comp I'm going to come home this time. I don't need to travel in between like I normally do, so I should only be gone for two weeks max each comp," I assure her, hoping it will stop her worrying.

"Oh, okay then, that's not too bad, I guess."

"Why, Jen, you worried you'll miss me?" I joke with her.

"No." She pauses, studying me. "Well, yes. I mean, it's just, I was getting used to having you around, that's all."

"Don't worry, I'm getting used to being around too. That's why I'm going to come home in between. I miss out on too much when I'm away."

Her worried expression has softened a little. It's nice to know she wants me around, but I haven't quite worked her out yet. Since that first week when we reconnected, she hasn't asked me another question about us or if anything will ever happen with us; we have just carried on like normal friends. Normal, but with a massive amount of sexual tension in the room every time we're together. And when we're not, she is on my mind constantly, and going away worries me just as much as I can see it's concerning her.

I have this need to be near her, to know she's alright, and it's becoming a little obsessive. Maybe it was unfair of me to say we could never be anything more than just friends. I'm crazy about her. Do I want more with her? Fuck yes, and my body craves it. I'm just not sure if I'm willing to put myself in that position again.

I run my hand through my hair, not quite sure what to say next. I want to have it out with her. Lay my cards on the table, because I'm going crazy over here. Normally my thoughts are consumed with how to be the best surfer I can be, where the next epic wave is coming from. I've been that way since the first day I popped up on a board and felt the rush I got when I rode a wave. But this summer, all I can think about is Jenna. Those red lips, how I want them on me everywhere, that thick brown hair, how I want to wrap my hand around it as I pull her head back and fuck her from behind. Those tits, fuck, she has the best set of tits I have seen in my life, and I'm going on memory here, of the night we met at the strip club, because it's been five fucking years since I have seen them without fabric shielding them.

She is doing that thing again where she bites her lip while she thinks. Does she even know she's doing it? She is driving me crazy. The fact that I won't allow myself to be with anyone else is also a major problem. If I could just fuck someone, I could get this all out of my system, but I can't bring myself to do it. Even thinking about another chick just feels wrong.

I shift in my chair uncomfortably.

"You alright, Drew?"

I shake it off. I don't want to fuck this up. I like her too much to stuff it all by telling her how I really feel and complicating things. Friends is good; she's in my life again, and that's all that matters. "Yeah, all good. Can't wait for this food to arrive, I'm starving."

"Me too. Must have been all the nervous energy from getting on that bike with you; I don't think you understand how frightening that was for me." She places her hand over her chest.

"I do, and I'm so proud of you for doing it with me. You need to live a little, do things that push you out of your comfort zone every once in a while. And I bet you secretly loved it."

"Oh, and this is coming from you, the adrenaline junkie. Not the person I'm going to take advice from on such matters."

I take her hand across the table, "Come on, admit it. For a second while you had your eyes open, you felt alive, like you were really living."

She looks down at our hands, then back up at me. "Is that why you do all the things you do? To feel alive?"

"Why not?"

"I don't know. I prefer to feel safe knowing I'm not going to die doing something reckless."

"But then are you ever really experiencing life if it's just a safe little bubble you're hiding in?" And as I say them, my own words come back to bite me. I have never erred on the side of caution, afraid to get hurt—that's not me. I go out there and take what I want. And I have a hell of a time while I'm doing it. Fuck the consequences. So why am I being such a pussy when it comes to her?

Our food arrives and we dig in. She's quiet while she eats; maybe she's thinking about what I said. I should take my own advice and be reckless with her, like I am with so many other things in my life. "You're right, these rice paper rolls are to die for. But I reckon I could have eaten two servings."

"You're always so hungry."

"It takes a lot of fuel to power this machine."

She laughs. "I bet." She checks her watch.

"It's time to go back to work, isn't it?" I say, disappointed. There never seems to be enough time with her. And the time we do have goes by so quickly.

"Yeah, sorry, this was so good, though. Thank you for taking me to lunch and sharing your news. I'm excited for you." She doesn't sound that excited, though. She sounds worried.

"You were the first one I wanted to tell." I make my way to the counter to fix up the bill, then come back to the table, handing her the helmet.

She looks at the helmet, then back up to me. "I was

thinking maybe I should walk back," she says, biting that bloody lip again.

"You are not walking back, missy. Get on my bike now." She takes the helmet with a pout, and I take her other hand in mine, pulling her back towards my bike. Really, I just wanted to touch her and have her close to me, hands wrapped around me while we ride. It might have been the reason I brought the bike today. I'm selfish, I know, because it's me who is stopping us from progressing any further, but that doesn't mean I don't want to. I'm just trying to protect myself.

But I think after the realisation I've had today, that's no longer an option.

CHAPTER SEVEN

JENNA

It's early Wednesday morning, the last day of me being a twenty-seven-year-old, and I sit at my breakfast bar with my laptop and a massive mug of coffee, typing away.

This story is writing itself. I've hardly slept after my chat with Ivy last night, my mind racing with everything we talked about. We both finally started opening up with each other after years of being friends and hiding our pasts.

I told her all my ugly truths, how I came to be working at a local strip club with not a cent to my name and a thug after me. I have hidden my past from her for so long, because after the boys helped me set up my new life here, with my job at the library and this townhouse, I wanted to totally reinvent myself. No longer was I the pathetic foster kid that no one wanted. I could make something of my life, and no one had to know about my past but me.

Ivy is a part of my new life, and I knew it would shock her to know where I came from, but she was Ivy, so kind and understanding. She's been through a lot herself. I don't know the full extent of it, but it sounds like her past was just as awful. Maybe that's why we found each other. We need a kindred spirit to move on from our past demons.

I started writing stories so long ago, I couldn't tell you when exactly it was. I would always be scribbling little notes in the back of my schoolbooks because I couldn't afford to buy books of my own to write in. It's my therapy and has pulled me through so many of my darker days.

I used to write urban fantasy. I enjoyed making up worlds completely different from my own. It was a place for me to escape to. Especially when things got too hard at one of the homes. I have a five-book series completed, just sitting in a file on my laptop. I would never have the guts to actually publish it. But it helped me get through so much, and I will treasure it forever.

The strange thing is this summer all I can write is romance. These two characters won't leave me alone, their constant chatter in my head. So, I keep writing it down. Every morning I'm up early, and at night I write until I'm too tired to keep my eyes open. I'm on to the second book in what is going to be a trilogy. They will get their happily ever after, it's just going to take them a little while.

I bury my head in my hands and massage my scalp, trying to clear the thoughts of Drew from my head so I can focus, but it's no use. My thoughts are consumed by him, now even more because he's going away.

I know it's selfish for me to be upset about Drew qualifying for the surf league again. I am happy for him, I really am. It's his life's dream to win, and I'm sure he will. He is so determined. It's just hard knowing he'll be away so much when I've gotten used to having him around. And not only that, but I know what the surf league means. He will be partying again, with a pretty new chick on his arm, and I will be an afterthought back at home.

I knew all this when I started pining after him. It's my own fault that I have fallen for him. He was never going to stay put for too long, he said so himself. He has been travelling the world in search of the next perfect wave his entire life, and he's not going to stay put for anything or anyone, especially me. Why would he? I'm just a friend of his. It's not like I'm his girlfriend or anything important.

And you never will be, I remind myself.

There is a knock at the door, and I glance down at what I'm wearing: black-and-white flannel pyjama pants and a black singlet. Oh well, it's probably only Ivy, anyway.

I open the door, and I was right. Ivy stands in the doorway, also in her pyjamas.

"Can I borrow a cup of milk for Harmony's breakfast? I was supposed to grab some on my way home yesterday, but I forgot," she says, holding up a pink plastic cup.

"Got other things on your mind, hey." I raise a brow at her. "Of course you can. You know where the fridge is." I let her in and rush through to close my laptop, so she doesn't catch a glimpse at what I'm writing.

She heads into the kitchen, opening up the fridge, then places the pink plastic cup on the counter and fills it with milk. "Thank you for last night, Jen. You opening up to me, it means the world to know I have such a true friend." She smiles a small smile and I know exactly how she feels.

"It means a lot to have you in my life as well. When you feel ready to finish what we started talking about, you just let me know. I will always be ready to listen."

"Thank you."

I don't like to pry too much, because I know she's going through some pretty heavy stuff, but I'm curious. "Have you decided what you're going to do about Theo?"

She gives me a look. "Have you decided what you're

going to do about Drew?" she says, throwing my question straight back at me.

"No! Now that he's going to be away so much, it hardly feels like there is any point in doing anything," I complain.

"Really? I would think that would give you every reason to make sure he knows how you really feel about him before he leaves."

"And how do I really feel about him, smartarse?" I sit back at the island and hold my coffee in both hands, taking a big sip.

She comes to stand in front of me with her cup of milk. "Um, it's obvious, you're totally in love with the guy. My guess is you want to marry him, fuck like crazy, and have a heap of babies."

I laugh, spitting out the coffee I had just sipped. "What are you on about, have you had too much sugar on your Weet-bix this morning? You're high!"

"I am not. It's that obvious, babe. There is no way Drew doesn't know it. You two need to talk about this before he leaves. I have seen the way he looks at you, and he might say he doesn't want anything more, but I call bullshit."

"Maybe," I say quietly. I'm sure she's right. I can feel it when we're together. This is so much more than just a friendship. But I'm not good at stuff like this, talking about feelings and laying my heart on the line, and I'm scared. What if I do then he leaves for his comp and goes back to his old lifestyle? That would be too much to take.

"I wouldn't leave it too long to make it official. A guy like that, I'm sure when he goes on the tour, he would have girls throwing themselves at him."

I throw her a dirty look. "Thanks, Iv, as if I wasn't already worried about that enough."

She gives me a sympathetic look and places her hand on

my shoulder, giving me a shake. "Do something about it, then. Make sure he knows how you feel. What's the worst that can happen?"

I shrug. "He can reject me and I will feel like a complete idiot."

"Yeah, I guess, but something tells me that's not what's going to happen." She makes her way towards the door with her milk. "Oh, and we're going shopping tomorrow for your birthday. Can you still meet me on your break? I'll pick you up at the library if you can."

"Yes, sounds nice."

"Okay then, babe, see you tomorrow."

I check my watch. I need to be getting ready for work. My story will have to wait now until tonight. Not that I could do anything more now anyway. My tummy is in knots with Ivy's words about leaving it too late.

Am I being just as foolish as my character by not telling Drew how I feel? Probably.

The buzzer to my gate goes off and I roll over in my bed to check the time: it's 5:45am. Who on earth—? I wrestle with my covers and slide out of bed, quickly running downstairs to the intercom. "Yes?" I grumble into it.

"It's Drew, let me in?" His way-too-cheery voice beams through.

I press the buzzer. What on earth is he doing here at this hour? I check my reflection in the hallway mirror. I look awful. My hair is a total bird's nest and I have no make-up on. I don't like to be seen without my face made up. I run my fingers through my hair and pull it into a high ponytail. I'm also in my pyjama bottoms and singlet top.

Looking good, Jenna, that's the way to get his attention.

He's going to be all over me now. Oh well, what does he expect if he rocks up at this time of the morning?

He taps at the door, and I open it in a rush. Of course he is the epitome of perfection, face shaved, hair neat in its unruly way, cheeky smile way too bright for the early hour.

I yawn, covering my mouth. "Drew, what on earth are you doing here so early?"

"Wishing you a happy birthday. I wanted to be the first." He smiles cheekily.

"It couldn't have waited till the sun was up? You don't have a lot of competition." I'm a little surprised he has even remembered it's my birthday. I think I mentioned in passing that it was coming up and Ivy was taking me shopping, but that was it. I really don't normally like to make a big deal about this day. It's sweet that he has remembered, though, so I can't be too annoyed that he's here so early.

"Sorry, not sorry. Go get dressed, we're going to watch the sunrise. Then I'm taking you for breakfast before you have to go to work."

"Really?" I ask, a little surprised.

"Do I look like I'm joking." He throws me his best serious look, and I laugh. He doesn't know how to give a stern look, he's too chill.

"Okay, I'll just be a sec." I run up the stairs to my wardrobe and rummage around, looking for something to chuck on quickly. It's still going to be cold out, so I need something warm.

Oh my God, I can't believe he is here on my birthday to take me to breakfast. This is just too perfect. *He* is too perfect.

I throw on a pair of black skinny jeans and a cream knit sweater with a V-neck. I slip into some ballet flats and run into the bathroom, brush my teeth, then quickly apply some mascara and my trusty red lippy. Then I rush back down the stairs. I wouldn't get up this early for just anyone, but he has a way of getting me to do things I wouldn't normally do.

When I arrive at the bottom of the staircase, Drew is leaning up against the door, waiting patiently, looking ever so dreamy.

"I'm impressed, you look good for someone who got ready in five minutes." He grins.

"Thanks, you could have given me the heads-up last night when we were talking that you wanted to do this and I would have been ready."

"And ruin the surprise? No way! It was better this way. I got to see how perfect you are when you wake up in the morning."

I turn away from him, grabbing my phone from the counter and hiding my smirk. He thinks I'm perfect when I wake up. I'm most certainly not, but I will take the compliment, especially when it comes from him, one of the sexiest men alive. Best birthday ever already, I reckon, and it's not even six o'clock yet.

Drew

Jenna stands at the bottom of the staircase, and I want to go to her, wrap my arms around her, make her mine. I have dreamt about her every night this week. She has invaded all my thoughts. If only she knew what kind of birthday present I really want to give her. But I don't reach for her. I keep my hands in my pockets, trying to get my feelings for her under control. Ever since I found out I made the wild card, my need for Jenna has ramped up. The waves used to be the only thing that drove me, gave me a thrill or any purpose in my life. Now she is the only one that lights that fire.

She looks me over like she wants to say something, but she doesn't. We both just stare at each other. Silence filling the space of all the things I want to say to her. I push off the wall. "Let's go before we miss it."

She grabs her purse, and we head out, walking in the direction of the beach. As we walk, we both keep our distance, but I'm so drawn to her. I want to be close to her. Yeah, she has hurt me in the past, but it was a hard time. She was hurting too. Things are so different now, and our connection over the last month is unlike anything I have experienced before. What she said when I told her we could never be more than just friends is correct, the heart does want what it wants, and I can't control mine no matter how hard I try. I thought keeping a physical distance would be enough, but it's not. I need to have her, and I can't wait any longer.

When we arrive on the beach, we find a dry spot to sit. The sky is already getting lighter. The waves crash into the shore, calling my name. I should be out there preparing. But right now, I want to be here with her more than I want to be in the ocean.

She shivers and runs her hands up and down her arms.

"Are you cold?" I ask.

"A little."

I wrap my arm around her, pulling her into me. "I'll keep you warm."

She nestles her head into my shoulder. I can smell the scent of her hair. In all these years, she hasn't changed what she washes her hair with. She smells the same as she did that first night I walked her home to my place, and smelling it brings back so many memories of that night.

I have never felt a stronger urge to protect someone as I did that night. She was so frightened, so fragile, and the most beautiful girl I had ever seen. Is that why I'm so obsessed with her? Why I still feel like I need to be the one to protect her?

I have no idea what it is about her, but I think I'm in love with her. It's stupid, I couldn't be. I've never been in love before, and we haven't even had sex. There is no way I'm in love with her, it's got to be just lust.

"Drew, what are you thinking about?" she asks in almost a whisper.

"The first night we met," I answer honestly.

She tilts her head to look at me. "Why? I wish you wouldn't think about that night. I don't want you to think of me like that."

I can see the hurt she still carries around with her in her eyes, but to me, that night will only ever be a good night because I met her. "I know that night brings up a lot of memories for you, but for me it will always be special because you came into my life."

She's still looking at me, straight into my eyes, our faces so close our lips are nearly touching. "You saved me from that life," she whispers.

"You saved yourself, I just gave you a little help along the way."

"No, you saved me. You showed me there are good people in this world. Until then, I could have sworn this world was out to get me. I had never met anyone like you, so good and caring. You wanted to help me, not for your own gain but because you are a good kind person. Drew, if I hadn't met you that night, I wouldn't still be here."

She wouldn't still be here. What does she mean by that? "Because of Vinnie?"

She doesn't answer, but the tears forming in her eyes tell me that's not the case. "I had nothing to live for, nothing. But I met you boys, you and Blake and your family. You all cared so much about me, someone you didn't have to even think about. Your mum helping me get my job. And I know you were the one who helped me get my house."

I helped her buy her house, but that's not something she's supposed to know. I wanted her to think she did it on her own. "You don't know that."

"Yeah, I do. Blake eventually told me it was you. If you hadn't done that, I wouldn't have been able to afford it, and you knew that. I owe you so much." She wipes away the tear that has escaped down her cheek.

"You don't owe me anything. You needed a little help. I would have done it for anyone in your position. It was just a bonus that we got on so well and I made a friend. I have always felt blessed that I grew up in my family. What you had to go through as a child, no one should have to go through that. You got your new start because you deserved a better life—and now look at you. I'm so proud of the beautiful woman you have become."

I take her face in my hands. She blinks back at me, but she doesn't pull away or tell me to stop. She wants this as much as I do, and I'm not waiting any longer. Cupping her face, I draw her toward me, our lips meeting in a perfect kiss.

I want to kiss her softly, take my time, like she deserves, but I have waited for this moment for so long. I pull her closer towards me, deepening the kiss, my tongue swiping through her open mouth, and I kiss her with force. Pulling her into me. I'm so desperate for her. She's the same as her hands go to the back of my head, and she clings to me like her life depends on it. I push her back down to the sand so

I'm on top of her. This moment is perfect. She pulls back breathlessly.

"Drew." She places her hand over her heart, trying to catch her breath. "Are we really doing this?"

"What is this? If you're asking if we're really making out down here at the beach, then yeah, Bamb, that's what we're doing."

She hits me playfully across the chest, and I catch her hand, wrapping my hand around her wrist. "Drew, you know that's not what I meant," she complains.

I roll off her and sit up, and she follows. All I want to do is make out with her, but we have too much history. We need to talk about all of this, so it won't get messy. "I can't answer anything else until you tell me what you want." And I'm dead serious. I need to know where she stands now as well. I want this, I want it so fucking much it hurts, but I need to know she's right with me.

She looks me over. "I want... I want you, but I know that's selfish. You have your surfing career to focus on this year. I don't want to get in the way of your dreams."

She's worried about my career. Not what I thought she would say at all. "Why would you get in the way?"

"I don't know. You go away in a few days and then what?"

"I'll be back. I told you, I'm going to come home after every comp this time. I want more to my life than just surfing. If my injury last year taught me anything, it's that my career can be taken away from me in an instant. I want something permanent."

"You think we could be something permanent?"

I cup her face; she looks at me so hopefully. "Bamb, I wanted to try this with you five years ago. Those feelings didn't just go away because you told them to and because I stupidly thought I could avoid them."

She looks down, ashamed. "I'm sorry, Drew, that was so awful, that day in the hospital. I didn't want to send you away. You were one of the few friends I had. But what Theo was going through... I couldn't be around you and your family knowing I was the cause of his pain, after how good you had all been to me as well. I felt like the worst person in the world."

"You know you're not to blame for all that happened."

"Maybe I wasn't the one who did it, but it was because of me."

"Jenna, we have been over this," I say, frustrated. She better not pull away from me again because of the past. I won't let her this time.

She reaches for me, knitting her hand with mine. "Yeah, I know, and I can't change what happened. I can see Theo is moving on with his life, and I'm so happy for him and Ivy, they are an excellent match. I know I can't let what took place in the past hold me back anymore. I want to try this with you... if you still want me?"

"If I still want you?" I pull her back to me and our lips meet again as we crash down to the sand, our bodies intertwined. We have missed the sunrise, too preoccupied, but who cares? We can see that another day. Finally, after years of wanting this, fighting it because I was a fucking idiot, I have my girl right where she should be, in my arms.

I kiss down her neck, biting and sucking as I go, pulling her jumper over her head. I need my hands on her body. I run them up and under her shirt as I kiss down her cleavage, taking her nipple in my mouth, sucking it through her T-shirt. I want her naked and under me now.

She pulls my head back up to hers, kissing me, our

tongues exploring, hurried, desperate to make up for lost time. Her hips roll under me, her pussy rubbing against me. I bet she is soaking wet under those pants. She is just as hungry for this as me.

She tugs my shirt off over my head and dances her fingers over my chest and straight to my pants, where she rubs my hard length through my jeans. I let out a groan. And run my hands up her shirt, cupping her breasts and yanking at the fabric of her bra, exposing her nipples. Man, her tits are massive, I need to see them. I pluck her nipples between my fingers, and she moans into my mouth, kissing from my lips up my jaw. I pull back from her and go to remove her shirt, and she shakes her head.

Her eyes are wide. "Drew, we're on the beach."

"So? There's no one around at this hour, no one will see. I want to give you something for your birthday."

She clings to her shirt, covering herself up. And I think she is going to shut this all down before I have even begun. But a slow, sexy smile crosses her face, and she pushes me back. "I'm not exposing myself on the beach, but you don't seem to mind, so how about you let me do something I've always wanted to, that can be my present."

"What have you always wanted to do with me?" I encourage her, cause I want to hear her say what she wants.

"To suck. Your. Cock," she purrs. Nudging me to get off her, and I play along. It's her birthday, and she wants to give me a blow job. Who is this goddess?

She pushes me down on to the sand and positions herself between my legs, undoing my pants and pulling them down just enough that my cock springs free. She bites into her lip, her hand palming me, stroking my length as she places kisses down my chest, my happy trail to my cock.

She licks the tip. "Mmm. So good." Then she takes me

into her mouth, swallowing me whole. My entire body shudders. It's been so long since I've been touched, and it's her. It's almost too much for me to take. She pulls back. "Fuck, you're big."

"That's right, baby, just wait until I fuck that tight little pussy of yours, then you're really going to know just how big I am."

She grins. "That's it, Drew, talk dirty to me. I love it." She licks down my length, then back up to the tip. Then she takes me in her mouth again, sucking back and forth slowly with just the right amount of suction.

"I love your pretty little mouth on my cock, it's the hottest thing I have ever seen." Her mouth feels so insanely good. I have to control myself or it's all going to be over very quickly. I rub her nipples through her shirt, and she moans on my cock. The vibration feels so good.

"Fuck, Jenna, this is too good." I grab hold of her ponytail, needing to control the pace, the overwhelming need to fuck her mouth too much. I pull her into me harder and faster as my hips rise, thrusting into her. "I'm going to... fuck." I lose control and release in her mouth. "Swallow all of me," I grunt out as hot, thick bursts slide down her throat.

She pulls back, gasping for breath, and I wonder if I went too far. Then she licks her lips and seductively wipes the corner of her mouth. I didn't go too far for her at all; she fucking loved it just as much as I did.

She pulls up my pants, and I drag her back to me, rolling on top of her. "That was so fucking hot, Jenna West. You're a dirty girl in the bedroom, aren't you."

"Guess you will just have to wait and see, Drew Walker." She smirks, and that's my answer. Have I just met my match in fucking, as well as my soul mate?

I kiss her, pinning her beneath me, rubbing slowly between her legs. I want to taste her so badly.

She pulls back from my kiss. "We better get going if we're going to have breakfast before I have to get to work."

"You've had yours, now I want mine." I lick my lips.

She shakes her head with a massive grin on her face. "Drew, we don't have time."

"But it's your birthday," I protest, still rubbing her through her jeans, her hips slowly rising to meet mine. She can't deny she wants this.

"You can give me my present when you get back on the weekend. I've waited for five years, what's a couple more days."

I check the time on my phone, and she has me. We have run out of time. If we're not quick, we won't get breakfast in time, and I bet she needs her coffee before she starts work. "Alright, we go for actual food and coffee, but you better be ready for me on Saturday, because I'm going to make you come so hard, you're going to forget who you are."

"I—" She kisses me. "Look—" She kisses me again. "Forward to it."

CHAPTER EIGHT

JENNA

It's Saturday afternoon. I'm with Penny and she's driving us to Theo's house for Drew's going away party. Penny has her music turned up loud and is singing at the top of her lungs. She is pumped up for the first house party we've been to in a while.

I wish I felt the same.

My stomach is churning. I'm so nervous about seeing the Walker family again. I have seen his mum in passing, and Elly I see sometimes when I catch up with Blake's wife, Indie, but all of them together seems like a lot. And what are they going to think about Drew and me seeing each other? The Walkers are the one family in this area who know the whole truth about my past. I'm sure I'm not the ideal girlfriend for their perfect superstar son.

I wish I was riding over with Ivy. I could have talked to her about this again. She knows the story, she could make me feel better about it, and she somehow knows how to calm me down. But she came over to Theo's early to help set up and see Theo before anyone else got here.

"You're quieter than usual, Jen, what's going on?" Penny

eyes me from her position in the driver's seat. Shit, she's on to me. Well, she's going to work it all out tonight anyway, so I might as well talk it out with her now.

"So, Pen, don't go making a big deal about this but, Drew —you know, Theo's brother—and I are kinda seeing each other now."

"No fucking way. I knew it! Just ask Ivy, I told her you were all loved up with him. So, give me the details. When did it all become official?"

"Nothing's official. He came to see me the morning of my birthday, early, and we kind of made out a little. A lot." I smirk, I can't help it. I've been on a high since our sexy morning at the beach. It was exhilarating, and my lady parts have been throbbing with need ever since. It was a shame we didn't have more time. But I had work, and he had to get to his training session. I'm hoping tonight will go differently.

She takes her hand off the wheel and slaps me across the arm. "You sneaky bitch, that's fucking fantastic news. You and Ivy both falling for brothers. What are the chances?"

"Yeah, I guess I never thought of it like that." It is pretty unlikely, I guess, but it works out well, then we can spend more time together. I won't have to give up my best friend because she's all loved up.

I can already feel the dynamic of our group changing, with Ivy spending more time with Theo and me with Drew. You'd think it would be Penny that was bothered by it, but nope, she doesn't care at all. I'm the one who doesn't cope with change well. And as much fun as I'm having with Drew, I don't want to lose my best friend.

"Is there another hot Walker brother for me?"

I laugh at her. "Sorry, hun, there's not."

"Oh well, guess I'll have to keep looking for my Prince

Charming." She shrugs it off, then turns back to me. "What's the problem then? If you're all happy and loved up, or sexed up, why do you look like you're going to puke?"

"Do I?"

She runs her eyes over me. "You look pretty pale for you."

"It's a little complicated. I've known Drew for a long time, and I know his family, but it's been a while since they've seen me. I have changed a lot in that time. I'm worried they will still see me as the old Jenna, the one who didn't have her shit together."

"Ha, yeah, you're funny, Jen. As if you were ever someone who didn't have your shit together. I bet you were born a mini mum, all organised and stuff."

I wince. Penny really has no idea who I was before she met me. "Not so much. Anyway, his family knows the old me. I'm worried they'll think I'm not good enough for Drew."

"Oh, relax, babe, they're going to love you. Everyone who meets you loves you, you're very likable."

I hope she's right, but as we pull into the driveway of Theo's house, I really don't feel so sure about any of this.

"Holy fuck, what is this place?" Penny squeals.

I take in the sight in front of me. Are we at the right place? This house is incredible. "Whoa," is all I can say. I'm blown away.

Theo's place is insane, sitting in amongst the rainforest. It's massive and unlike anything I have ever seen before. The only way I could describe it is like a gigantic treehouse, all timber and glass surrounded by greenery. I slide out of the car, being careful not to trip in my heeled boots and fitted dress. This place is tranquil. You could imagine, if there wasn't the sound of music coming from the party, it would be so peaceful to live here. God, Ivy must love it.

I run my hands through my long hair. I straightened it for tonight, and it drapes down my back, almost reaching my butt it's gotten so long. I turn to Penny. "Do I look okay? Not slutty, but nice?"

"You don't look slutty, babe. You look stunning. White is your colour, with your olive complexion. That dress is perfect, it's not too short, and there's a bit of a V, showing off the girls but tastefully."

I eye her suspiciously. Is she just saying what I want to hear? I can't tell, because I'm so racked with nerves. "Hmm, okay. Thank you. You look nice too, Pen. That skirt is something else." I don't know many girls who can get away with wearing short sparkly skirts like my friend Penny. But she looks hot, even if she looks a little like a disco ball.

"I'm going for more of a slutty look, myself. I don't look classy, do I?" She checks her reflection in the side mirror of her car and runs her hand over her skirt, playing with the sequins.

I laugh. "No, you're good, hun. I'm sure you will get all the attention you crave in that outfit."

Her face lights up. "Awesome." She scrunches her curls and stalks towards the house. I follow behind her, picking up the pace a little to catch her so I can link arms with her. I need her protection, still feeling very uneasy about the whole situation waiting for me inside.

The party is in full swing, music pumping, people dancing, and the sound of splashing and squealing in the pool. There is the aroma of something yummy cooking; it makes my tummy rumble and I realise I must have skipped lunch today. I was too preoccupied with making sure I picked the right outfit and looked perfect for tonight.

I'm not just on edge about meeting his family again. If tonight goes the way I want, and I'm pretty sure Drew wants it too, it will be the first time we sleep together, and after all these years of fantasising how it would be, it's a lot of pressure. What if we don't have chemistry between the sheets? But then I think back to the beach the other morning. That was hot. Like the hottest ever, and I know there is no way possible this isn't going to be the most epic sex of my life.

"I see who I'm looking for. Have fun, babes," Penny says, kisses me on the cheek, and takes off across the room. Damn, she was my shield. And she has left me for a boy within five seconds of getting here.

I scan the room, looking for Drew, but I don't see him. I find Ivy, so I head straight for her. Someone comfortable, safe. She can help me through this.

"Jenna," she squeals when she sees me coming, wrapping her arm around me in a hug as she balances a rather large cocktail of some sort in her other hand. By the looks of her, she has already enjoyed a few of them. I wonder if she's feeling as uneasy about the entire Walker family being here as I am.

"Looks like you're enjoying yourself. Where can I get one of those?" I point to her colourful drink.

She gives me a lopsided smile. "The bar over there. Theo's dad is mixing all sorts of wonderful concoctions."

I glance over to the bar and see Jim. He looks to be in deep conversation with Drew's brother-in-law, Fraser. I'm not quite ready for that yet. I might wait a bit for that drink, at least until I have Drew with me.

"Here, have this one, I'll get Theo to get me another." She hands me her drink with a knowing smile.

"Thank you." I take a big sip. It's fruity and delicious. "Yum." I take another gulp.

"I know, right? But be careful. They're potent."

"I can tell." I give her a look, and she giggles at me.

"Have you seen..." Before I have time to finish my question, I feel his warm hand slip to my waist and pull me towards him.

"Sorry, Ivy, I need to borrow Jenna for a little bit," he says, kissing my cheek. He has barely said anything, but my body is already reacting to that deep voice of his. I have never been so turned on so quickly by a man.

Ivy smirks at us, loving every second of this. I turn away from her and take him in. God, he looks so good tonight—white T-shirt, blue jeans, and that leather jacket, the one he was wearing when he took me on his bike.

"No worries, Drew, bring her back, though." Ivy is still talking, but I'm being pulled by the hand through the party, so I can no longer hear what it is she's saying.

He takes my drink from me, sips it, then pulls a face. "What is this?"

I shrug. He places it down on a table and then opens a door down a long hallway, dragging me into the room with him. Slamming the door behind us, he pushes me up against it. Within seconds, his hands are all over me, his lips straight to mine. His tongue swiping through my open mouth. His body is pressed so close, pinning me beneath his muscular frame, and it feels amazing.

Our kiss is desperate, hungry. His hands tug at my hair then move down my body, resting on my arse. I can feel his erection pressed into my belly. I didn't realise how badly I needed this from him, but I do. As we kiss, my hands roam under his shirt, over the ripple of his abs. Man, he feels so good, so strong. I'm dying to see him without his clothes on.

I'm sure his body is pure perfection, and his cock, well... I know it's sizable. The taste I had on my birthday has left me wanting to feel it inside of me.

"God, I have missed you." He sighs into my mouth, breaking our kiss.

I try to catch my breath. "It's only been a couple of days. How will you cope when you have to go away for weeks at a time?"

His eyes narrow as he studies me. "I don't know, maybe I shouldn't go."

Is he for real? He can't not go, this is his dream. "What? You can't do that," I say quickly, so he knows there is no way I expect him to put his dreams on hold for me. No way in hell am I having that kind of pressure put on me. God knows I'm not worth it.

He breaks into a grin. "I'm joking, Jen, but I am going to miss you." He strokes the side of my face, playing with my hair. "It won't be easy to leave this time, like it normally is."

"I'm going to miss you, too," I breathe. The unsettling pain I get in my chest every time I think about him going away is there again. I'm so worried that he'll go away and have so much fun without me that he'll break it off. I mean, we've barely had time to work out what it is either of us wants here. I know what I want, but will he go away and I'll just be a distant memory? A fling? Even if that is all this is, I want it. I want whatever scrap he'll throw me. I have waited so long to be with this man, I'll take anything.

I look back up at him with renewed purpose. "We need to make the most of the next few days."

"That's the plan, Bamb." He pulls me into him, devouring me with his mouth again. His hands roam up and down my body as our lips are locked, sending a scattering of goosebumps over my skin.

"And it starts right now. I need to feel you come apart in my hands." He reaches under the hem of my dress, exploring my bare skin, groping my arse as his fingers dig in. I let out an involuntary groan. I'm going to come as soon as he touches me.

His dark gaze is on mine, I can tell this is Drew in his element. "Spread your legs for me. I need to feel that hot little pussy of yours. I bet you're dripping wet for me already, aren't you?"

I do as he says, pushing my dress out of the way so he has full access to me. He smirks, enjoying the sight of me. Then he reaches between us, slipping his hand under my panties, exploring my folds. He's right, I have been wet for him since the moment he wrapped his arms around me tonight. His thumb teases my nub, and it sends a shiver through my whole body. His touch on my skin is so electric.

Fuck, it feels good to be touched by him. He knows exactly what he's doing, his movements slow, rubbing over my sensitive spot. It's almost enough to make me forget where we are.

God, I want him right here in his brother's house with the party going on just outside of this room, but that's crazy, and as much as I want him right now, we need to stop before this goes too far.

I pull away from him. "Drew," I pant. "We need to go back to the party. Your entire family are here tonight for you. I'm worried enough about what they're going to think of me, I don't want someone to walk in and see us in a compromising position."

"Not going to happen, baby. You had your fun on the beach and now I need mine. We're not leaving this room until my hands are drenched with your orgasm."

I gulp. Fuck, is he for real? No one has ever talked dirty

to me like this before, and I love it. He keeps rubbing me and I can't think straight.

"Why are you worried about what my family thinks?"

"Do you really think they'll be overjoyed to see you with the poor, pathetic stripper they had to save?"

He stops what he's doing, his hand still in my panties. "Whoa. You need to change your opinion of yourself, Jen. They're not thinking about any of that. I have already told them about us, and they couldn't be happier that we're together. My mum has always loved you, they're all really excited. Now get out of your head and let me..."

"Really?" It comes out so shaky. I just can't believe that his family would be happy about this.

His gaze pierces me. I can tell this conversation is done for him, and right now, I don't want to fight this anyway. I want what he's offering. Screw the rest of it, that's future Jenna's problem to deal with. Knowing he has won, he starts to move his hand again, and I melt further. This feels so good, *too* good. He kisses down my neck, his other hand gripping a handful of my hair, holding me in place, our bodies close, as he inserts a finger and then another into my dripping-wet centre.

"Shh." He smirks knowing very well it will be impossible for me not to be loud as he works his magic on me. He quickens his pace, and I know there is no turning back, this is too good. I don't care where we are anymore. I just want more of this feeling. I throw a hand over my mouth to cover the loud groan dying to come out.

He bites my ear hard. I mumble incoherent curses into my hand and I go weak at the knees as he applies more pressure to my clit, pulling the orgasm from me so quickly, I barely have time to prepare for the waves of pleasure pulsating through me. "Oh, Drew."

He kisses my mouth aggressively, his tongue taking over. When he pulls back from me to meet my gaze, I'm a panting mess, trying to catch my breath.

"Fuck, you're hot when you're coming on my fingers." He removes his hand, pulling my panties back in place, and puts his finger in his mouth, sucking my juices from his finger. I blink back at him. "You taste so good, Bamb."

He adjusts the tent in his pants then takes my hand. "Relaxed now?"

"I'm out of it." I giggle.

"Come on, let's go get you a drink. We have a party to enjoy."

I'm breathless and hot, and I must look a mess. I can't meet his family like this.

"The bathroom is down the hall. Get yourself sorted then we can go meet everyone," he says, reading my thoughts.

"Alright," I murmur, pulling my dress down and trying to straighten myself up before leaving the room. I can't even think straight right now.

He shows me to the bathroom, and I close the door, glancing at my reflection. Make-up is still intact, mostly. I run my fingers through my hair, trying to make it look like it was when I first got here. Okay, I can do this, it's just his family. I hope he's right and they do like me.

He's waiting for me in the hall and takes my hand. My tummy is still churning as we make our way back to the party. Our first stop is the bar that his dad is running. Jim, Drew's dad, embraces me with a warm hug then makes me a drink. Easier than I thought. I down the drink quickly.

Next, we find his mum, Anne. She kisses my cheek and pulls me in for the tightest hug I think I have ever received. She tells me Drew's and my relationship has always been fated, and she knew all along we would end up together. She fills a plate of food for us both, and we sit with her and chat for a while.

This is not what I expected at all. Elly and her husband Fraser are just as friendly and accepting. I really thought they all would hate me, try to talk Drew out of any type of relationship with me. But they're all so lovely. Our last stop is Theo. He and Ivy are so wrapped up in each other they barely notice Drew's hand in mine.

Just like that, I'm accepted into this amazing family. I can't believe it! This is not how things usually go for me. I'm waiting for the other shoe to drop.

Drew

I lean in and whisper into Jenna's ear, "Now that we've done the family duties, you're coming with me so we can finish what we started earlier. I won't wait another second."

She empties her second glass of punch, placing the glass on the counter. "Lead the way." I take her hand in mine, leading her out to the front of Theo's house. I know this party is for me, but all I want is to be with her, alone, before I leave. We stop when I get to my Aston Martin.

She looks over at my car. "Is this yours? It's different from the other one. I don't know anything about cars, but it looks expensive." She smiles, impressed.

We open our doors and slide in. "It's fast," I say with a raised brow.

She giggles, shaking her head. "You like everything fast, don't you?"

"Not everything. Some things need to be slowly enjoyed," I say, running my hand up her thigh.

"Some things." She gulps. I like that I make her nervous. She doesn't throw herself at me like so many other girls I've been with, and it makes me want her even more, if that's even possible.

"Yeah, like when I eat your pussy on the hood of this baby in about twenty minutes, *that* I want to enjoy slowly."

Her eyes go wide. "Fuck, Drew."

"Yeah, then I'm going to fuck you fast and hard while you scream just that." She looks a little worried, and I wonder if I've gone too far. She doesn't know this side of me yet, but if she wants this with me, she's going to have to learn about it sooner rather than later because I can't wait another day to be inside of her. "You up for that, Bamb?"

She nods slowly, a sexy smile crossing that seductive mouth of hers.

"Good, let's go then." I turn the key in the ignition, and we fly out of the driveway. About twenty minutes up the road, I pull into a lookout and put the car into park. Her teeth are buried in her bottom lip and she's quiet. I pull her into me and kiss her. She doesn't need to be worried or nervous around me.

"The view here is beautiful. I haven't ever been here before," she says, staring out the front window.

"Yeah, it's pretty sweet, hey, especially at night." I hop out of the car and go around to her side to help her out. Closing the door behind her, I lead her down to the lookout point and we stand in silence for a while. She shivers; she must be cold in just that dress. I take off my jacket and place it over her shoulders. She smiles over to me.

"Thanks." She slips her arms through the sleeves. Fuck, she looks hot in my jacket. I'd like to see her in that and nothing else. I pull her into me close, trying to warm her up. She smiles up at me. I tuck her hair over her shoulder and run my thumb down her plump lips. She's so beautiful. I press her into the fence and draw her in for a kiss. Her hands run up my arms and tug at my hair. My hands slip down her body and under the hem of her skirt to her arse; it's bare with just a thong on and feels fucking amazing.

I lift her up, pinning her to the fence, and her legs wrap around me as our kiss intensifies. I can't get enough of her—her taste, her smell, the way her body feels under mine. She bites my bottom lip and I nip at her in return. Then I drop to her neck, sucking and biting my way down to her breasts. My hands run up her body, cupping them. They're massive, and I can't wait to get my mouth on them. I suck her nipple through the thin fabric of her dress, the lace bra she's wearing now showing through the wetness of her white dress. And I smirk at her.

"Drew, you're going to leave a water mark."

"Like you care right now, your body is begging for me." I run my hand down her body and slip my fingers into her panties, feeling her wetness. "See, you're so wet for me, I could tear this dress right off you now and you would let me." I dip my finger in and she moans.

"You're right, I don't care, just keep doing that to me."

I pump my finger into her wetness again, then pull out. She glances at me in question. I bring my finger up to my mouth and lick her juices from it. Her eyes go wide. "Come on, I want you on the hood."

"You were serious about that?"

"Deadly, baby." I lead her back up the path. I open my boot and grab a beach towel. I feel the bonnet to make sure it's not still too hot then spread the towel down. I pick her up and place her down across the towel.

"Sure we're not going to scratch your pricey car?"

"Right now, I don't care," I growl, pushing the skirt of

her dress up so it bunches up round her waist. She looks perfect like this. I knew she would. Her white lace thong is the only thing stopping me from seeing what I'm desperate to. I peel it down her legs and tuck it in my pocket. Then push her legs apart wide so I can study her. She is wet for me, her glistening slit begging me to taste.

"What are you doing, Drew?"

"Admiring you. Told you I'm going to take this slow. I have dreamt about this for a really long time. I'm going to enjoy every lick."

She groans in frustration, and I love it; I have her just where I want her, at my mercy. I lick straight through her folds, tasting her honey. "You taste so fucking good, Bamb, I could do this all night." I lick her again, circling round her clit, sucking her sensitive bundle of nerves, and she arches her back off the car, moaning.

"So good, so so good."

My hands slide under her arse, pulling her into my face so I am surrounded by her delicious nectar. I lap it up, sucking, licking, nipping at her, continuing with my tongue, stroking over her sensitive spot. My finger moves to her wet pussy, dipping into her, then a second finger pulses in and out of her as my mouth concentrates on her clit. I push in a third finger, filling her, stretching her. She's tight, and she's going to need the stretch if I'm going to fit.

I pick up the pace, finger-fucking her harder. She moans loudly as her hips rise to meet my hand. She fucking loves this, and I can feel she's getting close. I continue at the same speed, curling my fingers as I go. Her faint cries of pleasure echo through the empty night sky of the lookout. Her body tenses as she falls apart in my hands for the second time tonight.

"Oh, Drew, that was..." Her hands cover her face. I slide

her down the bonnet to me and kiss her. She trembles, and I can't tell if it's from the chilly night air or the orgasm still rippling through her body. I hold her close to me, kissing her. We stand like this for some time, till I feel her hands roaming down my body. She fiddles with my belt, then jeans' zipper, until her hand is wrapped around my cock.

"Jenna, I have waited so long to do this."

"Me too, Drew. I can't wait a second longer, I need to have you in me."

"Turn around, baby." She does what I say, and I bend her over my car, slapping her on the arse. "Fuck, your body is gorgeous."

She giggles, arching her back so her arse is pushed out farther. I pull the condom from my pocket, rolling it down my length. I spread her legs open wider and line myself up with her entrance, pushing straight in.

"Drew," she cries my name. She steadies herself, her hands gripping the bonnet of the car as I move inside of her.

I want to take this slow, savour every minute with her, but after craving her for so long, my body is so desperate to dominate her, I can't hold back. One hand digs into her hipbone, the other wraps around her breast, pulling her into me, closer, as I thrust into her. It's hard and rough. The car park is silent except for her cries of pleasure and the sound of our slapping bodies as I plunge into her, repeatedly.

I know I'm getting close. I grab a handful of her hair, twisting it around my fist, pulling her back to me, kissing her neck roughly. "You're mine now, Jen, you understand? There is no going back from here." She turns her head to the side and I kiss her again, still thrusting into her body, held close to mine as I pump into her in short, sharp moves.

"I'm yours, Drew," she says breathlessly.

"You need to remember that every time I go away." I

keep moving, giving it to her, claiming her, for what she has always been. Mine.

"Always... been... yours." She cries out, her body convulsing around mine as she lets go.

"You're mine forever now, Jenna, I'm never going to let you go." I grunt out as I pump into her one last time and release my orgasm.

I place soft kisses down her neck and hold her as close to me as I can. Nothing will ever be more perfect than this moment.

CHAPTER NINE

JENNA

I squint, the light coming in the room almost blinding to my exhausted eyes. His warm body is pressed against mine, as close as he can be, and his arm rests over my chest. We must have eventually fallen asleep last night—or the early hours of this morning, it would have been.

I would love to stay like this all day, but I really need to pee. I carefully remove his arm from around me and roll out of bed, tiptoeing across the wooden floor so I don't wake him.

When I'm done, I wash my hands as I look at my reflection in the mirror. My lips look swollen and sore, and there are bite marks down my neck. My muscles ache, but it's the delicious ache of fulfilment.

I didn't know it could be this good. I mean, it's been a while since I've done anything with a man, let alone had a night of pure fucking perfection, but last night was something else. If we had left it with just what we did on the bonnet of his fancy car, it still would have been the hottest night of my life. But then he brought me home, and we continued until our bodies fell into an exhausted sleep.

Well, mine did anyway. If it were up to Drew, he would have gone all night. The boy doesn't have an off switch.

I splash my face with some water and tie my hair up in a high pony. That's as good as it's going to get without my bag, which is discarded in Drew's living room downstairs somewhere.

I walk back into his bedroom to find Drew awake. Sitting up in bed, his arms resting leisurely behind his head. He looks all kinds of sexy, with no shirt on and just the slightest covering of white cotton sheets strategically placed.

"Morning, gorgeous. How did you sleep?"

"Not very well. I was kept up most of the night." I laugh.

He reaches out for me, taking my hand and trying to tug me back to bed with him. "I didn't hear you complaining last night."

"I'm not complaining." I smile, slipping back under the sheet, his arms wrapping around me. He pins me beneath him, his cock hard again, pressing into me. How could he possibly be up for more?

"Your appetite for sex is insatiable." I giggle.

He kisses me. "I can never have enough of you." The way he looks at me has me believing every word. I knew us sleeping together would be a turning point in our relationship, but I'm falling for him harder and faster than I thought possible. It's so scary.

I know for a fact that Drew Walker has never had a long-term girlfriend—lots of girls in his bed, yes, but never anything real. And with him, I don't just want some fleeting fling. I want to be with him forever, but that's not something you can say to someone this early in. I mean, I know he said that I was his forever last night, but he was in the midst of his orgasm, and I'm pretty sure he would have said anything at that moment. It doesn't mean it's really what he wants.

I decided rather than bleed my heart out here for him before he leaves, I need to keep us busy so I can stop overthinking. "So, what do you want to do today? We only have three days until your first trip, and I have to work the other two. We need to make today count."

"You're the only thing I want to do today."

"Drew." I roll my eyes. "Come on, let's do something fun together, something you've always wanted to do."

"Okay, we can go and do something fun... on one condition."

"What?"

"You take a shower with me first."

I roll my eyes again. "Okay." I laugh. I mean, I don't really need convincing on that, but knowing how much he wants it makes me feel wanted, even if it's only for my body.

"Good girl." He leads me to the shower, turning it on and watching the steam fill the luxurious bathroom.

Two hours later, after a long hot shower and some breakfast, we arrive at the Brunswick River to do the activity of Drew's choice: a stand-up paddle boarding nature tour. Not the kind of activity I would have picked myself, but I do like how he pushes me out of my comfort zone constantly. I have lived in my safe little bubble for so long, and it's nice to try new things. And it comes with an added bonus of Drew without his shirt on. Well, a girl could hardly say no.

There are four other couples in our group. Judging by the accents, the others all sound like tourists. The instructor gives us a rundown on how to use the boards. I'm sure Drew is all over it, but I listen carefully to every step. I don't want to look like a complete idiot in front of him, and this is definitely not something I'm going to be good at. Then we're shown the course we will follow up the river. I have to admit it looks pretty straightforward and maybe a little fun.

Drew gives me a look with a sidewise smirk. "You going to be okay, Jen?"

I smile and nod, faking more confidence than I actually have. This is going to be easy, right? Follow the river, stay on the board by balancing, use the paddle to move forward. I can do this.

"Do you need to change into your swimmers or something?" he asks, eyeing the outfit I have on.

"Got them on." I show him the strap of the black-and-white-striped bikini that's under my dress. I have picked my nicest swimmers today. If I have to be doing an activity I'm not that comfortable doing, I can at least look good while doing it. Least, that's what I figured when I put them on this morning. This one is super cute, white and black stripes with one shoulder strap and a big decorative bamboo circle holding it together in the front.

"Nice. Well, come on then, let's get on the board."

"Okay." I place my bag in the locker provided. Drew takes off his T-shirt, and I shimmy out of my dress, placing it on top of my bag. His eyes roam over my body. I feel like I'm missing something. Should I be wearing more than just a bikini? "Is the water cold? Will I need a rash shirt?"

"You'll be fine. It's pretty warm at the moment and the sun is out. If you do this right, you shouldn't get too wet." He pulls me into him, kissing me. "Plus, you look fucking hot. I'm looking forward to following your fine arse up the river."

We move down to where the boards are lined up, and the other couples enter the water and slowly paddle up the river. I want to wait till last. I just know I'm going to make a fool of myself in front of Drew, I can feel it already, and I would prefer it to be just him. We walk into the water till waist deep, and Drew holds my board for me while I get on and find my balance. I take the paddle from him and drift through the water.

My balance is pretty good, I guess, from all the dancing, and my upper body strength is also pretty good, so I slip through the water with ease. This is actually fun. I look over my shoulder and Drew is right behind me, smirking. Okay, I probably look more unco than I feel, but I'm doing it and I haven't fallen in yet, so that's a plus.

I turn back to look in front of me, and as I do, the board wobbles a bit. I move my back foot to correct my balance but I'm too late. My sudden movement causes me to topple forward and dive headfirst into the river. I come up laughing at my stupidity. He's right, the water isn't that cold. But it must have looked hilarious.

Drew has abandoned his board and is next to me before I know it, helping me back on.

"Are you okay?" He laughs.

"Yes, oh my God, how embarrassing. I almost did like a full somersault into the water." I sit on the board, my legs dangling in the water, trying to catch my breath and calm my laughter.

"It looked pretty funny from where I was standing."

I hit him on the arm playfully. "You're not supposed to laugh at me."

"Sorry, but I did come to your rescue and get you back on your board so the creatures of the river didn't get you."

I smile at him and give him a kiss. "Thank you for coming to my rescue. Wait, what? There are creatures in the river I need to be worried about?" Oh God, I didn't even think about that. I curl a little farther up the board so my legs aren't hanging off the sides anymore. "Are there sharks in here or eels?" I was too busy thinking about how to do this to think about what might get me in the water. I need to stay on my board from now on. No looking around.

"Not that I know of, but there might be," he teases. He's not worried at all, still in the water holding my board.

I look down to the water. It's pretty clear, and I can't see anything too scary in there. I decide it's best not to think about it and try to enjoy myself.

He makes his way back to his board and we continue up the river. The rest of the journey is uneventful. I manage to stay on the board, and as I thought, Drew makes it look easy. The scenery is picturesque.

We sit on the riverbank with the other couples, having a gourmet sandwich lunch provided as a part of the tour. Mine is Turkish bread with avocado, cheese, and turkey with cranberry sauce; it's so good. I'm starving after the paddle. Drew has already scoffed his two sandwiches, and he is eyeing off the rest of mine. I want to talk to him a little more before he leaves, but I find talking about relationship stuff so difficult. It's silly, I just feel like I need reassurance from him.

"Drew, are you sure you're ready for this type of relationship? From everything you've told me, it kind of seems like you've never really had a serious girlfriend before."

He gives me a look. "I don't see how that's relevant now."

I fiddle with my hands, not sure how to get out what I want to say. "All the other times when you have gone away, you've been single, and I can only imagine what goes on while you're on the tour, especially with someone like you."

"What, you think I'll cheat on you because I can't go ten days without sex?" he snaps, obviously irritated by my question.

I take his hand in mine. "That's not what I said. I just meant you're very good-looking. I'm sure you have lots of girls after you, and it would be hard to resist the temptation." I shrug. "Wouldn't it?"

He narrows his eyes at me, assessing me. Then pulls me over to him. "Well, that's where you're wrong. I can resist the temptation. I've done it before." The way he looks at me makes me feel so guilty for even asking. "The first time we met when we were friends and I was sending you those letters... the relationship we had meant something to me. I didn't sleep with anyone that whole time. All I could think about was you. You were the only one I wanted to be with. I didn't even look at another girl. And this year has been the same. As soon as we reconnected, that was it, I knew you were the only girl for me. I wasn't sure if you felt the same, but I didn't care. I didn't want to be with anyone else, I just wanted you."

I lean up and kiss him. "I'm sorry, I didn't mean it to sound like it did. I just don't get it. If you could have anyone, why would you want me?"

He pulls me in closer to him, kissing me. "Because you're the one for me. I just know it, I have since the moment I met you. You will just have to trust me while I'm gone. I have to learn to do the same with you."

I look out over the river. I don't know if he gets it. I have been lied to and manipulated so much in the past that trust doesn't have a lot of meaning to it anymore, it's just a five-letter word. I look back to him. His eyes are so genuine. He's never done anything to hurt me or prove me wrong in the past. "I'm not the best with trust, Drew. Most people in my life have let me down. You don't need to worry about me, no one even comes near me. It's not like you have any competition."

He runs his hand down my arm, then pushes some hair behind my ear, his eyes meeting mine. "Hard to believe. You're irresistible. If other men don't pay you any attention, it's because they know you're too good for them."

"Ha, yeah, that's why." I laugh. Is he for real?

"It is." He gazes into my eyes. He's so intense, and I get lost in him. "You can rely on me, Jen. I know you've had lots of people let you down, but I won't." He cups my face in his hands. "You know I'm different. You have to trust that you know me well enough that I won't do anything to hurt you." He pulls me toward him, placing a slow kiss on my lips. I believe him; how can I not? He has never shown me otherwise, and I want so badly for this to work.

"Okay, I'll try," I whisper into his lips. Praying I'm right, because if I can't trust him, he will break me.

CHAPTER TEN

DREW

I hop off the plane at Kahului Airport. After a ten-hour flight, I'm glad to be on the ground. I don't hate flying; it's more the sitting still for so long that I can't stand.

I spent most of the flight with thoughts of the last three days going through my head. Everything just feels so right between me and Jenna, finally. I just hope me going away all the time won't mess with what we have, since we've only been together for such a short time. She has trust issues, and I get it, but she is just going to have to learn to trust me, because I really want this to work between us. Maybe even more than I want to win this title, and this has been a dream for me my entire life.

It's two days before my first comp in Maui, Hawaii, and since I have been out for a bit, I have some training to do with my coach, Ted, to be ready for this first event. I think I'm scheduled to meet with him in the morning, but I'll know more about my schedule over the next two weeks when I meet with my manager, Cobie. She should be waiting here to pick me up.

I grab my bag, and the line through customs moves

quickly. As I make my way into the arrivals gate, I see her. Our eyes connect as she notices me as well. Her smile when she sees me reaches her eyes; she's excited to see me, and I knew she would be. Cobie is a naturally good-looking girl, in a white tank and a pair of cut-off denim shorts. Her waist-length dark blonde hair is out, messy and untamed. I'd say she has come straight from a surf to pick me up.

It's been a while since I have seen her in person, as most of our contact since I got injured has been via email and phone, and I was wondering what it would be like to see her again after how we left things when I got injured. Admittedly, it's a little strange, and I get an uneasy feeling. Maybe now that I'm with Jenna I should have looked for a different manager to get me through this year. But I couldn't do that. Cobie has been my manger since the beginning of my career. She is organised and knows everything there is to know about surfing. She lives and breathes it just like me, and I need her on my team if I'm going to win. And that is why I'm here to get the win, then retire and settle down.

Cobie and I have been in each other's lives for as long as I can remember. We connected when we were both competing in the juniors. She has a twin sister as well, and it gave us something in common to bond over, both missing our siblings while away from home. When we got older, she couldn't keep up with the other girls, so she never quite made pro. That's when she decided to manage some of her mates who did make it. She has been amazing for me and my career.

She wraps her arm around me, and I pull her in close. It's good to see her again. She almost feels like my home away from home. I could never dump her as my manager.

"I almost can't believe it's really you." She looks up at me, her face bright with excitement.

"I thought you would have moved on to bigger and better things, been too busy to take me on this year, with all the names you have to manage now." I laugh.

Her smile is lopsided as she takes me in. "I am pretty popular these days." She slaps me across the arm playfully. "You know I will always have a place for you. You were my first big name, and you took a chance on me." She smiles sweetly.

"You took a chance on me too." I smile back.

She waves her hand dismissively. "Whatever, you were always going to be a superstar." She takes off in the direction of the door and I follow, dragging the bag trolley with me.

"This superstar needs food and sleep if I'm going to train in the morning. What's the plan for tonight?"

She stops in front of a black SUV. "Come on then, let's get you back to your room to unpack, then we're going for dinner. I want to catch you up on the program for this comp."

After loading my luggage, we jump in. She looks over at me from the driver seat and shakes her head.

"What?"

"It's nothing, I just didn't think you would be back. It looked so bad when you hurt your knee, I thought that was it." She smiles warmly, taking my hand in hers. "It's good to have you here."

I give her hand a squeeze. There are so many unsaid words between us, so much that should have been dealt with last year—or at least before I started dating Jenna. "Yeah, me too. But hey, look at me now. Good as new, just with a fresh scar."

Her face turns serious, and I know she's switching her role from friend to manager. "Are you performing good as new, or do I need to be worried?"

I raise a brow. Is she really questioning my ability? "I got in on the wild card, didn't I?"

"Yeah, you did. It was impressive, but I'll just feel better when I see you in the water tomorrow, and so will your sponsors."

I knew coming back this time would be different, after having time off, but no one had ever questioned my ability before. Especially not Cobie. She has always backed me a hundred percent. I guess it's good to be the underdog for once. I have something extra to prove to them all, and I intend to show them exactly why I'm back. To win the title that should have been mine last year.

On the way to the hotel, I send a quick text off to Jenna to let her know I'm here. After the last three days spending every possible second together, it feels odd to be without her. I miss her already.

Me: Got in safely x

It would be the afternoon there, and she should be at the library. I have a strange feeling of déjà vu; I have been in a similar situation with her, and last time we coped by writing to each other. She used to love my letters, and secretly, I loved hers as well.

She texts back straight away. She must have been hanging by her phone, waiting to hear I had landed. Knowing I have someone back at home waiting for me is so comforting.

Where is this shit coming from? Being in a relationship is making me mushy.

Jenna: Miss you already x

I smile to myself. Yep, this chick has me going soft. Who am I kidding? I have always been a big, soft, mushy, lovesick fool for Jenna. Now the feelings are just intensified because I know she feels the same.

Cobie and I drop my bags off to my room and head straight out for dinner at one of the burger places. I'm so glad too, because the food on the plane was fine, but I love my food, and it was no way near enough. We order and our food arrives quickly. Burger, fries, and a chocolate milkshake.

Cobie has been talking my ear off since she picked me up, filling me in with anything I've missed. Nothing much, really, a bit of gossip about who is sleeping with who, stuff she thinks I might care about, but that's about it.

She puts down her burger and narrows her eyes at me like she's assessing me. "So, what's changed since I saw you last? You look different, but I can't put my finger on it. But you have something going on, don't you?"

I was waiting for the right time to tell her about Jenna, but I guess there isn't ever really going to be a right time. I'm going to have to just come out with it. "Actually, a lot has changed." I pause, trying to think of the correct wording and how not to make this weird. "Most importantly, I started seeing someone." I keep looking towards her, waiting for her reaction.

Her brow knits together, like she's confused. She tilts her head. "Like you have a girlfriend?" She says it with sass, like the idea pisses her off. And I guess I kinda knew it would.

I massage my neck, uncomfortable to be having this conversation with her, but I know I need to tell her sooner rather than later. "Ahh, yeah, like things are kinda serious. Do you remember I told you about a friend I had a few years back, Jenna?"

She rolls her eyes. "The stripper you felt sorry for, yeah, I remember. You were moping around for like forever after she wouldn't talk to you anymore. She nearly destroyed your career." She huffs. Her eyes are burning a hole in me as she tries to work me out. Then realisation dawns. "She's not your girlfriend, is she?" she whines.

That was pretty much the exact response I expected from her. "Yeah, that's her. She's not a stripper anymore, she's a librarian, and we have worked through all that stuff from the past."

She rolls her eyes again. "Fulfilling all your fantasies then." She huffs, sipping on her shake.

"It's not like that, Cobie, she is someone special."

"Well, she must be doing something for you, because in the many years I have known you, you have never once had a girlfriend. Whatever this is between the two of you, though, I think it's best you keep it to yourself. You have an image to keep up, and you having a girl won't look good for that hot-single-guy thing you have going on."

That I didn't expect. But I guess that's Cobie, always thinking of how my image will help with the sponsorships. "Couldn't that be better for my image? I'm getting older now. Wouldn't it look good for me to be settling down?"

She shakes her head. "No, it definitely won't be. Keep this to yourself. They like you because you're the sexy bad boy with a death wish. No one chases the big waves like you, no one pushes the limits like you, no one parties like you, and no one fucks around like you. This is your image. You go changing that and you're no longer sellable." She gives me a stern look. She is more pissed about this than I thought she would be. "I'm serious, Drew, no photos of this girl on the socials, no mention in interviews. Trust me, your sponsors get wind of this and they will dump you for someone more interesting."

Her words sting because I know she's right. I have crafted that, as she says, *bad boy image* over many years, and until now, it has served me well. Made me a shitload of money, actually. And it all started after Jenna ended things last time. It changed the direction of my career completely because I just didn't give a shit about anything anymore, and Cobie made it work for both of us.

But there is that niggling feeling I keep getting that I don't want this life anymore, where I have to be that person. I'm so done with the fake bullshit of it all. And the thought that I have to hide Jenna makes me feel sick to my stomach, because all I want to do is show off how much I adore her. Once all this is done, she is going to be my future. How can I hide my excitement for that?

But I know what Cobie is saying, and for now I will play along. "Alright, I won't say anything. Not like she's here anyway, she's back in Byron."

She smiles that sassy smile of hers. I know it well, it's the one she wears when she has just won a great deal with a sponsor or gotten something to go her way. "Good, that's all sorted then." I get the impression that this is more than just to do with the right image for the sponsors.

"So, what's the plan for tomorrow?" I need this dinner to end so I can head back to my room and get in some sleep before I train tomorrow. I'm surprisingly really tired all of a sudden.

"You will meet with Ted at 5.30am. He has some spot he wants to take you and one of the other boys. Then back here for a rundown on the rest of the week, followed by a session in the gym. You in a rush to get back to your room or something? I thought you would have wanted to have a few drinks and catch up properly."

"Not tonight, Cobie, sorry. I'm tired from my flight."

"You're getting old, Drew. Having training in the

morning wouldn't have stopped you in the past. Or is it the girlfriend?"

"Yeah, maybe I am getting old." I shrug. Really, I think I just couldn't be bothered dealing with all this anymore. I'm getting over it. This life just doesn't seem as shiny and fun as it used to.

"Drew, before you go changing your entire life for this chick, I just want you to remember how she made you feel last time, cause I will never forget how broken you were, and I don't want to see you like that again." Her look is one more of sympathy now, and I know she was the one there for me last time. She probably thinks I'm nuts for even going there again. But it's different now.

I offer her a smile. She's just looking out for me like she always has. "I haven't forgotten, and that's why it took so long for us to reconnect, but she is the one for me, Cobie. I have to make this work."

"Okay, babe, but don't say I didn't warn you when it all falls apart. Not saying I won't be there to mop up the mess, cause you know I will always be there for you, Drew, but just hoped you learnt your lesson last time." She looks genuinely disappointed, and I get the sinking feeling that somehow our relationship has changed, not for me but for her.

It was all a bit uncertain exactly what we were to each other when I left last time, and that was probably my fault. We blurred the lines, and I wasn't man enough to deal with it, so I just didn't. Now she has to hear about this other girl. I probably deserve to have a drink thrown in my face. But things were never like that with us. Nothing has ever been serious. We have always just been friends, sometime friends that fucked a little.

Or maybe she really is just concerned. She was the one

who helped me put my life back together last time. She knows how bad it was, more than even Theo or Elly. Because she has always been that person I could rely on.

Jenna

I quickly scribble in my notebook the idea that has been playing over in my head all day. It's nearly my lunch time and I have been waiting till now to do it.

I go to put the notebook back and that photo I got of the two kids drops out, falling to the carpet. I pick it back up and study it. Who are these kids and why did some random guy drop it off for me? I haven't really put too much thought into it since I received it. I guess my mind has been on other things, but this is odd. Someone obviously wanted me to have it. I feel like I should have some idea of who they are. My guess is it's me as a baby; it could be. But with no other information on it, there is no way of knowing, and the thought of finding out anything more just makes me feel uneasy.

I know most people in my position would want to know about their parents, but I have never felt the need to know a thing. I think sometimes not knowing is better than hearing the awful truth.

I slip the photo back in the notebook and place it behind the counter. Out of sight, out of mind.

My thoughts go to Drew. He has only been away for two days and I'm really missing him. When did I become so clingy, waiting by the phone for a text? I'm waiting for Blake to meet me for our monthly catch-up. We either have lunch on our work break, or sometimes I go to his and Indie's place for dinner so I can see her and the kids as well.

Considering how much I hated him that first night we met, it's surprising that he has become one of my favourite people.

I scroll through my Instagram feed one last time while I wait for him to arrive. A photo instantly catches my attention—it's Drew, some girl hanging off him. She's pretty too, like fucking unbelievably stunning with long blonde hair and tanned skin. She's only wearing a bikini top and a pair of denim shorts, and her body is unbelievable. I wonder who she is. The caption reads, *'Back where he belongs'*.

"What's wrong?" Blake's deep voice breaks me from my internal freak-out, and I jump in surprise.

"Nothing," I say with a smile, tucking my phone in my back pocket and grabbing my purse from the counter. "I'm heading out for lunch," I call to Olive, who is stacking books in the returns trolley. She gives me a wave, and Blake and I make our way out of the library on our way to our usual sandwich place.

He gives me a look. "You know I don't believe it was nothing, I know you better than that, Jen."

Of course he doesn't believe me, he reads me so well. I stop walking and pull my phone out of my pocket. "It's this." I show him.

He scans the image on my phone. "Drew with some girl." He shrugs like it's no big deal.

I take my phone back and look at it again, my teeth grinding together and my muscles tense. Seeing him with some other girl gives me a sinking feeling. like, I knew he was popular with the ladies and photos like this would happen, but I didn't know how it would make me feel so uneasy. But with him so far away, it's harder than I thought.

"Yeah, who is she?" I snap at Blake. Whoever she is, I have decided I hate her already. Bitch touching my man. I shove my phone back in my pocket as we continue to walk. My entire body now feels stiff.

"You getting jealous?" He grins cheekily. I have no idea why he finds this so funny.

"Well, wouldn't you be, if Indie was ten hours away with some dude hanging all over her? How would you feel?" I raise a brow to emphasise my point.

"I see where you're coming from. But I don't think you have anything to worry about. Drew is all about you, Jen. This is probably just some groupie who wanted a photo with him."

"She's so hot, though, right? Like, ridiculously hot."

He gives me a sympathetic look. "She has nothing on you, Jen."

What guys say when they can't admit the truth. "You're full of shit, Blake," I mutter under my breath as we enter the sandwich bar and take a seat by the window.

I grumble. "I knew this would happen. I have seen lots of photos of him like this before, but it's different now, now that he's my boyfriend, and I hate that stupid girls think they can put their hands all over him. He has never been in a real relationship before. What if he forgets he has me back here waiting for him and takes some girl up on her offer?" I'm rambling all the stupid irrational thoughts spilling out of my head, but I need to talk to someone about it, cause I know it's going to drive me mad every time he has to go away, and Blake can give me a male perspective.

Blake's face is now serious in the way a dad is when he's trying to lecture you. "Do you really think he's going to do that?"

Probably not, but what do I know really? "I don't think so," I mutter, looking over the specials board for something yummy to take my mind off this shit.

Shaking his head at my behaviour, he picks up a menu and looks it over. "You're worrying for no reason then. You need to trust him."

"That's what he said." I huff, knowing how ridiculous I sound. But I can't help it. I'm crazy about him, and I don't want anything to stuff it all up. Like I did last time.

"Then maybe you should. Otherwise, you're going to make yourself crazy, because I'm sure this won't be the last girl to be all over him in a picture."

"Yeah, you're probably right." I sigh.

"You know I always am." He looks at me and pulls a face. "Plus, you're getting the crazy eyes."

I check my reflection in the window. I don't have crazy eyes. "What?" I look back at him quickly, and he laughs. He's just shitting me.

I laugh back. I'm being silly, I know I am, and he's right to make fun of me.

"I'll buy you lunch. What would you like?" He grins.

"The turkey wrap, thanks." He disappears to the counter, and I take another look at the photo. I know I shouldn't, but I can't help myself. Okay, decision made. If I'm going to survive this year with him away, I have to trust him, just like Blake is saying, and that starts with unfollowing him on Instagram. I'm going to go mad if I keep seeing photos like this every day.

Blake returns with our lunch and sits beside me. I take my wrap from him and unravel the paper, taking a big bite. I'm particularly starving today, nothing to do with the fact that I like to comfort eat when I'm stressed and that Drew being away worries me a lot. I'm going to be huge by the time he gets back if I keep this up.

"So, how's the family? You guys decided four is enough, yet?"

. . .

I'm just about to jump in the shower when I hear my phone ring on my bed, so I run back to my bedroom to answer it.

It's Drew. "Hey," I say, a little shy.

"Hey, gorgeous, I just got back to my room. I wanted to call you before I go out for dinner. Is it a good time?" It's so good to hear his voice.

I take a seat on the edge of my bed. "Yeah, I was about to have a shower, but that can wait. How are you? How is it all going?"

"Everything is going well, done all this a thousand times before." He sounds very confident. But it's almost like he's trying to convince himself that he has it all under control.

"Is your knee okay?" I ask, a little concerned.

"Not giving me any dramas at the moment. How was your day at the library?"

"It was good, just the same old stuff. I went for lunch with Blake, and he had photos of the new baby. She's so cute."

"That's good," he says, a little short with me.

I don't think he likes the fact that Blake and I are friends. I want to ask him about the girl I saw in the photo, but I know I need to trust him, so I decide not to. "Drew, I need to know we're okay while you're gone. This is already harder than I ever thought it was going to be."

"It's hard on me too, baby. I don't enjoy hearing that you went for lunch with another guy today, when I'm so far away."

"Not another guy. It was just Blake. You know we're friends, and he is one of your friends as well."

"Yeah, but I'm not stoked about it, especially while I'm not around."

"There is nothing to worry about with him. I don't like that I saw a picture of you with some girl draped all over you on Instagram today." Whoops, I was trying not to bring that up. But if he wants to have a go, then so do I.

"Not some girl, she's just Cobie, my manager."

His manager. Shit, that makes it so much worse. She's the one he has been spending all his time with. "Oh, your manager, she's beautiful."

"Don't be jealous, she has nothing on you, Jenna. You're the only girl I want to be with."

"Okay. I miss you, Drew," I breathe, almost unable to say it, suddenly overcome by emotions. Why am I getting emotional about all of this? It's so silly. I just really wish he wasn't so far away. Tonight, I feel like I need reassurance of what we have and he's too far away to give it to me.

"Hmm, why don't you prove it? Show me how much you're missing me, baby." I can hear his cheekiness coming through the phone. This is what I need.

"And how would you like me to do that from ten hours away?" I play along with his game.

"Hang on a sec, I'll call you back." Before I say anything else, he hangs up, then calls me again, but this time it's a FaceTime call so I can see him.

"Hello," I say awkwardly. I wasn't expecting to be on camera tonight. But it's so nice to see him. He looks good, really good, more tanned if that's possible, and his hair is wet like he has just got out of the shower or the surf. I wasn't quite prepared for a face-to-face. It's late and I probably look terrible. If I'd known I would have retouched my make-up and done my hair.

"Jenna."

"Yes, Drew?" I fiddle with my hair, trying to get it under control.

"You look beautiful." He smiles, as if knowing what's going through my mind. "Now you can show me."

I stop fussing, his words melting my worry about my appearance away.

"Thank you." I blush at his words. How can he reduce me to a giddy schoolgirl just by telling me I look beautiful? "Show you what, exactly?"

"Stop acting all shy, gorgeous. You know what I want to see. Show me how much you miss me."

He wants a show. Okay, I can do this. "Only if you're going to reciprocate. I want to see your body. All of it."

He props his phone up on the dresser next to him and removes his T-shirt. "This what you want to see?"

I nod and bite into my bottom lip. He is so ripped, his tan skin smooth over his muscular abs. God, I wish I could bite him, he looks so tasty. "I want to see more," I purr.

"You first," he says with a sexy-as-fuck wink. "Take your hair out."

I loosen the hair tie, letting my long hair fall freely down my back. Looks like we really are doing this. A thrill runs through me at the thought. I have been so good for so long, kept my body locked away, afraid to share anything with anyone, but that night with Drew where we fucked on the bonnet of his car has awakened the sex goddess inside of me, and now all I want to do is be so bad for him.

I prop my phone up on my bedside table, so my hands are free. I smile sexily over to him as I slowly unbutton my silk blouse, one button at a time, letting it drop to the floor, showing my white lace bra. "This what you wanted?" I turn around, unzipping my pencil skirt from the long zipper down the front and slip it off, revealing my G-string. I slide my hands down my body, feeling my arse, then turn around to face the camera again, gliding my hands back up my body to cup my breasts. "Your turn." I grin.

"Fuck, that was hot, Bamb. Your body is scorching. I'm so fucking hard for you, baby." He drops his board shorts and briefs, his massive cock springing free. He sits on his bed and grips himself, slowly stoking up his length. And if it's not the hottest thing I have ever seen, I don't know what is. My lady parts clench at the sight. "Take it all off, I want to see you make yourself come for me," he demands.

I swallow, trying to keep my breathing under control, and follow his instructions. I drop each strap off my shoulders one at a time, then unclasp my bra from behind, throwing it over my shoulder dramatically. I massage my bare breasts, then play with my nipples, rolling them between my fingers.

The entire time, my eyes stay on him. He watches my every move, his hand gripping his cock. I slowly run my hands down my body, over my tummy to my panties, where I slip my hand inside, skating my fingers over my dripping-wet pussy, teasing him because I know he wants to see so much more, but he can wait. I moan as I rub my hand over my clit. It's so sensitive, and even this small touch while watching him feels unbelievable.

"Jenna, you're killing me. Take them off, I need to see you. All of you." He groans.

I remove my hand and turn around, looking over my shoulder. I hook my thumbs in the sides of my G-string and slip it down my legs, bending over slightly, showing him exactly what he wants to see. I turn back around and stand before him, completely naked. I run my tongue along my lips, watching him. Man, I wish I could taste him right now.

The lack of contact is so hard. "I wish I was there with you so I could touch you."

"What would you do? If you were?"

"I'd drop down on my knees in front of you, take you in my mouth, suck you until you blow your load, then I would drink it down, enjoying every last bit as it slides down my throat."

His lips turn up at the sides into a sexy grin; he likes that idea. "Prop your leg up on the bed so I can see your pussy, then touch yourself for me. I'm not going to last long if you keep saying things like that, baby."

I play along, following his instructions, leaning one leg up on the bed and gliding my fingers through the wet folds. "Is this what you wanted, Drew?" I purr his name. I don't even know who the fuck I am right now, and I don't care. This is so hot, watching him watch me.

"Yes." He hisses, stroking himself harder and loving every second of this as much as I am. "That's what I need to see. Play with your clit. I want to see how you like to get yourself off when I'm not around."

I circle the sensitive nerves, my body becoming more aroused at his every command. I have done this many times before, way before I even knew he was into me like this. I used to imagine his instructions of all the dirty things I could do to myself to get him off. It works for me every time. But this is something else, watching him jerk himself off at the same time. This is fucking amazing, and it's not going to take long before I come undone, just playing with my clit. My other hand roams up to my breast, squeezing.

"Dip a finger in," he commands.

I do as he says, sliding one finger inside my core.

"Taste yourself for me."

Oh fuck, really? I give him a look, and he nods. He

wants me to taste my arousal. I slide the same finger into my mouth.

"Good girl. I bet you taste fucking delicious. What I wouldn't give to be there devouring that luscious cunt of yours."

I nod. "Mmm." I close my eyes and I can almost feel him doing just that to me. I return my finger to my excited lady parts.

"Two fingers now." His voice is low and so sexy, it's all I can concentrate on.

I push two fingers in. Moving them in and out slowly.

"Three, baby, stretch yourself for me. I fucking love watching you finger-fuck yourself for me. You look so goddamn sexy like this, your greedy pussy so wet. If I were with you, I would fuck you so hard right now." He's really giving it to himself now, his thrust almost aggressive. He's about to go over the edge.

I match his pace, moving my fingers quickly, my release so close, I can feel the familiar tingle run through my body. My eyes close and I tilt my head back as the sensation takes over, and I cry out loud. My body pulsing with waves of pleasure. I flicker my eyes open to see him empty his load, the fast squirts of hot liquid landing on his chest. God, he looks so hot like this. If I were there, I would lick it off for him, clean up every last drop.

He grins at me, the look on his face one of pure satisfaction. "You're a very dirty girl, Jenna."

I pick up my phone and collapse down on to my mattress. "You're a very bad boy, Drew."

"That's why we're perfect together. Do you feel better now?"

"Yeah, I do." How could I not? That was crazy good. Even from halfway around the world, Drew Walker can still leave me in a blissed-up state of euphoria. I have totally forgotten what I was so worried about all day. This man is all about me, I can feel it.

"Good, stop worrying. It's you I'm coming home to, Bamb, okay? And I'm counting down the days already."

"Okay," I say sleepily.

"I need to get to dinner with the others, but thanks for the chat," he says with a cheeky wink. "I'll talk to you tomorrow. Sleep well." He blows me a kiss and I do the same.

"Bye, baby, talk to you then." I disconnect the call. And feel a little empty as soon as he's gone. I do feel better than I did, but it's still hard knowing I'm heading to bed alone tonight and he is about to go out with all his surfing mates and his manager. *He is all about me*, I say on repeat, to remind myself everything is all good. He will be home before I know it and we can pick up where we left off.

I need a shower and it get into some writing to distract myself, before my imagination runs away on me. I'm tired from the day. I glance around my normally organised bedroom and giggle to myself when I see the mess of discarded clothing scattered around the room. That really was good. I gather them up and head for the bathroom. I need a shower even more now.

CHAPTER ELEVEN

JENNA

I'm sitting with Ivy in our favourite café. She's all glowing and smiley, filling me in on her latest date with Theo. I couldn't be happier for her. It's so nice to see her happy and giving herself a chance to move on with her life.

We're waiting for Penny, who is always late. I'm on my lunch break, and if she doesn't get here soon, I'm going to miss her. I'm sure she will have a fun story to tell us when she gets here, but she also drives me crazy. Would it kill her to be on time for once in her life?

She bounces through the door, in a cute, very short jumpsuit, unaffected by the look I'm giving her. "Hey, girlies. What's new?" she calls, taking a seat at our table.

"Not much?" Ivy shrugs. "We ordered for you."

"Thank you." She narrows her eyes at us and grins. "And likely story, you're both dating hot-as-fuck brothers, you must have something for me."

Ivy beams. The girl won't admit it, but she's totally head over heels for Theo. It's so cute. I can feel my own face warm up instantly, thinking of last night's phone conversation with Drew. I'm kind of head over heels myself. I have never done anything like that before; it was so hot. Even from nine thousand kilometres away, Drew has me all worked up the next day.

"Spill, Jen, your face just turned the same colour as the beetroot on your sandwich." She smirks.

Ivy glances back at me, also smirking. I cover my face to hide my embarrassment and the colour. "Oh my God, girls, you have no idea, last night was insane."

Penny twists a curl of her hair round her fingers. "What? He is overseas, isn't he?"

"Yes, but he rang last night, and I was all jealous about a photo I saw of him and another girl on Insta, and he was all crazy about my friendship with Blake. His answer to the problem was to show me how much he missed me. I guess that's what it was?" I say, trying not to give too much away. I know Pen is super open with her sex stories, but I don't normally have anything to share, and I can't just talk about it like her.

Penny slaps me across the arm. "You had phone sex, you horny little bitch! You couldn't even wait two weeks!"

"This coming from you!" I raise a brow in Penny's direction, rubbing my arm. Then pick up my sandwich and take a bite. Thinking about us last night, I couldn't write a scene that hot. His scorching-hot body, hand wrapped around his hard length. So fucking good.

She shrugs it off with a laugh, knowing the truth.

I shake my head, trying to come back to the present. "It was Drew. He can be very convincing." I giggle. "And it did make me feel better about the whole long-distance thing. I'm so worried about him being away. I just feel like if he can have anyone, why would he want me, you know?"

Ivy squeezes my arm. "It would be hard, but there is no

way that's going to happen. The boy is smitten with you, it's obvious."

"I hope so. We're going to need something, or our very new relationship isn't going to survive the year."

"Well, I think it's good. This is what you needed, some excitement in your life. It's what we both need, and the Walker boys do not disappoint." Ivy munches on a chip, then points it in my direction. "Some inspiration for your book, maybe?" She winks at me. If only she knew the full reality; Drew can be very... inspiring.

"It's pretty much finished, hey. I have never written a book so fast," I admit, knowing there will be more questions to come. I don't think I've even told Penny I was writing this type of book yet.

"You've finished already? You were only just telling me about your idea. Perfect timing, though, when you need something to take your mind off of Drew being away. Now's the time to do something with it, don't just let it sit there on your computer like all the others."

Penny claps. She's excited by this, which is maybe why I didn't tell her yet. "This sounds amazing to me, girl, you need to do something with it."

She must be joking. She knows I'm never going to do anything with it. Especially this one. Some of the racy scenes in there are too much, I could never publish it. "Ha, yeah." I laugh awkwardly.

Ivy grabs my arm, her eyes going wide. "No. I'm thinking you should send off your manuscript. It's time, honey, do it."

Penny taps on the table in a chant. "Do it, do it."

I give her a look like *are you kidding me?* She knows I don't have the confidence in myself to do anything like that. "Hilarious, Ivy."

She gives me her stern mum look, the one she saves for Harmony when she isn't doing as she is told. "I'm not joking, I think you should."

"Yeah, Jen. I want to read this thing. The world needs to see what's in that pretty little head of yours," adds Penny.

"The world is never going to see it. Even if I send it off to a publisher, they're not going to like it. It's not good enough."

She bumps her arm with me. "How do you know that? You won't let anyone else read it. You should at least let me take a look." She winks.

Could I let her read it? If I let anyone, it would be these girls, my closest friends. "Yeah, maybe." I shrug, looking into my coffee. It's a lovely idea, and it really is my dream, but I don't know if I can let anyone read this book, it's too personal somehow.

Penny taps excitedly on the table. "You should let us read it. We will tell you honestly if it's good enough, you know we would."

Maybe that's what I'm worried about. But the feedback would be nice. It might be complete rubbish, and I'm sure they would be honest. If I can trust anyone, it's my besties. And they're right, I do need a distraction at the moment or I'm going to go insane while Drew is away. "I'm probably going to regret this decision, but okay." I wince as I say it. I almost can't believe the words that have come out of my mouth.

Penny squeals excitedly while Ivy just grins. "Send it to me today. I have the afternoon off, and I need a distraction myself at the moment."

"I don't think it's ready yet."

"I don't care, just send it before you lose your nerve." Ivy is using her mum voice again.

"Okay, I will," I say, holding my hands up in defence. She is scary when she gets serious about something.

She smiles. "Good. I'm so excited for you, hun. I can feel it, this is the start of something big for you."

Penny gives me a squeeze. "I'm next, girl, send it to me too."

"Okay, I will email you both this afternoon."

"Good, then we can meet up next week for lunch to talk about it."

"Oh God, kill me now." I bury my head in my hands. I'm already embarrassed about the words they're going to read. This is one of the scariest things I have ever done. Worse than dancing on a stage for a room of sleazy guys. I feel like I'm letting them see my soul with every word I have bled out onto the page. "I'm just going to the loo before we leave."

I hop up and walk through the café to the bathroom. I can't believe I'm actually going to let them read it. But it's time to be a big girl and follow a dream I've had since I was a little kid. Hiding out in the school library with my stack of books, imagining what it would be like to be the one creating worlds and characters so real that people want to read about them.

I finish up and take a look at myself in the mirror, reapplying my red lipstick, flattening out my pencil skirt. I make my way back to the table. Penny is up and ready to leave, can't keep her sitting in one place for too long. They both turn to me, their eyes wide, and I wonder what could have possibly happened.

"Oh my God, Jen, you are not going to believe what happened while you were gone!" says Penny.

I was gone for all of five minutes, what could have possibly happened? "What?" I ask, mimicking her excitement.

I slip back into my seat and Ivy gives me a little smirk as she hands me a business card.

I inspect it; it says Reed Harrington Publishing. "What is this?"

"Apparently, the guy who was sitting at the table behind us is from a publishing house in Sydney. He overheard our conversation about your book. He wants you to send it to him."

"What? Why?" I ask, a thrill of excitement running through me. Someone who could actually make this all happen. But he hasn't even read it. Don't get your hopes up, Jenna. It doesn't really mean anything other than being a contact I can send it to, I guess.

"So he can read it, see if you're a good fit," says Ivy sarcastically.

Penny hits me on the arm excitedly. "What are the chances, Jen? You have to do it now, it's fate."

"It's a little coincidence, Pen, not fate."

Penny hugs me, and I peek up at her. "Don't be scared, you've got this, babe. I'm sure it's amazing. I've got to run now, places to go, people to see." She winks, and I wonder who the lucky guy is this time.

I can do this, I can do this. I will start with my best friends, see what they think, then if they like it, maybe I will consider sending it off to a publisher. Maybe.

I tuck the card in my wallet for later, then turn to my beautiful friend. She is so supportive of me, but something she said earlier has me thinking she might need me today as much as I need her. "Tell me, Ivy, why do you need the distraction so badly today?"

Drew

I've been away in Hawaii for nearly two weeks. Jenna and I have been getting by talking on the phone as much as we can, but I miss her. I need her body pressed up against mine.

My first comp went really well. I placed third overall and no sign of my injury. There are a few new up-and-coming competitors that I need to watch, but other than that, I reckon I've got this year.

Things with Cobie settled down a bit after that first night, as we got back into the swing of how things normally are on the tour. She seems to have accepted that I'm with Jenna, and there wasn't any more weirdness between us, and that's good, because I'm going to be asking Jen to come watch my next comp. I know Cobie carried on about not letting it be known I had a girlfriend, but after that discussion I had with her, I have decided I don't really care if I lose some of my sponsors, because I'm not the right fit for them anymore. I'm not forcing myself to be who they want me to be. For the first time since being on the tour, I have a girl that I want to show off, and I'm going to.

I've been home for a few hours; I've unpacked and been for a surf to kill time while I wait for Jenna to finish up at the library. Now I'm getting my place ready for her to arrive for dinner.

There is a knock at the door, and I can't answer it fast enough. I open it. There she is, my gorgeous Jenna. She squeals with excitement and jumps into my arms. I push her into the brick wall and kiss her. Her hands are on my back, nails digging in as she grips onto me. I have one hand under her arse and the other gripping her neck from behind, holding her body as close to me as I can. I slam the door shut and tug at her hair tie, and her hair falls down her back as my kiss moves lower down her neck to her open shirt. "Fuck, Jenna, I need you now." I rip her shirt open, the buttons flying, exposing her lace bra.

She laughs. "I liked that shirt."

"I'll get you another one." My hands are on her breasts, cupping them. Fuck, they feel good. I tear the thin lace fabric with my hands, and it comes apart. Hope she didn't like that one as well. Our kiss is desperate, hurried, and I run my hands over her breasts, tugging at her nipples roughly. I can't wait another second, I need to be inside her.

She undoes my fly, and I pull some protection from my pocket and roll it on, then tug her panties aside, line myself up, and push straight in. "Fuck, Drew," she cries, and I start to move inside her. Slamming her into the wall behind, in quickening pumps.

This is where I needed to be. This is coming home to my girl.

Our bodies slap together, and her arms are wrapped around my back as she clings to me. I move my hands farther down, gripping her arse, fingers digging into her flesh in my haste to get close enough to her.

Her head drops to my shoulder, and she moans incoherent sounds of pleasure as she kisses my neck. Her body tightens around me, and she cries out loud, "Yesss!" as she convulses, the ripple of her orgasm taking over her body.

I'm right there with her. I drive into her once more and fill her with my own release. Our sweaty bodies clinging to each other, I cradle her in my arms as our ragged breathing starts to calm. I have been thinking about fucking her for two weeks. But that was something more than just filling a need... That was everything.

. . .

Two hours later, we lie tangled in each other's bodies on my lounge. We didn't make it to the bedroom. The living room floor is littered with our clothes, and I couldn't be happier. This is where I want to be. Going away next time is going to be even harder. But right now, I have a few weeks at home, so I'm going to make the most of it.

I push some of her hair out of her eyes and behind her ear, and she smiles up at me. She is so beautiful like this. Hair out and messy, her face flushed. I could lie here like this all night.

"So, I know I only just got home, and we want to spend as much time together as we can while I'm here, but Elly is pestering me to catch up, and she is dying to get to know you better, and she has suggested we go to a game tomorrow night. The Titans are playing on the Gold Coast. Would you be keen to go?"

She thinks for a bit. I can see her overthinking it, and I hope she will be okay to do it. I know she struggles with my family, and they're a lot, but I think if she gets to know Elly, she will find they aren't so scary.

"Alright, I think that sounds like a good idea. I would like to get to know your sister. Plus, we can't just lie around your place naked the whole time you're home. Probably should do some normal things as well."

"I'm pretty sure I could just lie around like this for the next two weeks." I squeeze her arse and pull her into me, kissing down her neck.

She giggles. "Drew, how could you be hard again already?"

"Always ready to go when you're around, baby."

She shakes her head. "I'm hungry. I need to eat before we go again."

"I'll let you eat." I thrust my hips into her, implying what she can eat.

She slaps my chest. "Drew, I need food."

"Okay, but I'm ordering takeout. You can stay there just like that."

"If that's what you want." She bats her eyelashes at me dramatically.

I roll out from under her and get up, standing back to study her perfect body. "That's exactly what I want, baby doll. You naked all night. What do you want to have for dinner?" I laugh, walking into the kitchen to grab some menus.

"Um, I don't know, you choose." Her voice is a little shaken.

When I walk back in the room, she is sliding her shirt back on, gripping it at the front. The look on her face tells me I've done something wrong. But what? "Everything okay?"

She pulls on her skirt, not even looking at me. "Ah, yeah, you order us something. You know I'm not fussy, just whatever you want. I need to go to the bathroom."

She tries to push past me, and I grab her hand. "What did I do?"

"It's nothing, just give me a sec." She fakes a smile. But I can read her, and something's not right.

I drop her hand, so confused. One second, we were having fun, and now she looks like she's seen a ghost. I decide I should get dressed as well. Then I order some Thai takeaway because I know how hungry she is and it will be fast. I sit and wait for her to return.

She takes a seat next to me. Looking almost normal again.

"What was that all about?" I ask.

"I'm sorry, you just threw me. No one has called me baby doll for a very long time."

Oh, it was the nickname I called her, not what I did. That makes more sense. I sometimes forget how many triggers she has to her terrible past. "Was it Vinnie?"

"No, it was my first boyfriend. I haven't had a very good track record, have I?" she whispers, and I can see she's reliving something. I don't want to pressure her to talk about her past if she isn't ready. She's never mentioned this first boyfriend. I want her to know I'm here if she needs to talk.

I take her hand, lacing her fingers through mine. "You got it right this time."

She offers me a small smile. "I did, I know that for sure."

The doorbell rings. It must be our food. I go to answer it, taking our food from the delivery guy. It smells so good. I carry the food to the kitchen, where Jenna is now taking bowls from the cupboard and placing them on the counter.

"I hope you like Thai."

"You know I do." She smiles, but it's not her normal happy smile; she's in her head.

I open the plastic containers, and she places a fork in each. We both dig in, filling our bowls. Something I love about her is that she enjoys all food just as much as I do. She takes a seat at the dining table, and I fill her a glass of wine.

"Thank you." She smiles back at me. I love her smile. From the moment we met, all I wanted to do was take away her pain from the past and make her happy.

I take a seat across from her, and we both devour our food. She is quietly trapped in her own thoughts. She's often like this, where I can see her battling with whatever it is. I want her to open up to me. I need to know her pain so I can take it away.

"What happened with your first boyfriend? It must have

been bad, you looked like you had just seen a ghost when I said that pet name."

She swallows. Looks down at her bowl then back at me. I can see her internal struggle. "He was the reason I left my last foster home." She pauses. "He was my foster brother and my first boyfriend." She winces.

"Oh!" What the fuck. I know that's technically okay, but it seems really weird. Just the thought makes me feel really uncomfortable, and I have a thousand questions. How old were they? Did the parents know? What the hell did he do to her that she had that reaction to a name?

"Yeah, I know, bad idea, right?" She takes a big sip of her wine, places it down, then goes back for more, draining her glass. Her hands are shaky. She is really affected by this guy; whatever it was must have been bad.

"More?" She nods and I top up her glass. I have to agree with her, that sounds like a terrible idea. I guess there isn't really anything wrong with it, but it just sounds completely inappropriate. I wonder what the boy's parents thought about it.

She nibbles on her bottom lip. "I was fifteen and stupid, and he was the first guy that was nice to me, paid me attention. He made me feel special in a world where I wasn't anything much to anyone."

I don't like where this is going. "What happened then, if he was nice to you? Why the bad reaction when I said that word?"

She gives me a look, getting irritated that I'm not piecing it together and she has to explain.

"I'm sorry if this isn't something you want to talk about. You don't have to. But if you want to, you can tell me anything, I won't judge you. I want to be able to help you deal with your demons."

She takes my hand across the table. "And I have so many. You must think I'm such a mess. You're so sweet to me, Drew. Other guys just haven't been like that, and it's hard for me to talk about the past, my life was so messed up. I don't see how you could understand any of it. It's so different to the upbringing you had."

I grip her hand tighter. She's right, I have no idea what it would have been like to be her. I had an ideal family, really. But I want to be her strength, the one here for her whenever she needs me to be. "I might not be able to relate, but I want to be here to support you through all your past trauma. You're my girl now. Let me take on your pain so you don't have to feel it anymore." I hop up from the table, taking both our bowls to the kitchen. "Grab your wine and come and sit with me on the lounge."

She follows my suggestion, taking her drink and sitting with me, curling her legs up underneath her. She sips her wine. "He was being nice to me to get in my pants, Drew, and once he did, he turned into a controlling arsehole. He was three years older than me and was the one who was supposed to be driving me to school and picking me up. Both his parents left for work at eight and didn't get home until six. They had no idea what was going on under their roof. He was a massive bully, and I had no one to go to and no way of escaping him."

I'm so fucking mad. That was what I was hoping she wouldn't say. Fucking cunt scum. "Are you kidding me? This eighteen-year-old arsehole was taking advantage of you and bulling you into sleeping with him. In the place that was supposed to be safe, your home. That's, like, against the law. Isn't it statutory rape?"

Her eyes are wide as she assesses me. "Drew, how was I going to prove that? His word against mine, and I agreed to have sex with him. It was on me." She shakes her head sadly. She has lived with the guilt of this for so long, you can see it. If she didn't tell me about this all those years ago when she started opening up to me, it could be she hasn't told anyone. It's fucked up.

I want to lose my shit about it, track down this fucker and mess him up. But I know right now that what she needs is to have someone to talk to about it, and I promised I wouldn't judge. I would just listen and be here for her, so that's what I will do.

"There's no way that was on you, you were fifteen. Just a kid." My voice is raised, and I can see her reaction is to shut down, but fuck, I'm so annoyed about this. How could someone take advantage of her like that? She was so little and vulnerable, no real family around her to protect her. It makes me so mad. I try to calm myself down, so she won't shut down. This isn't about me. I need to be here for her, and right now she's talking, so I need to calm the fuck down and just listen to her. "How long did you stay at that house?"

She places her wine on the coffee table in front of us. "I was there about six months, three months with all this going on. One night while his parents were on a weekend away, it all got too much. I couldn't handle it anymore. I weighed up my options: stay and be controlled by him, go back into the foster system—and really, I was a messed-up fifteen-year-old at that point, not fun for a family to take on—or I could go and start my life looking after myself, where I had some control over what was happening to me. So, I waited for him to be asleep, I packed up the very few possessions I had into my backpack, and I got the hell out of there."

I pull her into me, hugging her to my chest. I don't know if this is what she needs right now, but it's what I need. Her as close to me as possible. I may not have been able to help her back then, but now I can, and no one will ever be able to hurt her like that again. "I'm so sorry you had to go through that." We stay like this for a long time. She doesn't cry, but I can feel the tremble through her body. "Was that when you started stripping?"

"Yeah. That was the start of all of that. I met a girl who was doing it, and she let me tag along to her club, got me a fake ID, showed me what to do."

This makes me so angry. I hate that she had a life before me, when I couldn't protect her from the evil scum out in this world. I need to look after her now, though. "What was this guy's name?"

Her eyes go wide. "I'm not telling you his name. What, you think you can do something about it now? You can't."

"I can go mess him up."

Her face is stern. "Drew, it was years ago. I don't want you to go get yourself into trouble with the law for doing something stupid."

"But you still have to live with it. This fucker needs to pay for what he did to you at such a young age."

"Drew, that's not what I need from you. I will tell you, but you have to swear you will never do anything with his name."

"Okay, I won't." I won't, but she doesn't know how hard that actually is for me. All I want to do is be able to protect her from her awful past, and it's so hard when it's all things that happened before I had the chance to save her.

"His name was Damien. I have no idea where he is now, it's been years since I've seen him."

"Alright. Jenna, how do I fix this if you won't let me go mess him up?"

"I need you to take my mind off it. Distract me, make me forget that I ever had a past before I met you." She tugs at my shirt, pulling it over my head, running her hands down my chest.

If this is what she wants to be able to deal with it, I can give her that. But I'm not going to forget about this. If I ever get the chance to find out who this guy is, I will mess him up. "Your wish is my command." I kiss down her neck.

CHAPTER TWELVE

JENNA

It's Saturday, and I'm sitting between Drew and his sister Elly. Fraser, Elly's husband, sits on the other side of Drew. They have been chatting away since we got here.

Drew and I spent the morning together. Then this afternoon, we picked up the others and drove to the Gold Coast for an NRL game, Titans versus Dragons. I'm not fussed on sports, but I know Drew loves anything competitive, so this is for him, and I'm looking forward to getting to know his sister better. I know how important she is to Drew, they're super close, so hopefully I can make a good impression and she likes me.

Last night felt like a big deal for us. Drew knows everything about me now, and he hasn't run for it because he's concerned about how the past might have messed me up. He wanted to make it all better. For the first time with a man, I feel like he is in this to make me happy. This relationship isn't about what I can give him or do for him. He just wants to make me happy, and it's the most amazing feeling in the world. To know I am that important to another human being, especially one as amazing as him. How did I get so lucky?

Elly leans into me. "So, I hate these games. Do you like sport?"

"Not really. Wasn't this your idea?" I asked, confused. I was assuming she was just like Drew and into sports.

"Yeah. Look at them." We both look over at the guys. Their faces are fixed on the game. A call is made that Fraser doesn't agree with and he yells at the ref like he can hear him. "They're distracted, so we can get to know each other, and Cooper is with my mum." She beams like her plan was genius.

"You know, next time you can just take me for coffee, less effort." I giggle. "But the boys do look to be in their element."

She laughs. "I know these two very well."

I've been watching the two of them interact all afternoon. I wonder how she and Fraser started out, since they seem so good together; I bet it was love at first sight. "So how did you and Fraser meet, anyway?" I ask, curiosity getting the better of me.

"He was Drew's best mate in high school," she answers, her eyes wide, like there's an entire story behind the comment.

His best mate. I can only imagine how much trouble that would have caused. I raise a brow at her. "Bet that was awkward. Have you been together since then?"

She shakes her head and laughs. "No, not at all. It seems silly now, but in high school Drew and I had this pact, no dating your twin's best friends. We were really close, and we didn't want to do anything to change that, so we came up with the pact. But I fell for Fraser anyway. Shit sister, I know."

"I think it's cute. You found your person when you were just a teenager."

"We had a little thing in high school, but we didn't really get together until about six years ago. Around the same time you met Drew."

"Oh, really? And look at you guys, married with a sweet little boy. You're so lucky." I watch the game for a bit. I have no idea what's going on, footy make no sense to me. I look back to Elly and lean in so Drew can't hear what I'm about to say. "I feel like Drew and I have wasted so much time. We could have been happily together all this time if it wasn't for me."

She gives me a sympathetic smile. "Maybe, but sometimes we take a little while to really know what we want. It took me and Fray years, and even then, it wasn't simple or easy. We had to fight for it. Love is complicated. But now you guys have each other, I'm sure things will be just perfect for you. I can see how happy you make Drew."

That feels good coming from his sister. I can feel the love that she has for him, and she really wants this to work out for him as well. It's so nice to be accepted. "Thank you, I hope I do. It all just feels so right when I'm with him."

"And if he drives you nuts and you need a break, that's when we go for coffee so you can vent. I get how annoying my brother can be more than anyone. Growing up with two of them is why I'm so grateful for you and Ivy right now."

"Thank you, I appreciate the offer." I laugh. Drew's sister is so lovely.

The rest of the night was just as good. The team the boys were going for won, so they were both on a high as we left the game. The four of us went for a late dinner and a few wines at a little Italian place. Fraser was driving, so Elly and I opted to sit in the back together and have a few wines on the way home. I was silly being so nervous about his family and coming tonight. Elly's a hoot and has been treating me like I'm a part of the family already. It makes me wish I grew up here with this group. I can only imagine how much fun we would have gotten up to.

CHAPTER THIRTEEN

JENNA

THE LAST FEW WEEKS HAVE BEEN AMAZING. WHEN I wasn't working, Drew and I were together. I spent most nights at his place, and if I wasn't there, he was with me. He came to girls' night on Tuesday, and Thursday night he hung out with me and Harmony while Ivy taught her class at the yoga studio. It all felt so normal, just what a relationship should be.

But it's comp time again. Drew left two days ago, and I have asked for a couple of days off work so I can go and watch. It will be so much fun to cheer him on and feel a part of something that is so important to him. This comp is in Newcastle, which is about six hours' drive away, so I left early and I'm going to stay the night, then drive back tomorrow.

Penny is with me for the trip. As soon as I told her I was thinking about coming, she had a room booked. She's keen to see all the hot bodies or something along those lines. And the truth is, I needed her here with me. I'm a little worried about meeting this stunning manager of his, on top of the fact I have no idea about surf comps. How do you even win one? Something I should know when I'm dating one of the best in the world. So Penny tells me she'll help me work it out.

We arrive at the beach and find a spot to park, then make our way down to the water. I have butterflies in my stomach, and I'm not sure if it's because I get to see Drew again or because I'm nervous about meeting his manager. I turn to Penny, grabbing her arm to stop her walking any farther. "Do I look okay?" I'm in denim shorts and a black top, my hair down with a wide-brim hat.

"So cute, babe, just relax."

She would have said that regardless of how I looked. I let out a sigh. "How can you tell I'm worried?"

"You went quiet on me and you're fussing; you've changed your hair style like three times already this morning."

"I just feel out of place here."

"That's why you have me, I fit in everywhere." She takes my arm and leads me down the beach in the hunt for Drew. She's right, she fits in everywhere because she just doesn't give a fuck about anything. She chats to whoever she sees and makes sure everyone knows she's around.

Luckily, Drew sees us and runs straight over, kissing me then slipping his hand in mine. The connection is so nice and just what I needed. "Come on, I have some people you have to meet." He drags me back down the beach to introduce me to some people he works with. Penny follows along.

I'm a little surprised, I wasn't sure how he would be with me around this crew. This is his world. But he's so excited to show me off to all of them, it helps to make me feel like I am someone to him.

"Jen, this is my coach, Ted, and manager, Cobie." He

introduces me to a good-looking man, probably in his late forties and the girl from the photo. She is better in real life, and I instantly hate her even more. I'm such a bitch, she is probably the nicest person ever. Except why can't he have a man as his manager, not this stunning woman standing in front of me in nothing more than a short pair of denim shorts and a tank? Her body is insane, I feel self-conscious just being in her presence.

Drew smiles at me proudly, presenting me to them. "This is my Jenna and her friend Penny." My Jenna. That's sweet, he must have already told them about me.

Ted shakes my hand with a warm smile, and Cobie looks me up and down, a fake smile across her face, and she throws her arms around me in a hug. I take a step back to balance myself, hugging her back awkwardly. I wasn't expecting her to hug me, and I'm taken off guard.

"Hi, it's so nice to meet you both. Drew talks about you so much I feel like I already know you," I say in a small voice. I know Drew adores both his coach and manager, but the way he talks about them, I get the impression that they're his home away from home when he's on the tour. I hate meeting new people, though, and knowing that they mean so much to him makes it worse.

"It's so nice to meet you as well. You're just as beautiful as Drew said you were. I can't wait to get to know you better. I think we're going to be fantastic friends." Cobie thinks we will be friends. Maybe I shouldn't be so quick to judge her. She might be nice.

Drew gives her a look, obviously surprised by her comment. I'm a little surprised as well, I always thought she would hate me. Or maybe that was just me projecting my feelings because I was so jealous of her. She gets to spend so much time with Drew, and they obviously have a long history of being friends... at least I hope only friends. Knowing Drew's past reputation, it could have definitely been more. I really hope not. Maybe Cobie and I will be friends. I know how important she is to Drew. They've known each other a long time.

Penny says, "Hi," to them both, then looks at me like we need to talk. "I'm sure we will," I say to Cobie, with the most genuine smile I can muster.

"You should both come out for dinner with us tonight. If you're staying, the whole crew will be there," offers Ted.

"We would love that." Penny grins. *She* would love that. I'm not so sure about myself. I just want Drew all to myself.

Like he can feel my internal thoughts, Drew wraps his arm around me, ushering me away from the tent. "Nice to meet you, Jenna," they both say as we walk away. I smile and wave.

"Penny, I'll introduce you to some of the other boys," says Drew. Feels like he can't get me away from Cobie fast enough, and I'm so thankful for it.

"Good idea, Drew, there is a nice-looking group gathered over there. Do you know them?"

He laughs and shakes his head. "Yeah, I know them."

"Good." She smirks.

He introduces us to a few of his friends, and Penny strikes up a conversation with one of the guys, so we leave her to it and walk a little farther up the beach. Finally, I have him alone.

"I'm sorry about Cobie, she can be a little weird when you first meet her."

I look at him, trying to read him. Why did he think she was weird? "She was lovely, Drew. I'm not sure what you mean."

He shrugs, but he looks uncomfortable. I get the impression that I'm missing something. "Yeah, I don't know, she was just all super nice to you. I don't know, it was strange."

"What, did you want us to hate each other or something? She's your manager, isn't it good if we get along?"

"Yeah, of course it is," he says, looking off into the distance. Weird?

He's hiding something from me, I can tell. "Is there something I'm missing?"

His attention comes back to me. "Nope, all good, I've just missed you, I guess, and wanted some time with you all to myself." We stop walking by a picnic-style table and chairs. He wraps his arms around me.

"Is that right?" I ask.

"Yes, I haven't seen you for two days. I want your body wrapped around mine." He kisses me. As he picks me up, my legs instinctively wrap around his waist, and he leans me onto the table, his lips on mine, kissing me with force. I love it when he gets like this, doesn't matter where we are. I'm the only one around, and nothing is more important than the connection we have. At least that's what it feels like.

I pull back from him, already breathless. "You miss my body, you mean." I laugh.

"Well, there is that, but I miss all of you." Before I know it, his hands are in my hair and his lips are on mine again, pulling me to him so closely. My hands roam up under his shirt and around to his back. I cling to him as our kiss intensifies. God, if he said he wanted to, I would let him take me right here on the picnic table in the light of day with hundreds of people around. That's how crazy he makes me when he kisses me like this.

"We should go somewhere."

I laugh at him. "You're that desperate, you can't wait till tonight?" I know exactly how he feels. I don't want to wait another second before he's inside of me.

"Yes." He groans into my neck.

This man, he kills me. And right now, I miss him so much I would do whatever he wants, go wherever he wants. "Where?"

Drew

I need her now and scan the beach for somewhere we can sneak off to. My train of dirty thoughts is rudely interrupted by a message on my phone. It's Cobie letting me know I'm needed back in the tent. My heat isn't far away. Damn.

"Got to head back now, Bamb, sorry. We will have to continue this later," I whisper into her neck. I kiss her once more. I need to go, but my body wants to stay here with her.

"Okay," she whispers. She's just as disappointed as me.

We wander back up the beach and I spot Penny still talking to the same guy.

"Guess I'll go join Penny so we can find a spot to watch you from. I'm looking forward to being your cheerleader. Good luck." She kisses me.

"And what a cute cheerleader you make, as well." I kiss her again, really not wanting to leave, but I need to get my head into my comp. "I don't want you hanging round with that group of guys. That's for Penny. Grab her and find a spot on the sand."

"Bossy." She laughs.

"I don't trust that lot with my girl."

"Good to know."

"See you after, baby." As I kiss her goodbye, I pull her into me hard, grabbing her arse; it looks so good in these short shorts she has on. I know I'm only tormenting myself. She pulls away.

"Drew, you need to go." She gives me one more peck on the lips then pulls away completely.

I watch as she wanders off down the beach to Penny, and they walk away from the group of guys to find a spot on the sand. I make my way back to the tent. I need to get my head into what I'm about to do. Right now, all I can think about is her. Might not work to my advantage, having her here. But I'm glad she is.

As I enter the tent, Cobie grins at me. "She's very pretty, Drew. I can see the appeal, on top of the whole stripper, sexy-librarian thing, I guess."

Catty Cobie, she's jealous. "What was the whole bestie thing you pulled with her? You don't normally act like that when you meet someone."

"I was just being friendly. She is your girlfriend and I'm your manager—we should get along, shouldn't we?" she says so sweetly I almost believe her. Almost, but I know her too well.

I start to get everything sorted. I have a whole routine I go through before a comp.

Cobie is acting weird. I thought she would have been pissed at me for bringing Jenna here today after her whole no-photos, no-mention-to-the-press talk, but she is happy about it? "I thought you were dead against the whole girlfriend thing, cause it would ruin my image."

She fakes a smile. "I have changed my mind. I'm thinking a pretty girl like that and the whole 'Drew Walker settles down' could work just as well. Besides, not like you were going to listen to me, anyway." She rolls her eyes. "She's here, isn't she? I'm sure there will be a photo of the two of you together soon enough. So now I need to make it work for us."

I'm pleasantly surprised by her change of mind. "Well, good, cause I'm happy with her." My heat is called, and I turn to grab my board.

She rolls her eyes. "Good luck, Drew, bring me home a win, baby."

"I'll do my best," I say with a wink as I turn to walk away.

"Drew?" she calls.

"Yeah?" I turn back towards her, irritated she's messing up my calm.

"Does Jenna know we've slept together in the past?"

What the fuck, is she trying to put me off my game? "No, Cobie, she doesn't, and I would prefer to keep it that way." I throw her a look, telling her this isn't up for negotiation. If I feel like she should know about it, I would want it to come from me so I can explain to her it's nothing.

"Not good to keep secrets, Drew," she tuts. "But my lips are sealed, I won't say a thing." She zips across her lips as if to prove it.

Great, now all I'm going to be thinking about out in the waves is Jenna finding out about my past with Cobie. It was only a few times, and it wasn't like it meant anything—not to me, anyway. We were just friends who got carried away. I was a single guy back then, it didn't matter who I fucked, but I know Jenna is a little jealous of her already, and I don't want to add fuel to the fire, so that's why I haven't told her about it. I don't want anything to fuck up what we have going on, but I'm sure Cobie won't say anything. Why would she?

I take a deep breath and try to clear my mind and get in the zone. I want this win, and today's conditions are perfect for me.

CHAPTER FOURTEEN

JENNA

I've been sitting on the sand with Penny all day. The weather is perfect—warm sun heating up our skin, not a cloud in the sky, just a small breeze off the ocean. Drew has competed and won his event, like I knew he would. It was inspiring to watch him out there doing what he loves. It makes me think that what the girls were saying about following my own dreams is right. Maybe I should listen to them and just go for it. What have I got to lose? If I send off my manuscript and they hate it, I'm no worse off than I am now with it just sitting in a folder on my computer.

Penny snaps her fingers in front of me, pulling me from my thoughts. "What you thinking about? You're very quiet."

"I don't know, just thinking about following dreams. It's inspiring to watch Drew in his element, don't you think?"

Penny smirks. "I would have said more hot, but yeah, I guess you could say inspiring. Why are you being all philosophical?"

I nibble my bottom lip, not sure if I should ask her about this or not, because I'm scared her answer will be something along the lines of, "It's great you wrote a book, but it might be better off left for the professionals." Or maybe she will just say it's shit. She is pretty bluntly honest. "You have read my book, haven't you? Should I send it off to a publisher? Or is it shit. Be honest, I can handle it." I bury my head in my hands with my eyes shut tight. I want to hear her opinion, but I don't. Maybe if I have my eyes closed, I won't be able to hear the bad stuff.

She rubs my back in a comforting gesture. "Jen, it was amazing. I don't read as much as you and Ivy, but you have a talent for storytelling. I found it hard to put down, and that is saying something for me. You know how hard I find it to sit in one spot and do anything. Definitely send it off."

I look up at her, still feeling so unsure.

"Back yourself, hun." She smiles.

"Really?" Just the thought of actually doing something with it has my tummy churning.

"Totally. I'm not shitting you. I was so impressed. I couldn't believe one of my friends came up with such a fantastic story."

I study her face; she looks impressed and excited, but that is Penny. She is our resident woo girl and is that way about most things. I need Ivy's practical thoughts on it before I decide completely. "Okay, maybe. Thank you."

"Stop thinking about it so much, you think too much about everything. Just take a chance and send it off."

I look out over the beach. All these people here are chasing their dreams. I can do this. Penny is right. I need to get out of my own head and just take a chance.

"Jenna, Penny, come and sit with me." I hear a female voice call from behind, breaking me from my thoughts, and turn to see Cobie coming our way. She looks stunning in a casual understated kind of a way I wish I could pull off.

Penny turns to me and whispers, "What do you make of this chick?"

I shrug. "She seems nice enough and she and Drew are really good friends. I want her to like me. But I reckon there is something with her and Drew, so if you can get to the bottom of that, I'd love you forever."

"You would love me forever anyway. I'll play nice then," she says with a smirk.

"Please try, Pen." We stand, brushing off the sand, and walk up the beach to where Cobie is setting up some chairs.

She takes a seat, then pats the one next to her. "This will be heaps more comfortable. When you come to these things as much as I do, you come prepared." She smiles, and it seems more genuine this time.

"Thank you," we both say, sitting down next to her. It's definitely more comfortable than sitting on the sand for hours on end.

"You must be happy Drew won today," I ask, trying to make conversation.

"Always happy when one of my boys gets a win. Especially Drew." She pauses, looking towards me for some sort of reaction. "He's been with me since the beginning," she says finally.

"How many boys do you manage?" asks Penny.

"A few. This year I have signed a number of new names, some of the up-and-comers, I'm hoping they will achieve some big things for me this year. Helps with the sponsors."

Penny is staring at her, a little too interested. "Will they be at dinner tonight as well?"

"Probably. Why, you got your eye on someone?"

"She has her eye on everyone," I say, rolling my eyes so Penny can see, and she hits me in the arm. I rub it. The girl is violent, always bloody hitting me.

"Not everyone. This guy here, you know him?" She motions with her head to where a young guy probably early twenties stands, waxing his board. His hair is long and shaggy in a shade of brown and his skin is tanned. He's nice to look at and I can see the appeal.

Cobie raises a brow, and her lips turn into a curved smile. "You're in luck, Penny, that's Hutton, he's on my team. I'll introduce you tonight."

"We kinda met already today. Drew introduced us. He is mighty fine," Penny says.

"He is, but I have got to warn you, the boy is a major player. Kinda like Drew used to be," she says, giving me a look like, "Whoops, did I just say that out loud?" And yeah, bitch, you did. I'm off this girl again. She acts super nice, but I get the impression there is more to the super niceness.

Penny shrugs. "Doesn't bother me. Means he won't get all clingy when I'm done with him."

Cobie winks at Penny. "Well, good for you, girlfriend, I like your style. Too bad you're with Drew, Jenna, cause I think the three of us could've had some real fun together if you were single."

I smile at her smugly. "Yeah, but I'm not, sorry. Maybe you two can go party together tonight while I catch up with my man." I know it was a bit of an immature dig to say my man, but I feel like I need to make it clear where we stand right from the start. Drew is mine, and she better just keep it professional and keep her hands off him or I will unleash my crazy on her.

She fakes a smile. "Of course he is, and you two must miss each other while he's away. It must be so hard not knowing what he's doing." She puts her hand over her heart. "I mean, I don't think I could handle knowing my boyfriend was Drew Walker, when he's away all the time

—not with his reputation." She pauses, all serious, then she smiles. "But you obviously have nothing to worry about. He is crazy about you. I don't know how you did it, Jenna, but you're one lucky girl. Most chicks around here, including myself, would have killed to have tamed the beast."

My eyes flick to Penny, wondering if she just heard all of that the same as I did? "Thanks, I guess." I don't even know what else to say to that. She really lays all her cards out on the table. She's happy to tell me she has a thing for my boyfriend right to my face. Rude.

She touches me on the arm playfully. "Oh, sweetie, you should see your face." She laughs. "You have nothing to worry about, all that was in the past. You know Drew is so into you."

Penny narrows her eyes, her brow frowning. "So you had a past?" There she is, the Penny I love, straight out with it, and I thank God that my ballsy friend has the guts I don't to ask that question.

I'm getting overwhelmed by this whole situation. This is always what happens to me with people like this. I let them walk all over me, make me feel like shit, then later, when the whole scene is playing over in my head, I realise that I should have said something to stick up for myself, but it's too late.

Cobie shrugs like it's no big deal. "I guess you could call it that."

Penny eyes her suspiciously, then looks back at me. I shrug. I don't know what else you say in this situation. "So, you slept together then? Friends-with-benefits type of arrangement?" Penny asks.

I cover my face and shake my head, surprised she went that far and actual said it. Cobie hasn't responded, and I look towards her. Wanting to know the answer but hating what I know I'm going to hear.

"Something like that." She smirks.

Bitch! She knows what she's doing here. She isn't sweet at all. She is a fucking cow after my man.

And that is exactly what I didn't want to hear. My sexy-as-fuck boyfriend, who I already know has a reputation for sleeping around and has never had a girlfriend, has slept with his hot manager, who he will go away with on the regular for the rest of the year. Why has Drew not told me about this? I look at Penny, and her face says it all. This is not good.

Drew

Cobie has organised dinner and a few drinks at a local Mexican restaurant with Ted, some of the other competitors, Penny, and Jenna. She is being sickly sweet to Jenna. It's kinda weird and makes me feel a little uneasy. I don't really want them to be friends. I mean, I love Cobie, she has been in my life for a long time, but I haven't been totally honest with Jenna about my past with her. There could have been a little something there between us once, and we have slept together a few times. I just know how unsettled Jenna already feels about me going away. I didn't want to tell her and worry her any further when I know there's nothing there anymore. Jenna is the only girl for me, and now that I have her, I'm not going to do anything to screw that up.

The table is noisy with chatting and laughing. Penny has taken a liking to Hutton and is hanging on his every word as he tells an animated story. Jenna sits between her friend and me. I'm on the corner. She rolls her eyes dramatically at her friend, and I chuckle.

Jenna wasn't that keen to come tonight, and I have to say I was the same. All I want to do is be back in my room with her body wrapped around me, celebrating my win. I run my hand up her leg and lean into her neck. "We eat, then we're going back to the room. I'm not waiting any longer to have you."

"What about Penny?" she whispers. Jen has been acting a bit funny since I finished up this afternoon. She is standoffish, not her normal self with me. I can't tell if she just feels out of place or if there is something actually wrong.

I look toward Penny and Hutton. I think we all know how that is going to end tonight; Penny could care less about what we're doing. "Penny is fine, look at her," I say. She glances at her friend, then back to me.

"What about Cobie? Don't want to make her even more jealous." The look she gives me. Fuck, she is pissed. My guess Cobie has said something and now I'm in shit because I didn't say something first. That's the only explanation for her iciness tonight. How do I fix this?

I lean into her, my hand on her leg. "I'm sorry, Jen. I should have told you," I whisper so no one else can hear.

"Yeah, you should have. Wasn't fun finding out from that smug bitch." She gives Cobie an evil look. I haven't seen Jenna pissed off like this before, and it's my fault.

"I would have told you. I just didn't want to cause a problem when she's my manager and I just have to get through this year."

She removes my hand, pushing it away. "Yep, I get it," she snaps.

I give her a look, and she stares intensely back at me. "Jenna, we need to go out the front now," I say under my breath. I don't need to be having a fight with my girlfriend in front of everyone.

We push out our chairs and Cobie glances our way. She's watching us. She has caused this. She smiles my way, and I shake my head at her. Why did she put me in this position? I need to have words with her about all of this.

Jenna storms out the front, and I follow closely behind her. She leans up against the wall at the front of the building, arms crossed over her chest; she is mad. I have to remind myself I'm grovelling right now, because she's cute when she's mad, and fighting with her is the last thing I want to do right now.

I stand in front of her, keeping my distance in case she hits me or something. Not that I think she would, but her face is murderous. "Jen, I promise you there is nothing to worry about there. Cobie is jealous because she's not used to me having a girl in my life, but Jen, you have always been the only girl for me."

"But you're friends with her and she's your manager and I could handle that, but knowing you have slept together, it's too much."

"Did she tell you that?"

She kicks the dirt around at her feet, her eyes down to the ground. She's frustrated, and I get it, I would be too if the roles were reversed. "Drew, she didn't have to. Her behaviour was enough to tell me. She acts all sugary sweet but throws in enough comments that I could piece it all together. I don't trust her, and I hate that she is around you so much." She looks into my eyes, her bottom lip trembling; she is trying not to cry but she's on the edge. "Did you have feelings for her? Be honest with me." She blinks back at me.

I wish I knew the right thing to say. I want to be honest with her, but I know that won't be the easy option here, because it's complicated. But what's the point if I can't be truthful with her? I would be more of an arsehole than I already am.

"She is a close friend, and yes, we did sleep together a few times, but it wasn't because I was in love with her or anything. It was because I was drunk and she was my friend, we were hanging out together having a bit of fun. I care about her, but not in the same way I care about you."

I dust my hand along her arm. She glares up at me. She looks so sad, and I feel terrible. This is what I was trying to avoid by not telling her, and now I have made it so much worse. "I know that sounds shit, but I haven't done the whole relationship thing until you. It's not like I had anyone to answer to. It didn't really matter who I slept with back then, and I don't know... I'm probably stuffing this up."

I run my hands through my hair. I wish I knew how to fix this. "What I'm trying to say is, even if there was a little of something there between us in the past, it was only because I thought I would never have a chance with you again, and now that I do, you're the only girl for me. Nothing will ever happen between me and Cobie again. You have to trust me on that." My eyes plead with her to understand. I don't want anything to jeopardise what we have, she means too much to me.

She lets out a big sigh, unfolding her arms, letting them drop to her sides and relaxing a little. "Yeah, and now you have me being a pain-in-the-arse girlfriend. Questioning you. I'm not pissed that you slept with her—well, not really. It's that you didn't tell me and I had to work it out for myself. Made me feel stupid, like we're not as close as I thought we were."

"I know, that was silly of me. I'm sorry. I'm not good at this boyfriend stuff." I take a step towards her, closing the gap between us, taking her face in my hands. "But if you can stay with me through all these teething issues, I'm sure I will be worth it, baby. We're a good match, Jenna, you are the perfect girl for me. I can't even tell you how much I adore you."

She nods, and I see some of her anger fade away. "How can I stay mad at you when you look at me like that? Those big, blue puppy-dog eyes." She smiles softly, and I know things are going to be okay.

"You can't." My lips meet hers and my hands run down her body, pulling her towards me as I kiss her deeply. I need her to know what she means to me, and if I can't tell her, I'm going to fucking show her the only way I know how. She runs her hands under my shirt, feeling up my back. As my hands slip down her body to her arse and I pull her into me, her legs wrap around as I press her into the wall behind.

I'm so hard for her right now, she must be able to feel me pressed into her, so needy to be inside her. I kiss down her neck and she moans out loud, her eyes closing. She craves me just as much. I need to get her home and show her just what she means to me.

Someone clears their throat. We look over to where the voice comes from. It's Cobie. Of course it's her, as if she hasn't caused enough trouble for tonight. "Dinner is ready," she says shyly.

Jenna tries to push me off, feeling awkward by the situation, but I keep my hands where they are, her pressed against the wall. "Tell them all something came up, and I had to take my girl home."

"Oh, you sure?" She looks confused.

"Drew, we should go back in," Jenna pleads with me. I can tell she's uncomfortable making a scene. But I need to prove a point, as juvenile as it might be, and I don't want to go back in there right now. All I want is Jenna.

"No," I growl, looking straight into her eyes. "I'm taking you back to our room." I kiss her and she melts into me. "See you tomorrow," I call to Cobie, not moving my eyes from Jenna.

Cobie disappears back inside the restaurant.

"What will we have for dinner, then?" Jenna asks.

"I'm having you." I smirk before I kiss her passionately again. Tonight might not have gone exactly how I had planned, but it's going to end just how I want it to.

CHAPTER FIFTEEN

JENNA

We slam into the door outside our hotel room, and he kisses me again. His hands are everywhere. Hard, rushing forcefully, his stubble scratching my face. His lips pressing into me. I want him so badly. I grip onto him. I don't want to let him go; I haven't since we left the restaurant in a rush and headed back to his room.

The way he looked at Cobie back there. He was so pissed with her for making us fight, and the entire time, he didn't let me go. He was happy to stay in that compromising position to show her he was serious about us. I needed that.

I need him so badly after that fight. I had been so worried all day about what him and Cobie sleeping together meant. Were they more than friends? But him like this, I feel it. I know it's only me. This is his way of proving it, and it's just what I need.

I'm pressed into the door as his hands roam up my body. My hands tug at his shirt. I want it off. I need his fucking hot body on mine.

He pulls back and kisses and bites down my neck. It's hard and rough and feels so good.

"Where's your room key?" I breathe.

"In my pocket." I slip my hand down into his pocket, retrieving the key, and swipe it through the door. The door swings open and we stumble through it. Tearing at each other's clothes, grabbing and pulling them off before we've even closed the door.

His shirt is first to go, and I run my hands over his chiselled chest. I fumble with his belt, his fly. He helps me to remove his jeans quickly. His hands return to me, his lips on mine, as he pushes my dress straps off my shoulders, and it pools on the floor.

He slams the door shut, and his hands go to my waist, pushing me back into the door. Our bodies press together, his lips on mine, his hands are everywhere. His hard cock digs into my stomach. His mouth devouring me. My leg hooks around his waist as my nails dig into his back. I can't get close enough to him. His fingers run back and forth over my soaked panties, teasing me.

"I need you in me," I pant desperately. "Now."

"What's the rush, baby?" He chuckles, but this isn't funny. I'm serious.

"I need to know what I mean to you, show me," I plead with him. I feel so desperate to be seen by him. To know I'm the only one. "Fuck me."

His face breaks into that cheeky smile of his. Then he drops to his knees in front of me, pulling my panties down my legs, running his nose along my pussy.

"You smell delicious." He groans.

Oh God, this man is too much. "Not what I asked for."

He pulls back from me. "You asked me to show you what you mean to me. You're my queen, Jenna. I'm going to worship you." I smile down at him, the way he looks at me so intensely, then he licks his lips and my insides clench. I need him to touch me.

He lifts my leg over his shoulder, placing kisses down my thigh until he gets back down to my pussy. He runs his tongue through my dripping-wet folds, and I have to press my hands into the door behind me to stabilise myself.

"Is this what you needed?" He licks through my flesh again.

"Yes." I moan.

"I could do this all night." He flicks his tongue out and turns his attention back to my lady parts. His mouth back on me, right where I need it, sucking my clit, circling his tongue in small motions, then sucking vigorously, repeating the pattern.

The world around me disappears, along with all my fears. What he's doing is everything. I run a hand through his long hair, tugging the ends as my hips rock slowly towards his hungry mouth that devours me. My body tingles with anticipation, and just when I think I can't take any more, he slides in a couple of fingers, pushing in as deep as he can.

The pressure of his pumps, along with the sensation of the sucking, is so mind-numbingly good. It only takes a few quick forceful pumps and I lose control completely, my body tightening and convulsing with the ripple of the orgasm that radiates through me.

Whoa, that was something else. My head is foggy. My breathing is ragged. My heart feels like it is going to hammer out of my chest. With Drew, every little sensation is just so good. He pulls back from me, taking me in, his grin reaching those fucking dimples. He is proud of himself—and he should be, as he has a gift.

He slides his hands up my body as he rises up to me. "You're on the pill, aren't you?"

He's asking if he can go bareback? "No, but I get the depo shot."

"Good. I have never slept with anyone without protection, but I need to with you tonight."

I blink back at him. No condom? Not a discussion we've ever had before, it has always just been non-negotiable. When we're ready to go, he has the thing on. So I believe him when he says he never has before. But why now?

"Get out of your head. I can see the tennis match going on in there. I need nothing between us," he growls, kissing down my chest as his hands work on removing my bra. It falls to the floor and his hands cup my breasts, massaging them as he teases my nipples into hard peaks. My hands run down his front, tugging his briefs down his legs, his massive cock jumping free.

"Do you trust me, Jenna?"

Do I trust him? I don't have to think about it. "Yes," I whisper, and I do. As much as I have my insecurities with other women around him, I do trust him.

"Good girl." His fingers dig into my hip bones as he lifts me up, my legs wrapping around his body, my back resting against the door behind. He slams into me balls deep in one action. Almost knocking the air from my lungs. He stares straight into my eyes. "Jenna, you are the only girl for me. I have to have you forever."

I cling to him, unable to take my eyes away from his. Every second that passes, the more convinced I am, I can feel exactly what he does. This must be what love feels like, a connection so deep with another person that the feeling can only be explained as love.

I thought he was going to fuck me hard and fast against

the door, but this is something else. This is intimacy I haven't ever had before. I'm scared and excited at the same time. I want everything he offers. "I'm forever yours," I whisper into his lips as I kiss him.

As we kiss, he moves, rocking his hips to me slowly. It's almost too much, this feeling of closeness. It has me on the verge of tears.

As if he can feel my mood shift, his kiss turns from slow and sweet to aggressive as he picks up the pace. His teeth biting into me. This is the Drew I'm used to in the bedroom. My head falls back to the door as he fucks me with everything he has. Beads of sweat forming on his forehead, his fingers dig into my hips so hard I know there will be marks there tomorrow, but right now I don't care. This is perfect, our bodies moving together in perfect timing.

With every hard pump I cry out louder. The pleasure builds and takes over my body till I'm a trembling mess, weak like jelly in his arms. The only thing keeping me against the door is him. He pumps me three more times then grunts into my neck as his orgasm takes over and he fills me with his hot cum.

He pants into my neck, out of breath, and I cling to him, too weak to move.

"We should fight more if this is how we make up." He's such a smartarse.

"Really?" I laugh. He loosens his grip to look at me, and I slip down the wall to standing, my body slowly coming back to life. "That was insane. I think you still have some grovelling to do. I haven't totally forgiven you yet." I take off across the room.

"Is that right?" He chases me, tackling me to the bed and encasing me in his arms. "I'm only just getting started with you. By the time you wake up tomorrow, your sore body will be well aware of how much I made it up to you."

"Promises, promises," I tut, even though I know I'm going to regret pushing Drew. He is insatiable enough.

Drew

I wrap my arms around her and pull her body closer, inhaling her scent before I even open my eyes. Her skin feels so good on mine. I could lie like this all day, both of us naked, our bodies tangled around each other.

She has to go home today without me, while I stay on and finish the next week of the competition. After last night, I don't want to be apart from her. Something shifted between us, and now there is a closeness that I can't even explain. Feelings I have never had before. I always knew she was someone special to me, and I felt like I was in love with her in the past, but this feeling of attachment to her is crazy. Is it normal to feel like this? It couldn't possibly be.

"I don't want to go home today," she mumbles into my chest.

I stroke her long, silky hair. I can barely stand the thought of her not being here with me. But I need to get over that and quickly. We both knew it would be like this all year when we started this, and we still have months to go. "Can you stay another couple of nights?" I ask, hopeful but knowing the answer before I asked.

She pulls back to look at me. "I wish I could, except Ivy messaged me last night. She's going through something and needs a friend. And there is work."

"What has Theo done?"

She bites her lip nervously. This is where it gets a little

strange, when your brother is dating your girlfriend's best friend. "I don't know, but she seemed pretty upset in the message, so I think I should go home. We have each other's backs, and she needs me. Plus, if we let Penny stay any longer, she'll get a name for herself." She giggles.

"Yeah, Penny is a worry. That girl is going to get herself in trouble hanging out with guys like Hutton."

"Sorry I have to go," she says softly. Leaning up to kiss me.

I roll on top of her, pinning her beneath me. "It's okay. I like that you and Ivy are so close, you're like family to each other, and if it were my sister that needed me, I would go as well."

"She is my family, definitely." She leans up, kissing me again. "I'm going to miss you until you come home, though."

"I'm going to miss you, too. Are we good after last night? You know you can trust me, right?" I'm scared to ask, but I have to know everything is alright between us before she goes.

"Yes, I trust you, Drew. We're all good. I wouldn't be leaving you with Cobie for another week if I didn't. I don't trust her, though, you need to be careful there. She likes you more than you think."

"I will be. I know how to handle Cobie. And by my calculations, I have you for another two hours and I'm not due at the beach until midday, so I'm going to make the most of every second." I roll my hips into her, and she laughs.

JENNA AND PENNY LEFT AFTER OUR LAZY MORNING IN bed and a late breakfast. I have just arrived on the beach and head straight for our tent. I need to talk to Cobie. Her telling Jenna we had a past was exactly what she told me she wouldn't do. I need to understand why she would put me in that position. I thought we had an understanding, but maybe things are worse than I thought, and Jenna is right.

"Ted, morning," I say, arriving at the tent.

"So nice of you to join us, Drew. Late night?" He smirks.

"Nah, just making the most of spending time with my girl before she had to go home."

Cobie's eyes land on me, and she gives me an awkward look.

"Hey, Cobie."

"Drew, can we go for a walk?" she says softly. She seems sheepish today.

"Sounds like a good idea," I offer.

We walk out of the tent, and Ted calls after us, "Don't take too long, I need to go over a few things with you before you get out there today, Drew."

I turn back to him. "No worries, Ted, this won't take long." I smile cheekily, and he shakes his head. He's probably wondering why he even bothers with me. I don't listen to his advice half the time. I have always been shit at taking directions from others. But he loves me, that's why he sticks by me. Most of the risks I take pay off and make him look good anyway.

I turn to Cobie, needing to get this conversation over with. "Why did you tell her?"

She shrugs. "I didn't really tell her. Her friend Penny asked if I had a friend-with-benefits kind of arrangement with you in the past, and I just didn't deny it." She stops walking and turns to face me. "I wasn't lying, Drew. You know I think honesty is the best policy."

"You could have told her to ask me about it, though. It was for me to tell her. It was so much worse coming from you, can't you see that?"

"Maybe she doesn't trust you, that's why she got her friend to question me. I would be careful with her, Drew. Girls like that, they're only after one thing."

What is she on about, girls like that? Like what? I don't like this side of Cobie. I haven't seen it before this year. She has always been so loyal to me, but trying to make out that Jenna is a problem, it's a low blow. "And what would that be?"

"Your money, honey, you know that, right?" She gives me a sassy look, like she is really trying to sell this idea of Jenna being a gold digger. She has to be kidding, though, Jenna is as far from being after my money as anyone could be. She is so different to the other girls around here, that's why I like her so much. She's real, not out to be something she's not or hanging off my every word because she wants people to know she's with me. I know that's what Cobie sees a lot and it might be why she's jumping to that conclusion, but it's not fair. She doesn't know Jenna at all.

"Jenna's not like that," I snap at her.

"Maybe." She shrugs smugly, like she knows better.

"She's not, and anyway, I was the one who was after her, so that doesn't even make sense." I glare at her, and she smiles at me. "Cobie, are we going to be able to finish this season together? Because I don't like where this is all going."

She runs her hand along my arm. "Drew, stop your worrying. We will be fine. I just have to get used to you in a relationship. It's odd when I've known you so long, I guess."

"And you will be nice when you see Jenna next?" I ask, trying to be as diplomatic about it as I can. But the need to protect Jenna from her is real, and I need to know if Jenna comes to another comp that she will feel welcome.

Cobie's eyes flick back to me. "I was nice to her yesterday," she snaps with attitude.

"You know what I mean, don't say anything that will cause trouble."

She fakes a smile. "Anything for you, Drew baby." She gives me an awkward hug. "Come on, you have a comp to win." She stalks back up the beach and I follow her. I think Jenna might be right, I need to be really careful. I'm not great when it comes to reading chicks, but things are not okay here, not by a long shot. Cobie is acting weird and none of what happened yesterday was an accident.

CHAPTER SIXTEEN

JENNA

It's now May, two months since I let the girls read my story. I'm staring at my laptop screen, frozen. It feels like a lot has happened over the last two months, and nothing at the same time. I found a publishing house that looks right for me. Actually, it was the one that Ivy got the business card for that day in the café. I was looking into them, and they look perfect. They specialise in romance books and have been around for a long time.

The email is written, the manuscript attached. Should I send it or not? I have no idea what to do. *No, just do it, Jenna. What have you got to lose?* Especially now, after what happened to Ivy a few weeks ago, when her ex-husband turned up and wreaked havoc on her and Theo's life. The two of them are lucky to still be alive, and I won't take my life for granted anymore.

It's like Drew says, life is meant to be lived. If we spend all of our lives playing it safe, too scared to take any risks, then what is the point? You're not really living.

And I'm talking to myself again. Olive has caught me doing it a lot lately, and I'm pretty positive she thinks I'm going crazy—and maybe I am a little. You can't live in an imaginary world half of the time and not be a little nuts.

I hit send and let out the breath I have been holding for what feels like five minutes. Too late to back out now. They will probably hate it, but at least I have given it a go. I feel proud of myself, regardless of what happens. I close my laptop and slide it into my bag. I look around the library and daydream about how amazing it would be if they like it and I actually publish a book. It's probably never going to happen, but I can imagine how it would feel, anyway.

Stop being so negative. This is your time to shine. You have done the work. Now back yourself, Jenna, you've got this.

"What're you doing?" comes a deep male voice.

I jump and place a hand over my heart. I was so deep in thought I didn't see Blake walk into the library and he's right in front of me. "Ha, yeah, I don't know, I was just thinking."

He narrows his eyes, as if assessing me. "Okay, it looked very serious."

"Nah, just giving myself a bit of a pep talk. You know, when you put yourself out there and you don't know what's going to happen, so you feel a bit down about it. I was just telling myself it's okay." I try to brush it off as no big deal because I haven't told Blake about writing the book. I'm scared if I tell too many people and it doesn't happen, I'll feel like a failure.

He rests his hand on my shoulder. "Yeah, I get it. Is something wrong? I'm sure I can work out a way to fix it if there is."

I shake my head at him. Typical Blake wants to fix what's not even broken. He has to feel like he's helping in some way. I think it makes him feel needed or something. "No, I don't need you to do anything. Why do you guys always want to fix everything?" I roll my eyes, and he frowns at me.

"I don't know, just want to help if I can. How about lunch at that rice-paper-roll place you like so much. Will that make you feel better?" He grins.

I smirk back at my friend. "You know me too well. Food is always the answer. Thank you, but I'm fine, really." I look over my shoulder to see Olive. "Just going for lunch, be back in an hour," I call to her.

"No worries, hun, have fun," she calls over her shoulder with a wave.

We exit the library and hit the warm sunshine outside. It's a beautiful day for this time of year, no sign of the cold hitting us yet.

Blake looks down at me, a look of concern still on his face. "Is it Drew you're worried about?"

"I'm not worried about anything." I shake my head. He gives me a glare like he doesn't believe a word I'm saying. He will not let this go. I'm going to have to tell him all about it now. "It's not anything to do with Drew. It's silly, I'll tell you about it at lunch." I huff, not really wanting to give my secret away just yet, but it's nice that he cares so much. I imagine this is what it would be like to have a big brother looking out for you. He really has taken on that role for me over the last few years, and I adore him for it.

We walk through the car park, arriving at his car. "Okay, then. When will Drew be home? Where is he this time?" he asks, unlocking the vehicle.

"He will be home from Rottnest Island today. Won this comp as well, so he is well on track to winning the title." It has been a couple of months since we had that fight at Newcastle, and he has been away a few times since then. I'm okay with the whole situation with Cobie. That night I could see I was his number-one priority, and she was just his manager and an old friend, who he fucked. That part is harder to accept, but I'm ignoring it because it was in the past.

Once I let go of my anxiety and jealously over the whole situation, and the truth was out in the open, it got easier when he went away. I know I can trust him now. And what we have developed is a connection, a closeness that I have never had with anyone else before. It's the way he makes me feel desired, but not just in a sexual way, in a way that he can't breathe without me, and I can't without him. I have never felt like this about anyone. I can't imagine my life without him in it anymore, and I think he feels the same.

"That's amazing. We all knew this would be his year." He smiles, pleased for his friend. We all are.

"Yeah, he's doing so well. I'm so excited for him. Looks like the dream he's had since he was a kid will finally be a reality."

As I go to step into his car, I see Drew's bike ride into the car park. My heart kicks up a beat—it's him! His presence still has this effect on me. I'm like a kid on Christmas, suddenly filled with such excitement. I run to him as he parks the bike. He takes off his helmet and there's that cheeky grin, dimples and all. I wrap my arms around him, reuniting my lips with his. God, I have missed him. My hands run through his hair, and I cling to him like my life depends on it. He smells so fricken good. It's him, he's home.

"This is a bit cute," I hear Blake tease from behind us. For a second, I had forgotten he was here.

Drew glances over to him, and he forces a smile; it is becoming more obvious that he doesn't love our friendship.

I turn to Blake, a little embarrassed about my teen-like

behaviour and over-the-top public display of affection. "Sorry, Blake."

He laughs, totally unfazed. "You joining us for lunch, Drew? We're going to Jenna's favourite place."

"I could eat." But the way he looks at me, I don't think he is talking about food. He makes my lady parts throb with need. I wish we could skip lunch and go home for a quickie, but I need to get a hold on it because I still have an afternoon of work to get through. And I only meet up with Blake once a month these days. I don't want to blow him off because I can't control my desire for the sexy man in front of me. Blake is important to me as well.

Drew takes off, and I hop into the car with Blake. I'm a little torn. I almost feel like I should have gone over with Drew, but I was already about to hop into the car with Blake, and there is the matter of what I'm wearing. Butterflies dance in my tummy because I get to see Drew again.

We arrive at my favourite spot for lunch, placing our order and taking a table down the back in the courtyard. Drew shuffles his chair a little closer to mine so he can sling his arm around my shoulders. The caveman-like show of ownership is not lost on me. He is making it very clear to Blake that I'm his. The funny part is Blake doesn't care at all.

As we wait for our order to arrive, Drew tells us the dramatic story of how he managed to win his last comp. He's so animated as he retells what happened, it makes me wish even more that I was there watching him, so I could share his joy when he won. As he talks, his free hand runs up and down my thigh, sending a thrill through my body. I have missed him so much, and tonight, he will be all mine again. I have a little surprise for him, to help him celebrate his win properly as well.

Our food is delivered to our table, and we all dig in. I crave these rice paper rolls at least once a week. They are so light and fresh but filling as well. I love the way they wrap little mint leaves in there too, and the peanut sauce is to die for. I moan a little when I take my first bite. "So good," I say.

Drew leans into me. "I can think of something even better to fill your mouth with, and it's going to have you moaning louder than that all night." He kisses my neck before pulling away.

"You two need a room." Blake shakes his head.

"We do," he says back to Blake, deadpan. And I'm mortified. I throw him a look, telling him to control himself. He isn't going to make this lunch easy for anyone. When Drew wants something, he keeps pushing until he gets it. Right now, he wants to be alone with me. It would be cute how badly he wants me if it wasn't so obsessive and in front of one of my friends.

"Drew," I chastise him. "Sorry, Blake. How's Indie? Is she back at work now?" I say, focusing my attention on him, trying to change the subject to make all of this less awkward.

Blake shrugs it off; I don't think he really cares. "She is, just one day a week in the office and the rest she works from home. She is amazing." He bursts out laughing. "You two are never going to believe what happened with the twins the other day. It will put you off ever having kids of your own, probably forever."

Blake tells us the latest stories about his family. As he talks, you can see how much love he has for them all. His twin boys sound like hard work, but it doesn't seem to bother him. He makes it all just sound like so much fun. I don't know why Drew has such a problem with Blake. Surely he can see how crazy he is about his wife, even after four kids. His face still lights up when he talks about Indie. That's the kind of love I want. Someone who adores me no matter what and still talks about me with such love, even after the honeymoon period has worn off and the realities of life have taken over.

Is that what I could have with Drew? It's too early to tell, but I hope so. Love like that and a family of our own would be beyond anything I ever could have imagined in my life, but I've always wanted kids. A big happy family around me with a noisy, messy house, just like Blake and Indie have. I envy them, it must be so wonderful.

I glance at Drew. He thinks Blake's story is hilarious. He laughs with his head back, full chuckles coming from him. Watching him makes me what to laugh just as hard.

"So, what's this thing you were going to tell me at lunch, then?" asks Blake.

Oh, he had to bring that up, didn't he? I knew he wouldn't let it go. Drew raises a brow, wanting in on this chat as well.

I rub my hands nervously together. "Well, this morning I did something I have always wanted to do but never thought I would have the guts to. And I don't want either of you to make a big deal out of it, because it will probably never go anywhere. But it feels good that I had the guts to give it a try."

"Go on," says Drew.

"I sent off a manuscript of a romance novel I wrote to a publishing house." I nibble my bottom lip nervously, waiting for their response.

"You did it, you sent it off. I'm so proud of you, Jen." Drew pulls me into him and kisses me.

I glance to Blake nervously, wanting his approval. I have no idea why, but I need it.

"That's amazing. Good on you for following your dreams. I couldn't be more thrilled for you." He beams with excitement for me.

"Thank you both so much for your support, it means so much to me." I smile at them. These two men changed the course of my life. If it weren't for them, who knows where I would be today, and getting to share my wins with them, even if they are small, seems like such a big deal. I can't help but think how lucky I really am.

"Better get you back to work. And I need to get to my next building inspection," says Blake.

I check the time. He's right, it's nearly been the full hour I get for lunch. It went by so fast. I don't want to go back to work this afternoon. But I guess I better.

We pay the bill and make our way to Blake's car. Drew has his arm wrapped around me. "Jen can come on the bike with me, so you can get on back to work, Blake."

"I'm happy either way," says Blake.

"Drew, I'm wearing a pencil skirt and pumps, there is no way I'm getting on that bike like this. It's just not going to happen. Sorry. I'll see you at my place after work."

"Settled then, see you later, Drew," calls Blake with a wave, hopping into his car.

"Jenna, I want to take you back to work. I want to give you something," he growls into my neck.

He's being dirty, I know he is. I can feel his hard-on through his jeans. My hands slide down his sides and into his back pocket, pulling him closer to me. "I get that, baby, but it's not possible right now, so you're just going to have to wait till I get home to *give it to me*."

"You're going to get it, alright, and I'm going to punish you for making me wait so long."

I kiss him. "Promises, promises," I say, pulling away from

him. Then turn and open the car door, sliding into the seat. Drew watches me. He should be jumping on his bike and heading home, but he doesn't. He stands by the car, his eyes glued to me, hands in pockets. Probably adjusting that hard-on before he attempts to ride away.

I glance at Blake, who is on his phone, scrolling. "You two finally done."

"Sorry, Blake, so embarrassing." I bury my head in my hands because I'm sure I'm bright red.

"It's fine, Jenna, it's actually pretty funny. You're torturing the poor boy, you know."

"He'll be fine. Delayed gratification." I laugh.

"This is a side to you I have never seen, and it took Drew Walker to bring it out in you. Who would have thought the two of you would eventually work out that you were meant to be together." He smiles cheekily as he takes off through the car park.

I look over at him, waiting for his reaction to what I'm about to say. "He's the one, Blake. He's my Indie." I can't help but cover my smile with my hand.

"I know, Jenna, you can see it when you're together."

I'm surprised it's that obvious. I feel like we've had no time together to even seem like a couple who's good together. "You can?" My goofy smile grows.

"Yeah."

"I hope I have everything you have one day. You're so lucky."

"I know I am. That's why even when things are shit with the kids and they're driving us crazy and we're running on no sleep, I look around at what we have and just think how grateful I am. I have a beautiful family who I love more than anything. You and Drew will have that as well. I'm sure of it."

"I really hope so."

He smiles over to me, patting me on the leg. "You will."

I want to imagine that for us, a future that looks very similar to what he has, but every time I do, the feeling of losing it overwhelms me. There are too many questions of what if it doesn't work out. I just need to keep focusing on getting through this year with him still travelling so much. Then we can think of the future.

THE AFTERNOON AT THE LIBRARY SEEMED TO GO FOR A week. It's like time has literally slowed down, and when I check how much longer till the end of the day, it's only been five minutes. I wander around the aisles with the trolley, finding homes for the returned books. Truth is, I haven't got much done all afternoon, I'm so desperate to get home to Drew. I have a little surprise for him and I'm excited to show him what it is.

A text pings on my phone, and I roll the trolley out of sight and pull it from my pocket to check. It's Drew, I knew he wouldn't be able to wait until I got home.

Drew: You were a naughty girl today, choosing Blake over me. You will be punished for it tonight.

I laugh when I read it. I'm so scared. Big, bad Drew. The thought of being punished by him sends a thrill through me. But I doubt he will punish me when he sees what I have in store for him tonight.

Me: It wasn't safe for me to go on the bike today, Drew! I didn't choose him over you!

I hit send. Then type again.

Me: Oh, and I think you will want to hold off on the punishment when you see the surprise I have planned for you.

I hit send again and then wait. I know I'm smirking to myself, staring at my phone like an idiot in the middle of the library. But I'm just so excited about tonight, so I really don't care.

Drew: We will see. Your place or mine?

Me: Mine, 6pm. I need a little time to get ready after I finish work.

Drew: You expect me to wait longer? I'll be there at 5.30!

Me: Might ruin your surprise, but that's up to you.

Drew: I'll take my chances. I'm not waiting another minute to see you.

I'm not shocked at all. He is the most impatient person I know. I decide to leave it there and not message anything back, because I know that will annoy him and I'm in the mood to stir him up.

I continue placing books back on the shelves and move to the next aisle. I feel a bump on the arm and look back. It's Olive, of course. Is that the only way this girl can get my attention? "Go home to your man. There's no one here, I'll lock up tonight."

I smile at her. We work together too much, it's like she can read my mind. "You sure?"

"Yes, I have it under control, and you're no good to me anyway. You're all spacey this arvo." She pulls a face, mimicking me with my head in the clouds.

"I'm so sorry, I'll catch up in the morning. It's just been two weeks since I've seen him. I'm going crazy."

"You horny little bitch, go home." She laughs as she shoos me away with her hands.

She's not wrong. I have one thing on my mind. "Okay, see you tomorrow."

Home to my man. I need to enjoy this time with him while I can, and tonight is going to be fun.

Drew

I buzz her gate at exactly 5.30. "Hope you're ready for me," I ask, but I don't really care. I'm not waiting any longer to see her.

"I think everything is under control. Let yourself in, the door is unlocked. I'm finishing up in the kitchen," she calls through the intercom.

I walk up the driveway and open the door. She has music playing, something old; I think Etta James. She loves her old music, and I can hear her humming along.

The aroma coming from the kitchen makes my stomach growl. I hadn't realised how hungry I was until I smelt it. But I'm starving, and whatever this surprise is must be what she's cooking. Smart girl, she knows the way to this man's heart is through food... and sex.

I round the corner into the kitchen, and my mouth nearly drops open at the sight of her. Fuck, she is amazing. She really knows me well. Not only is she cooking me dinner, but she's dressed in only a red lacy bra and thong set with red stilettos, her long hair out and running down her back, and a frilly white apron tied at the waist.

She glances over her shoulder at me, a sexy-as-fuck smile on her red lips. "Dinner won't be long," she calls, then continues to stir whatever she's cooking on the stove.

I come up behind her, wrapping my arms around her, kissing her cheek. "This is a nice surprise." I run my hands down her body, feeling her curves.

She places the wooden spoon on a plate and slowly

spins around in my arms to face me. "You like my chef outfit?" She gives me a little shimmy.

"I love. Hottest chef I have ever seen." She gazes up at me, teeth digging into her bottom lip. I brush her hair over her shoulder, pulling her into my chest, our lips meeting. I'm no longer hungry for anything but her.

She pulls back from me with a sassy smirk. "I better finish dinner. Why don't you pour us a wine and relax."

Is she kidding? I can't relax now. My mind is running through every possible scenario of us fucking in her kitchen. Her bent over the bench top, or maybe standing up against the pantry, her legs wrapped around my waist. Or the table, it's not set, I could lay her down, spread her legs wide.

She gives me a look. "Drew, take a seat, chill out for a bit. I won't be long."

"Alright," I huff, pulling two glasses from the cupboard and filling them. I slide her glass over to her and take a seat at the breakfast bar.

"Thank you." She smiles sweetly, taking a sip, then returning to the pot on the stove, pouring in more liquid and stirring.

My knee bounces on the spot. I hate being told to sit and relax. Fuck this, I can't sit and watch her when she's dressed like that. I have waited two weeks to see her. I need to be buried deep inside of her right now. I go around the counter and take the spoon from her. I taste what she's cooking. "Mmm, very good." And it is, she can really cook. It's like a chicken rice thingy, and I could eat it every night of the week, it's that good. But right now, I don't care. "I think we should turn this off, tastes done to me."

She grabs the spoon back, dipping it into the pot and tasting the flavoured rice herself. She shakes her head. "We can't do that, Drew, the risotto will be destroyed if I turn it off now. The rice is still hard. It needs to be stirred until all the stock is absorbed." She tuts, a sassy smirk on her lips. Feels like she's doing this on purpose. Or maybe that's just me being impatient.

I place my hands on her arse, slipping them around to her front, pulling her back into me so she can feel the effect she is having on me. Like she didn't already know standing half naked in the kitchen was going to drive me crazy. Such a tease. "I don't like waiting, you know that. And you look so good right now," I growl into her ear, biting her lobe.

She giggles, pushing her arse back into me, trying to push me away. "Drew. Just think how good it will be when you finally get what you want."

"This was your plan all along. To tease me, was it?"

She tilts her head back to look at me, eyelashes batting. "I thought you would like this sexy chef thing I have going on." She pouts. "Drink your wine and relax. Dinner won't be long, then you can have me for dessert."

I pull away from her and sit up on the kitchen counter. She is going to pay for making me wait. Two can play this game. I sip my wine, watching her. She sways her hips to the music as she continues to add herbs and spices to the risotto mix. She goes to the fridge, bending down in front of me slowly, looking for something. She closes the fridge, empty-handed, then comes back to the stove. "Silly me, I already have the butter over here." She smiles sweetly.

I slap her arse playfully.

She gives me a look. "Ouch, what was that for?" She giggles.

"You're teasing me, and if you continue, I will have to come up with a better punishment for you."

She raises a brow. "Is that right?"

"Yes," I say, sliding a fresh wooden spoon out of the

canister on her bench and slapping it against the palm of my hand. Her lips curl into a sexy smile. She likes this idea.

She adds a scoop of butter to the rice then turns off the stove, moving the risotto to the back burner and placing the lid on. It's finally done.

I slip off the bench, wrapping my arms around her, kissing along her neck as I run my hands down her body, untying the apron. She turns in my arms to face me, revealing more of the sexy lingerie. She is scorching hot in this; she should always wear red lace.

She runs her hands through my hair and pulls in closer, kissing me. My hands settle on her waist, and I lead her over to the pantry, away from the heat of the stove. I press her into the door as our kiss deepens. I take both her hands in mine and raise them over her head, pinning her to the door. I have her right where I want her.

She pulls back from the kiss. "Drew, the dinner," she mumbles into my lips. Her eyes are still closed. She couldn't care less about the dinner, she wants this right now just as badly as I do.

"Dinner is made, we won't ruin it anymore by stopping. And I'm not waiting till after dinner for my dessert." I hold her hands in one hand and slide the other into her panties, my fingers slipping through her wetness. Like I thought, so ready for what I have in store for her. "Have you been getting yourself all excited while you waited for me dressed like this? You're so wet for me already, baby."

"I've missed you," she breathes.

I slide one finger in. "How much?"

"So, so much." She whimpers.

I push in two more and her hips thrust towards me. "I missed you too. You should always be dressed like this for me when I get home. It's my new expectation now."

"Yes," she groans, tilting her head back to the door, taking the pumps as I fuck her with my fingers. My thrusts getting harder, my palm applying pressure on her clit, teasing as I do. "Yes, Drew, I'm so close," she cries.

I slip my hand out of her panties and drop her pinned arms.

Her eyes flutter open. "Why did you stop?" she complains, looking dazed.

I step back and take my wine from the counter, slowly taking a sip as she watches me. "You were teasing me, so that was payback." I give her a wink. "So, this dinner, then? I'm pretty hungry now."

She crosses her arms over her chest. Making her breasts look even more enticing. "No way you're getting dinner until you finish what you started," she demands.

"Bossy little thing when you want something, aren't you." A slow smile crosses my face. She knows I won't be able to resist her, even if I wanted to try. I curl my finger, signalling for her to come to me. She slowly closes the gap, her heels clicking on the floor and her hips swaying as she moves closer.

When she gets close enough for me to reach her, I pull her towards me. "You're too gorgeous to resist dressed like this. I would like to tease you like you have me, but I can't. The need to be buried deep in you is too powerful." My fingers dig into her arse as I pull her into my body. She tugs at my shirt, pulling it over my head, then runs her hands down my chest. She places kisses where her hands have just been. Her teeth dig into my flesh, just a little nip before she pulls back.

"Sorry," she purrs, her teeth grazing into her bottom lip.

"You're not sorry at all." She wants to play it like this. This is the most surprising part of our relationship. She likes it rough, a little pain with her pleasure, just like I do. We really are perfectly matched in every way.

She shakes her head and nips at me on the chest again, her hands wandering lower. I lace my hands through her hair, yanking her back up to me, kissing her aggressively, my tongue invading her mouth. She's in a mood to play rough, and so am I.

I tug at her lip as I pull away. I lift her onto the counter, removing her bra, grabbing her large breasts and sucking callously as I tug at her other nipple, twisting it roughly between my fingers. She moans loudly as her hands go to my hair, drawing my head closer to her breast. I switch to the other, giving it the same attention, sucking and grazing my teeth along her hardened nipple.

She is perfect like this; her head tilted back, small moans escaping her lips, her hair long and messy, her body craving every little scrap of attention I care to give it.

She pulls my head back up to her lips. Her eyes are hooded when she focuses on me, kissing me desperately. "Since I brought the apron and lingerie last week, I have been imagining you bending me over this bench and taking control of my body in the way only you know how to. I can't wait another second, Drew," she breathes into my lips.

Music to my ears. I smash my lips back with hers, my tongue exploring her mouth. She slips off the counter into my arms. Tugging at the button of my jeans, her fingers quickly undo them, pushing them down to the floor, followed by my briefs, and I kiss and suck along her neck.

"Turn around and I will bring your little fantasy to life."

She follows my command and spins around to face the bench. She moves her hair to one side, giving me access to her neck, and my lips kiss as my hands run along her skin from her breast down to her arse. She grinds back on my length, greedy for me. I hook my thumb in her panties, dragging them down her long, tanned legs. I return my hand to her arse, slapping it hard.

She turns her head over her shoulder. "Ouch!" she cries. "Do it again."

I grab the wooden spoon I left on the counter earlier and smack it across one arse cheek, then the other. Then I immediately line my hard cock up and thrust into her, filling her.

"Fuck, Drew, yes," she calls out.

My hands go to her hips, getting a better grip so I can thrust harder, as my carnal desire to control her body takes over and I really let her have it. Over and over again. She moans my name in pleasure, crying out for me to give it to her harder. I give her everything I have. Two weeks of pent-up sexual frustration of being away from my girl is slammed into her steadily and repeatedly as I take what I need and give her what she calls out for. She is fucking amazing, and I will never have enough of her.

Hours later, we're lying in bed wrapped in each other's arms. She has been clinging to me like she can't let go, and I feel the same. I need to have contact with her the entire time we're together.

Her risotto was the best I have ever eaten. Is there anything this amazing woman can't do? She's lying in the crook of my arm, her hand resting on my chest. It's so nice to have her in my arms again. Fucking Jenna is out-of-this-world amazing, but it's this I miss the most when I'm away. The intimacy we share after, holding her close and the conversations about the little things. This is why I know I always want to have her in my life. Through all the other bullshit, these little moments together are so real.

She moves in my arms so she's glancing up at me. Her eyes are glassy. "It's so hard when you go away. Drew, I don't know how to get through this year." Her lips tremble as she gets the words out, and I wonder when her mood shifted. She was on cloud nine just moments ago.

I brush the hair away from her face and place a soft kiss on her lips. "It's difficult for me as well, beautiful. It has been so much harder than I thought it was going to be, and I don't love coming home to see you going for lunch with Blake." I know I shouldn't bring it up when she is being so understanding about Cobie. But it's the truth. I can't stand the fact that she and Blake are so close. Why are they? He has a wife, he should be with her, not taking my girl out to lunch.

She rolls her eyes. "You know you have nothing to worry about there." She goes to roll away from me, and I catch her arm and roll on top of her, pinning her below me so she can't escape this conversation.

"I know you're friends and I know I don't have anything to worry about, but it just sucks that I'm missing out on so much time with you by being away. And Blake already got to have your friendship all those years while we weren't talking. It's my turn now."

"I know exactly how you feel, it's the same for me with Cobie. I know you're just friends, I can tell that's all she is to you now, but it's still hard. I want to be the one handing you a towel when you come out of the surf and celebrating your wins." She blinks back at me like she has more to say. Is she hiding something from me?

"What is it? You can tell me anything, you know that, right?" I know it must be hard for her, but she is trusting me, and I need to do the same with her and Blake. As hard as that is, when I know I have the most amazing girl in the world and I'm sure every other hot-blooded male out there must be after her. I want the world to know she is mine.

She sighs. "I still find it hard to believe that someone like you wants me. We're so different, not like you and Cobie. Why do you even want to be with me?" She turns her head away so she's not looking at me anymore.

I had no idea she was still feeling like this. I need her to know what she means to me. She is everything to me. How could she not realise that?

I cup her face, forcing her to look at me. "Because I have been in love with you for five years, Bamb. She was never even an option." I lean down and my lips meet hers with a soft passionate kiss. "I love you. You are the only girl for me," I whisper, almost afraid to say it out loud because I have never even been close to saying those words to anyone before.

She glances back at me. "You love me?" she murmurs.

"For five years."

She blinks back tears as a smile crosses her features. "I love you too, Drew." I take her face in my hands and pull her towards me, rolling her on top. Our lips meet in a slow and sensual kiss. I love this woman with everything I have, and I need her to know it. I wish there were a way we could spend more time together this year. And there might be...
"Jen, I have an idea. Do you have a passport?"

She frowns. "No, I've never been overseas."

"Well, you have three weeks to get one. I want you to come with me for the next trip to the USA. I don't want to go away without you again."

Her eyes go wide. "Are you serious?"

"Deadly, baby, do you think you can swing a couple of weeks off work?"

She beams with excitement. "I'll see what I can do. I can't believe it. This is going to be so much fun." She hugs me, her lips pressing into mine again.

I hope she can swing it. This trip could be a really good opportunity for us to have some real time together, and it would be an amazing trip for her when she hasn't been overseas before.

And I have some big plans I want to share with her for our future.

CHAPTER SEVENTEEN

JENNA

I step onto the beach with Drew. It's early morning. We got in last night and headed straight for our hotel, so this is the first I have seen of sunny California, and it's beautiful. A long beach lined with colourful umbrellas and a long pier to one side. The sheer number of people is overwhelming; it dwarfs the comp we attended in Newcastle.

I grip his hand a little tighter, and he gives me a squeeze back. He seems so happy, so at home when he's at these things, and I feel so out of place. I guess he has been doing these comps for most of his life, so it would feel natural for him.

"Where are we going?" I ask.

"Just looking for our tent. Over there." He pulls me in the direction of the tent, weaving us through all the people sitting on beach towels and foldout chairs. They have the whole set-up with them; I guess they plan on spending the entire day here. We get to the tent, and I recognise his coach Ted and manager Cobie from when I met them last time.

There are another couple of guys hanging around as well, I assume some of the other Aussie boys that Ted coaches.

Cobie comes running from the tent to greet us. Her arms are around me before I know what is going on. My body immediately stiffens under her hold. This woman makes me so uncomfortable.

She turns her attention to Drew, still holding me. "Drew, I'm so excited you've brought along Jenna for this trip. It's going to be so much fun having another girl around."

I pull back from her embrace and offer the best smile I can when I can't stand the girl. "Thanks, Cobie, that's very kind. I'm excited to be here. I have never been overseas before."

"Oh, that's so cute. Well, you can hang with me while the boys do their training."

I look at Drew, hoping he can read my mind. I need a way out of this before it gets more awkward. Drew, however, is already on top of it. "Maybe another day, Cobie. Jenna is hanging with my cousins today, they're taking her shopping. We're going to meet them now."

I look at him, confused. This is the first I've heard of cousins. Is he making this up to get me away from her? I fake a smile at Cobie. "Sorry, maybe another time."

"Bye, Cobie. I'll be back in a sec, Ted," Drew says, pulling me away from the tent by the hand.

I lean into him. "Did you just make up a lie to get me away from her?" I whisper.

"No, I don't lie. But I thought you would like the opportunity to do something else today."

I kiss him. "Yes, thank you. So, your cousins are really here?"

As I ask the question, two blonde twenty-somethings

run towards Drew, nearly taking him out as they barrel into him with a hug. He laughs and hugs them back. "Andy, Jasmine, this is Jenna, the girl I was telling you about."

"Hi." I offer a little wave shyly. These two are stunning. You can see the family resemblance, they're like younger Ellys, with their pretty blue eyes, porcelain skin, and fair hair.

"Jenna, so nice to meet you," says one of the girls, the one with her hair in a short bob. I think Drew called her Jasmine. She hugs me warmly. The other stands back, assessing me from afar. Looks like she has attitude.

Drew turns his attention back to them. "I didn't think you girls would be able to make it. How did you get time off from training, Andy?"

"Season hasn't started yet. We're just playing some trial games so I had some free time."

"Andrea."

"Andy," she corrects Drew, giving him a look.

He turns back to me. "Andy is playing professional soccer in the National Soccer League." He beams at his cousin; you can see how impressed he is by her.

"Oh, really. Another professional athlete in your family. You guys must have some good genetics." I smile towards her, hoping she will warm up to me.

She shrugs it off. "Yeah, I'm pretty good. Haven't made a name for myself like Drew here, though." She pokes him in the chest.

"Modest too," her sister says. "Give her time, though, Drew. The way she behaves, she'll have more of a reputation than you in no time." Jasmine rolls her eyes dramatically.

Drew wraps his arms around Andy and gives her a

squeeze. "That's why you're my favourite, Andy." She pokes her tongue out at her sister and Jasmine shrugs it off.

"I don't compete until this afternoon, but I have a few things I need to do with my team this morning. Did you girls want to take Jenna shopping for a bit, show her around?"

"Sounds good to me," says Jasmine.

I turn back to Drew. I have only just met these girls but they seem nice enough, and it's going to be better than taking my chances with Cobie at the beach. "You okay if I go? I'm supposed to be here to support you."

Drew gives me a kiss goodbye. "Totally, babe, you'll be bored here all day. You girls have fun." He leans into my ear and whispers, "You can support me tonight." His words send a thrill of excitement through me. I literally can't control myself around this man. I give him a little smirk.

He looks back at his cousin. "And, Andy, be nice and no telling stories."

"I'm always nice." She smiles sweetly.

"You know what I mean. I like Jenna, make her feel like a part of the family."

"Anything for you, cuz." She winks at him.

"See you girls later." He wanders back toward the tent, and I wonder who he has left me with. Why did a grown woman need a warning to be nice? Maybe I would have been better off on the beach with Cobie. At least I already know she's a bitch.

We walk along the Venice Beach boardwalk, stopping into each shop and flicking through the racks. Most of the shops are touristy gift shops or knick-knack hippy jewellery. It would be good to bring something back for the girls and Harmony.

As I walk around, I keep thinking about my manuscript, wondering if anyone has read it yet. I haven't heard a thing from the publishing company I sent it off to, and it's been nearly a month. I was silly to let myself get my hopes up. I probably gave someone a good laugh at how bad it was before he or she threw it in the bin, not bothering to email me back with any response. Least I'm guessing that's what happened.

But I'm okay with that. I'm back to working on the second book in the series. Every second I sit at the computer typing the words that come to me is liberating. It frees my demons and gives me an inner confidence I've never had before. I feel so at peace with myself when I'm writing, like this is something I was born to do. It must be what surfing is like for Drew.

It's better than paying for expensive counselling sessions like I used to, so I could deal with the shit in my head, and it's more cathartic than meditating. I know Ivy loves it, but I just can't get my head to stop for long enough to relax. But when I write, the world makes sense to me. I feel calm and alive at the same time. I don't care if I never get published, because just doing this is enough for me.

THE GIRLS HAVE DRAGGED ME INTO A TOURISTY SHOP now, and I search the T-shirt rack for Harmony's size, something cutesy to bring her home. I decide on a pale pink T-shirt with a palm tree that says, 'California love'. I'll find her some bracelets as well; she loves to wear them up her arms just like her mum. I hold up the shirt to show Jasmine. "For my friend's daughter," I say.

"Cute. I'm sure she'll love it." She puts a long, beaded necklace up to her chest and inspects it in the mirror. "So, Jenna, what do you do? You know, for work?"

Andy is hanging around us flicking through racks but hasn't said much since the beach.

"I'm a librarian. What about you?"

"A psychologist."

"Really?" I give her an uneasy look. "Should I be careful what I say around you?" I laugh a little nervously. If only she knew the shit in my head, her answer would definitely be yes.

She grins. She must get that a lot. "I won't judge you too much." She laughs. "I mainly work with children."

"Oh, really, you would like my friend Ivy. She's in the process of setting up a yoga and meditation program in some of our public schools to help kids with their mental health. Actually, she's working with Drew's mum on it."

She holds up another necklace, shakes her head, then looks at some earrings. "Mum told me about your friend. She's the one dating Theo, with the little girl, yeah?"

"Yeah, that's her. You should get those, they would suit you," I say, pointing to the earrings.

"Thanks, I think I will." She smiles and takes them to the counter. I follow her with the top I picked out for Harmony.

She turns back to me. "I love her idea. So many kids will benefit from such a program. Auntie Anne is so impressed with her initiative, she was telling Mum about it just last week."

"So, it's your mums who are related?" I've been trying to work out the family dynamic and how Drew's cousins came to live in the US.

She pays for her new earrings and the lady at the

register wraps them up and places them in a bag for her. "Yes, my mum is Anne's younger sister."

I place the shirt on the counter and the lady rings it up, and I pay. "Thank you," I say with a smile. We start towards the door. "If she's an Aussie, how did she end up in the US?"

Andy walks around the corner, following us. "She gave up her opportunity to travel the world because she fell in love with a guy in the first country she visited. Ack!"

We stop to wait for her. She clearly isn't finished with this shop. Jasmine gives her sister a scowl, then smiles all dreamily back at me. "It's actually really romantic. She met our dad in a laundromat here in the US on her first week away from Australia. She was supposed to be on a round-the-world trip, but fate had other plans. There she was just doing her laundry and *bam*! It was love at first sight, and so she stayed. They've been together for nearly thirty years and have four kids. Still just as in love. I hope I have the same someday." The way Jasmine talks about her parents, you can see she is a hopeless romantic, the type who lives for love and a happily ever after.

"That is so romantic." I hope I have the same with Drew. Our story of how we met is maybe not so idealistic, but I could do with being together for thirty years with four kids.

"Wasted a good trip around the world for a dude. As if you would," Andy grumbles, flicking aggressively through the rack in front of us. I don't know if she is always like this, but the chick is hostile, so different from her sweet sister.

"That *dude* is our father, and you wouldn't be here and neither would your three sisters if she didn't," Jasmine tells her off.

"Yeah, I guess," she huffs.

"Is she alright?" I whisper to Jasmine.

"Guy troubles, that's why we're here to watch Drew.

We've been a few times in the past, and she loves to watch him. Mum and Dad thought it might get her out of this funk. You know, getting away for the day, change of scenery and all that."

"I can hear you," Andy calls over the rack.

"Jenna's family now, and it's hard to miss your mood. She can know what's going on."

Andy comes to stand with us, her face softening a bit. She must realise she's coming across like a massive bitch. "Fine. Why don't we grab some lunch, because I need comfort food, then I will fill you in on the joys of being a Harper girl." She hooks her arm in mine, and I'm surprised by the contact. She has been so standoffish until now.

I give Jasmine a look and mouth, "Harper girl?" confused by her statement.

"It's our surname, and yeah, all four of us are just as unlucky in love. Super successful in our careers but can't find the right guy for the life of us. The latest story of our older sister is a doozy. You'll need food for that one."

I feel so special that they are accepting me into their family and telling me their secrets. I have never been a part of a family before. I mean, I have Ivy, Harmony, and Penny, but not like this. This feels important. Drew's cousins who he's close to are accepting me.

We grab some burgers and chips for lunch and head back down to the beach to watch Drew compete. And get the inside scoop into the Harper family. I really like Jasmine; she's lovely, warm, friendly, and super smart. Her sister Andy is a firecracker, but I'm warming to her as well. She's not as tough as she looks when you first meet her. Just pissed at some guy and maybe the world.

DREW

I see the three girls as I come in from my heat. They wave and smile. Jenna looks like she's had a good day. Unfortunately, not my best heat, but it's nice to know I have a cheer squad watching. I head for the tent to grab a towel and leave my board.

Cobie comes running over to me and hugs me. "Nice job today, Drew."

I pull out of her embrace. She doesn't normally throw her arms around me when I come in from a comp. I'm assuming this would be for Jenna's benefit. "Thanks, not my best, though. Going to have to pick up my game on the next two heats to get the win."

I glance back to Jenna, but she's not looking our way. She and the girls have walked down to the water and are paddling their feet in the shallows. She laughs at something Jasmine has said, and Andy kicks water at the two of them. Looks like they're getting on well.

Cobie touches my arm, bringing my attention back. "You still beat the other guy. Stop giving yourself a hard time. You don't have to be perfect. You should be happy."

"I'm happy I beat him, but it wasn't my best result," I say, distracted, still watching Jenna.

Cobie glances over in the girls' direction. "You and your friends coming for dinner tonight?"

"Not sure yet, I'll see what they want to do."

Her face drops. "You're changing, Drew. You get a girlfriend and you're too cool to hang with the crew now."

"Cobie. Not too cool, I just have different priorities now." I turn to walk away. I've had enough of this conversation. Her jealousy over Jenna is getting a bit much.

"Don't forget about your friends, cause when she breaks it off with you, you're going to need us."

I give her a look. That was a harsh dig. Even for her at the moment. She has been like this with me since Newcastle. Not happy with my situation, so having a dig at my relationship whenever she can. It's getting old fast and making our working relationship difficult.

"Why are you so convinced she will?" I snap at her. She has hit a sore point and she knows it. I know things are different this time with Jenna but still part of me has concerns that something will happen, causing her to run again, and the last thing I need is Cobie bringing it up like it's definitely going to happen.

"I just know you, and the two of you, you're not right for each other. But I'll let you see that for yourself." She goes to walk off. She always has to be the one to have the last word. But I'm not going to let that slide.

"You're wrong. She is the one for me, and in a few days, everyone will stop asking me stupid questions and telling me this won't last. You will all see this is forever."

She turns back to me. Her eyes go wide, and she looks worried. But I don't care, I'm sick of it. They all think they know me so well and that I'm supposed to party forever because I did for a few years. It's not me. I don't want this life anymore; all I want is her.

"Don't do anything stupid or impulsive, Drew," she pleads with me.

I shrug and walk away, over to my girl. I'm not doing anything impulsive. I have given this a lot of thought, and I know exactly what I want. I want Jenna with me for the rest of my life, and I'm going to make that happen.

With the weather and conditions being so perfect, I finished up all three heats of this comp in just eight days, so we have a little time to do some travelling. We hired a car and set off driving to my Auntie Rose and Uncle Will's to spend the night. They live in a small town just outside of Palm Springs, in a luxurious house. Will was a pretty big deal movie producer back in the nineties, did well enough he could go into early retirement. Their four daughters live close by in the same town and all joined us for dinner at their parents' place. Jenna and Jasmine have hit it off and become instant friends. She fits into my family so perfectly.

This morning, we left early for Las Vegas with a scenic but remote drive along route 62. Four hours later we arrive at our hotel. I knew we would be tired after the long drive, so hopefully the room is all set up the way I asked. We check in and make our way up to the room. I'm so excited for tonight. Since the idea came to me last week, I knew it was what I wanted to do. I just hope Jenna is happy about it; she's not as spontaneous as I am.

I flash the security key to the door and push the handle. Everything is set up perfectly. The room is pretty flashy, all in various shades of white, with flocked wallpaper and plush carpet, a massive king bed in the centre, and a luxurious-looking ensuite off to the side. The view of the busy city below is impressive from the large glass windows that wrap around the room.

Jenna follows me in, and I watch her as her eyes go wide. She drops her bag by the door and stares into the room.

"This room is like the best hotel I have ever stayed in, it's crazy good." She beams. I take her hand and walk a little farther into the room so she can see the surprise. She turns back to me, a look of shock on her face.

"Drew, what is all of this?" Her words are slow and drawn out.

I place my hands on her shoulders and direct her, encouraging her farther into the room because she seems to be frozen to the spot. "This is a little surprise I had organised for you."

In the kitchenette area of the room, there are rose petals scattered all around, with grouped tall candles in vases. In the centre of the timber floor is a large heart shape made up of rose petals, and in the middle are the words 'Jenna marry me' spelled out in tea light candles.

She glances between me and the display on the floor, her hands covering her mouth. Her eyes glisten with tears. I take the ring box out of my pocket and get down on one knee in front of her.

"Jenna, I have loved you for five years, and in that time, I thought my love was a lost cause, that we would never be lucky enough to find our way back to each other. But we did, and on your birthday when we kissed at the beach, I knew right then and there that I wanted to marry you. I went out that day and bought this." I open the small, square jewellery box to reveal an antique engagement ring with the band in rose gold with a massive oval-cut diamond in the centre. "You're my person, and I want to spend the rest of my life with you, if you can put up with me. Will you marry me?"

Jenna hasn't said a thing as she stands in front of me, her eyes wide in shock, a lone tear rolling down her face. And for a second, I think she's going to turn me down, tell me this is all too quick, that I'm crazy. But her face breaks into a stunning grin that reaches her eyes. She nods her head slowly up and down. "Yes." More tears follow the first and trickle down her cheeks.

I remove the ring from the box and take her hand in mine, sliding the delicate ring onto her finger. It fits perfectly. Standing up, I pull her into me, kissing her lips, though not rough like I normally do. This moment needs to be perfect, so I kiss her slowly. She melts into me, and I feel like the luckiest man alive. I *am* the luckiest man alive—she said yes.

She pulls back and looks at me. Her eyes have a happy twinkle to them. "I can't believe you bought this ring the day we first kissed. How did you know?"

I take her hands. She is trembling slightly. "I knew when I saw you dancing on that stage for me all those years ago. I told you that night that you were going to be someone special in my life."

"And you were right. I don't know how you knew."

"It was love at first sight, Jenna."

"I felt it too. I thought it was just all the adrenaline because I was scared, but I felt it."

I'm so glad it's not all just in my head and she feels the same as I do. Because I have so much more planned for this trip. I take a deep breath.

I don't know how the second part of my plan is going to go down with her, I just hope she is where I am and thinks this is a good idea. "There is one more thing, and I hope you don't think I'm completely nuts for saying this and take back your yes, but I don't want to wait. I want the world to know you're mine now. I don't want to wait a second longer. If you agree, everything is already arranged." I pause, waiting for her to catch up with me. I know what I'm about to say is crazy, but that's how I do things. I want something and I go for it. What's the point in waiting? "I thought we could get married here this week?" She blinks back at me, the look of shock back in her eyes. "If you think it's a terrible idea, we can wait, I just don't want to."

"I do think you're crazy, Drew, this is insane!" She pauses. "And Penny and Ivy will kill me for agreeing to marry you without them by my side... but I don't want to wait either. We have waited long enough to be together. Let's do it." She squeals, wrapping her arms around me.

Kissing her, I pull her into me and slide my hands down to her arse, picking her up as our lips are still locked. I carry her to the large bed in the centre of the room and place her down. She lies back before looking up at me, blissfully happy. She is the most beautiful woman I have ever seen, and my heart feels like it's going to beat out of my chest. The adrenaline rush I get with her is like no other.

This has gone exactly how I wanted. A few more days and she will be mine forever.

CHAPTER EIGHTEEN

JENNA

We spent last night celebrating. We drank cocktails and explored the casino on the bottom floor of our hotel. We were both on such a high from getting engaged that the night flew by, and we didn't climb into bed until the sun was nearly coming up.

My eyes roam over Drew's naked body, and I sigh. He's lying on his tummy with the sheets just covering his legs, his perfect arse uncovered enough for me to perve. I can't believe this dreamy man wants to marry me. And even more, that someone in this world wants me as their own forever. My bad luck in life must be shifting. It's all so quick, I know it is, but I don't care. For once in my life, I'm going to be spontaneous and just go with my heart, no overthinking!

Today we need to organise the marriage licence with the Clark County marriage licence bureau and do some shopping to get ready. I'm so tempted to sneak out of bed and call Ivy, spill to her what I'm about to do. She has been my sounding board for so long, and I feel like I need to see if she thinks it's a good idea or not. But I won't. It feels kinda special that this is Drew's and my little secret. This is the start of our new life together, and it's all just between us.

I should be fast asleep like Drew after such a massive night, but I lie awake, unable to sleep any longer. My mind is buzzing, listing everything we need to organise before we get married tomorrow.

I don't need the fanciest dress, but I want something special, memorable. I want Drew to remember how I looked on our wedding day forever. This whole thing is so unlike me, but there is something about Drew that brings out this more impulsive side, and I like it. It's exciting. I can see why he lives for his next adrenaline rush. I want to be more like him. Just do stuff without thinking it over for so long the fun is drained right out of the idea. I know this is a big place to start, and I could have maybe started with something smaller first, like getting a tattoo or jumping out of a plane, but I want this. I want him. I know without a doubt I want to spend the rest of my life with him, so why not dive in headfirst.

Drew stirs, rolling onto his back, turning to look my way. I love him like this, all sleepy, his hair messy. He rakes his hand through his curls. "Morning, baby. How are you awake after such a late night?" he asks with a yawn.

I clap my hands like an excited kid would. "I'm too excited to sleep! I have a million things going through my mind."

"So you're still keen to go ahead with the elopement?"

Don't tell me he's having second thoughts. "Yes, of course. Why, have you changed your mind?"

He grins and shakes his head. "God, no! This is happening, baby, just wasn't sure if I was going to have to convince you a little more first." He sits up in bed and grabs the phone. "Why don't you go have a shower while I order some room service for us? We can have something to eat and plan what we need to get done today to make it all happen."

"Okay, sounds like a good plan." I slip out of bed and tie my hair up in a loose messy bun and sift through my suitcase for something to wear. I pull out some casual clothes and head for the shower.

The bathroom in this place is gorgeous, marble tiles floor to ceiling, with a large circle bath down one end and a double shower at the other. Turning on the water and letting the room fill with steam, I step in under the warm spray. My head is foggier than I would like it to be this morning. I wash my hair and massage my scalp, trying to get it back to some sort of normal function so I can plan today. What do you even need to get married? It's not something I have given a lot of thought to before.

I list off items in my head.

A dress, shoes, a veil... Do I even want a veil? Nah, I don't think so. Drew will need a suit because it's unlikely he has one in his suitcase, and we each need wedding bands. I can't even think of what else. I need to check with Drew if the package he has organised with the chapel has flowers included, or do I need to get a bouquet as well? I let out a little squeal and do a happy dance. I'm so excited. I can't believe this is all happening.

I shower quickly then turn off the water and dress in my black skinny jeans and a white off-the-shoulder top. Apply my make-up with red lips. I feel like I have to look my best today. Even though we're just shopping and organising, it still feels important.

The smell coming from our room makes me finish up swiftly. I open the bathroom door, taking in the sight before me. I know the boy likes to eat and probably has one hell of a hangover, but this looks like major overkill. The dining table is overflowing with items off the room service breakfast menu. Scrambled eggs, bacon, waffles, fresh fruit—and most importantly, coffee. From the looks of his plate, Drew has already tried a bit of everything.

"This looks delicious. Did you order everything on the menu?" I ask, giving him a peck on the lips.

As I go to take my seat, I can feel him watching me, and I turn to him with a brow raised in question. His gaze roams down my body. He looks hungry for more than food. I would have thought he would have had his fill well and truly after last night.

"You look delicious." He smirks, pulling me back into him. He's wearing low-slung pyjama pants, and he looks so damn fine himself. I could forget the rumble in my stomach for a taste of what he has in those pants. The way he kisses me has my mind going hazy all over again. I'm tempted to forget the mission I'm on, but then I remember we have a long list of jobs to get done today and have already wasted most of the morning sleeping, so I take a step back and slide into the seat next to him.

"There will be time for that later, but we have so much to do today."

He pushes his seat back. "I will let you get away with turning me down just this once because I know you're right, we have a lot to get done."

He makes his way towards the bathroom and drops his pants in the doorway. I giggle and bite into my bottom lip. This is his cute attempt at teasing me; he knows I can't resist him when he's naked. God, the man is perfection, no woman could resist.

Right now, I have to, though. I pop a couple of strawberries in my mouth and take a bite out of a waffle. I can barely taste a thing. My eyes are glued to him, and he knows it.

He jumps in the shower, bathroom door wide open. He soaps up his athletic body, his eyes coming back to me, as his hands roam over his torso and down to his massive cock. He gives it a couple of strokes. This is hot and very distracting. Breakfast with a view. One I can't resist, even with my analytical brain telling me there is no time for playing around this morning.

I pop another strawberry in my mouth, then make my way into the bathroom, stripping off my top. He smirks at me, knowing all too well he has got his way yet again. Right now, I'm not fighting it, this man is too good to be true. The sexy-as-fuck Drew Walker, and soon to be my husband, who wants me. How on earth did I get so lucky?

After finally leaving our room, our afternoon is spent sorting out the marriage licence paperwork and walking through the strip of shops they recommended, trying to find all the items we need. Lucky for us, this town is set up for people just like us, unorganised and last minute.

We have rings sorted, simple rose-gold bands to match my engagement ring. Drew has selected a navy-blue suit with an off-white shirt that makes him look super dreamy, and now I just need a dress.

Drew waits in the lounge area while I try on a few different designs. I don't want him to see what I pick but I need him close for moral support. I have the option of a long vintage lace that is fitted and falls off the shoulder—beautiful but too much. A below-the-knee princess-cut A-line with a lace overlay—it's stunning but it feels too fancy for a chapel elopement. The last one is also a princess-cut ivory A-line that falls to just below the knee, but this one has a tulle overlay with little white polka dots all over, the sleeves are a three-quarter, the back is low, and there's a waistband in ivory satin with a bow that ties at the back. It's perfect!

I do a little twirl, checking myself out in the mirror. "I found it," I call to him.

"Perfect. Put it in the bag and I'll take it to the counter." He won't let me pay for anything; he wants to be the one to do it all.

"You in a rush to get out of here?" I say, changing the subject. I'm paying for my dress.

"Yes, I want to get you back to our room." His tone of voice says it all. I know what he wants. The boy is insatiable.

I dress quickly and zip the chosen dress back into the garment bag. Slinging it over my arm, I open the door, heading straight for the lady at the counter. "Just this one, please," I say.

She smiles at me, takes the bag, unzipping it a little to see which dress it is. "Nice choice. Are you two eloping on your holiday? You're obviously from Australia."

"Yes, tomorrow. My friends will probably kill me, but I'm so excited."

Drew comes to stand by my side and tries to hand over his credit card. "No, Drew, let me pay for my dress. You have organised everything else, I want to do this."

He takes his card back. "Okay, fine," he huffs.

I pass my card over to the lady. "Thank you." I smile. My face must be ridiculous. I'm so excited I can't stop smiling like a bloody Cheshire cat.

She processes the sale. "Congratulations, have a wonderful day tomorrow, dears."

"Thank you," I say as Drew takes the garment bag from her, and we leave hand in hand. I have never been so happy in all of my life. Tomorrow I marry the man of my dreams, and it's going to be perfect.

Drew

The chapel is just as you would expect from one situated in Las Vegas. A flashing neon sign on the street highlighting a cute—if not a bit tacky—white chapel, with a path through artificial grass leading to the front door. Once inside, the tiles are white marble, the windows are stained glass, and there are rows of white pews with over-the-top fake flowers in whites and greens on either side of the aisle. I can only imagine what Elly would have to say about the place. I'm sure she would be mortified that I'm choosing to get married here. And that makes me laugh. I actually can't wait to see her reaction, it's going to be funny.

I wait for Jenna with the officiate, Judy, at the altar; she is a dear old lady who says she has owned this chapel for nearly forty years.

The music changes, and Jenna comes into view. She is stunning in her ivory dress, and her hair is out and curled down her back, just the way I like it. I'm marrying the most beautiful woman in the world. I can't believe she agreed to be my wife. I know, for her, this probably isn't what she imagined as a little girl, but we can have a party with our friends later. With each step she takes closer to me, my heart beats a little faster. I'm actually nervous. She's so radiant, and her smile reaches her eyes that sparkle with the hint of tears. I have no question in my mind that she is my future.

She places her hands in mine, and we gaze into each other's eyes. The nervousness I was feeling washes away.

Judy stands beside us. "Look at you two lovely young people, so in love. This is why I still do this job. I can feel the love you share for one another." She smiles over to us. "We come here today to join Drew and Jenna in marriage. Marriage, as most of us recognise, is a voluntary and full commitment. It is made in the innermost sense to exclusion of all others, and it is entered into with the desire and trust that it will last forever.

"Before you declare your vows to one another, I want to hear you confirm that it is indeed both your intentions to be married today."

Judy smiles towards me. "Drew, do you come here freely and without reservation to give yourself to Jenna in marriage? If so, answer I do."

"I do."

Judy continues, her eyes on Jenna. "Jenna, do you come here freely and without reservation to give yourself to Drew in marriage? If so, answer I do."

"I do."

"Drew and Jenna, having heard that it is your intent to be married to each other, I now ask you to state your vows. Please face each other and hold hands."

She looks at me. "Drew, repeat after me. I, Drew Walker, take you, Jenna West, to be my wife. I will share my life with yours and build our dreams together, support you through times of trouble, and rejoice with you in times of happiness. I promise to give you respect, love, and loyalty. This commitment is made in love, lived in hope, and made new every day of our lives."

As I repeat my vows, it feels like time slows down. My eyes are locked with Jenna's as she blinks back at me, tears in her eyes.

Judy faces Jenna. "Your turn, dear."

Jenna drops my hands and takes a folded piece of paper out of her dress's waistband, handing it to Judy. "I added a few words I needed to say." She smiles shyly as a blush rises on her cheeks.

Judy looks over the paper. "Lovely, dear."

"Drew, from the moment I met you, you have improved my life so much. You made me feel important and cared for and like I belong somewhere in this world. When I was a little girl, I always dreamed of growing up to marry a man just like you, and today I feel like the luckiest girl in the world because all my dreams have come true. You're my person. I, Jenna West, take you, Drew Walker, to be my husband. I will share my life with you and build our dreams together, support you through times of trouble and rejoice with you in times of happiness. I promise to give you respect, love, and loyalty. This commitment is made in love, lived in hope, and made new every day of our lives."

"Have you got the rings?" asks Judy.

I reach into my pocket and hand Jenna my band.

"Your wedding rings are the outward and visible sign of the inward and invisible bond which already unites your two hearts in love. Drew, place the ring on Jenna's finger and repeat after me:

"I give you this ring.

Wear it with love and happiness.

As this ring has no end,

My love is also forever."

I repeat each line, my eyes never leaving Jenna's.

"Jenna, place the ring on Drew's finger and repeat after me." She slides the ring onto my finger. Still gazing at me.

"I give you this ring.

Wear it with love and happiness.

As this ring has no end,

My love is also forever."

Jenna repeats the words, and I feel every one of them. My love for this woman is forever, nothing will change that.

"May the wedding bands you exchanged today remind you always that you are surrounded by lasting love. And so now, by the power vested in me by the State of Nevada, it is my pleasure to declare you husband and wife. You may seal this declaration with a kiss."

I slip a hand around Jenna's waist and pull her into me, kissing her lips softly. She pulls back with a giggle. "I love you, Drew Walker."

"I love you, Mrs Jenna Walker." She beams with happiness, and I kiss her again, this time letting my tongue sweep through her open mouth, showing her every bit how much I intend to love her forever.

CHAPTER NINETEEN

DREW

It's Sunday afternoon and we have just arrived home from the airport. We're high from our amazing time away together, and I'm excited to share our news with my family, so we're heading home to my parents' place for Sunday family dinner.

"Are you okay, my wife? If you're too tired, we can head home and tell them all another day." I grin over to her. I love calling her my wife.

"That's going to take some getting used to." She giggles. "Um, I don't know." She looks down at her ring, twisting it in her fingers.

"Your knee is bouncing like crazy, so I would say you're nervous about family dinner?"

She throws me a look. "Oh my God, why are you not? They are all going to kill us, getting married without telling them."

I run my hand along her leg, trying to calm her down. "They're not going to kill us. They will be excited for us. Just relax and stop the bouncing knee, you're going to wear a hole in the carpet." I'm actually excited to see their reactions. Elly and Mum will be the worst to deal with, but I'm sure they will still be happy for us.

Jenna sucks in a deep breath. "I wish I could relax. Just drive faster so we're there already."

I laugh at her dramatics. I'm not worried at all. I know I've made the right choice to marry her. I love her and that is all that matters. My family will be okay, or they'll just have to get used to it.

We pull up out the front, and by the number of cars that are parked in the driveway, I would say that the entire Walker clan is already here.

I wrap my arm around Jenna protectively, and we walk out the back together. "Just breathe, Bamb, it's going to be fine." I kiss her forehead.

She grips my arm tighter. As we get closer, the noisy chatter and squeals of all the kids playing in the yard offer a much-needed distraction, and I see the smile return to her face. I'm sure she is dying to see Harmony; I love how close she is with her.

Elly is the first one to spot us and comes rushing over. "Drew, Jenna, you're finally here." She throws her arms around me, then Jenna, and stands, holding her hands when she pulls back. "I want to hear all about your trip. I'm so jealous. How are the Harper cousins? How was California? I bet it's ama..." She stops mid-sentence and holds up Jenna's hand, inspecting her rings. She looks at me, her head tilted to the side. "You got engaged? Oh my God, I'm so excited for you! Welcome to the family, Jenna. I knew you were planning something, Drew, but this was a big surprise." She squeals and throws her arms around Jenna again.

Jenna is frozen to the spot and looking overwhelmed by a very excited Elly. I take her hand and pull her towards me.

"I'm glad you're so excited, because we actually got

married," I correct Elly, kissing my wife. Elly's jaw nearly hits the ground in shock. I chuckle at her response. I love to be able to throw her off balance, and she wasn't expecting that.

Elly looks between us, then settles on Jenna. "Did you really? I can't tell if Drew is just shitting me."

"We really did. In Vegas. You're not going to kill me, are you?"

Elly squeals and grabs Jenna's arm, hooking it with her own, and drags Jenna along with her to where the rest of the family are gathered.

"We have a new sister!" she announces to everyone. The whole family looks towards Jenna, and I see her face heat. She is hating the attention. I quickly catch up to them and pull her out of Elly's grip, wrapping my arms around her protectively.

"Drew, what is Elly talking about?" asks Mum.

"Hi, everyone. What my sister was trying to say is... while Jenna and I were in Las Vegas, we eloped." I grin, hoping the response from the rest of them will be as good as Elly's. My family breaks into cheers of celebration.

Ivy is the first to grab Jenna, and Theo hugs me, leaning in to whisper, "Congratulations, but Mum is going to kill you for taking away her chance to throw a party." Then he chuckles to himself and walks off. Dad is next, then Fraser and Blake and Indie. Everyone is excited for us. I knew it would be fine.

Mum comes over at last. I can't read her. She looks unsure of all of this, I think. She hugs Jenna first. "Welcome to our crazy family." Then she hugs me and stands back to look between us. Her face is serious. "Are you pregnant?"

I laugh, and Jenna's eyes widen; she looks mortified. "No, Mum, we're just in love." Truth is, we have kind of moved so fast on this, so I don't even know where Jenna stands on kids and all of that. Probably should've had that conversation before we got married. Because I definitely want kids someday. Whoops.

"I wouldn't have cared if you were. I want more kids around here. I just wanted to be the first to know."

I squeeze Jenna's hand. She plasters on a smile, but I can see her overthinking all of this. She's having an internal freak-out. "Okay, Mum, when that day comes, you will be the first to know."

"You do know I will have to plan a wedding reception for you back here, as well. You can't just go overseas to elope and get away with no party. We need to celebrate." She tenderly clutches Jenna's shoulder.

"Yes, of course," Jenna answers, looking at me for help.

I kiss her cheek. "We would love that, Mum. Thank you."

"Perfect. Jenna, I will be in contact." She beams, and I can see Jenna relax a little, knowing the worst is over. My family loves her. I knew they would be just as excited as I was.

I turn to Jenna. "You okay?"

"Yes, I think so," she replies softly.

I kiss her. "I'm sorry they are full-on."

"No, it's fine. I love your family. It's so nice to have a big family around, I feel very lucky, just a little overwhelmed."

"We can eat quickly, then sneak out if you like?"

Ivy wraps her arm around Jenna. "Drew, I'm stealing her away for a minute. We have some catching up to do." Jenna gives her a look of apology, and they wander off together.

I go stand by my dad who is cooking the BBQ. "Need a hand?"

"Sure, grab yourself a beer from the esky. I want to hear all about how you talked such a wonderful girl into marrying you." He laughs.

Jenna

Ivy drags me down the yard to a quiet place where we can still see the kids playing.

"Oh my God, Jenna."

"I know, right, it's crazy!" I shake my head, glancing at my beautiful ring.

"So crazy!"

"So, you're not mad at me, that I didn't tell you?"

"No, but we do still need to celebrate this together. I will organise you a belated bachelorette party. I'm so excited, this is a start to a new life for you. If things work out with me and Theo, we will be like related." She grips my hand tighter.

If they get married as well, we will be. Not something I had considered, but I love it. She has been family to me since I met her. "Ha, yeah, we will. That's so cool, I hadn't thought of that. And what do you mean by if? You two are so perfect for each other. Now you're all living together, you're a beautiful blended family."

"I guess now you're married to Drew, you will be leaving the townhouses as well. So much has changed this year. Who would have thought back at the beginning of this year when we were whinging about our pathetic love lives, this would be us? You married and me living with the man of my dreams, brothers." She laughs.

I give her a look because I know this is what being married is, but leaving my place makes me feel extremely anxious and I really hadn't considered it before. "Yeah, brothers, moving, married."

"You okay, Jen? You don't look so good."

I take a deep breath, trying to calm myself down. I'm feeling a little light-headed. "Yeah, I think I'm just exhausted. It's been a long few days, and the flight. I think I just need a good night's sleep in my own bed, you know."

"Or Drew's bed, I guess." She gives me a look, like she can read my mind, and I don't like it. She has a way of knowing what I'm thinking like no one else.

"Yeah." I look at Ivy, unsure of how to say what is really going through my head. "Is that just assumed? That we will live at Drew's place?"

"You don't want to live there?" she asks, her brows knitting together. She must think I'm nuts. Drew's place is lovely.

"I don't know. Ivy, this is going to sound so dumb, but we haven't talked about the future at all."

A worried look crosses her face, and I can see the protective mothering side in her take over. "What do you mean?"

"Like, we just agreed to get married, and we haven't talked about anything. We spent the last few days having a fucking wild time. It was the most fun I have ever had. I just let go of all the chatter in my head and went along with Drew's crazy ideas. It was insane, but I loved every second of it. But now realisation is settling in, and we haven't talked about anything. Like where we will live. I don't even know if he wants kids or not. I got swept up in the excitement of it all, the romance, and now I think my head is catching up with my heart, and I'm panicking a little."

She pats my arm. "Oh, honey, I think that would be normal. This was all quick, but also you have known each other a long time, you know each other well enough. You two are so perfect for each other, you will work out all the other stuff together as you go."

"Of course, yeah, you're right, we will," I say to keep her happy.

Drew's dad calls everyone for dinner, and the family make their way to the large table. Drew fusses over me, organises my food, and sits me between him and Ivy, and I let him. I'm so overwhelmed I can barely function, or maybe it's just jet lag.

I sit quietly and watch the family interact. There is so much love here. I know it's something really special to be involved in this family. But right now, I feel like an outsider looking in, an imposter who hasn't earned her place at the table. I know it sounds ridiculous, but I do.

HOURS LATER, WE WALK THROUGH DREW'S FRONT door, and I collapse onto his lounge. I am completely exhausted, so many questions thrown my way all night. Are you moving in with Drew, or will he move in with you? If you do, will you sell your place? When are you going to start trying for a family, how many kids are you going to have? How will you cope while Drew is away?

My head is spinning. The conversation I had with Ivy plays over in my head the most. She says we will work it all out together. But tonight, I have no answers for any of them because, well, we haven't had any real-life conversations about our future. I got swept up in the romance of it all without thinking too much about the details. It's very unlike me.

Drew walks through the door with some of our luggage. I should help him. I go to get up and he stops me. "I'll finish unloading the car. Why don't you go have a shower and jump into bed." He places the first of our bags down and comes over to kiss my forehead. He is so sweet and thoughtful.

"Thanks, I think I will. I can't keep my eyes open."

He cups my face and kisses my lips. "I know my family are a lot. They would wear anyone out."

He takes my hands, pulling me up. "Your family are lovely," I say, "it's just been a really long day. Week, I guess."

"Go have a shower, jump into bed, and I'll meet you there and make you feel better." He pats me on the arse as I walk by, and I don't even have the energy to respond. How is he still so energetic after a long flight and dinner with so many people? I really hope I do feel better after my shower, because right now I feel like I'm getting vertigo from all the thoughts going through my head. Did we rush this a little? Or a fucking lot.

Freshly showered, I curl up in Drew's bed. It's so cosy and warm, and his sheets feel luxurious. I could get used to his fancy place. Maybe I should give up my townhouse and move in with him. But is that really what I want?

I'm too tired to even have this conversation in my head with myself. I just need to sleep. I'm sure answers will come in the morning. I try my hardest to stay awake until Drew comes to bed, but as soon as I hear the shower turn on and him jump in, the sound of running water is too relaxing, and I drift off to sleep.

Drew obviously got into bed with me at some stage. I wake with his arm over my tummy and the light of day streaming into his room. I must have slept all night, which is unusual for me but not surprising. After yesterday.

I slip out of bed to use the bathroom, splashing some water on my face and trying to wake up. I feel like I could sleep for another couple of days just to catch up. I try to creep back into the room so I don't wake Drew, but he is lying in bed already awake. He gives me a sexy smile, and I have to wonder again just how I got so lucky to be able to wake up to this man every day for the rest of my life.

He looks so good like this. The ripple of his muscular chest is just yummy. I know I should be getting my head straight to have a real conversation with him about our future, but right now, all I want to do is enjoy my husband. Do we really have to deal with any of it? Our lives can just stay the same, can't they?

"Come back to bed, my beautiful wife."

How can I resist? "Just for a little bit. I have work today, and I need to go home so I can get ready." I jump back into bed with him, and he wraps his arms around me, pulling me into his body so he's spooning me.

He brushes the hair away and places gentle kisses down my neck. "We need to fix this living arrangement, so we have more time for cuddling in the morning."

"We do." I sigh, knowing we do need to have this chat, even though I don't want to.

"When can you move all your stuff in?"

He, just like Ivy, assumes I will move in with him. I turn round in his arms to face him. "So I'm moving in here?"

"Of course." He looks confused by my question.

"Why is it assumed that I move in here? Your place is lovely and all, but I'm quite fond of my place. Everything is just the way I like it to be, and my furniture, it's all pieces that I have collected over the years. I can't just move into your place."

"But I'm here," he says, trying to be cute.

"You could be at my place as well," I add, a little more serious.

"Hmm, if that's what you want. But you do realise I'm like a few steps from the beach and I have a pool."

I know what he's saying makes total sense and I should just give in. "Yeah, you have a point. Your place is pretty sweet. I could move here... I just don't want to completely lose my identity and just slot into your life. Does that make sense?"

"How about we do a few things around here to make it more homely for you. We can set up one of the guestrooms as a library and office for you to write in. You can also move in whatever furniture you like. This place needs a bit of a change-up anyway. I want this to feel comfortable for you. This is your home now as well."

I want to put up more of a fight for him to move into my place, but he is being so sweet, and I can't deny that his house is way better than mine. "Okay, I like the sound of all of that. What do I do with my place?"

"You could rent it out, like I do with my other investment properties. It's easy, I can help you with all the logistics."

"Alright."

"Perfect, I can help you. We can start to move your stuff in this weekend if you like."

"Yeah, okay, maybe."

"Maybe?" He kisses me.

This is all happening so fast. I thought I would feel better once we started to talk about it all, but I just feel more overwhelmed. Moving out of the only stable home I have ever had is a really big deal for me. I want to be here with Drew, but I'm not really ready to give up my place just yet. "I mean, yes, thanks." I kiss him back, trying not to show the panic I feel inside. "Drew, will it be weird that I'm in your house while you're away?"

"It's going to be our house, so no, not at all. But you will come with me when I go from now on, won't you?"

I pull back from him, assessing his expression. Is he for real? I give him a look, like what are you on about. But he looks dead serious. "Drew, I can't, you know that, right? I have a life here, a job. I can't just leave every couple of weeks."

"But you don't need to work anymore. I can take care of you."

I sit upright in bed. What the fuck is he talking about? "Um, I like my job. I enjoy working. I'm not going to give that up to follow you around the world."

He sits up next to me, obviously getting irritated by my mood shift and the fact that I'm not just agreeing with what he wants. "You could spend your time writing, and it's only until the end of the year anyway, then I'm done. It won't even be that many more trips."

"Sounds like a nice idea, Drew, but I don't want to do that. I like my life the way it is, and as much as I hate it when you go away, I couldn't handle travelling about everywhere. I need stability." I pause, looking at him. He doesn't look impressed. Whatever else I should say, it feels like this is going to turn into a fight, and I don't want to fight with him. "I need to get to work," I say, slipping my legs off the side of the bed.

"Jenna, I—"

I cut him off. I can't keep on talking about all of this. If I do, we will fight or I'll cry. I'm feeling so inundated with all of this. I need to clear my head before we talk about it any more. "We can talk about this tonight, okay?" I bend down to kiss him.

"Alright. I love you."

"I love you too."

But we didn't talk about it again when I got home from work. We didn't the next day or at all that week. Instead, every night when I arrived home from work, Drew had dinner made for me and we distracted ourselves with food and our usual go-to, mind-blowing sex. Everything between us is perfect as long as we live in total denial and nothing has to change. As soon as l even think about all the changes, I start to get the feeling of panic wash over me.

I think Drew knows it as well, because every night is the same. We do what we're best at as a couple—fuck in every room, every position. I don't know about Drew, but I feel like when he's buried deep inside of me, our connection is stronger than ever, and all the other stuff just doesn't matter.

And while we don't talk about all the real stuff, it doesn't matter, and we are happy to just continue on as we are. My fear is what happens when the avoidance catches up with us.

CHAPTER TWENTY

DREW

Today I leave for my next comp, and I wish Jenna was coming with me. She is driving me to the airport and has been quiet the whole drive. She's been quiet a lot lately.

I know she's trapped in her thoughts, and I wish I knew how to talk to her about everything, but she is shutting me out. Every time I try and bring up talking about the future, she changes the subject, usually by removing her clothes. She knows all too well how to distract me, and while I love that type of distraction, I'm also very aware that we have a real problem.

I get it, she has her own life, and she needs to be able to keep things the way they are. She has so many demons from the past that it must be hard for her. I don't want her to have to change everything for me. I just wish she wanted to, so we could be spending this time together as husband and wife. I want her by my side.

She pulls into the airport drop-off zone. I hate this so much. "I love you, Jenna. Stay safe while I'm away." I pull her towards me, kissing her.

"I love you, Drew." As she says it, her phone rings, and she hits the speaker button.

"Hello." She looks at me and shrugs, like she has no idea who it is.

"Hello, Jenna West, is it?" says a female voice.

"Yes, that's me. Actually, it's Jenna Walker, I just got married." She smiles over to me as she says it.

"Oh, how lovely, I will fix that up on your paperwork. It's Natalie here, from Reed Harrington Publishing. I'm calling on behalf of Mr Stone, one of our head publishers. He has read your manuscript and would like to set up a meeting with you to talk about getting your book published."

Jenna turns to me in total shock and mouths, "Oh my God," her hand over her chest. This is so exciting for her.

"Oh really, thank you, thank you so much!" she says into the phone.

"That's alright, dear. Mr Stone is quite booked up at the moment, but I have an appointment time in a month, Tuesday the 24th of August at nine am if that will suit you?"

"Yes, that sound perfect, thank you."

"I'll send you an email confirmation and all the details about how to get to our offices. See you then dear."

"Thank you again." She disconnects the call and turns to me. "Can you believe it?" She is so excited. And I'm so happy for her. She deserves to follow her dreams, and this is such a big opportunity for her.

"Yes, I can. You're so talented, and this is going to be the start of something big for you."

A car toots its horn from behind us, and I realise we have been sitting in the drop-off zone for way too long. "I'm so excited for you, Bamb. I better go, though."

"Yeah," she says sadly. "I'm going to miss you."

"I'm going to miss you, too. Love you." I kiss her again. "See you in two weeks."

I turn to get out of the car, and she pulls me back to her, kissing me again. "I love you, Drew."

I kiss her one more time, then make my way out of the car, pulling my luggage from the boot. I turn back to her, and she gives me a small wave, then blows a kiss. These two weeks are going to be hard.

It's been two weeks since I have seen my beautiful wife, and I'm tired from the flight and one of the shittiest comps of my career in Oaxaca, Mexico. My knee is playing up, and I'm praying with a couple of weeks' rest now, I will be ready to go for the August comp in Narrabeen.

I can't wait to see Jenna after the week I've had. I know she will make it all okay, take the pain away and the edge off of losing. The waves were bigger than expected in that last race, and normally I would be all for it, but I have been off my game this whole comp. It didn't help that my injury flared up right from the first heat, but it's more than that. I'm distracted.

Being away from Jenna was hard. And then there's Cobie. I thought telling her I got married would put a stop to the weirdness that had been between us all year. But if anything, she has been making it obvious that she wants something with me. She's not taking no for an answer, and it's becoming almost impossible to work with her, but I only have a few months left of this tour. It's too late to look for another manager.

I wish Jenna would have taken me up on my offer to

come travelling with me. I just know if she were by my side things would be different.

I ended up taking an earlier flight home. I didn't want to stay for the last night of celebrations. All I wanted was to be at home with my wife. So, I have decided to come and visit her at her dance studio. Surprise her that I'm home early. From all of our phone conversations, she has been struggling just as much as I have these past couple of weeks, and I can't wait to see the look on her face when she sees me.

I pull up to the dance studio car park. This place has always been a bit of a mystery to me. She rarely talks about her class, just sneaks off to it on a Sunday afternoon.

From what Ivy said, the class should have finished twenty minutes ago, but I can still hear music blaring from the studio. I go up to the door and peer through the little window to see if I can spot her.

It's a large dance studio with timber floors and stripper poles, about twelve of them. The room is empty except for Jenna. She is dancing to the beat of the music, then she takes hold of the pole in front of her and pulls herself up. I stare on in disbelief. What the actual fuck is going on here? The class she teaches is a pole-dancing class?! She never mentioned that to me. I always assumed it was just a dance class, ballet or some shit like that, whatever girls are into.

My mind starts to race with all the possibilities. Is she still fucking stripping as well? And she is keeping that from me?

I don't get angry over many things, but something about seeing her doing this really aggravates me. Partly because the last time I saw her doing this I had to rescue her, and it brings back those memories, and partly because I don't even know if I can trust my wife.

This feels like a huge betrayal of my trust. I knew there

were things we didn't know about each other, and there was still a distance between us. She was having a hard time really committing to being my wife and living with me. Now I see this...

It all makes sense. She's not who I thought she was at all. She wants to keep her life separate because she has this whole other side to her. One she knew I wouldn't like.

I push open the door. Of course it's not locked, she really doesn't care for her own safety. I clear my throat loudly to get her attention over the music. My heart beats fast in my chest. I don't know how to handle this. I wish I had just waited at the house for her, I didn't need to see her like this. It brings back all the memories from that night... the fear in her eyes, my overwhelming need to protect her. And now that she is my wife, the need is even stronger. But how can you protect someone when they continue to put themselves in harm's way?

JENNA

I hear someone clear their throat and turn to see who it is. Drew, he's home!

I'm so happy to see him, it feels like forever since I have seen his handsome face. I slide down the pole and run to him as best I can in these ridiculously high heels. I have missed him so much this week. I throw my arms around him and kiss his lips. He kisses me back, but he's stiff, he hasn't put his arms around me. I take a step back, taking him in. His features are hard, his gaze cold. He's pissed at me.

"What's wrong? You're not happy to see me?" I say, a little wary but trying to keep it light.

"I *was* happy to see you. Until I saw what you were

doing. What is this all about, Jenna?" He gestures to the studio.

I knew this was going to be an issue for him, that's why I haven't said anything more than I teach a dance class, and he asked nothing else about it. "Um, this is the dance class I teach," I say defensively. I know I have stuffed up by not telling him the whole truth here, but I also knew this would happen, and I really didn't want to deal with his reaction.

"You're a pole-dancing teacher. What the fuck, Jen, are you stripping again as well?" He is so mad. I thought he wouldn't like the idea but didn't realise he would be so angry about it. I have never seen him like this before. Drew doesn't get mad. I don't quite know what to say.

"No, I'm definitely not stripping again, I haven't since the night I met you. This is totally different. I just teach a bunch of girls how to dance. This class is about having a positive attitude towards your body, empowering women to feel strong and good about themselves. It's not about stripping."

"It might as well be, the moves are the same," he huffs.

I take another step back from him, my hands going to my hips defensively. This is bullshit. I know I should have told him what this class was all about months ago. That is on me. But really, his reaction is over the top. "It's not even close to being the same thing. I can't believe you're so annoyed at me about this."

"Yes, you can. You knew I wouldn't like this, or you would have told me this is the type of dance class you're teaching, but you strategically left that out each time you said you were off to dance class. You're my wife, and I feel like I don't even know you. What else have you been keeping from me? Is this why you won't move into my place properly? You still want to have a fun single life on the side?"

Wow. This side of Drew is something entirely new to me, and I don't like it. He is acting like a total dick. "I'm sorry, okay, I just didn't want this to be a big deal. You know me, this is just one little thing. I don't need a fun single life. I haven't moved all my stuff in yet because..." I say, reaching up to him, trying to get him to calm down.

He pushes me into the wall behind us, pinning me beneath him, kissing me. It's aggressive and passionate, just like I expected when I haven't seen him for a couple of weeks. My hands go to his hair, and he pulls me closer. His hands roam up my body, and I cling to him. I need this, I have missed him so much.

Then he pulls back, looking at me, his gaze so intense, his pale blue eyes now dark, steely. We both struggle to catch our breath, panting. Neither one of us moves or says anything. He is so intense. What is going through his head?

"Because why? Why won't you move in with me properly?" he asks, and I feel terrible.

"I don't know, I just feel rushed. I'm sorry, I'm not ready to give up my place completely." How do I explain to him I literally can't give it up and let some stranger just move in there? That place is more than just somewhere to sleep for me; it is the only place I have felt completely safe. It is my little piece of the world. I have been there for five years, and there is nowhere else I have stayed that long. I don't have a family home to go to like him. This is all I have, and every time I think about giving it up, I feel like I'm losing control and I start to have a panic attack. "I don't know how to explain it to you. I'm living at your place, my clothes are there, I just need to hang on to my place for now. I'm sorry."

He shakes his head, and I can feel the distance between

us grow. It feels like he doesn't believe me. "I don't want you teaching this class anymore. This body is for my eyes only. I don't want you flaunting it around, it gives off the wrong idea," he growls. His lips are back on mine, kissing me aggressively. This is how we deal with our problems. We go to what we know—sex. But we can't this time. As much as I would like him to take me in his arms and make me forget, there is a real problem here, and I feel like we need to deal with it.

My hands go to his chest, pushing him back. I need distance. I can't be this close to him and have him demanding that I do as he says. But he remains firmly pressed into me. He has to be kidding me. He can't just say things like that to me and expect me to fall under his spell again because he kisses me after and he knows I can't resist him.

"And what idea would that be?" I ask, probably a stupid question. But I need to know exactly how he feel about all of this. Why is it such a big deal to him?

"That you're easy." The words roll of his tongue, like this is how he has felt about me all along. And as he says them, my body physically reacts with a terrible sinking feeling. I don't want his hands on me anymore.

I try to push him off me to get some distance, but he is locked in position, pinning me beneath him. "You think people will think I'm a slut because I teach a pole class to empower women," I spit back at him. I'm so hurt by his words.

"It gives a bad impression is all I'm saying, not anything else." The way he says it, though, is all smug, like he knows better than me. Who even is this Drew Walker? Not the man I married. I don't know him at all.

I need space from him. "Whoa! If that is the way you feel, you need to get off me. NOW!"

"I'm not trying to tell you what to do, but you're my wife. I don't want you doing this anymore," he pleads with me. He won't let me go, but I'm not scared of him. He looks desperate, like the very thought of me doing this pains him. His eyes beg me to agree with him, put him out of his misery. But I don't get it. He couldn't be so jealous of me dancing with other women.

"Drew, there is nothing for you to worry about here, it's just a bunch of women dancing. You're blowing this way out of proportion," I try to reason with him. I don't want to be some pushover who gives into what her man wants. I have been that girl, and you start by giving up one thing and end with losing everything. I won't do it again.

"Well, I don't think I am overreacting, and you should know better, especially where you came from. I don't want this for you. I want to protect you. If you need extra money, I can give it to you, I can give you everything you need. You don't need to teach this class."

"Drew, you really need to watch yourself. Yes, I'm your wife, but you don't get to tell me what to do. I have been looking after myself for a really long time, and I can't handle having you boss me around. I enjoy teaching this class; the girls are a lot of fun and I can see the difference I make in so many of their lives. They feel good about themselves when they leave here. I like to know I'm making that difference in their lives. That makes me feel good, and it shouldn't change the way you or anyone else looks at me. Being your wife doesn't give you the right to tell me what to do." I push on his chest again to emphasise my point.

He takes a step back from me. "So, you're going to keep

doing this, you don't care what it looks like or how I feel about it?"

"You're the only one that is looking at it like there is a problem." I'm trying to keep my cool, but he is making it really hard. I'm not going to back down on this, it's too important to me and my class.

"Yeah, that's because there is a problem. I'm not comfortable with you doing it. Someone else can help your class feel empowered. I need you to stop it."

I laugh at him sarcastically. He has flicked my crazy switch. Is he fucking for real? "Or what, you'll divorce me? Are you kidding me? You're being a fucking arsehole, Drew, and if you're not going to listen to reason, I think we're done here today."

"Well, if I'm being an arsehole for looking out for my wife and hating that she is doing the very thing I helped her get out of, then I guess I'm an arsehole. I'm not apologising for loving you so much that I can't stand to see you doing this."

I glare at him. I'm so mad I'm shaking. Why is he making this about him? Why can't he see this from my perspective? I get it that he has some issues with it, all because of the way we met, but really, this is insane.

"We're done here, we're not going to see eye to eye on this. You need to leave before you say anything else you're going to regret later," I scream at him. Who the fuck does he think he is talking to me like that, making me feel so fucking small?

He opens his mouth as if to say something, then closes it and turns towards the door. He's just going to leave? What did I expect? He can't see it from my side. I had hoped that might snap him out of this shit. Why would he stay and make this better, fight for me like I'm worth it? I'm not. I never have been to anyone else—or him, apparently. I thought he was different, but he's not. He just wants me to be his perfect little arm candy who doesn't think for herself. Not going to fucking happen.

I have fought hard to have this life. I'm not giving up something I love just to placate him. My heart is hammering in my chest and my hands are shaking, the adrenaline pumping through me. He's not going to fight for me, he's just going to leave. I can't help but have one last dig. "Is this even about me or is your ego just so wounded because I won't just do what you want? Is that what this is, Drew? The superstar Drew Walker doesn't get what he wants for once so he's throwing a hissy fit. You have a lot of growing up to do if you want a future with me."

He spins around to face me; he is fuming. "This has nothing to do with my ego," he yells at me. "I saved you from the shitty life of a stripper and you throw it back in my face by doing this and lying to me about it. You're right, we don't have a future if this is the way you want to live."

I glare at him. Why is this so bad to him? We're both angrier than we have ever been with each other. I never thought we could fight like this. I can't even say anything back. He is going to throw that shit back in my face; he saved me from my fucked-up life, so now I should just do whatever he says and be happy about it. Fuck no. He might have helped me back then, but now I'm strong because of it, and I know my worth. I don't have to put up with this shit from a spoilt brat who is used to getting his own way all the time.

He stares back at me. He is just as furious, but it's something more as well. He looks wounded, like I have hurt him! He tells me what to do, and I have hurt *him*.

Without another word, he turns and walks out of the

studio. I can hear his car start, and I slam the door shut as hard as I can, my back pressed against it. I try to catch my breath as angry tears trickle down my face. My heart pounds, and I bury my head in my still-trembling hands.

That escalated so quickly. One minute I was ecstatic to see him after missing him so much the last two weeks. Now it's all fucking over. I slide my back down the door till I hit the floor, and the tears overwhelm me. I cry so hard I feel like I'm going to be sick. The man I love thinks I'm a slut. What did I expect? We met in a strip club, while I was stripping. Deep down, that is the way he will always see me, some trashy girl he needs to save from her own bad decisions. That truth hurts so much more than I thought it ever could.

I hate him for making me feel like this, but I hate myself more, because I should have always known the truth: I wouldn't be good enough for him and he was always going to leave. I should have known better. I did, but I let my heart lead me astray, thinking I deserved a life filled with love and happiness.

What a fool I was.

CHAPTER TWENTY-ONE

JENNA

AFTER I DON'T KNOW HOW LONG, I HEAR THE KEY IN the studio door. I move out of the way to let Mia in.

She walks in, dumps her bag, then looks in the mirror. I don't want her to see me like this. I don't want anyone to see me like this, but it's too late. She's here and I'm a fucking mess. Mascara stains run down my face. My nose is red and my eyes swollen and sore. There is no hiding it.

"Jenna!" She runs to me, ducking down to my height and pulling me to her in an embrace. "What's going on, beautiful girl?"

I shake my head. "He's gone. I'm pretty sure it's over."

"Drew?"

I nod my head.

She sits on the floor opposite me, legs crossed, and takes my hands in hers. "I'm sure we can fix this. Everything is fixable, right? Why don't you tell me what happened?"

"Drew came to see me here just after I had finished up class. I was working on the new routine. He's been away for nearly two weeks, I was so happy to see him."

She eyes me over. "What happened then, why are you like this now?"

"He wasn't happy about the type of class I was teaching. I hadn't told him it was a pole class, and he was so angry about it, asked if I was stripping again, and he demanded I stop teaching. He was being a total controlling arsehole about it."

She narrows her eyes. "Are you kidding me?"

My lips tremble as I feel overwhelmed by it all over again. "I wish I was. I saw a whole other side to him today. It was awful. He was not the man I thought I married." The tears tumble down my face again, and I bury my head in my hands. "I rushed into all of this too fast, didn't I? Who gets married after just a couple of months? It was crazy," I mumble into my hands. I can't look up and see the truth in her eyes. Then it really will be real.

She rubs my back in slow, circular motions. "It was romantic, honey, and you two have known each other a lot longer than a couple of months, really. Some guys just have a jealous streak, and maybe he will be fine when he calms down. It might have just taken him off guard, because of how you met. I was there that night, and it was pretty scary."

I look up at my friend. She smiles at me sympathetically. "There is so much I don't really know about him, though," I say, "and I guess stuff he didn't know about me. I probably should have told him about the class. It might have avoided this complete mess."

"Honesty is the best policy, but with the way he reacted, I get why you didn't say anything. Men can get funny about stuff like this, I should know. Especially when they find out you used to strip."

"Right. I can't even remember, it was all so heated. He

did bring up why I hadn't moved my stuff in yet. I feel so bad, but I'm not ready."

"You just need time, hun, to adjust to all the changes." She hugs me again. "Come on, let's get you home. You can't stay here all night."

I shake my head. I can't think of anything worse than going back to his place right now. I need to be surrounded by my things, and right now, I'm so glad we still haven't moved any of my furniture into his place. Maybe this is one of the reasons I didn't move my stuff. Deep down, I was keeping my safe place for when things fell apart like I knew they would. Why wouldn't they? "I don't want to go back to his place. I can't see him again today after all that," I whisper.

"You still have your place, so we'll go there."

"Alright, thank you."

"Let's get you back to your place, then we can work this all out. It's going to be okay."

She holds out her hands to help me up from the floor. "Thank you." I smile sadly.

She rubs my shoulder and leads me to my bag, helping me gather my belongings. "One way or another, you're going to be alright, Jen."

I want to believe her words, but the way I feel right now, it hurts too much to even think about. I don't want to be okay without Drew. I can only see my life with him in it, but if he really loved me like he said he did, how could he have said all those awful things to me and then just walked away?

Since we got married, I have been a little worried that we may have moved things too quickly and needed to talk about what we want for the future, that was the most of my worries. But now I'm wondering if we even really knew each other at all or if it was just lust-filled desire driving our relationship.

DREW

I jump in my car and speed away. I need to get away from her. She was right about one thing; if I stayed, I would have said something I regretted. I do like to get my own way, and it's very clear that wasn't going to happen. She is so stubborn!

I have gone from having a shitty week to a completely fucked-up one. That got out of control so quickly, I don't even know what the fuck just happened. I was so excited to see her until I saw her dancing like that—then I just saw red. I have never felt so furious in an instant. It triggered me in a way I didn't expect. I don't even know exactly what tipped me over the edge, being lied to all this time or what she was actually doing. Her legs wrapped around that pole in short shorts, thigh-high boots, and a crop top that just covered her boobs. She looked unbelievably sexy, it should have been a turn-on, but it took me back to that night when we met and the months afterward I spent so worried that I wouldn't be able to protect her, that Vinnie would get her. And he did.

She was lucky to escape with her life. Why can't she see that? She could have died because of that life she was living. She got a second chance at a better one, so why would she want to revisit the past every week by putting on those boots and gyrating on a pole?

I pull into my driveway and run my hands through my hair in frustration. "Fuck!" I scream in the car as I hit the steering wheel with my fist.

I should have stayed, made her see my point of view. Seriously, though, how did I not know this is what she was doing every Sunday? I feel like a total idiot. Was she hiding those fucking boots at the dance studio? I have never seen them before.

My mind is running through every scenario it can. What else don't I know about her? Is this why she hasn't moved her stuff into my place properly? Because she hasn't, and she won't even talk about what she wants for the future. I have tried to bring it up, and she gets all deer in the headlights about it and changes the subject. Why can't she just see that I'm trying to offer her the best life possible with me? I want to take care of her. She's my girl, I need to protect her from everything bad in this world, including her past.

It's one reason I hate going away so much. I was overseas when Vinnie kidnapped her. I should have been here to protect her, and it never would have happened. She would have been safe, and Fiona wouldn't have died. At the time it absolutely killed me Jenna didn't want me in her life anymore, because my need to protect her after what she had been through was so strong, and I had to just walk away. That day when Blake rang me, I thought I would come back home and take her into my arms and never let her go again. That's what I wanted, what should have happened.

I know that threat is no longer something we need to worry about, but I want her with me all the time, so I know she's safe. Is that really too much to ask? She could come away with me when I go overseas; she hasn't been able to travel before, and I could take her places she wouldn't be able to go otherwise. She could do her writing while I surf. It would be perfect. But she is grasping on to her independence like her life depends on it. I don't get it. I know all her life she's the only one she has been able to rely on, but she has me now.

Since she came back into my life, I have had this nagging feeling that she would end it all again, run from commitment like last time. I know she lives with lots of demons from her past and they still haunt her, I'm sure. That's why she reacts the way she does. But I don't know how to deal with it. Part of that is why I proposed so quickly. I was stupidly thinking if we got married then that was it, we would make it all work. I could protect her from the world and take care of her. She couldn't run or shut down on me.

But that was stupid. I know that now. It's nothing more than a certificate, a piece of paper. She can still run, she can still block me out of her life.

Hours later I'm pacing around my house, waiting for her to come home. It feels so empty without her here. I knew she would need time to cool off, we both did, but now I'm starting to worry. It's getting late. Where is she?

I send off a text because I'm not ready to call her, but I can't stand not knowing where she is.

Me: Are you coming home?

Jenna: No.

That was a blunt response. She must be really pissed. I should just leave it at that. I'm majorly pissed at her as well. But I need to know she is safe.

Me: Where are you?

Jenna: At my place.

And there it is, the reason she was hanging onto her place, so she could run from me when it all got too hard.

Makes perfect sense now. But I'm not going to let her run. It was a stupid fight, and we need to sort it out. She needs to be in my bed tonight with me so we can work this all out.

Me: Come home, we need to talk.

Jenna: Not tonight. I need some space.

Fuck, is she kidding? She's not even willing to come home and talk to me? I will give her the night, but that's it. Tomorrow we work this shit out.

CHAPTER TWENTY-TWO

JENNA

My house feels different.

I sit in my library trying to write, but no words will come to me. It has been two days since the fight at the dance studio, and my heart still hurts. Drew messaged me the first night, but I wasn't ready to face him. The way he looked at me at the studio, I can't forget. He tried to call me the next morning as well, then messaged me in the afternoon. He has been persistent. But I can't face him. The way he made me feel in the studio, the way I know my past has affected him... We are just two very different people, and he won't ever see things from my perspective because he hasn't lived my life.

Mia has been amazing and has stayed with me the last two nights. She gets it. Her background isn't that different to mine and look at her now. She has this amazing business empowering women. She is inspirational. I wish I had half of her strength. But I don't, and that's half the reason I can't face him yet.

I'm on my own tonight, and I miss Drew like crazy. I needed the space until I had it; now I just feel empty inside without him around. But I'm still angry with him for wanting me to slot into his life and do as he says. Not only that, but I'm so panicked that this was all too fast, and it's just not going to work. What if we really are just too different to be able to make it work? I can't see him ever understanding why I have to keep my independence. My whole life, I have been the only one I can rely on. I shouldn't really say that because Ivy has always had my back. But now because of her and Theo, I feel like I can't even really turn to her. It's too messy since Theo and Drew are brothers. So, I really can only depend on myself again.

I've been staring at the screen for an hour now, and I have three words written. I need a break. I head downstairs and turn on the coffee machine. While I wait for it to heat, I decide to check the mailbox. It's a beautiful sunny day outside; I have been missing out on it cooped up inside. I would take my laptop down to the beach like I normally do on pleasant afternoons, but I'm worried I'll run into Drew. And then what? I have to deal with this mess. Nope, not ready to do that.

I flip open the box and pull out the pile of mail. I flick through the letters, mostly bills, apart from a large yellow envelope. Weird, it looks just like the one I got a few months back at the library. It hasn't been posted, there's no delivery address or stamp on it, just my name in large black letters. What the hell? This is so strange. I tear open the end and tip the envelope. Out falls another photo.

I look in the envelope. That's all there is, just another random photo, like last time. This one is of a couple. The woman is young with long brown hair. She would be in her early twenties, at most. The guy is older, with dark hair and a full beard. She smiles at him with her arm wrapped around his waist.

Who are these people? I have never seen either of them

before in my life. I wander back into the house to the sideboard, where I stored the other photo. I rummage through the drawer, finding it. This one is of two small children. I look between the two pictures.

Is there something I'm missing? Am I supposed to know who these people are? The really strange thing is this woman, she looks kind of like me. Her hair is just like mine, her lips are full, her eyes like a duplicate of mine, actually. Could all just be a coincidence, but it's weird that it was put in my mailbox with my name on the envelope. It's like someone is sending me clues to my past, maybe? Creepy fucking way of doing it if they are.

I place both photos in the drawer and close it. Don't let your imagination run away on you, Jenna. Could it be one of my parents trying to get in contact with me? Is it possible they are still alive? If they were, why wouldn't they just call or come and see me? Whoever is sending me these photos, they know where I live and work. I don't like how that makes me feel, so vulnerable.

I make my coffee and stare out the back window, letting the heat of the mug warm my hands. The buzzer goes off and I jump. My nerves are totally on edge. I put my mug down and answer it.

"Hello."

"Hey, honey, it's me, let me in," comes a warm voice.

I press the buzzer to let in Ivy. I haven't talked to her at all this week. I can only assume she's here because Drew has told Theo about our fight. I open the door for her, and she wraps her arms around me. And tears break free at her gesture.

"What happened?" she asks, ushering me inside the house and closing the door.

"It's so stupid. We fought over me doing a pole-dancing

class, and Drew got all controlling and tried to demand I stop. Then he was pissed at me because I hadn't moved into his place properly yet. It's all a mess."

"Yeah, you hid that class well from all of us. Why, hun?"

"I don't know, I didn't want to be judged."

"I would never judge you over that. God, I would have come and taken your class, it sounds like fun."

I laugh. "It is fun. You would be so good at it too, you have great upper body strength from all the yoga." I smile at my beautiful friend, feeling silly for underestimating her. Of course she would be understanding. "Do you want a coffee?" I offer.

"I'll take a tea, too late in the day for me to have a coffee. I'll be up all night."

We head into the kitchen, I make her a tea, and she sits at the breakfast bar. "Where's Harmony?" I ask her.

"I left her with Theo. All the kids are at Elly's place, we're having dinner there tonight."

"We used to have dinner together on a Tuesday night," I say sadly.

"Is that what all this is about, Jen? Everything is changing?"

I shrug. "I don't know, I just feel like everything has moved so quickly, and yeah, if I'm honest, you're with Theo all the time. And I love you two together, but I miss you, and I don't get to have Harmony on Thursday nights anymore. I miss her too. Everything is changing. For the first time in my life, I had this comfortable life. Yeah, it was boring, but I had a place of my own, a best friend who's like my family, and a great job. I know when we sat down at the beginning of the year, I was all sad because my life was going nowhere, but now I'm scared of how fast everything is changing."

"That was the night we ran into the boys at the pub. Everything changed after that. Funny, it must have been the universe answering your prayer for something more." She smiles, remembering that night, I'm sure.

"You know I don't believe in all that. It is funny, though."

"Look, I know it's all changing, and I'm sorry you feel like we don't get to see each other enough anymore. I need to make more of an effort to make that happen. You're so important to me and to Harmy. The only reason I don't have you look after her anymore is because I don't want to be a burden on your life. You're newly married, I figured you needed time with your husband."

She takes my hand across the bench, and I smile back at her. "Yeah, I know. I just miss our old life as well, you know. It was us girls against the world."

"It still is, baby. I got you, that's why I'm here. We can work all this out. It's just a fight, right? You two just need to talk."

I come around the counter to sit next to her. Taking a drink of my coffee, I let out a sigh. "What if it's more than that? What if we're too different to make this work? What if this was all one really big mistake?" I spill out all of my concerns to her quickly. It feels good to talk to her, she always knows what to do.

She narrows her eyes at me. "Do you really believe that?"

"I don't know," I huff, dropping my shoulders, feeling so defeated over all of this. I don't even know what I think anymore. I've thought about everything all too much, and it's making me crazy.

"Only you can know the answer to that, hun. But I will be here for you with whatever you decide. Do you love him, Jen?"

I answer without even thinking. There is no question in my mind about that. "More than life itself."

"I think that is the only answer you need, sweetie. You love him. Everything else will work itself out once you two start communicating properly. Be open with him, tell him your fears. I seem to remember you giving me similar advice not that long ago and look how it worked out for me."

"Maybe you're right." I smile at her.

She gives me a warm smile back. "You know I am." She checks her watch. "I have to get going to dinner. You should come."

"Thanks, maybe another time. I don't think I can face the Walker family tonight."

"Okay, hun, but the offer stands whenever you're ready."

Ivy leaves, and I'm left to myself again to think. Not ideal.

Drew

I feel the thump of my head before I even attempt to open my eyes. The bottle of scotch last night was a bad idea. I'm not a big drinker these days, but when I came back here a week ago and saw all of her things here, I just wanted to block it all out. Our fight, what I said, the fact that I married her after no time at all together.

I barely know how to be a boyfriend, let alone a husband. And I have already fucked it all up. Then there is how majorly I sucked in my last comp and everything with Cobie... My life is turning to shit and it's all my fault.

At first, I was really mad at Jenna for not seeing it from my perspective and spent my days in the ocean and on my bike trying to block it all out, but last night, a week after our fight, it got the better of me. I knew she would have done her dance class again yesterday, and it pisses me off. But most of all, I miss her. I want her back here with me. This is where she belongs.

I saw the bottle of scotch in my cupboard, and it was way too tempting. One glass led to another as the memories blurred. I must have eventually passed out.

I crack open my eyes to look around the room. I groan out loud. I must have passed out face down on the hardwood floor in my kitchen. There is a loud pounding at the door, and I sit up slowly. Running my hands down my face, I try to get my head together. If I ignore whoever's at the door long enough, they'll go away. They thump on the door again.

"Drew, it's Theo, open up," I hear my brother yell through the front door.

Shit, Theo. He won't just leave. He'll keep at it until I let him in. I bring myself up to standing by gripping on the kitchen counter. I'm wobbly and the room spins. Am I still drunk? I kick the empty bottle, stubbing my toe as I try to walk. "Fuck," I call out as I hobble my way to the door. That answers that question—I'm definitely still smashed.

I open the door, the sunlight almost blinding me. Theo looks pissed, and standing behind him is Ivy. I don't like the look on her face either.

"You look like shit. Are you drunk?" Theo says, pushing past me.

I run my hands through my hair and try to focus on him. I'm so not in the right frame of mind for a lecture from the big know-it-all brother and his missus. "Thanks, nice to see you too, big brother." I leave the door open and sway my way back towards the kitchen. I need water and something for the constant pounding in my head. I pour myself a glass of water and throw back two painkillers, while Theo and Ivy make themselves at home. Ivy glares at me, and I can't say I blame her. None of this looks good.

Theo picks up the empty bottle and places it on the kitchen counter. "Big night, Drew? Is that such a good idea?"

"Fuck off, Theo, I don't need you here lecturing me. So I had a fight with my wife and a few drinks to help me relax. It's been a shitty week. You can't tell me you wouldn't do the same."

"Yeah, but I'm not an elite athlete. You have always been really careful about drinking."

The truth is Theo really has no idea what I get up to when I'm away and still manage to compete. "Well, I had a slip-up," I say to appease him. I take a seat at the counter, praying the painkillers kick in soon.

"What's going on, Drew?" asks Ivy.

"I don't want to talk about it. What happened is between me and my wife."

"I care about her just as much as you do, Drew, and I don't care how messed up your head is right now from the alcohol. You need to hear us out. She is hurting, and clearly you are too. You need to talk to each other, make it right." Ivy gives me a look. She's not as angry as I thought she would be, here trying to protect her friend, but she looks sympathetic to me somehow.

"I don't know how to make it right. I've tried to call her a few times, and she hasn't picked up. When I text her she just says she needs space. I'm starting to think she doesn't want this at all. It's just like last time, she has shut me out."

"I'm sorry, Drew. I talked to her, and she is just overwhelmed with all the changes and she's worried."

"What is she worried about?"

"You two should be talking about this."

"She won't talk to me, Ivy. I need to know what it is so I can fix it."

Ivy looks at me like she's trying to find the right words or something. "It's not my place to say all of this, but I can't stand to see you two like this. She's worried you're too different, that you will never understand where she's coming from because you haven't lived her life. She needs her independence, Drew, it's her way of coping. She has never had someone she can rely on before."

Ivy is a good friend to Jenna, and I can see she is just trying to help. But hearing her say that just pisses me off. She has had someone she can rely on. Me. I haven't let her down. I have offered her everything. "Well, she does now, and she is throwing it all back in my face."

"You are asking her to stop doing something she loves and enjoys, and not only that, but move in with you and fit into your life. What about the life she has created? There has to be give and take."

"I know that," I snap.

"Good," she huffs, rolling her eyes in Theo's direction.

"I just need her to see what it's like from my perspective," I say. "I was shocked to see her dancing like that. I know I overreacted, but I still don't want her to do it. So how can I make this better? I have no fucking idea what I'm doing here."

Theo takes a deep breath. "Drew, in a relationship, there are always going to be things you don't agree on. You two just have to talk about it, come up with a compromise that works for both of you," says Theo. Like he can talk, he has only just figured all this shit out for himself. Now he's some relationship expert, giving out advice.

Ivy comes around to my side of the counter. I don't look up from the spot I've been staring at on the kitchen bench.

Out of the corner of my eye I can see her looking me over, as if assessing me. "Do you love her, Drew?"

My eyes snap up to Ivy. How could she even ask me that? "Of course I love her, that's why I was so angry with her for not being open with me."

She gives me a little smile, and for the first time since we had the fight; I feel like there might be some hope in me fixing all of this. I mean, if her best friend is here trying to help, there must still be hope.

"Well, you need to start with that. Tell her you love her and try to work it all out. You two just need to communicate better. Relationships aren't easy, it's hard for everyone. But I'm sure you can make it work if you just talk to each other. The longer you leave it, the harder it's going to get." She looks me over again. "Maybe fix yourself up first. Theo is right, you don't look your best."

"Thanks," I huff.

They say their goodbyes and leave me to it. I look around my place; it's a totally pigsty. I need to get myself sorted and go and talk to her. I'm not leaving it like last time just because she has asked me to give her space. She has had time to herself. Now we need to sort this out.

CHAPTER TWENTY-THREE

DREW

I pull up out the front of Jenna's townhouse. I leave to go away to Narrabeen today, and I know I need to make amends with her before I go. I can't leave without her talking to me.

The silence between us is killing me. I should have come around here sooner and demanded that she see me. I let my stupid pride and the desire to be right cloud my judgement for what's most important. I love her, and we should be able to work through anything as long as we do it together, like what Ivy said a few days ago. At least that's what I'm here to tell her.

I'm still not sure if we didn't rush into getting married too quickly before we really knew each other. But I know I love her, and that is all that matters. We can work the rest of it out.

I press her buzzer and wait. No response. It's late afternoon. She should be home from the library now. I press the buzzer again. Fuck. I kick the dirt on the sidewalk and stub my toe on the concrete path. Shit. This is so fucking annoying. Why isn't she here? I need to fix this before I go. I turn around to leave and hear someone call my name. I turn to see Ivy running down from her place.

"Drew, you okay?" She leans on the fence.

"Yeah. What are you doing here? Don't you live with Theo now?" I ask, confused to see Ivy here.

"Just catching up with Fay, our old neighbour. She's missing the company of having us girls here, and I had some stuff to get done with my place."

"Where's Jen? I wanted to see her before I go away."

"She left for Sydney yesterday, for that meeting she has today with the publishing house for her book."

Fuck, I really am the shittiest husband ever. I totally forgot about it, and it's so important to her. "Oh yeah, of course. How was she? Did she seem confident? I should have called her."

She raises a sassy brow. "Yeah, you should have."

I pull out my phone and try her number. No answer. Damn.

"She might have it on silent while she's in the meeting," offers Ivy. Why do I feel like that's not true?

"Yeah, maybe. Ivy, can I ask a favour?"

"Shoot."

"Can I come in and use a piece of paper and a pen? I need you to give her a letter for me. I need her to know how I feel about her and how sorry I am."

She gives me a sympathetic smile. "I think that's a good start. Come on."

I follow her into her house. "I thought you would have this place rented already, now you're living with Theo."

"Actually, that's one of the reasons I'm here, waiting for the real estate agent to get here. They want to take a couple of photos for the listing."

"Well, I'm glad I caught you."

"Here you go." She hands me a sheet of paper, an envelope, and a pen.

I get writing, trying to come up with exactly what I need to say. I really hope this works and she can see just what she means to me. Once I'm done, I hand it to Ivy. "Please make sure she gets this."

"I will. Drew, I hope you guys work this all out." She offers me a sad smile.

"Yeah, me too, thanks for your help, Ivy, see you when I get back."

"Have a safe trip. And Drew, keep trying to ring her, she will pick up eventually if you wear her down."

Eventually. So she is avoiding my calls. This is her running when things get too hard, I know it. But I'm not going to let her do it this time. "Thanks, I will."

I wander back to my car with a sinking feeling. Why did I wait so long to come and see her? I'm a fucking idiot. All I want to do is see her and make this all right. It was all so silly, really.

I should be with her for this important meeting. That's what a good husband would do. But I will be heading to my next comp to follow my own dreams. If I don't, I will lose my chance to get to the top spot, and I can't do that, not after everything I have been through to get where I am. This is the closest I've come to winning the title. I have a real chance this year. I need to win to prove to myself and my family and friends that all the hard work my entire life has been worth it.

Don't I?

I'm not even sure anymore.

Jenna

It's been over a week since our fight, and I know I need to talk to him and fix it. I just couldn't deal with all of that on top of having this meeting as well. Every time I think of having a real conversation with him, the panicky feeling is back. I've tried writing to get a hold of my anxiety over all of this. I thought it might work for me, because it has always worked so well in the past, but nope. I couldn't even get any words down.

Once I get through today's meeting, I will make sure Drew and I talk it all out. I have no idea why I find it so easy to write a character's story full of deep emotions and conversations about very real things, but when it comes to talking to the man I love and opening up, I can't do it. I can't tell him my fears for the future or even what I want or that I'm scared he will realise I'm not good enough for him. It all plays on repeat in my head. I know what I want to say to him, and after Ivy came over the other day, I felt like I would have the confidence to march over to his place and tell him it all. Lay my cards on the table, see what he thinks.

But with every day I tried, I failed to get the courage to do it.

And now I'm wondering if he has just given up on me completely. I wouldn't blame him if he did. I know he goes away to Narrabeen this week for his next comp, so I guess that's it, he really has given up on us. I'll be divorced at the age of twenty-eight. Just another fuck-up to add to my long list.

I sigh loudly as I take one last look in the mirror of my hotel room. I straighten my pencil skirt and reapply my red lippy. Today is too important to be thinking about my messed-up love life and Drew Walker. I'm in Sydney for my chat with the publishing house, an absolute dream come true for me, and I'm not going to let anything ruin this for me. I flew in yesterday and stayed the night in a hotel not far from their office so I could be all sorted for the nine am meeting.

I walk through the busy entry to Reed Harrington Publishing. Men in suits and women in nice business attire all busily rush about, making their way to work for the day. It's a little intimidating. I'm used to the quiet and familiar environment of my library; this is so far from my usual day at work. I feel out of my depth. Can these people all see I don't fit in here? I'm sure they're all looking at me like *what on earth does she think she's doing here?* Yeah, the imposter syndrome is real, and I have it majorly today. I half feel like turning and running for it, but my black pumps won't take me far, and I'll probably end up on my arse and make a total fool of myself.

I stop when I get to the elevator and check my phone for the exact address. The elevator arrives and I step in, pressing the floor I need. I try to calm my breathing while I wait for my floor to arrive. You can do this, Jenna. For once in your life back yourself, fake the confidence you don't have. If this doesn't work out, you will never have to see this person again.

There's the ding of the elevator arriving, and I step out into a massive room. Everything is sleek and white with marble floors. I feel even more out of place. I walk straight for the receptionist before I really do lose my nerve and just leave.

She's young, probably early twenties, with her blonde hair in a neat bun. She smiles at me warmly. "How can I help you?"

"Hi, my name is Jenna Walker, and I have an appointment with one of your publishers."

She scans through the computer in front of her. "Yes, here it is. Follow me."

She comes around the corner of her desk and briskly walks away from me. I follow her through the long corridor as her heels tap on the marble floor to an office. She's wearing a white pant suit and looks like she's out of the pages of a fashion magazine. I wish I had half her style. She raps on the door and pushes it open. "Your nine am, a Mrs Walker."

"Send her in," I hear a deep voice say.

She turns to me with an encouraging smile. "Mr Stone will see you now."

Stone. I hate that name. Until I had the phone call to book this appointment, I haven't heard of someone with that surname since high school, but it still makes my stomach churn. Not going to let that ruin today either. There is no way it's the same person I knew, what would be the chances. I laugh to myself.

I plaster on my most confident smile and walk through the door to his office. I stop dead midway through the doorway. The chances are pretty fucking high, I would say, since it's him. Instant panic washes over me at the sight of him. My palms are sweaty and my heart is hammering. This is probably the worst thing that could have happened today. I knew I should have run for it when I got into the foyer. Why didn't I listen to my intuition? It's too late now. His eyes meet mine and send a shiver down my spine.

"Mrs Walker," he says, emphasising my surname. "What a pleasant surprise."

I stand in the doorway and blink back at him. I'm frozen to the spot, unsure if I should even go any farther. I think I'm in shock. I am in the same room as Damien Stone, the reason I ran away from my last foster home.

"Mrs Walker, why don't you close the door behind you and come and take a seat." He gestures to the seat across from him. I blink back at him. I feel winded, like the air has been knocked from my lungs. I'm a fifteen-year-old high school girl, all alone in this world, vulnerable and scared, looking for love and acceptance from anyone who would give it to me. He promised me he was the one I was looking for.

He pushes his seat back, frustrated, and stands, walking past me to close the door behind me. Then his hand goes to my elbow, guiding me towards the seat. My feet move involuntarily, not obeying my brain to stay as far away from this man as possible. I know nothing of him as an adult, it's been a long time since I have seen him. But the boy I knew was not a good person, and the thought of being in the same room as him, with my chances of publishing my book in his hands, makes me feel sick to the stomach. Why is this happening to me?

He reclines back into the large leather office chair, the hint of a smile playing on his lips as his eyes roam over me, taking me in. His posture is relaxed and comfortable, total opposite to what I'm feeling. "Little Jenna West, don't be so shy," he says playfully, grinning back at me.

His smile is pleasant, friendly even, large full lips, perfectly straight teeth. He's a nice-looking man. The kind you would definitely give a second glance to if you saw him walking by. Sandy-blond hair and piercing green eyes that haven't left me for even a second since I entered the room. If I didn't know better, I would think time has changed him, softened him, or maybe he has just grown up and he has a heart after all. I guess people can change. "It's so nice to see you again after all these years, and what a coincidence. I work in publishing, and you want to publish your manuscript."

"It's Walker. I'm recently married," I blurt out, trying to make it obvious I'm taken, and the look in his eyes telling me he wants to eat me alive can fuck right off. And he's right, this is a fucking huge fluke. What are the actual chances? I got the number for this publishing house from Ivy. She was handed a business card that day in the coffee shop. Is it just a coincidence? I shake my head, trying to clear my thoughts. My imagination is running wild again. I need to stop. Of course it's just by chance this all matches up.

His smirk is lopsided. "Yes, I see that here in your email, but you will always be little Jenna West to me." That would be about right, he is going to ignore that fact that I'm married because it's not what he wants to hear.

I force a smile. I want the earth to swallow me up. I can't believe I finally get this opportunity and it's going to be destroyed because it's with him. There is no way in hell I can work with him, it's not even a possibility. I'm not even sure why I'm still sitting here, but I think it's because his presence has me unable to move.

"I enjoyed your manuscript. I'm surprised now that it came from you. Sweet little innocent Jenna, wouldn't have thought you'd have it in you to write a dirty romance novel."

Find your voice, Jenna. You are not a teenager anymore. You can talk back to him. I glare at him, finding my inner strength. "How is it that you would know anything about me? I haven't seen you since I was fifteen." This whole thing turned to shit the moment I walked through the door and it was him. I'm not going to pretend to be nice when I despise the man.

"Let's not be like that now, hey. We both know all sorts

of things about each other. We were very good friends once. Have you told your husband about me?"

"Why would I have done that? You're not anyone to me," I snap.

"Ha, we both know that's not true. I was someone to you alright. There is no way you could forget what we had. I never forgot about you, Jenna. You have a special place in my heart, and you always will." He smiles kindly.

It makes me feel like a bitch. I'm here hating him, and he is being so uncharacteristically pleasant. Maybe my memory of him is worse than it actually was. I soften a bit; it's hard not to when he's being so nice. "I don't see how any of that is at all relevant now. Shouldn't we be talking about my manuscript in this meeting, not our past?" I say, trying to keep us on task. Maybe my dream is salvageable. God, I hope it is.

He steeples his hands and presses them to his lips, as if contemplating what I have just said. "Okay, lets." He looks over at the stack of papers in front of him. "As I said, I like what I see. It's written well. I like your take on the modern fairy tale, and after a few tweaks, I think we could have a marketable book. I want you to take a look over my notes and let me know what you think. If you can see this relationship working?"

He hands over the printed manuscript and I flick through. There are a lot of notes, it's overwhelming. How can he possibly make so many notes when he doesn't even know where I'm coming from? But I guess I should put my feelings towards him aside. He is the expert in this area, and I should take into account what he has to say. "Alright, I will take a look. How does this work? Do I just send it back to you with my changes?"

"No, not yet. Just take a look, see what you think of my

suggestions. How long are you in Sydney for?" Why does he even need to know that? The less information I give him, I feel, the better. "Just so I can work out my schedule as to when we can go over this again." He rises a brow as he says it.

"Just for two days."

He hands me some more papers; I glance over the contract.

"Okay, we will meet for dinner tomorrow. If you're keen to work with me, I will need you to read and sign the contract as well."

I scan over the papers. If I'm keen to work with him? What am I doing? I can't work with him, and I definitely don't want to go for dinner with him, business related or not. "I'm sorry, I don't won't to sound ungrateful, because I'm glad you like my story, but is there someone else here I can work with?" I gesture between us. "This isn't going to work for me." I did it. I stood up for myself.

"Yes, it is. The past is in the past, we were silly teenagers. I forgive you for leaving me, if you can forgive me for being a hormone-fuelled arsehole. Don't let all that stuff ruin your chance for an exciting future as an author."

Hormone-fuelled arsehole? That is an interesting take on what happened between us. But I feel like I have to give him the benefit of the doubt. He does seem like a completely different person. Does he really think I could be an author? Or is this all some bullshit game of his? "Don't you think dinner is a bit over the top then? Couldn't I just come back here tomorrow during work hours or something?" I suggest, hoping to get out of what can only be a very awkward situation.

His eyes narrow and I shrink back in my seat. "Jenna, I know you're new to all this, but this is how it works. You're not getting treated any different to anyone else just because you were my foster sister when we were teens. I don't do special treatment. I have a business to run here, and if you don't like the way I do it, then maybe this isn't the right industry for you."

He did always have a way of making me feel unimportant and small. But this time maybe he's right, this is just what they do with every new client. And if this is what I want, I should just do what he says. I wish I could call Drew and talk it all through with him. He would know what to do. But I don't even know if I will ever be able to do that again. It's probably over with him, and if it is, I'm going to need this distraction more than ever.

"Alright, I will take a look over it all," I say, still a little unsure.

"And meet me for dinner tomorrow night. Where are you staying? I'll meet you in the hotel restaurant, easier for you."

"Okay. It's at the Vibe Hotel."

He comes around behind my chair and pulls it back for me, standing over me. His eyes burn into me. He's a big man, and even though I know I shouldn't, I still fear him. He has a hold over me I don't want him to have. "Jenna, this is a really big deal. We don't take on that many new authors. Make the right choice."

I grip the papers to my chest and swallow the lump in my throat. How can he still scare the shit out of me? He doesn't have power over me anymore. I'm not a fifteen-year-old orphan without another soul in the world to care for her, him three years older, holding all the power.

He ruled the school, a footy-playing jock with top grades. Teachers doted on him because he was smart and charming. The other students loved him because he was gorgeous and a footy star. He had some sort of weird power over all of us. I was just his insignificant foster sister, new at the school and in need of friends. He helped me, looked out for me. I needed the protection he provided, and at first, I looked at him just like the rest of them, in total awe.

He takes a step back, giving me some much-needed space. I suck in a deep breath and get to my feet. I'm a grown woman with a support system around me, people who care about me. I am strong. If I do this, it will be because it's the right decision for me, not because he's telling me to do it. "Thank you. I will see you tomorrow," I say with a smile. I hold my head up high, shoulders back, and leave his office. Coming across as strong and as in control as I can.

I will fall apart in the elevator.

CHAPTER TWENTY-FOUR

DREW

IT'S THE FIRST DAY OF THE COMP HERE IN NARRABEEN on the northern beaches of Sydney. I have been on fire today, carving up the waves like the pro I am. I'm back in full form, and I'm relieved after the last comp that my knee is feeling fine. My personal life might be in complete ruins, but at least I can still surf.

It's just past eleven at night. The whole lot of us have been out for dinner and drinks. I've probably had a few too many, but since Jenna is still ignoring me, I have slipped easily back into my old ways. Lots of booze and late nights. It's mind-numbing fun, but it's not enough to block out the fact that all I want is Jenna.

Cobie wraps an arm around me. "Come on you, it's time to get you home or you'll be useless competing tomorrow."

I look down at my friend and smile. No matter what, she always has my back. She is the voice of reason when I've lost my mind. She was that for me last time I fell apart because of Jenna as well. "Okay, I'll walk you back to your room," I offer.

She looks at me like I've lost my mind. "Drew, you're

very drunk. I will walk you back to your room. I don't need any of my boys going missing tonight."

"Alrighty then, Mum, lead the way," I tease.

She throws me a dirty look for my comment, and I laugh at her as I follow her in the direction of our rooms.

I'm a bit wobblier than I thought, and Cobie grabs my arm, hooking hers through to balance me as we walk. She is quite a bit shorter than me and it must look awkward as fuck from behind, her steering me in the right direction, down the path from the restaurant to my room.

"What's going on with you, Drew? You're acting like... well, like you did when Jenna broke up with you all those years ago. Has something happened with the two of you?"

I glance at her. I haven't said a thing to her about it, but she's worked it out. Shit, she really does know me. "I fucked up and now she won't talk to me. It's been over a week."

"Oh, I'm sorry to hear that. I'm sure you two will work it out, though, right?"

I stumble on the uneven concrete, and she corrects me, guiding me as best she can. "She's back living at her place," I confess. I didn't want to say it all out loud before, because I was scared if I did, it would be real. But I think it is. I think I might have fucked up so badly she is already done with me.

"I'm so sorry, Drew, that sucks."

"Yeah." We walk a bit farther up the path and stop when we get just outside my room. "Cobie, do you think I rushed into the whole marriage thing?"

"Just a bit. It was pretty quick." She offers me a small smile. And I know she is dying to tell me she told me so, because she did, and I didn't listen to her.

"I know, but it just felt right. I thought we knew each other well enough. But I guess we've both changed a lot in our time apart over the last few years. Maybe I don't know her as well as I thought. And part of me is just scared I'm not ready for this type of commitment and neither is she."

"Marriage is a big commitment. You know how I feel about it. I think you're nuts, but you love her, don't you?"

"Yeah, I do." Her eyes drop when I say it, and I feel like a dick talking about this with her. It's not right, we have history, and I should just keep my problems to myself. She doesn't need to hear about it. "Hey, do you want to come in for a drink or something? There is no way I'll be able to sleep just yet. You can fill me in on what's happening with you."

She smiles sweetly. "Okay, just a quick one. We both have big days tomorrow."

I open the door to my accommodation and we both go in. I head for the fridge. "Beer?" I call.

"Drew, I think it's time for coffee, don't you?"

"Yeah, I guess. You really are like my mum tonight," I tease her.

She pushes past me into the kitchenette. "I'll make it, you sit," she demands.

"Yes, sir." I give her a solute and laugh. Shit, I am really quite drunk. Being this drunk makes me want to call my sister, so I dial her number and wait for her to pick up. Come on, Elly, where are you?

"Drew, how are you?" Her voice is quiet, like she's whispering.

"Elly, oh shit, what time is it there, did I wake you up?"

"No." She laughs. "You're in Sydney, it's the same time zone as you. I'm still up. What's going on? You sound drunk."

"I may have had a few beverages."

"Where are you?"

"In my room, Cobie walked me back."

"Good. You need to sleep it off, little brother, or you're not going to be able to compete tomorrow. Are you forgetting you want the win this year?" she says in her mum voice that she reserves for Cooper. I must be bad, I'm getting the mum tone from everyone.

"I haven't forgotten, I just... I miss you, Elly."

"I miss you too, Drew." I can hear her smile through the phone. "Are you okay?"

"She hasn't rung me yet. Did Ivy give her the letter?"

"I don't know, Drew. I think Jenna is still away for the meeting. You just have to be patient, she must just need some time. You guys rushed into all of this. Maybe she just needs a minute to breathe. She'll come round, Drew. You two are perfect together. It will all work out. I'm sure of it."

Cobie comes to sit with me, placing my drink on the table in front of me. "Drew, your coffee."

"Who's that in your room?"

Cobie takes the seat opposite me and sips on her drink. "It's just Cobie, my manager."

"Do you think that's a good idea?" Her tone has shifted to super serious.

I shuffle in my chair, getting more comfortable. "It's fine, Sis. Got to go, though. Love you, talk soon."

"Love you too, little brother, try to keep yourself out of trouble, will you."

"I'll try. Laters." I disconnect the call, not needing a lecture.

"My sister," I say to Cobie, who is smirking at me.

She shakes her head and laughs at me. "I figured. You two are cute."

"I'm not cute."

"You so are. I don't know many guys who tell their sister they love her over the phone."

"We're close." I shrug and take a sip of my coffee.

Cobie watches me. She's been funny towards me since Jenna and I got married. Something has shifted with our friendship.

She darts her eyes away from me.

"You okay?" I ask her.

"Drew, do you ever wonder if we could have been something?" She sighs, looking down into her drink. "I mean, before you got hurt last season, I felt like we were getting close, and then when you came back, you had Jenna." Her words are a whisper, like she's scared to say them out loud, and my heart drops.

"I don't know, Cobie. You have always been such a good friend to me, and I adore you." I rub her arm.

"Drew, I think I'm in love with you." She blinks back at me hopefully, but with tears forming in her eyes. I don't know what to say to her. I didn't expect her to say that she was in love with me. I don't want to hurt her, but this is not good. I pull my hand away from her.

I'm sure she regrets the words as soon as she says them. "I'm sorry, I know you're married. I shouldn't have said that, but you're having troubles in your marriage already, and I have always thought we could be such a perfect match. We come from the same world, and we get on so well. Why didn't we ever get any further than a few sleepovers?"

I look at her, really taking her in. "I honestly don't know." I don't. She is a beautiful girl, and we do come from the same world and get on famously and always have, but there is something missing with us. The spark I felt with Jenna was instant, like the stuff they write about in novels, where you just know that person is for you and you would do anything to make sure you spend your life with them. That has never been there with me and Cobie.

She pushes her chair back and comes around the table, kissing me on the cheek. "I'm going to go. I'm sorry, that was... I shouldn't have said it." Tears well in her eyes. She's upset, and I feel terrible. Because I can't make this right with her, and I know this will be it for us. Our friendship will be over. She makes it to the door.

I follow her. Not sure what to say, I'm not in the best state of mind to handle this. "Don't be upset. You're a beautiful girl, you will find the right person for you. I'm sorry things never worked out for us."

She turns back to me, taking a step to close the space between us, and reaches up to cup my face. "They could work out for us, though, Drew." Her thumb runs along my stubble, and it's familiar and comforting. I have been right here with her before, and it was always amazing. We did fit together nicely. We do come from the same background, and we get the lifestyle.

But she's not Jenna.

"It's not too late," she says. "You just give me the okay and I'll stay the night. It will be just like old times." Her lashes flutter as she looks back at me. She closes her eyes and tilts her head towards me, her lips almost grazing mine.

My brain kicks into gear and I pull away from her. "No, Cobie, this is not going to happen. I can't. I love Jenna, I'm so sorry."

She takes a step back, blinking up at me, wounded. "She's not the right person for you, Drew. When you work that out, you know where I'll be." She storms out and slams the door.

I feel sick to my stomach. Everything has completely turned to shit. I should have known better than to let her in my room. I didn't kiss her back, but I could have. It would have been easy to fall into old patterns, and I nearly let it happen. I have let Jenna down and upset Cobie, someone I really care about.

There will be no coming back from this for us. She can't be my manager anymore, not now that I know how she feels. Jenna has to be my priority. I need to get my shit together and sort all of this out before it's too late and I really do lose her, because I know for sure that is the last thing I want to happen.

CHAPTER TWENTY-FIVE

DREW

Day two, the waves are big, a little messy at times, but mostly they are perfect conditions for me. I'm up against my top competitor, Hutton. I've competed against him many times before, I have studied his technique, so I'm not worried. I know I've got this, it's my comp to win.

Hutton is still fairly new to all of this, and he just doesn't have the experience I do. He is also managed by Cobie, and he's young and reckless and after my title. I just need to block out all the drama of the last few weeks and focus on what I'm doing here today. I watch the heat before ours, reading the waves. It's going to be a piece of cake.

On the third wave of the day, I have priority. I see it coming and start to paddle madly. As I pop up on my board and start to ride the wave, I see a flash out of the corner of my eye just before I feel the impact of the other board. My knee buckles, and the next thing I know, I'm on the sand coughing up salt water.

"Drew, Drew, can you hear me? It's Ted." I see his face come into view. It's a little blurry but it's him.

"Ted, what happened?" My voice is croaky. I must have swallowed quite a bit of water.

"You fell, mate, your board hit you in the back of the head."

I try to get up, but my head spins. "The comp, I need to finish," I get out before he pushes me back to the sand.

"It's over, Drew, just relax. Your first two waves got you good scores, you didn't need this one. You need to go to hospital, you probably have a concussion."

"I'm fine, it's just a concussion. I've had one before, I'll be fine." I try to sit up and my head spins. I blink my eyes, trying to focus.

"You're not going back to your hotel room by yourself, mate."

Cobie comes into view. She kneels down beside me. We haven't talked since last night, and I need to talk to her. But when I can't even string two words together is not the time.

"It's okay, Ted, I'll keep an eye on him," she offers, and I'm thankful. I'm starting to feel really unwell.

"Thanks, Cobie, let me know how he's going, will you," I hear Ted say.

"No worries." She looks down at me. "Come on, Drew, let's get you back to your room." She helps me up to standing and wraps her arm around me, walking me away from the crowd that has gathered.

"Thanks, but I think I'm okay to walk on my own."

She looks up at me. "You sure? You hit your head pretty hard."

I feel the back of my head; it hurts like a fucking bitch, the throb radiating through my skull. The pain is suddenly overwhelming. Fuck, I'm going to be sick. I push Cobie out of the way and fall to my knees, emptying the contents of my stomach on the grass in front of me.

She looks down at me, worried. "Do you want me to take you to the hospital? I think you're worse than you think."

"No," I snap. I'm not going to the fucking hospital. "I'll be fine, I just need to get back to the room."

"Let me help you then, come on." She helps me up, leading me to the car, her arm wrapped around me, and I let her.

I feel a little better after being sick, but my head still bloody hurts. She starts the engine, and I lie my head back, trying to work out what happened. I think Hutton and I both went for the same wave, and our boards must have collided. That's never happened to me before. What the fuck was he doing? It was my priority. Jenna will be pissed at me for being so stupid.

Jenna, I need to call her. "My phone, I left it back with my stuff at the beach. I need to call Jenna."

"Don't worry, Drew, I will call your mum. She will let them all know. I'm sure Jenna will call you soon and check on you. Your phone is in the back of the car with all your other gear. All good, you just relax."

"Thanks, Cobie. What would I do without you?" She smiles at me sweetly. After last night, I didn't even know if she would be talking to me today, but she's acting like nothing happened. I really appreciate her today. We've been friends for a long time, and she has my back when it matters most.

We get back to my room and Cobie helps me into bed. She gives me some painkillers and water for my head, but I'm not really focusing on anything much. "Come wake me up if Jenna calls, I need to talk to her," I mutter as my eyes close.

I just need to sleep. I'm sure I'll feel better in the morning. Cobie whispers something to me as I fall asleep, but I don't catch what.

Jenna

I wasn't sure what to wear for this dinner since it's really a business meeting, so I just went for a simple black dress with a high-roll neck and my ankle boots. Hair neat in a high pony. Professional business look.

After tossing and turning all night, I rang Ivy today, and she convinced me to go for it. Stop letting the past get in my way. She might not have been so persuasive if I'd told her the entire story of how well Damien and I know each other. He wasn't just my foster brother, he was also my first boyfriend. How fucked up is that!

I was stupid. He was the first guy ever to show me any attention, and I was so starved of it that I let him treat me terribly. To the outside world, including his parents, he was charming and charismatic, everyone loved him and thought the sun shone out his arse! And he was like that towards me to start with, but as soon as I gave him what he wanted, things changed very quickly. He turned into a controlling, jealous, narcissistic arsehole.

No way I was telling Ivy the full extent of all of it. It got so bad at the end I took off in the middle of the night, actually scared of what he was going to do to me next. I feel slightly better about tonight now, though, knowing someone will know where I am—you know, just in case I disappear or something.

I'm being overly dramatic, letting my mind run wild. That's the problem with having an imagination like mine. You can write a wonderful story, but you also spend half your life trapped in your thoughts of all the things that could go wrong. The shit that happened between us was just immature teenage stuff, but he's an adult now. I'm sure he has come a long way since all of that, and it really did seem like it was yesterday.

Ivy also mentioned Drew left a letter with her. She said he hates himself for the fight we had, and he wants to fix things. I was tempted to have her read it out for me over the phone. He tried to call me a few times yesterday, but they were when I was in the meeting. And I thought of trying to call him back, but I can't bring myself to do it. I'm dying to know what the letter says, but it will have to wait until I'm home tomorrow. Right now, I need all the energy I have to get through this weird meeting and work out what I'm going to do. Do I sign the contract and go for it?

I walk into the hotel restaurant, my shoulders back, head held high. If I'm going to do this, I'm going to fake all the confidence I can and show him who I am now. Not the pushover I was when we were kids. I scan the tables, and I see him towards the back as he watches me like a lion stalking his prey. It's kind of creepy and sends an uneasy feeling through me.

Don't let him get to you. You've got this, Jenna.

"Mr Stone," I greet him, and he gestures for me to take a seat.

"Miss West."

"Mrs Walker," I correct him. I take the seat opposite, not the one next to him. He smiles smugly. Is he trying to get under my skin? I get the impression this is a bit of a game to him.

"Wine?" he asks, holding up the bottle of red.

"Yes, please, just a small one." I need to keep my head as

straight as possible around him. But a little wine to take away the churning in my tummy would be nice.

He fills my glass to the top. I give him an irritated look. He is going to do whatever the fuck he wants—and why am I surprised? I take a small sip and place the glass back down in front of me.

"I have ordered for us. Something you will like."

Control freak, of course he has. "Oh, okay, thank you," I say super sweetly with a smile, trying to show him his behaviour no longer has any effect on me.

His eyes roam down my body, then land on my face. He is an attractive man, but the way he looks at me gives me the creeps. "You have changed so much, Jenna. It's a shame you're married, you're one gorgeous woman, and it would have been fun to take a trip down memory lane with you. I'm sure with your colourful past career you would be amazing in bed."

I'm mid-sip of my wine and nearly choke on his words. Fuck, tonight he came prepared to push my buttons. He has looked into my past. Did he know it was me coming in yesterday? Was he the one that day in the café, sitting at the nearby table listening to the girls' and my conversation? Surely if it was him that handed Ivy the business card, I would have recognised him sitting there, but I didn't notice him. Maybe it wasn't a coincidence he called me in, because he knew it was me. I don't like that he knows anything about me and what I went through after running from him.

The waiter brings over our food. It gives me a second to give myself a pep talk. *Keep it professional, Jenna, so he has nowhere else to go. Don't show how he affects you, you're stronger than that now.*

He thanks the waiter and digs his fork into his pasta, twirling the long strands, then placing a forkful in his mouth. I glance at the plate in front of me, and I'm pleasantly surprised he has ordered some sort of pasta with a creamy sauce and sundried tomatoes for me as well. It looks and smells delicious. Least if the rest of the night goes pear-shaped, I got an enjoyable meal out of it.

I straighten my shoulders, debating how to reply to his comment. "I guess working at a library for so many years, I have learnt many colourful and interesting things. They do help with my writing, but I can't see how any of that would relate to anything else." I take a bite of my pasta. It's as good as it looks. "And we are here to discuss my writing, aren't we, not my marital status or anything else?"

He chuckles. He got a rise out of me, and that's what he wanted. Damn it.

"I'm here to see if you're a good fit as a client for me. And you know I wasn't referring to the library, but that was an interesting choice for you. I'm talking about your many years as a stripper. I would have paid good money to see that. You must have been very young when you started, not even legal to drink in the club you were working in."

I can feel my face heat, but it's not because he turns me on—it's because he makes me fucking mad, and I don't want to talk to him about my past as a stripper. I knew it was a mistake to come here tonight.

His eyes run down my body, settling on my breasts. I don't even want to know what is going though that sick mind of his. "How did you end up stripping, anyway? I can't imagine how sweet little Jenna got up there dancing around a pole. I mean, you have great tits, I can see why they would have given you a job, but why stripping? You were always a smart cookie, you could have done anything."

I glare at him. So much for not showing how he affects me. Does he want me to say it? That it was all because of him? He is so sadistic he needs to hear me say my life was practically destroyed at such a young and vulnerable age because of him. "How do you think? There aren't many job opportunities for a fifteen-year-old with no family who hasn't finished school. It was that or live on the streets." I spit venom in my tone. I hate this man, and I can't believe I fell for his charm yesterday.

He gives me a slow clap, and I look at him dead in the face. Is he fucking for real? "Jenna, such great theatrics. You always did have a vivid imagination. You had other choices. You could have stayed with my family. We had a good thing going on, you didn't have to run away."

"I'm not being dramatic. That was my reality. I couldn't stay with you and your family because you were a controlling arsehole, and I couldn't get away from you in that house. I had no one to run to because the whole town thought you were the shit," I hiss at him, the suppressed anger I've had towards him for so long now unleashing. I want to hit his fucking smug pretty-boy face.

He sits there trying to say I'm being dramatic? I know what it was like living with him. I remember clear as day, and him sitting there trying to act like it was in my imagination, that's fucking Damien all over. Always making you believe the fucked-up shit he does is in your head. I'm not a callous person but marking this arsehole's face would feel good. Really good.

"And here I was thinking I couldn't be any more turned on by you. But angry Jenna is fucking hot. The colour in your cheeks, the pout on that pretty little mouth of yours." He smirks, the smug bastard.

I grab the papers I came with, preparing myself to leave. I want this but not to the point I'm willing to put up with him, and right now I'm ready to walk. "Can we keep this professional and just talk about the book? If you can't do that, then I'm leaving."

He places his hand on my wrist. "Settle down, I'm just trying to get a rise out of you. I'm not serious. You're so easy to work up, you make it fun. It really is just like old times."

Prick! The worst part is I can't tell if he's serious. I narrow my eyes, glaring at him. Do I stay or not? I really want this deal, and this might be my only chance. I'll give him ten more minutes, and if we haven't sorted it all by then, I'm leaving.

I put the papers back down on the table and take a sip of my wine, trying to get my anger towards him under control. "It's not fun for me. This is your last chance. We talk about the book or I'm out."

"Alright, Jenna." He relaxes back in his chair. "So, what did you think about my suggestions?"

I take a few more mouthfuls of my dinner. "I agreed with most of them." I shrug.

"And the contract? Have you signed it?"

"I've read through, but it's not signed yet."

He reaches into his suit pocket, handing me a pen. "What's stopping you?"

I look over at him. I can't read him. There is something stopping me from signing them, even more so after that last weird conversation. I don't trust him, and as much as I want this—and I do so much—I don't feel right about it. "I need some more time to decide if this is what I want to do."

He frowns. Seriously, what did he expect? "You don't have forever, Jenna, there are lots more talented authors out there who would gladly take this opportunity. Don't miss your chance."

Nice! Why is he even trying to get me to sign the papers if I'm so crap and there are so many others better? "I'll send them back to you once I sign them." I glare at him, trying to work out what the hell is going on here. Is he even working at a publishing house? Or has he somehow set this all up? It would be a lot of effort to go through just to get at me, so I doubt it. "Tell me, how did you get into publishing?" I ask, curious to know more about him and how much of a coincidence this all really is.

"When I finished school, I went to university and studied communications and media studies, with the idea of going into journalism, but when I finished my degree, my stepdad had lined up an internship with a publishing house. They liked me, and after not too long, I was promoted to join their editing team. It hasn't been hard to work my way up the ladder, so here I am now." He scoops another mouthful of pasta into his mouth.

His story sounds legit, but how can I be sure? Because he really could have just done some research about all of this and faked the whole thing.

"I see what you're trying to do, Jenna. You think this is too much of a coincidence to be true, you're trying to work me out."

He's got me, that's exactly what I'm trying to do, because I don't trust him one bit. I shrug. "I'm just interested in your career, that's all."

He pulls out his phone and types something in, passing it to me. "I'm legit, Jenna. I have worked for this company since I finished uni." What I'm looking at is the company's website. Why I didn't think to do a little research of my own, I don't know. It has his photo and his role, along with a whole heap of info on how wonderful he is at his job. There are write-ups from other authors who have loved working with him. It seems he is still everyone's golden boy.

I hand his phone back. "Happy now?" he asks.

He's not impressed, but I don't care. I'm not going to let him bully me into this. It has to be the right choice for me, and I'm just not sure that it is. Even more so after tonight. Surely there are other options for me. I could always try sending it to another publisher.

"When do you fly home?" he asks.

"Tomorrow morning."

"I'll give you till then." He pushes his seat back. "I'll fix up the bill. Make the right choice for your future, Jenna. You will regret it if you don't."

I stare at him as he walks away. He gives me no opportunity to say I need more time. He has said his piece, and he's just going to leave mid-dinner. Okay. Fine. Whatever!

I know one thing for sure: I'm doing some more research of my own when I get back to my room.

I finish my meal. I'm in no rush to get back to my hotel room, and this is so good. As I eat, I watch the people in the dining room. It's busy, the room is alight with chatter.

There is one couple I focus in on. They're elderly and have finished their meal. They're sitting hand in hand over the table; they're so sweet. I can only imagine they have been together for many years and still look so in love. I want that. Is that what I can have with Drew, if I just give in and stop fighting it? I hope so.

I finish my pasta and wander back to my room and plonk down on my bed. My head is going crazy after tonight. I don't know what to do. That meeting was strange and kind of creepy, but I can't really put my finger on why, other than we have a messy past. I could call Ivy and talk it through again, but really, all I want to do is be able to talk to Drew.

God, I miss him. I keep going over the fight we had at the studio in my head. I have been doing that for nearly two weeks, trying to make sense of it all. Most of what we fought about was so silly and just got blown out of proportion in the moment. We can both be hot-headed when we want to be.

Now that I've had time to think about it all, maybe he wasn't totally in the wrong. He did majorly overreact, but I was the one who hadn't told him about the type of class for a reason, I knew he would feel that way about it. And the more I think about those weeks when we got back from Vegas, the more I know all of my concerns were in my head. It was just me panicking because things that had been so safe and comfortable for me were changing.

But change doesn't have to be bad, especially when it's someone like Drew I'm adapting my life for. He was trying to offer me a chance to spend more time with him because he loved me, and all I could see was how he was asking me to change my life. I let out a sigh. We just need to talk and work it all out.

This trip to Sydney has been good for me. Time away from everything to clear my head and work out what I really want for my life, and I know one thing for sure: I want Drew in it.

I wonder what his letter said. I don't think I can wait until I get home to find out. Without another thought, I dial his number and wait. I'm an idiot for not calling him sooner. I need to hear his voice. The phone rings and rings, then clicks over to his answering message. I try again, and it's the same. It's not that late, I'm sure he's not in bed, but maybe he's out still with the surfing crew. That's probably more like it. I'll send him a text.

Me: I miss you, we need to talk and work this all out. I'm sorry I waited so long x

Texting is frustrating, I can't say what I want to say, but

I send it anyway. Hopefully he will call me as soon as he sees it.

I hit dial and get Ivy next. "Hey, honey, I hope I didn't call too late. Are you in bed?"

"No, all good. How did you dinner meeting go?" She sounds tired, and I feel bad for calling.

"I don't know, it was strange. I'm having major second thoughts about all of this. I have until the morning to work out what I'm going to do."

"Oh, why was it strange?"

"Just a feeling I was getting, and he said a couple of things that didn't sit right with me." I wasn't going to tell Ivy the entire story, but I feel like I need to talk to someone about it, and since I can't talk to Drew, I need to confide in her.

"You have to go with your gut, hun. If it's not right, you will work out another way to get your book published."

"Actually, Ivy, it's more than just a feeling. He wasn't just my foster brother when I was younger. He was..." Ahh, I don't even know if I can say it to her. I wish she were here, and I didn't have to be talking about this over the phone.

"He was what, Jen? You know you can tell me anything." Her kind, comforting voice comes though the phone, and I know I can. She understands a shitty past more than most would. She won't judge me.

"He was my first boyfriend, and it was an extremely toxic relationship," I get out, the only details I feel like I can share over the phone.

"Oh. Are you scared of this guy? Worried for your safety?" I can tell her tone of voice has changed. She is just as worried.

"I don't know. I mean, as a kid I was, and if I'm being honest, as much as I don't want to be as an adult, he still makes me really uncomfortable, and he said some stuff that gave me the creeps. I don't trust him, Iv."

"I think you have already made your mind up. You know in your gut that this is feeling heavy for you. Don't go there."

"Yeah, you're right. I'll think on it overnight, but you're right. There is one other thing I wanted to talk to you about tonight. I was wondering if you have that letter there with you?"

"The letter from Drew?" She perks up.

"Yeah, could you screenshot it or something and send it to me? I tried to call him tonight but no answer, and I can't wait any longer to see it."

"Sure thing, I'll do it for you now," she says excitedly.

I smile because I love my friend. She is so desperate for this all to work out for me. "Thanks, Ivy. I'll see you tomorrow when I get home."

"See you then, and Jen? You have options. Don't do anything you feel uncomfortable with. There is always another way, you know."

"Thanks." We disconnect the call, and I wait for her text to arrive with Drew's letter. It's not quite the same reading it like this, but I really can't wait any longer.

My Jenna,

I can't even tell you how sorry I am for the way I acted. I was shocked to see you dancing like that, and it took me back to that night. It scared the shit out of me.

You were right—I have a lot of growing up to do.

I have lived my whole life with everyone doing what I wanted. I'm used to getting my way. But I should have stopped and taken the time to listen to you. I know I can't take back the awful things I said to you. I'm so sorry, though, and I hope you can forgive me for it.

I have never been in this type of relationship before, and I was forgetting about your needs and wants. I was selfish. I won't be anymore. You're too important to me. I'm sorry that it took me so long to try to make things right between us, but this past year my life has changed so much, and that fight with you rattled me. I needed a minute to process everything.

I know we rushed into getting married, but I have no regrets, that is the one thing I am certain of. I didn't get to do our wedding vows properly on the day because it was all so rushed, but there are so many promises I want to make to you for our future, so here goes.

Since the day I met you, I wanted you to be mine. You were the most perfect woman I had ever seen, and when I looked into your eyes, I saw my future. I knew that moment you were the one for me. I can't promise you I will always be the perfect husband, but I will take care of you and love you with everything I have. I will respect and support you, and I will put your needs first and make sure every day you know how important you are to me. I will be patient with you, and I hope you can be patient with me, because at times I'm sure you will need to be. I want to work together with you on our goals and dreams and to share my life with you forever, because I don't want to live my life without you in it.

I love you, Mrs Jenna Walker, always and forever,
  Drew

Tears roll down my cheeks, and I let them. Tonight, I need to cry. His words are beautiful, and I love him so much. I feel so stupid for waiting so long to talk to him or for worrying so much about all the small things. I know we can work this all out. Things will be okay. They have to be.

CHAPTER TWENTY-SIX

JENNA

I can barely lift my hands to wash the conditioner out of my hair, I'm that tired. I've had another sleepless night, tossing and turning until the sun came up. I didn't hear back from Drew, and I just don't know what to do about Damien and the contract.

Something feels off with Damien. I did as much internet research into him as I could last night. From what I can see, he checks out. He has been in this line of work for years, has awards even. So I know meeting him like this is just a massive coincidence.

I can't tell if the uneasy way I feel about all of this is just the way I feel towards him because of our past or if I'm just having second thoughts about the whole getting-my-book-published thing. But the more I think about it, I know I can't trust Damien. And Ivy says I need to trust my gut.

I'm going to march myself into his office this morning before I leave to tell him it's not going to work. I have resigned myself to the fact that I'm probably going to lose my chance to publish, but maybe there is another way I can do it. I haven't really looked into it, but if there is, I feel confident enough now to explore other avenues.

I have also decided that if I do publish, I'm using a pen name. After Damien's comment last night, I don't want other people to be able to know my business. My past. It hadn't even crossed my mind until last night when Damien was talking about how easy it was to see what I've been up to. It's scary, and I really don't want the entire world to know all that about me.

After I drop into his office, then I'm going to surprise Drew by turning up at his comp in Narrabeen. I haven't seen him surf since California when we got married. And I can't wait until he comes home to talk to him; I need to see him now. I looked up the schedule this morning and his final is on at midday, so I should have time to make it. I can't lie, I'm a little nervous to see him again. We have a lot to talk about, but I can't wait any longer either. I need things to be okay with us.

I finish in the shower and turn the water off, hand-drying my hair and wrapping a towel around myself as I head into the room. My heart nearly stops when I see Damien sitting on the end of my unmade bed. He is dressed in a navy-blue suit, his posture oozing confidence and major sleaze. I feel a cold shiver run up my spine and feel physically sick.

"How the fuck did you get in here?" I force out through my fear. My hands have a little tremble as I cling onto my towel, hugging it closer to my chest, making sure I'm covered up.

Damien's hungry eyes roam down my body, eating me up in my lack of clothing. Could I feel any more vulnerable? Just out of the shower.

He smirks, and the icky feeling I have in the pit of my

stomach increases. "I told you, I was giving you until this morning to make your decision. I'm here to get the signed contract."

"You couldn't have waited for me to come into your office?" I snap with venom in my tone. He has to know how majorly fucked up it is he just turned up and let himself into my room. "I'm going to get dressed, and you'd better be gone by the time I get out," I demand.

I grab my clothes from the end of the bed and rush back into the bathroom, locking the door while I dress. Jeans and a T-shirt on, I brush my wet hair, putting it up in a neat bun. Giving him time to leave and me time to get my frantic heart under control. I knew he was giving off a creepy vibe last night, and turning up in my hotel room while I was in the shower is kinda terrifying. How did he even get in?

I can't hear the sound of any doors opening and closing in my room, no sign of him leaving. I want to cry, I can't deal with him, he's too much. But I'm left with no choice. I take a breath, trying to compose myself as best I can. It's obvious he is still here. I need to regain some control. I'm going to demand he get out of my room, that I will meet him at his office.

I stalk back into the room, posture straight and in total control. Shoulders back, head held high, faking as much confidence as I can. As I expected, he hasn't moved. "Seriously, you're still here? How did you get in here, anyway?" I keep my distance from him, standing close to the bathroom.

"Told the chick on the counter I was your husband. It was that easy." His smirk is smug. He's proud of himself for manipulating yet another person to do what he wants them to.

"You're kidding. That's scary that she could have let

anyone in," I mutter almost to myself. I'm going to be having words with the manager of this place.

He raises a brow sarcastically. "Yeah, and she did!" The look on his face makes the hairs on the back of my neck stand up. He's not here for the contract. I'm so screwed.

I cross my arms over my chest and stand a little taller. "You need to leave. I will drop the contract off to your office when I'm ready."

He laughs. "It's funny, you think you have some sort of say as to what happens now. If you know what's good for you, you will do what you're told."

Was that some sort of threat? Whether it was or not, with those words, I'm transported back thirteen years to my little bedroom in his family's house. Doing what I'm told because Damien says so. He was a bully then and he is now, but I don't have to put up with his shit anymore. He has no power over me. I'm done with this whole thing. I don't need to publish my book this badly.

"No. You don't have any power over me anymore. Leave or I'll call the cops," I yell at him.

"With this?" He slides my phone across the bed to me. I take a step closer, picking it up, and I glance at the screen. No fucking service. The arsehole has taken the SIM card out. My stomach drops. Maybe this is a little more serious than I originally thought. He is still that same sick monster he always was, and I'm trapped in his game yet again.

"What do you want?" I stammer.

He licks his lips. The movement is slow and intentional. "You, baby doll, you know that's what I want. I need you to move back to the city and start a life here with me."

Is he for real? Why would I even consider something like that? He eyes me, waiting for my reaction. This is his way of having fun. Messing with me. Scaring me. It's all about control with him, it always was. That's why he liked me, because to start off with, I was so naïve, I just followed his lead. But the more I gave him, the more he wanted. I can't give him anything today. I'm not going back there.

I need to get out of here, and fast. I shake my head slowly. This is not going to happen, not today, not fucking ever. My eyes dart to the door, the only way out of this room. Without another thought, I run for it, pulling it open. Only to have it slammed shut and my body pushed into the wall, pinned beneath a wall of muscle. *No*, I cry silently. *This is not happening.*

He lowers his face to my ear. "Jenna, I'm trying to help you. You have no life waiting for you back in Byron." His hot breath is on my neck and sends shivers through me.

"I have Drew and my friends," I cry. What is he on about?

"What, your friends who have moved on with their lives? Your bestie, Ivy—she is just lovely, by the way—it was such a pleasure meeting her that day in the café. She will be marrying Drew's brother Theo, and do you really think you will still be friends once you get a divorce?"

God, how much does he know about my life? It was him in the café that day. How did I not notice him? Wait, how could he possibly know about Ivy and Theo and that things with Drew are strained? "Wha... what are you talking about?" I splutter.

He loosens his grip on me, taking a step back. I turn around to face him, not sure what to do. "You think I'm out to get you. You're so scared of me, aren't you, baby doll? You were about to run again. But Jenna, I'm here to help you. I know I was a total prick to you when we were younger, and I understand why you might not think very much of me now. But I'm not the same person I was.

People change. I only came here this morning to help you."

Is this all just more games? I look at my phone, trying to make sense of what he is saying. "Why would you take the SIM out of my phone then?" Because he is full of shit!

"Something happened overnight that I didn't want you to see until you felt like you had options."

What could have happened overnight? And what options is he talking about? His offer for me to stay here with him? "What are you talking about?"

He takes my hand and leads me to the small table and chairs. I wouldn't go with him so easily, but he isn't giving me a choice with the way his hand grips mine. He encourages me forcefully to sit at the table and he takes the seat next to me. His body is an imposing presence over me. "I will show you, but just know that I'm here for you, I can help you through this mess."

"Just show me," I demand. I'm sick of his games already. I want to know what's going on.

He puts the SIM back in my phone and hands it to me. It loads up and a heap of missed calls and messages flash on the screen. They are all from the last thirty minutes. Ivy, Theo, and lots from Drew. What's going on? Why are they all trying to contact me? I hope something hasn't happened to Drew! "What am I looking for?" I snap at him, just wanting this over with so I can call Drew and Ivy.

"This morning's paper, it will all become obvious."

I type it in, and the headline reads: *Bad boy surfer at it again*. There is a photo attached, and it looks like Drew with his manager Cobie, in front of a hotel room, arms linked, at night.

I swallow the lump in my throat. What am I seeing? There is also another picture of them at the beach. She is nuzzled in close to him. What the actual fuck am I looking at? We have a fight and he runs straight to her? Is that what this is?

My eyes dart between the phone and Damien. This couldn't just be his games, he couldn't have made this all up. This has to have happened. It also explains all the calls; if the others have seen this, they will be trying to contact me, Ivy to make sure I'm okay and Drew—well, he has a shitload of explaining to do. I don't really know how he could talk himself out of this one, though, it looks pretty obvious what he has been up to.

DREW

When I wake up, my head is still thumping, but it's more of a dull pain now, and a feeling of nausea, not like that throb it was yesterday afternoon. I must have slept all night. I roll over to find my glass of water on the nightstand. I take a big drink, emptying the glass, then set it back down. When I do, I notice a handwritten note. I pick it up, it's from Cobie.

Drew

I can't be your manager anymore, it's too hard. It hurts too much to see you all the time and know you're in love with someone else. And I can't move on while I still have you in my life and keep hoping that you will see me and love me back the way I do you.

I'm sorry that this leaves you without a manager at such short notice, but seeing you with the injury last night, I wanted to be the one there for you, to comfort you and take care of you, and you kept asking for her. She is your wife, why shouldn't you?

I only hope that one day I can find a man who loves me the way you love your Jenna. Because the love you have for her is true and beautiful. You're very lucky to have each other. I hope you can work out your differences and enjoy a wonderful life together.

Cobie

Her words make me feel awful because she deserves so much better, and I feel like I have let her down, but I love Jenna. And I guess she's right, we can't work together anymore. I was trying to hang on to her, but things have changed too much, and it just won't work anymore. She had the guts to make the hard decision I couldn't.

Today is the final for my division, and I need to get myself up and sorted so I can be there for it. But first I need to call Jenna. I can't wait for her to call me anymore after what happened yesterday. I just need to hear her voice and tell her how much I love her.

I dial her number and wait, but the line is dead. That's odd. I check I have the right number then try again—same thing. I dial Theo instead. Maybe Ivy will know what's going on. He picks up quickly.

"Hey, man, you okay? Mum told us what happened."

"Yeah, I'll be fine, just a concussion," I huff, less concerned with myself than why Jenna's phone is dead. "Have you guys heard from Jenna at all? I tried to call her, and her phone has gone dead."

"That's strange, maybe she has blocked your number." He chuckles at his joke.

"Ha, very funny. Is Ivy with you? Can you get her to call Jenna just to check? I have a bad feeling about this, Theo."

"Yeah, sure. Ivy, can you try and call Jenna?" His tone changes as he calls to Ivy. He must be able to hear the panic in my voice. I don't know what it is, but something is telling me she needs me. "She's trying now."

I sit at the little table and lean on my hand while I wait, my head still not feeling right. "Okay, thanks, Theo. I have a bad feeling something is wrong."

"You're just feeling bad because the two of you haven't sorted your shit out yet."

He thinks he is funny or something, but I'm not in the mood for him. I just need to know she is alright. "Has Ivy got her yet?"

"Drew, it's Ivy." She sounds worried, and I know she's feeling it too.

"Did you get her?"

"No, her phone is dead or something. I'm a bit concerned. She's in Sydney for that appointment with the publishing house for her book."

"Wasn't that a couple of days ago?"

"Yes, but she was staying a few days for a bit of a getaway. There is something that's bothering me. I'm sure it's nothing, but when I talked to her yesterday, she said something about the guy she had the meeting with, the publisher, being one of her foster brothers. Someone she dated as well? She was a bit worried and really shocked to see him after so long. I convinced her to go to the dinner, but now I'm worried that was the wrong thing to do."

Now I feel really sick because there is only one person I know this could be. "Are you fucking serious? Not a Damien someone."

"Yes, that's what she said, Damien Stone. He's with the publisher. They were having dinner last night, and she called me when she got back to her room, said it didn't go very well."

"Fuck, Ivy, he's not just some foster brother. He was the creep she ran away from. From what she's said to me, he's a total psycho." I drag my hands through my hair in frustration. I knew something was wrong.

"What do you know about him?" She sounds panicked. "Theo, look into Damien Stone from Reed Harrington Publishing. See what you can find out," I hear her say to Theo, and I'm glad she is taking this as seriously as I am. After everything Ivy has been through with her ex, she knows how badly things can go wrong very quickly.

"Yes, she's told me some stories. He's not someone she should be anywhere near." I need to stay here and compete today. This is a final, and if I don't, that's it for this season. There will be no possible way I can win.

"Drew, I'm sure it's okay, she was back in her room safe last night. She just felt a bit creeped out by him and wasn't sure if she should go through with the contract or not. She's a big girl, I'm sure she can handle it, right?" Ivy is trying to sound unfazed, but I hear it. She is just as worried as me.

I hop up and grab my jeans and a T-shirt, throwing them on while I wait. "Has Theo found anything?" I ask impatiently.

"He's working on it now, I'll call you back."

"Okay." I hang up the phone and start packing up my

room. Fuck it. I throw my stuff in my travel bag. I don't even care if Theo doesn't find anything on this guy. We can't get hold of her, and I feel it in the pit of my stomach. Something isn't right.

I'm not meant to win this comp this year. It doesn't even matter anymore. The safety of my girl is so much more important. I hurry to my car and start the engine. I don't even know where she's staying. I dial Theo again.

"Where is Jenna staying?" I demand.

"We were just about to call you. I dug up a bit on this guy. If she was my wife, I would be getting to her as fast as I could." He has changed his tune, his voice deadly serious now.

"What did you find?" I stammer, my heart now in my throat. I'm having flashbacks to when they rang me last time to tell me she was missing and Vinnie had taken her.

"He has had numerous sexual assault cases filed against him in the past. All seem to be work related. I don't know how he's done it, but they have all been thrown out of court."

What the actual fuck. "Where is she staying, Theo? I'm leaving now."

"Vibe Hotel in the city."

I type it into the GPS and take off for the hotel. "Got to go."

"Don't do anything stupid, Drew, just check on her. Call me back if you're in trouble. I'll see if I can get a car down there just to check things over as well."

"I won't, just getting my girl back." I disconnect the call and speed through the streets of Sydney.

Please let everything be okay with her.

CHAPTER TWENTY-SEVEN

JENNA

My heart pounds in my chest. I'm wounded and so upset with Drew. Is this real? Can I even believe what the paparazzi write? Most of it is bullshit anyway, isn't it?

I want Damien out of my room so I can process what I just read. I know I need to keep my cool until he's gone. I'm not going to fall apart in front of him.

I need to ring Ivy. I need answers. She will know what is going on. Maybe that's why she has tried to call me so many times this morning already. I place my phone back down on the table.

"Okay, I have seen what you needed to show me. Thanks for bringing it to my attention. I don't need any more of your help. I'm a big girl, and I can handle all of this on my own. So you can go now," I say, as emotionless as possible.

His brow knits together, and his eyes narrow, staring straight through me. "That's it? You have just seen proof that your husband is cheating on you, and you say *thank you for bringing it to my attention*? Was it a sham marriage or something? I thought you would be devastated."

He was hoping I would fall apart, and he would come off like the hero here. That's what this all was. "It wasn't a sham. I just don't need to discuss my personal life with you. This is none of your business—and I don't even know why you're here, getting yourself involved in any of this."

"Because like I said earlier, I think you should move to Sydney and start a new life with me." He comes around behind my chair, placing his hands on either side of my arms, and I jump at his touch. He bends down, and I can feel his breath on my neck. "I care about you, Jenna. I always have. I was devastated when you took off in the middle of the night. You were so young. I was worried that something had happened to you. I looked for you for weeks. Even years later, when I saw a girl with long chestnut-brown hair, I would do a double take hoping it was you."

I'm sure he was upset because he no longer had someone to cater to his every desire, and he was probably worried that I told the authorities and he would get arrested. I'm sure eighteen-year-old him would have been shitting himself when I took off.

I don't respond to him, so he spins my chair to face him. He makes me feel small under his stare. Why does he still have this effect over me? I feel like I'm right back there in my bedroom.

It's the night I ran, just past eleven pm, and his parents have gone away for the weekend. My door creaks open, waking me from my sleep.

"Shh, baby doll, it's just me."

I groan inwardly. All I want to do is sleep, I'm utterly exhausted. Lately, he has been visiting my room every night, as soon as his parents are in bed. Tonight, I just can't do it. I have had enough, and I need my space.

At first, sex with him was exciting. He made me feel

special, cared for, even. The boy every girl in our school wanted to be with was secretly with me. But now it all feels like some sick game to him, and I'm the doll he's playing with. He's no longer caring or loving towards me, and he doesn't care if I don't want to take part in whatever he has planned.

If I try to stick up for myself and fight him on it, he gets violent with me. Most of the time, I don't bother fighting him anymore. I think he likes it more. He climbs into bed with me, and I lie still, hoping that it will all be over quickly and I will just be able to go back to sleep.

"Don't act like you're asleep, baby doll, I know you're not." He turns on the bedside light and shakes me. I flick my eyes open, and he looks deep into them. He is the devil.

"Jenna, where did you go?"

I snap back to the present, to those same green eyes, same intense stare. He hasn't changed a bit. For as long as I live, those eyes will haunt me. A sick feeling washes over me. Letting myself remember that night, it makes me sick to my stomach, and I feel the panic rise.

"Don't you need to be getting to work?" I stammer, hopeful the answer will be yes. But knowing in the pit of my stomach that he's not leaving anytime soon.

"I'm not going anywhere, baby doll. I have finally found you after all these years. Do you really think I would let you go so easily?"

I cringe at the use of that name and his words that followed. I knew last night I was in trouble. There was no way he was just joking around with me. "This was all a set-up, wasn't it? Running into you at the publishing house?"

"Just a coincidence."

"Was it?"

He throws his head back, laughing, then flicks his eyes

back to me, the delight in them evident. "The coincidence is that I worked for a publishing house. I found you that day when we bumped into each other in the street. I knew it must've been fate."

I rack my brain. When did we bump into each other on the street?

"You look confused, you don't remember me that day? You were walking with your lippy friend Mia, and you had on the most adorable shorts and sports top. I knew it was you right away, and I could see the connection we had all those years ago was still there between us."

Oh my God, he has lost his shit completely. I remember a man bumping into us that day, but I had no idea it was him, and there was definitely no connection between us.

I should have gone home while I had the chance, now I'm stuck here. My eyes flick quickly down to the table where my phone still sits, then back to him. I weigh up my options, but there aren't many. I could scream, but last time that backfired very badly. Screaming is a last resort.

He has removed my pyjamas and his hungry eyes eat up my body. He's so close to me tonight, and it's turning my stomach. I'm so physically repulsed by him, I can't just lie here and take it.

Something kicks in, and without another thought, I scream. I don't know why, there's no one here to hear me, but I hope someone will. Before I have barely made a sound, his hand covers my mouth, silencing me.

Tears of frustration prickle in my eyes and trickle down my face. That was my chance and I fucked it up.

"Silly girl, you've been warned before what happens if you try and tell my parents or make a sound. You know I have enough photos of you on my phone to destroy that good-girl reputation you have at school. I have all the power. You *were a nobody when you got here, they only include you because of me, and if you tell a soul about any of this, you will go back to being a nobody."*

I can't scream, that is a last resort. I need to distract him. He will not lay a finger on me this time, I won't let him. "Alright then. Well, if you're staying, I'm starving. Should we order breakfast?"

He looks at me, a hint of confusion appearing in his features at my change of tune. He was expecting me to fight him, that's what he wants. I just need to keep my cool and outsmart him, that is really my only hope here.

"Okay, that's a good idea. I will order us something from room service." He walks to the side of the bed, picking up the phone and dialling room service. I wait until he is distracted on the phone ordering breakfast, and I grab my mobile, sliding it into my pocket just in time before he hangs up the phone and pats the bed next to him. I get that cold shiver again. There is no way in hell I'm going over there near him.

"Um, I'm just going to the bathroom, then I'll come and sit with you while we wait for our food." I offer a smile. I sound like such a gullible fool, but I'm just saying whatever I think he will be happy to hear, to keep this situation calm until I can get help. I know from experience he can snap at any second, and then I'm going to be in danger.

He eyes me suspiciously. His fingers rubbing through his stubble. "Okay, hurry up, our food will be here soon, then I have plans for you."

I'm not going to find out what those plans are. I rush off to the bathroom before he has time to change his mind and close the door. I turn my phone to silent and madly start to text.

I know Drew and I are on rocky grounds right now, and

there is a very large possibility that he has cheated on me with his manager, but I also know... well, I *think* I know he would do anything for me, and he's in Sydney at the moment competing. If I can just get hold of him, he might come and get me out of this mess. I just pray he isn't in the water already and out of reach of his phone. I type out a message.

Me: I'm in trouble. I need you. Damien Stone won't let me out of my hotel room at Vibe Hotel in the city, room number 510. Please get me out of here.

I hit send, then copy the message and send it off to Ivy as well. If Drew doesn't get it in time, hopefully, she will, and Theo can call his cop mates or something. No reply bounces back, so I tuck my phone back in my pocket and flush the toilet to make it seem like I have just been. I wash my hands and open the door. And thud straight into Damien's chest. What the hell, he was standing at the door listening.

I glance up at him. He's pissed, and I know I'm in big trouble. My heartbeat increases and panic starts to take over.

"What did you just do?" He glares at me.

Fuck, fuck, fuck. He couldn't possibly know what I was doing. "I used the toilet," I answer innocently.

His forehead is creased, his eyes narrowed. "Don't lie to me, Jenna."

Before I can think of what to say in response, he has me pinned to the wall, wrists grasped in one of his large hands. With his other hand, he removes my phone from my pocket.

"Stupid girl, did you think I wouldn't notice it missing?" He gets right up in my face as he glares at me. I did exactly what I was trying not to do—I have pissed him off. Fuck! "Lucky I had the foresight to know you would try something stupid, and I have another room, the one I stayed in last night."

He stayed in another room in this hotel last night? So creepy. I can't go with him to another room. No one will know where I am. Think, Jenna, think. "What about our food?" I ask, trying to distract him because I have nothing else. All I know is if I go with him to another room, I'm well and truly fucked.

He grabs me by the throat, lifting me off the ground. He's so much stronger than he used to be. I fight against his hold, but that makes the struggle for breath harder. Tears of fear threaten to break, but I won't let them. He will not get the satisfaction of seeing me cry because of him.

"You should have thought about that before you snuck into the bathroom to use your phone. I no longer care what you want. You're going to give me what I need." My skin prickles all over. I have heard that line before. I know what is coming next. Last time I was covered in bruises, ones his parents would be able to see, but it was like once I pissed him off enough, he just snapped and he didn't care anymore. The monster had taken over, and he was going to take whatever he needed.

He releases his hands and I drop to the floor, gasping for breath. I rub my hand over my throat, swallowing.

"Get up, on your feet. We're going to walk down the hallway like a normal couple. Don't try anything stupid again or you're going to be in more trouble than you already are."

I shakily get to my feet. I know I can't go with him, but what choice do I have? He holds all the power. I'm not strong enough to fight against him, and if I try to run and he catches me, it's only going to be worse.

I follow him to the door, and he wraps an arm around

my waist and tucks me in close to his side, his fingers digging into my flesh. He's not taking any chances of me running. To anyone else, we would look like a couple in a loving embrace. My only hope now is someone will be out in the hall and will notice us.

He directs me down the hall to another door not far away, room 505. I note the number just in case I need to know it for later. There isn't another soul in sight. He has to loosen his grip a little to swipe his card and push open the door, and even though I know I shouldn't, something comes over me. I take the opportunity to make a run for it.

"You fucking little bitch!" he calls after me, but I got out of his hold, so I run as fast as my feet will take me down the hall.

I can see the fire escape, and as I push on the door, his arms wrap around me, lifting my body off the floor. "Nooo," I cry.

I kick and scratch at him. I know now is the time I have to fight. I can't go back there with him. I have to get away. I have gone completely feral as I muster up all the energy I can, trying to push him off me as he drags me back down the hall to the room. He slams me up against the door, pinning me between him and the door.

There is no escape now.

Drew

As I speed through the busy streets of Sydney, all I can think is *please, let her be okay*. This all could just be some sort of misunderstanding. Maybe she had her phone off so she could sleep, and that's why none of us can get hold of her.

In my gut I know that's not the case. I can feel it, something is wrong.

From what she has told me about this Damien guy, he was awful to her. She hasn't told me all the details, but he was the reason she ran away from her foster home and started stripping at such a young age. She wouldn't have done that unless things were really bad. And from what Theo said, he has done this to other women as well, and somehow the bastard gets away with it.

What are the chances that he was the publisher she met with? This is a total nightmare.

I pull up at the Vibe Hotel and look for the car park. There is a sign pointing in the direction of the parking garage, and I follow. All the spots are full, and I drive through layers of parking, trying to find a spot.

I'm getting so frustrated, I'm half thinking about just illegally parking and dealing with the consequences after I know she's okay. Finally, I see a spot to park, but I'm miles away from the front of the building. I lock my car and run towards the elevator.

The elevator is ridiculously slow coming down, and I run my hands through my hair as I wait. This fucker better not have anything to do with the fact we can't get hold of her. There is a ping of the lift arriving, and I step inside, hitting the button for reception.

Taking in my reflection, I look terrible. My hair is all over the place and I have dark circles under my eyes. My head thumps with a dull thud, and I feel sick to the stomach, the after-effects of yesterday's head knock. None of that matters, though, I just need to find Jenna.

Inside, I run to the reception desk. The young lady on the desk eyes me curiously. "Can I help you, sir?"

"Yes, I need to see my wife, she's staying here. Jenna Walker. I'm not sure the room number."

Her eyes widen as I say her name, and she glances at her computer. "What name was that again?" she asks.

"Jenna Walker," I snap. Why is she looking at me like I'm crazy? "I can show you my licence. I pull out my wallet and show her my driver's licence. "See, same last name."

Her eyes dart from my licence to me, a look of concern washing over her. "If you're her husband, who did I give a room key to an hour ago?"

My skin prickles all over. What did she just say? "What the hell are you talking about?"

"There was a charming man here in a suit. Not more than an hour ago, he said he was her husband and had locked himself out of the room when he went for a walk. I thought he must have been her husband because I saw them in the restaurant eating dinner together just last night."

"What the fuck are you on about? Some guy is in her room with her right now?"

"You need to calm down, sir, or I will need to call security to have you removed. I have seen things like this before. I'm sorry to be the one to break the bad news, but perhaps your wife is having an affair?"

"She's not having an affair!" I snap at her angrily. As I say it, a message pings on my phone. It's from Jenna.

Jenna: I'm in trouble, I need you. Damien Stone won't let me out of my hotel room at Vibe Hotel in the city, room number 510. Please get me out of here.

She's in trouble. That fuckwit is going to pay. "You need to call security, send them to her room. That arsehole you let in is her crazy-as-fuck ex." I hold up my phone, showing her the text.

Her eyes widen. "I'm so sorry, sir, I will call them now," she stammers, picking up a phone, dialling.

I'm not waiting for security. We know this guy is dangerous, and I have the room number. "Give me a key to her room." She types something on the computer and hands me a key, still waiting on the phone to security.

I take off for the elevator, hitting level five. My mind is running a million miles a minute. I just need to get to her, I need to know she's okay. I knew I should have been here with her for this. If I were, none of this would have happened.

The elevator arrives at level five, and I run out, looking both ways for her room number. It's right down the end of the long hallway, and I slip the key in the lock, opening the door and bursting through. There is no sign of anyone. I can see this is her room, her clothes are here and her phone, her bed has been slept in. Where is she? It couldn't have been over five minutes since I got the text from her. Where could she have vanished to in that time? My head pounds, and I feel dizzy as I try to think about my next move. There is a knock at the door.

A lady in a hotel uniform is standing with a trolley of food. "Room service." She smiles warmly.

She ordered room service? "Just through here, I guess. When was the food ordered?"

"I would say about twenty minutes ago, sir."

"Okay, thank you," I offer.

She leaves.

I dial Theo. He'll know what to do next, because I have no fucking clue. Jenna has just vanished.

"Did you find her?" he asks.

"No, I'm in her room; she's gone."

"Drew, Ivy got a message. She said she was in trouble, that Damien guy was there."

"Yeah, I know, I got the same message and to say what room she was in. But she's not here. This room is empty except for her belongings. Her phone is sitting on the table in here. Her message was only five minutes ago. They couldn't have gone far in that time, could they?"

"You need to talk to the hotel security to see if they have video surveillance of the halls and lobby. You might be able to see if they've left the building or not."

"Yes, that's a good idea." I hang up the phone and run back down the hall, taking the elevator to reception. I arrive back at the desk just as a middle-aged slightly overweight security guard wearing a uniform all in black slowly arrives at the desk.

"The room was empty," I pant. "Can we access the security footage to see where she is?" I say to the girl on the desk, who looks completely overwhelmed by the whole situation.

"I'm sorry, sir, we can't just show you the security footage."

"So, you mean to tell me that you let some random guy into my wife's room. She is now missing, even though all of her belongings are in the room, and you're going to do nothing?"

She blinks back at me. "I... I—"

"Sir, I'm Joe, head of security here. I can take a look at the footage for you. Come with me," the security guard says, directing me to a small office off to the side of the reception desk. Here, take a seat. I'll go over the floor she was on first. How long since she went missing?"

"Ten minutes at the most. Her room was on floor five."

Joe types away at his computer and footage rolls of the hallway. "I could get in a lot of trouble for having you in here, but you seem so distressed that I just had to help you. If it was my wife, I would want someone to help me," he says kindly, and I'm thankful someone wants to help.

It all feels like a bad dream where I'm trying to save her, but I can't get there fast enough, and new obstacles keep getting thrown in my way every time I think I get a breakthrough. I wish this was a bad dream.

"Thank you. I appreciate your help. They can't have just disappeared. Something has to show up on the footage. Right?"

He gives a nod, not turning away from the screen for a second as it fast-forwards through the last hour of recording.

"There," I say pointing to the screen, "slow it down."

He goes back to the spot, slowing it down. The camera angle is from right at the other end of the hall to her room, but you can see clearly enough that it's her and some guy. He has his arm wrapped around her and they're walking from her room to another room. Just as they are about to go in, she escapes his grips and runs down the hall. She looks so scared! He catches up to her and drags her back to the room, kicking and screaming, the door closing behind them.

"Oh, shit! I need to call the police," Joe says, grabbing a phone in his office.

"What room?" I yell.

He zooms in and it looks like 505.

I take off for the elevator. I can't let my mind take me to what is happening in that room, I just have to get there as fast as I can and stop it. The look on her face as she tried to escape him will haunt me forever.

As the elevator takes off, my head spins again, and I steady myself for balance against the wall. I just need to get her to safety, then I can sit down. The elevator arrives on level five, and I slowly pull myself from the elevator. My vision is now blurry, and the hall looks like it's on an angle.

I just have to get to her...

I steady myself with the wall and pull myself along to the room. I can't even get in there without a key, and Joe is still behind, calling the police. How the fuck do you get into a room without a key? I can't even think, my head is so foggy from the pain.

I make it to the door with the number 505 and try to listen. I can't hear a thing. Are they even still in there?

CHAPTER TWENTY-EIGHT

JENNA

THE DOOR SLAMS BEHIND ME, AND THE FEAR OF MY reality hits me with a thud. The tears I have tried to hold back now stream down my face. I don't even care anymore. I'm too tired to fight. I gave it all I had out there, and he still won.

He throws me down on the bed and stands back, nursing his arm. He removes his suit jacket and blood seeps through his shirt. Must have been where I bit him, and I feel some pride that at least I was able to hurt him this time.

"So fucking feisty these days, aren't you." He removes his shirt and wipes away the blood with it. Then he turns his attention back to me. He crawls onto the bed on top of me, his legs on either side, pinning me beneath him. "You know how much a of a turn-on that is, letting you run and seeing the fear in your eyes as I caught you? You were like a scared little deer caught in the headlights. Now look at you, you're exhausted, no fight left, and I have you just where I want you. Your gorgeous hazel eyes blinking back at me from under a layer of thick, dark lashes." He lifts my chin so I'm forced to look at him. "Long, tanned legs." He runs his hands along my thighs. "Bambi really was the perfect stripper name for you, not just because you look the part, but so fitting since your mother was also shot dead when you were just a baby."

My what? My mother was shot dead? Back at the club, when I said my parents were dead, it was made up, pretend, because I had no idea what happened to my parents. I never saw the paperwork and no one ever told me. All I knew was I didn't have any parents, and that's why I was in the foster system. I never looked into any of it further because I always assumed I was unwanted and dumped, so why would I want to find them if they never wanted me? "What do you know about my parents?" I cry.

"Everything." He snickers. This is all a big fucking joke to him. More games. He probably doesn't know a thing and is just trying to upset me more.

"I bet you want to know it all. A curious girl like you would hate not knowing what happened to her parents and where she came from. I bet you wonder every day what they were like, if you took after them, looked like them?" He touches my lips, running his thumb over them. "Who gave you these full, luscious lips?" He tugs at my hair. "If it was Mummy or Daddy who had the thick, chestnut waves." He cups my breasts, squeezing them aggressively. "I'll tell you one thing: your mum had the big tits just like you. Least that's what it looked like in the photos. But you should know that, I gave you the photo of your parents."

That was him? He sent those photos in the yellow envelopes, and it was of my parents? How did he even have access to photos of them? "You gave me those photos? What do you know about my parents?" I ask without thinking, because I know that's what he wants, for me to play along with his game.

But if this isn't a game, and he knows about them, I want to know the truth. The night I left I searched through my foster parents' office for my birth certificate and found a photocopy of it. That was good enough for me. I was in a rush and didn't know to look for anything else. Were there photos of my parents that no one had ever shown me? Or some sort of written document that said what happened to them? I've put it to the back of my mind all these years, but now I want to know. Does Damien have this information about them?

He grins, the sides of his lips turning up slowly. I have played right into his hands. "I'd be happy to tell you. Why don't we play a little game? You do something I'm pleased with, and I will tell you another thing I know about them."

I knew it, it's all fucking games with him. He is full of shit. "You don't know anything about them," I spit back at him angrily. I always knew he was a sadistic fucker, but this is low even for him. How dare he!

He grabs my chin. "That morning you took off, I overheard my parents talking. They were so upset with you. After everything they had done for you over the years."

What is he talking about over the years? I was only with them for about six months.

"They said you went through their stuff and took your birth certificate, but you must not have known about the package your mum had left for you. They were supposed to give it to you on your sixteenth birthday. My mother was beside herself. They looked for you everywhere. And when they couldn't find you, she felt like she had failed her best friend. She was devastated." He shakes me in frustration, letting go of my face.

"Our mums were best friends?" I ask, now even more confused. His anger has simmered down, and if I can get him talking about this long enough, I might just buy enough time for Drew to work out where I am, if he even got the message and is looking for me.

"Yes. My mum tried to look after you when your mum died, but she was only young herself, and she had me to take care of. It was too much on her own, that's why you ended up in the foster system, but after she found my stepdad and married, she found out where you were and tried to get you back. Do you believe me now? I know everything about you. What wasn't left by your mum, I have researched ever since running into you that day. Now let's play my game."

He says he knows everything about me. This could all be totally shit. This guy reads manuscripts of people's stories for a living. This could just be some made-up story he is borrowing to trick me.

I try to remember his mum. She was always kind and caring towards me, a little distant, but I got the impression she had her own shit going on. She mentioned nothing about my mum and her being friends. That's something she would've talked about if she had known her, isn't it?

I look back to Damien. I can't tell if this is all true or not. Come on, Drew, where are you? I can't see any other way out of this, but I'm not giving in to him. "No. I don't want to play your game. All of that stuff is in the past and it can stay there."

"Do you really think you're able to deny me? Cause the way I see it, I have all the power here. Nobody even knows you're here with me. So here is how this is going to go. You do what I say, and if I'm pleased with what you do, you will earn one thing out of the parcel you were supposed to receive on your sixteenth birthday. I have already sent you two items, so you owe me."

He has it here? Even if he does, I'm not playing his

fucked-up game... but I would like to kill as much time as possible. "Prove it, show me the envelope."

His eyes narrow. "Okay, fair request. But I don't trust you not to try running again, so while I do, I'm tying you up."

Fuck, that was exactly what I was going to do while he was distracted. "You don't need to tie me up, I'm not going anywhere. I learned my lesson last time."

"Cute, but for what I have planned, I would prefer you tied up anyway."

Oh hell, what has he got planned?

He reaches into the bag he has on his bedside table, pulling out cable ties. He binds my hands together all too easily, then loops them over my head and through the bed head. This creep has done this before, and a wave of nausea washes over me. Has he done this to other women because I didn't report him all those years ago?

"You're not going anywhere now, are you, baby doll?"

He slides off the bed. I turn my head as best I can from the position I'm in, trying to see what he's doing. He has a black duffel bag and rummages around in there, pulling out a large yellow envelope; he brings it over to me, holding it up for me to see. There is writing on the front: *'Jenna West on your 16th birthday.'* It says just what he has already said to me. It proves nothing, really. He could have done all this himself.

He places the envelope down on the side table and slides onto the bed next to me. "Now the real fun begins."

Fuck, Drew, if you can hear me, I need you now. Stop fucking around and save me. Damien leans in to me to kiss me, and I turn my head away. He growls.

I'm going to fight him with everything I have. I don't

care that it all seems hopeless. I'm not giving in to him like I used to, no fucking way in hell.

He grabs my face, pulling me back to him, kissing me aggressively, and I bite him hard enough that I have the metallic taste of blood in my mouth when he pulls away.

"You fucking little bitch." He licks the blood from his lip, then he slaps me across the face with the back of his hand, so hard I hear ringing in my ears. Tears instantly sting my eyes.

He moves down my body, undoing my jeans and tugging them off. I buck off the bed, trying to kick him, and the cable ties cut into my wrists. It burns but I don't care.

He grabs my feet in his hands. "As much fun as it is to watch you fight, baby doll, you keep kicking me and I will tie your legs up as well." He spreads my legs and positions himself between them.

I know this might be the stupidest thing I can do, but I scream at the top of my lungs. This is a fucking hotel, someone has to hear me and do something, right? I scream until his hand clamps over my mouth, his angry eyes piercing through me.

There is a knock at the door, and he looks at me. His eyes flick between me and the door.

"Room service, delivering the breakfast you ordered," we hear a male voice come through the door.

"We didn't order anything, you must have the wrong room," Damien calls back.

"It is definitely for this room."

"Just leave it out the front," Damien calls back.

"Sorry, sir, I have to bring it in, company policy."

He bends down low, his face right next to my ear. "Don't say a fucking word or I will kill you, understand?" he whispers to me.

I nod. He removes his hand from my mouth and goes to open the door.

Drew

As soon as he opens the door, I ram the breakfast trolley at him. He didn't see it coming, and he is forced backwards and stumbles over, landing on his back on the carpet. The trolley goes over as well, its contents scattering everywhere.

I search the room for her, my eyes landing on the bed where Jenna is restrained, her pants off. He better not have touched her or I will finish him off. I hope I got here in time.

"Drew!" she calls.

I want to run to her, take her in my arms and tell her she's safe, everything is going to be okay now. But I don't know that myself. I hardly have the energy to continue to stand, let alone fight this fucker, and with security still nowhere in sight, I don't see another way for how this is going to end.

"The fucking husband," snarls the guy I knocked to the ground. Damien Stone. He gets to his feet lightning fast and launches himself towards me.

I'm knocked to the ground, my pulse thumping through my skull. Jenna is all I can think about. I block out the pain and focus on her and the need to get her to safety and away from this monster. I have to fight for her.

"Drew!" Jenna calls. I glance back to her, and she looks so scared.

Damien wrestles for the upper hand, but I use all the strength I have and force him off me, elbowing him in the face as hard as I can. Blood gushes from his mouth as he flies back.

CHAPTER 28   351

I crawl over him, punching him in the face as hard as I can. His head launches back, and he stops moving. From what I can tell, he's out cold. I take the chance to drag myself back to the bed to Jenna, pulling her towards me. She cries as I hold her as close to me as I can.

I reach for her hands. "How the fuck do I get these off?" I try to break the cable ties with my hands, but it's no use.

"Drew, the knife," she cries. Tilting her head toward the floor where the catering trolley has gone over.

"I see it." There's food and cutlery spilled all over the carpet. I reach for the knife, grabbing it and running it back and forth along the cable tie, trying to be careful not to cut her wrists as I go. Eventually, it snaps, and her hands are freed. I take her sore hands in mine; they're all cut up from where the tie had bitten into her skin. She must have really fought him.

She wraps her arms around me. "Drew, I didn't think you were coming," she sobs, tears streaming down her face.

"I've got you, baby. You're safe now." I pull the bed sheets around her, covering her up, and pull her into me again. "Did he—?"

She shakes her head on my shoulder, and I feel the relief. I made it here just in time.

Joe, the security guard, has finally caught up and runs through the door, panting. "The police are on their way," he announces.

"Bit late," I say, suddenly feeling a lot worse. The room is spinning, and I feel like I could pass out at any time.

Joe assesses the body lying on the floor, checking Damien's wrist. "Still has a pulse. But we're going to need an ambulance." He radios to reception to get an ambulance.

Jenna pulls back, looking at me. "Drew, are you okay? You don't look so good."

"I'm okay. I got taken out on a wave yesterday, it's just a mild concussion." I lie down on the bed, unable to sit up anymore from the spinning.

Her eyes narrow in fear. "You have a concussion and you just got knocked over by Damien? I think you need an ambulance yourself." She brushes the hair back from my face, inspecting me.

"I'll be fine, I just needed to know you were okay. Let's get you back to your room so we can pack up your stuff and get you out of here."

"You're not going anywhere until someone takes a look at you."

CHAPTER TWENTY-NINE

JENNA

Drew keeps trying to convince me he's okay, but there is no way he is. He looks terrible. I'm really worried.

The police and ambulance arrived not too long after Damien came to. Joe sat with him until he was wheeled from the room on a stretcher. The paramedic that came to help him had a look over Drew as well. It's a concussion alright, and he needs to rest and take it easy over the next few days.

The police interviewed us both, and as hard as it was to go over it all again, I'm glad I did. Drew told me that Damien has done things like this to so many other women, and every time, he's gotten away with it. No fucking way he will this time. I'll make damn sure of that. Knowing that Damien has been able to do this to others makes me feel sick to my stomach. If I had only said something all those years ago, he never would have had the chance.

I won't ever let it happen again.

We're back in my room and Drew is lying on the bed, his eyes closed. Just resting, he says. He needs to.

I'm trying to pack up my stuff, but I can't make my body move. I glance at the yellow envelope I took from Damien's room before we left. I want to look inside and see what it holds from my past, but now isn't the time.

My skin is crawling. I need a shower; I need to wash this morning off my body.

I drop what I'm doing and head straight for the bathroom, turning the shower on to scorching hot, letting the room fill with steam, before I strip off my clothes. They will need to be burnt. Anything that reminds me of Damien, of what almost happened this morning, will need to be destroyed.

I feel so stupid for not turning and running from his office as soon as I walked in there and saw him. I knew what he was capable of and let him manipulate me yet again, this time into thinking he was different, that he had changed. How wrong I was. He is worse than ever.

I let the hot water wash over me. It stings at the cuts on my wrist, and I close my eyes, letting it. I want to block it all out. I want the water to cleanse me, make me feel normal again, the way I did before this all happened. I got there after last time, I know I can again.

But right now, I close my eyes and I can still see him, feel him pressed to me. I have no escape, and I'm so scared. My breathing gets shallow, and I can feel the panic rise. Tears break free and stream down my face. My back slides down the tile wall to the floor, and I sob. I hug myself, holding my knees as close to my chest as I can. The devastating tears trembling my entire body.

How did this happen? The events of the last twenty-four hours keep playing through my head like a scary movie. How did it all happen? I'm angry and hurt and so confused.

I hear the click of the door opening, and Drew comes into the bathroom. He hops into the shower fully clothed, sitting on the floor next to me. He pulls me on top of him, cradling me as I weep.

"No one will ever hurt you again, I promise you," he whispers to me, stroking my soaked hair.

I don't know how long we stay here like this for, but my tears eventually stop, and he helps me up, taking a towel and hugging it around my body. I wander back into the room in a daze. I'm utterly exhausted. The adrenaline has worn off, and my body aches from head to toe. I climb into the bed and wrap the covers over myself. Drew climbs in behind me; he has changed out of his wet clothes and has on a robe. He wraps his arms around me, and I fall asleep. Safe in his warm, protective arms.

I WAKE GASPING FOR BREATH, HANDS AROUND MY throat—then I realise I was having a nightmare, and I relax when I feel Drew's arm still over me. He's asleep, and I don't want to disturb him. He needs the rest with the head injury he has.

I know I need to talk to him about the photos I saw in the paper, but now is not the time. He came to save me, and I know he still loves me, I could see it the moment he rammed through the door and our eyes locked. He fought a concussion and a madman to get me to safety. No matter what happens with us, I will be forever grateful he stopped what he was doing and came to me because I asked him to.

Stopped what he was doing.

He's supposed to be competing today, and he's here.

He moves behind me, pulling me in closer, and I let

him. It feels so good to be in his arms again. He places his lips to my neck and kisses me softly. I roll over in his arms, brushing his hair away from his eyes. He blinks up at me sleepily. "Sorry," I whisper. "I didn't mean to disturb you, I know you need your rest."

"You didn't. I was awake already, I just didn't want to move. This is the closest we've been in weeks. I have missed you so much."

"I've missed you too." Our eyes are locked. I want to melt into him, but there are so many unanswered questions. "Aren't you supposed to be competing today? If you're here with me, what will that mean?"

"Don't worry about any of that right now, Jen, it's not important anymore."

"Drew, it has been your dream since you were a kid. How could it not be important anymore?"

He reaches up to me, cupping my face, and I flinch from the pain in my cheek. Ouch, that arsehole got me better than I thought earlier. My cheek must be bruised. "Is you face really sore?" he asks.

"Yeah, a little." I wince, touching it.

"I'm so sorry this happened to you. I should have been here with you for this meeting, then it never would have happened." He looks so sad, broken.

"You can't blame yourself, Drew. You can't be with me every second of the day."

"I can try." He looks deadly serious, and I'm sure he is. But we both know that's not going to be the way we live our lives.

"You know that's not practical," I say with a small smile.

"If anything bad ever happened to you, I couldn't live with myself. I can't even bear to think of how awful it must have been for you this morning. If I didn't get here in time..."

"But you did. It's over now, and thanks to you and your timing, you put a stop to it."

I sit up in a rush, thinking back to what he said about his comp today. "Is there still time to get you back to compete today?"

"No, Jen, it's too late, and I'm not well enough."

I drop my head, deflated. He missed out because of me. "I'm so sorry, Drew," I say, tears breaking free again.

"You're the most important thing in my life. My surfing career was just killing time until I could be with you. I don't need it anymore. I don't need to win. I just need you."

He's willing to give up the win for me? What about Cobie and those photos? "But what about Cobie?"

"She'll understand. She knows what you mean to me. Wait, what do you mean what about Cobie?" He looks confused, and I have to wonder if his head knock was harder than he says, maybe he has some memory loss or something as well.

"This morning Damien showed me the photos of you two together. The news article."

"What article?"

I bring it up on my phone and show him. He reads it and shakes his head. "Jen, this is what they do—get a scrap of photo, spin it into a story. This one here must have been taken yesterday after I was knocked out in the surf. See? You can see blood on my head. Cobie was helping me to my car because I literally couldn't walk alone." He points to the other one. "'This one must have been the night before." He pauses, as if contemplating what to say next.

There is more to all of this, and I feel that sinking feeling. I waited too long to contact him. She moved in and he wants her now. "Drew, what is it?" I ask, unsure if I really want the answer or not.

"She walked me home because I had too much to drink. I was a mess. You wouldn't talk to me, I was worried you were done with me. I didn't handle it well."

I give him a look. "So you slept with Cobie?"

"No! God, no. I would never do that to you. I just had too much to drink, that's all. Cobie did tell me she was in love with me that night, and she tried to kiss me, but I explained that it was only you for me. Even if you didn't take me back, you would still be the only girl for me, and I would be forever lonely because I could never move on to anyone else. Never."

"Really?" I ask, cupping his handsome face.

"Yes, really."

"Even if I'm fiercely independent and it drives you crazy?"

"*Because* you are." He kisses me, and when our lips meet, it's soft and sweet and everything I have been missing. I love him so much my heart aches. But I still have no idea how we make it all work for the future.

"Drew, how do we do this? You know, everything we fought about, you were so angry with me."

He smiles. "We make it work together, because we love each other. I know I was angry, but that was because I was surprised. And I've had time to think about it all now. You need your independence, I get it. I don't want to control you, that's not what I was trying to do. I just wanted to protect you. But Jen, I need to know I can look after you. I love you, knowing you're safe is so important to me. That's why I acted so crazy."

"I think I get it now." And I do. His need to be in control isn't like it was with Damien or with Vinnie. He doesn't want power over me. It comes from a place of love and wanting to protect me. It's hard to accept someone feels so strongly about you when you didn't even have that from your own parents.

Now that I have found it, I'm not going to stuff it up. I'm going to hold onto it.

CHAPTER THIRTY

JENNA

"Where do you want this one?" asks Theo.

"What's on the side?" I ask.

He glances at the side of the box. "Books."

I smile, trying not to laugh at him, because he is helping me, but I know that box is bloody heavy. I couldn't even lift it once it was packed, and he's trying to act like it's not. "Umm."

"Hurry up, Jenna," he grumbles.

"Straight to my office upstairs. Thanks." I flash him my most appreciative grin.

He mumbles something to himself about how much he hates moving and struggles up the stairs.

Ivy stands at the bottom of the stairs with a much smaller box, laughing at him. "What's all the working out in the gym for if you can't help your sister-in-law move?" she calls after him, throwing me a wink.

Drew bounds through the house with the next item of furniture. He has been more of an Energizer Bunny than normal today. He is so excited I'm officially moving my things in. It's been one month since what happened in Sydney, and things couldn't be better between us.

We're working on being a team, as best we can anyway, when we are both so fiercely independent and have been single for so long.

I go out to the truck, jump in, and struggle trying to manoeuvre my coffee table. Shit, I should have waited for help. I feel the weight drop, and I think it's fallen out the back of the truck when I see Drew catch it.

"I've got you." He grins, and we lift the table out of the truck together and carry it into the house. Drew has moved some of his furniture out so we can have a mix of mine and his together, and as I stand back to look around the living area, it's definitely starting to feel a lot more like home. A huge luxurious mansion that I now live in, it blows my mind.

Ivy and Theo come back downstairs and meet us in the living room. Ivy tilts her head and the smiles she wears tells me something is going on. "Have you been upstairs to your office yet today, hun?"

I wonder what's going on with the office. I haven't had time to look, I've been focusing on getting the truck unpacked and everything inside before the ominous clouds looming overhead open up and all my stuff gets wet. "No, why?" I ask.

Drew throws her a look.

She bites her lip. "No reason," she mutters, walking away.

Drew takes my hand and leads me up the stairs. "What's going on, Drew?"

"Just wait and see." He grins, dimples showing. Whatever this is, he is so excited about it.

We get to the hall right before the entry to my office,

and he stands behind me, covering my eyes with his hands. We slowly walk to the doorway. "You can look now." I peel his hands away to see an exact replica of my library from my townhouse. The shelves Blake had built for me. Everything is the same.

"It's my library!" I squeal. "But how did you do this without me?"

"Blake and I got it all done yesterday while you, Ivy, and Harmony were out shopping."

I turn to face him. "It's perfect. I love it. Thank you." I kiss him.

"You're perfect," he mumbles into my lips, kissing me again.

I know that's not true, but I'll take it from him. I walk in and look around the room. Opening a box of books, I start to unpack them onto the shelves. Drew sits on the desk, watching me.

I finish unpacking the first box and open the second. The yellow envelope from Damien sits on top. I haven't opened it yet. I've been too scared to. Do I really need to know where I come from?

"You going to open it?" he asks.

I nibble my lip, picking the envelope up and inspecting it. "Maybe one day."

"Why not today, Jen? Aren't you dying to know about your parents? This envelope might contain all the information." He looks so hopeful, and I wish I could feel the same.

"Yeah, I know. I am curious, but I'm scared. What if I don't like what I find?"

"I think you can handle whatever you find." He says it with such confidence I actually think I can. This is something I love about him so much, the supportive way he encourages me.

Can I handle it, though? I really don't know. Damien said my mum was best friends with his mum, and she promised she would look after me because my mum was shot, but I can't believe a word he says, really. It was probably all just made up. How do I know whatever is in here isn't just made-up bullshit? It could be.

Drew pats the desk next to him and I go and sit. He wraps his arm around me, kissing me on the cheek. I take a deep breath and tear at the end of the envelope, letting the contents fall to my lap. There are more photos, mostly of a baby. A marriage certificate with the names Mrs Madaline Northwell and Mr Julian West. Those are my parents. I knew that already because they're the names from my birth certificate.

According to the date, they were married for four months before I was born. The witness was Cora Stone, Damien's mum. They *must* have been friends.

The second paper is a death certificate. My mother. It's six months after I was born. I don't know why, but as soon as I read it, tears roll down my face. I didn't know her, and all this time I knew she could have been dead, but somehow seeing it in black and white makes it all real. She died when I was just a little girl. She was so young herself, only twenty-two.

Drew is reading over my shoulder. "Your mum?"

"Yes. She's dead, a really long time ago. I will never meet her."

"Is there anything in there about your dad?"

I look over the photos and papers. "No, nothing."

"Maybe we can look into it, try to find him?"

"I don't think I want to know."

"Really?"

"Yeah. Maybe one day, but right now, I don't."

There's a knock at the door and we both jump. "Sorry, guys, just letting you know, we're off if you don't need any more help?" says Theo.

"Got to save Elly from the kids," laughs Ivy.

"Yeah, of course. Thanks so much for your help." I hug them both.

"See you tomorrow for family dinner," adds Drew as they leave.

I look around my new special space. I love it so much, and the fact that Drew thought to do it for me makes my heart so happy. He is such a wonderful man, and he gave up so much for me.

"What is it, Bamb?"

I walk to him, taking his hands in mine. "Drew, would you try again for the win next year if you had the chance?"

He looks me over. "I can't be away from you again. I'm happy here starting my surf school."

"What if I came with you? Would you then?"

"You want to come with me?"

"I was thinking maybe I could be your manager, write in my downtime. I want you to have the chance you missed out on because of me."

His arms wrap around me, pulling me into his body close, his eyes locked with mine like he's trying to read my mind. "I want this for you, baby," I say. "Let's make it happen. Then we can come back here and settle down... maybe start a family?" I raise a brow to see what he thinks of that idea.

He grins. "I think we should do that now."

I look at him, confused. "Start a family now?"

"Well, at least practice." He smirks, and I reach up on my toes and kiss him.

"What exactly do you have in mind, Mr Walker?" His

hands roam down my body, landing on my arse with a hard squeeze. He lifts me up, my legs wrap around him, and he walks us backwards till I'm up against the bookshelf.

"Let's give you something to write about," he says cheekily, and I giggle. I will never get enough of this amazing man.

EPILOGUE
JENNA: TWO AND A HALF YEARS LATER

We flew in yesterday from Brazil to spend Drew and Elly's birthday with the family. Drew is so excited because everyone is going to be here. I have no idea how Anne is going to cope, there are so many of us now.

This is Drew's first season back after taking last year off to spend with me while I was pregnant. It wasn't quite what we discussed; I wanted him to get straight back to it, but he didn't want to miss a thing during my pregnancy, and it was going to be difficult for me to travel, so we made the choice together.

The little joke Drew made in the library that day about starting a family turned out to be not such a joke, because that month we got pregnant. Our little darling, Tia, is now one and a half already. She's the cutest, with blonde ringlets and blue eyes, and she also has the cheeky smile just like her dad.

Tia is the easiest baby, and that's why we have been able to travel around with her so much this year. It's not quite what I was imagining for us, but somehow, life has a way of working things out for you, and I couldn't be happier with how things have played out. My little family means the absolute world to me.

I scoop Tia up out of the car seat and pass her to Drew. She cuddles into him, all sleepy from the ride in the car.

"Everyone must be here already," says Drew, looking up the street.

"I'd say so." Judging by the line-up of cars in the street and the noise coming from the yard.

We make our way in together. Jim is on the BBQ with Fraser. The older kids have water pistols and are running around the yard in their swimmers, squirting each other. Blake seems to be the king of the kids and has a Super Soaker, getting them as they run past. Drew hands me Tia and grabs a Super Soaker from the lawn, taking off through the yard after a screaming Jasper and Cooper. I head up onto the deck and find Ivy, Indie, and Elly sitting in the sun with the little ones. I can see Anne in the kitchen, and I offer a wave. She smiles and mouths, "I'll be out in a sec." Ivy and Theo had a little girl, Zara, one month before Tia was born. She's sitting on Harmony's lap. Harmony is the best big sister, so helpful to Ivy.

"You girls look so comfortable," I say, taking a seat and sitting Tia in front of the pile of toys on the mat.

"Not poor Elly," says Indie, giving her friend's leg a squeeze.

"What's wrong, Elly?" She looks like she's going to be sick. She jumps up, grabbing her mouth and running inside the house. I look at the other two with a questioning gaze.

"I'll let Elly fill you in on that," says Ivy. "How was the flight?"

"Yeah, it was good, Tia slept for most of it."

"You're so lucky. I would have no chance of getting Zara on a plane. She won't even sleep in her own bed."

"Is she still that bad?"

Theo comes over, picking up his daughter. "She is. It's lucky she's cute." He tickles her belly, and she giggles.

"I'm going to check on Elly," says Ivy, hopping up and heading inside.

"What's going on with Elly?" asks Theo.

"Mega hangover? She must have drunk too much for her birthday, that's my guess," I say with a shrug.

"Drew said you went to see your old foster mum?" says Theo.

"Yeah, we did. I know it took me a bit, but I finally felt ready to find out what Cora knew. I thought she would have hated me after what happened with her son, but she was so lovely. Apologetic for everything that happened."

"Could she tell you about your dad?"

I nod. It was a few weeks ago now, but I'm still not sure how much I want to say. I'm still trying to process what she told us.

"She told us what she knew of him. But she hasn't seen him for years, not since my mum was killed. Apparently, he felt responsible somehow, and that's why he took off and left me."

"Are you going to try and find him?" asks Indie.

"I don't know. Can I ask you something, Indie?"

"Anything."

"Did it help when you tracked down your dad?"

"It offered some closure and meant I found out that Fraser is my brother, so I'm glad I did. Neither of us have a relationship with him, but that was his choice."

"You might have other siblings as well?" adds Theo.

"I did a little research about him. It doesn't look like it. He lives alone in Sydney. Never re-married. He spent some time in the prison system then worked as a mechanic."

"Why did he go to prison?"

"Assault. Got into a fight in a bar."

"It's your choice, hun, but it might give you some closure."

"You know what? I think I have all the closure I need."

Anne calls us all for lunch. We make our way to the table, setting up the kids with their food then sorting our own. Elly wanders back through the house, and Fraser wraps his arms around her. "We have a little announcement," says Fraser.

Elly takes one look at the food on the table in front of her. "Oh God, not again." She runs for the bathroom.

Fraser looks back at the group. "If you can't already tell, we're pregnant," he says, then takes off after his wife. Poor Elly, I feel for her. But I'm also super happy. Cooper is nearly eight. And I know she has been wanting another kid for a while.

In their absence, everyone continues on with serving up their food and sit at the table to eat. Fraser and Elly re-join us, and she looks slightly better with a cold ginger beer in her hand. She sits next to her mum. "You sure it's not twins?" asks Anne.

Elly looks like she's going to cry. "You would think so, hey, with how horribly sick I am. But no, just one that hates me already." She slowly sips her drink.

I offer her a sympathetic smile. I was sick with Tia as well, couldn't hold anything down. One of the reasons Drew stayed with me the entire time. He had to be the one to take care of me, and for once I let him.

The rest of the table breaks off into chatter about everyone's lives.

I sit next to Drew and across from Blake and Indie.

"How's the surf school going, Drew?" asks Blake.

I'm so proud of what Drew has created with his surf school. At the moment, he's focussed on eight to thirteen-year-olds. But he has plans to expand when he's back here full-time.

"It's taken off, hey. There is so much interest we're going to have to run a few extra afternoons next term."

"That's awesome, mate. Congratulations."

"What about you, Jen, how is the new series coming along?"

"Good, the next book releases in two weeks, and I hope to have the entire series out by Christmas, if I have the time. It's hard to tell if I will around Tia's schedule and our overseas time with Drew, but hopefully."

After the horrible experience I had with Damien and the publishing house, I decided to go down the path of indie publishing and haven't looked back since. I have published a total of seven books in the last two-and-a-half years, and I feel more content than I ever have in my life. It might have been a struggle to get here, and at times my life hasn't been the easiest, but now that I'm here I feel so blessed to have the life I do. My wonderful family and extended family, all the people at this table mean so much to me. A career I'm so proud of and enjoy with all my heart—writing isn't just a passion for me, it's my therapy, my sanity, and my escape when I need it.

Jim and Theo clear the table and Anne brings out Elly and Drew's decadent-looking chocolate birthday cake.

"I would like to say a few words," says Jim, standing up and addressing the table. Everyone gives him their full attention. "I just wanted to say how nice it is to have all my family here together today to celebrate the twins' birthday. Anne and I have always felt so blessed to have our three wonderful children, and now our little family of five has expanded to include all of the amazing people I see here before me—Fraser, Ivy, and Jenna who have chosen to marry into the Walker clan, and Blake and Indie who weren't born into our family, but we love as our own, and all of our little grandbabies."

Anne has tears in her eyes and stands by his side. "I second what your dad says. We are very lucky to have each other. Now let's eat some cake."

I still can't believe I got so lucky to be accepted into such a beautiful family, but I feel very grateful every day that I am. And that this is all Tia will know, the love of a big, warm family supporting her throughout her life. Drew squeezes my leg, and I know he's reading my mind.

"We're lucky to have you too, Bamb."

All my childhood dreams have somehow come true. I have the man of my dreams by my side, a large family to call my own, and a career I'm truly happy doing for the rest of my life. I never used to believe in happy endings, but the Walker family have proven me wrong.

Happily ever after truly can exist.

The End

ALSO BY A K STEEL

Always Fraser — Broken Point book 1
Eventually Blake — Broken Point book 2
Only Theo — Broken Point book 3
Forever Drew — Broken Point book 4
The Coach — Harper Sisters book 1 (Coming soon)

If you enjoyed Forever Drew, please leave me a review. Reviews really do make such a difference. Even a short one-liner is a big help.

ABOUT THE AUTHOR

I'm a steamy contemporary romance author of books with swoony men, twists and turns, and always a happily ever after.

I'm a busy mother of three pre-teens, who lives on the beautiful South Coast of New South Wales, Australia. I have always been a creative soul, with a background in fashion design, interior decoration, and floristry. I currently run a business as a wedding florist and stylist but have always had a love for reading romance novels. There's just something about how the story can transport you to another world entirely.

So, in 2020, I decided to jot down some of my own ideas for romance stories—always with a happily ever after, of course —and from that came my debut novel, *Always Fraser*. From that moment, I haven't looked back. Writing has become a part of me. I have a long list of stories plotted, and I look forward to being able to share them all with you soon. I hope you enjoy reading them as much as I loved writing them.

XX

For all the news on upcoming books, visit A.K. Steel at:

Facebook: https://www.facebook.com/a.k.steelauthor
Instagram: @aksteelauthor
www.aksteelauthor.com

ACKNOWLEDGMENTS

My partner, Kiel, you have changed my life in so many wonderful ways. Thank you for pushing me to start writing. Without your encouragement and love, I never would have put pen to paper and started this fantastic journey in the first place. I feel like I found myself this year, and I'm finally where I'm supposed to be. Without you, this never would have happened.

My amazing mum, Kay, thank you for your constant love and support. You read every word I write and have always been my number-one fan. You put up with my meltdowns and endless questions, you are my best friend, and I'm grateful every day to have you in my life.

My dad, it's been seven long years since you left us, but the outlook you had on life still inspires me every day. It's the reason I believe that if you work hard enough, you can achieve any dream, no matter how impossible it seems.

My kids—Hamish, Marley, and Quinn—thank you for looking at me like I'm amazing and can do anything, even when I don't feel like I can. Everything I do is for you. And I hope I have shown you that with a bit of determination and hard work, your dreams really can come true.

Karen, my friend and mentor, you made this dream feel possible. Every time I thought I couldn't do it, you encouraged me to keep on going. I couldn't have done any of this without your knowledge and friendship.

T. L. Swan and the girls from the Cygnet Inkers group, I'm loving being on this journey with you all. You girls keep me positive and motivated, and I love you for it.

Lindsay, my editor, thank you for your patience with a new author. Your knowledge and expertise have made this book what it is.

Sarah, for my gorgeous cover design, and your patience with my indecisiveness. I love the cover you created for me.

Photo credit, Michelle Lancaster for her wonderful cover image, www.michellelancaster.com

www.instagram.com/lanefotograf.

Cover model tommyfierce.

Give Me Books Promotions, thank you for your help spreading the word about my books in the book community and helping me share my stories with the world.

My beta readers—Elise, Shelly, Kirstie, Bek, Francesca, Jemma, Patricia, Tobie and Anita—thank you for your time, honesty, and support. Without you lovely ladies I wouldn't have had the courage to publish and share my story.

My proofreader Kay, thank you for double and triple-checking every word.

To my friends and family who have been so supportive along this journey—you have all been so amazing—thank you.

And lastly to my readers, thank you for taking the time to give a new author a chance, and making my dreams become a reality.

Printed in Great Britain
by Amazon